8/17

Ascension
of
Larks

Center Point
Large Print

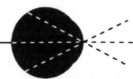

**This Large Print Book carries the
Seal of Approval of N.A.V.H.**

Ascension

of

Larks

Rachel Linden

CENTER POINT LARGE PRINT
THORNDIKE, MAINE

This Center Point Large Print edition
is published in the year 2017 by arrangement with
Thomas Nelson.

The text of this Large Print edition is unabridged.
In other aspects, this book may vary
from the original edition.
Printed in the United States of America
on permanent paper.
Set in 16-point Times New Roman type.

ISBN: 978-1-68324-483-7

Library of Congress Cataloging-in-Publication Data

Names: Linden, Rachel, author.
Title: Ascension of larks / Rachel Linden.
Description: Center Point Large Print edition. | Thorndike, Maine :
  Center Point Large Print, 2017.
Identifiers: LCCN 2017018793 | ISBN 9781683244837
  (hardcover : alk. paper)
Subjects: LCSH: Women—Fiction. | Family secrets—Fiction. |
  Women photographers—Fiction. | Large type books. | GSAFD:
  Christian fiction. | Love stories.
Classification: LCC PS3612.I5327426 A54 2017b | DDC 813/.6—dc23
LC record available at https://lccn.loc.gov/2017018793

For Yohanan. Wherever you are, I am home.

If the skies fall, one may hope to catch larks.
Francois Rabelais

All shall be well, and all shall be well,
and all manner of thing shall be well.
Julian of Norwich

Chapter One

"Come on, come on. I know you're here somewhere" Magdelena Henry murmured, squinting through the viewfinder of her camera at the ragged line of coffee pickers sorting their day's yield. Standing in the dust on a narrow dirt lane, she panned over the workers, looking for the perfect shot. Behind her, the late-afternoon sun spread light like butter, soft and golden, over the Nicaraguan landscape, across the high, dense, green mountains and ribbon of road winding back through the coffee fields. Birdcalls blended with the screeching of howler monkeys, creating a cacophony of sound in the treetops above.

Adjusting her 55mm camera lens, Maggie focused on a young girl in a grimy rainbow-print shirt as she worked through a large woven basket full of coffee cherries, separating the ripe red ones from the young, bitter green ones. Inside each cherry lay two small coffee beans. The girl looked up at Maggie and grinned, holding out a handful of red cherries. Her baby teeth were all rotten, a line of black against her gums.

Maggie caught her breath with the familiar thrill of recognition. Every so often the elements aligned and offered her a perfect shot. She paused for one split second, focusing intently on the girl amid the dust motes and shafts of sunlight. Then with speed and precision born of long practice, she pushed the shutter once, twice, again in quick succession. She glanced briefly at the digital image frozen on the screen. Beautiful. The colors were crisp and striking. The light was excellent. At least one of these shots should be good enough for the magazine cover.

Maggie was known for photos like these, intimate portrayals of daily life around the globe that highlighted people often unseen by the camera's eye. She captured images that were striking in their display of basic humanity, their sense of real life in all its grit and vibrancy, its specific and often brutal beauty. Her ability to reveal hidden and forgotten things was a gift, a skill that took her to some of the most isolated corners of the earth. It was also quickly making her one of the most acclaimed documentary photographers in the world. Maggie Henry's star had been rising for almost seven years. It showed no sign of slowing.

Lowering her camera, Maggie walked to the edge of the dirt lane, stretching to ease the tension in her shoulders. She was standing on one of the largest fair-trade coffee plantations in the country. It spread around her as far as the eye could see, with a bevy of coffee pickers harvesting the grounds and two guards armed with machine guns at the entrance.

Earlier the temperature had been almost cool in the shade of the high mountain coffee fields, but it had risen in the late afternoon. The sun was fierce now, and she felt a prickle of sweat beginning to bead under her quick-dry shirt, already rimed with dried salty blotches from her earlier hike. She didn't bother to blot it away. Sweat came as part of the job.

Maggie took a deep breath. The air smelled like dust and lush vegetation, a sharp, fertile scent that clung to the creases of her skin at the end of the day and had to be scrubbed away with her almond castile travel soap. She tucked a stray, dark curl back into her ponytail and let her gaze drift over the rolling terrain.

"Here, you need to stay hydrated." Sanne, Maggie's assistant for the shoot, appeared at her elbow and handed her a bottle of water. "I know it doesn't feel hot, but the sun's strong this close to the equator." A photojournalism student from South Africa, Sanne was interning with Maggie's photography agency for the summer. Her job was to provide whatever Maggie might need on the shoot, from paper clips to toothpaste to international dialing codes, a role she fulfilled with brisk efficiency.

"Thanks." Uncapping the bottle, Maggie took a long swallow of water, watching a tiny woman in a stained blue blouse as she hoisted a large basket of coffee cherries onto her back. Her face was tanned to the color of strong tea, her shoulders permanently sloped from years of picking on the steep hills.

"How's it going?" Sanne asked, surveying the line of pickers sitting along the lane with their baskets of cherries.

"Good. The light's perfect," Maggie replied, pleased with the afternoon's work so far. "I've got at least a dozen we could use from today."

On assignment for *TIME Magazine*, Maggie was shooting a photo spread for a feature article on fair-trade coffee. The article promised to reveal the truth behind the fair-trade label. Did the label make a difference in the lives of the pickers? From what Maggie had seen in the last week, the answer was no. The pickers and their families looked like countless others she had photographed in the slums of Mumbai, the sun-dried plateaus of sub-Saharan Africa. They bore the telltale signs of malnutrition and a lack of basic hygiene or medical care—missing teeth, leathery skin, a faint orange tinge to their hair. Poverty was a familiar story, but one that never grew easier with the telling.

Maggie gulped a few more swallows of water. It tasted of minerals. She lifted her face to the sun, closing her eyes and enjoying the brief respite. She loved the feeling of the sun's rays on her skin, the warmth seeping into her bones. She never burned, thanks to the complexion she'd

10

inherited from her Puerto Rican mother. She just tanned a dark, burnished gold.

Maggie sighed, trying to tamp down a creeping sense of weariness. Another day or so and she would be done, flying back to Chicago to prep for her next assignment. This was normal life for her, jetting to far-flung places and for a week or a month immersing herself in a remote area of the globe, reemerging with a handful of marvelous photos to share with the rest of the world. In the past seven years, she'd tucked over ninety countries under her belt.

Bolstered by the momentary rest, Maggie tossed the half-empty water bottle into the leather backpack that seldom left her side. "I'm going to take some more shots before the light goes," she told Sanne. "We should have enough after today to wrap up by tomorrow."

Her assistant's face brightened. Although Sanne hadn't once complained, Maggie knew she had struggled with the ever-present dust, sparse living conditions, and multitude of insects. The first night rats had chewed through Sanne's backpack to reach her stash of organic granola bars. Maggie shrugged when she saw the gnawed hole. She accepted the more unsavory aspects as part of the job. Centipedes in the shower and grit in her teeth were standard fare. After years of working in primitive conditions many people would consider unlivable,

11

very little was outside her comfort zone.

"Great." Sanne flashed a relieved smile. "I'll call the office and let them know our schedule." She was already moving before the words were out of her mouth.

Maggie lingered for a few minutes near the little girl in the rainbow-print shirt. She'd noticed the family at the beginning of the week. The girl and her brother were young. The plantation overseer claimed the girl was twelve, the age when children could begin picking coffee on the farm, but Maggie guessed she was no more than seven or eight. The boy appeared to be a year or two older.

The girl pranced in a circle in front of Maggie, imitating a rooster, showing off. She had a mop of frizzy curls, and her belly was slightly distended from malnutrition or parasites, probably both. Her mother worked silently nearby, sorting cherries while keeping a sharp eye on her daughter. Maggie snapped a few more photos, and the girl offered her a handful of coffee cherries, proudly telling her in Spanish that she had picked them herself. The arm she held out to Maggie was scabbed between the wrist and elbow from the tough coffee bushes. Maggie met the girl's eyes, seeing in that dark gaze a fierce independence tinged with a hint of desperation. Maggie had encountered that look countless times—in the faces of children indentured as cigarette rollers in Bangladesh, in the lipstick-painted smiles of Thai bar girls too young to fill out the sequined bras they wore. It was the look of a child forced to grow up too quickly.

"*Gracias,*" Maggie responded easily, taking the cherries and carefully tucking them into her backpack, switching from English to Spanish without hesitation as she spoke. Her mother had often spoken Spanish to Maggie in their home. It didn't trip off Maggie's tongue as easily as English did these days, but Spanish was still a language that warmed her heart.

"*Cómo te llamas?*" Maggie asked the girl. *What is your name?*

The little girl giggled at Maggie's accent, so different from her own. "Carla," she answered.

"*Que linda,*" Maggie responded. *How lovely.*

Leaving the mother to her work, Maggie walked slowly down the line of coffee pickers, camera in hand, alert for a potential angle that might catch her eye. Carla followed her, chattering away, asking for candy and chewing gum. She scuffed the dust with her bare feet as she ran alongside Maggie, keeping up a constant stream of conversation, both of them speaking Spanish.

"How old are you?" Carla demanded. "What's your name?"

"My name is Magdalena, and I'm old. Almost thirty." Maggie smiled, remembering how thirty

13

had seemed impossibly ancient when she was Carla's age. She would be thirty in just a few months, and she had to admit that sometimes she felt old beyond her years. This kind of work exacted a toll. She loved it and couldn't imagine doing anything else, but she paid a price to do what she loved. Every year it seemed to cost her a little more.

Carla beamed at Maggie's attention.

"*Estas bonita!*" the little girl said admiringly. *You're pretty!* After a moment she asked again, this time more slyly, "Do you have any candy?"

"No. And you shouldn't eat candy. It isn't good for you," Maggie chided, smiling in spite of herself at the girl's obvious attempt to curry favor in the hope of getting a treat.

Carla grinned, showing her rotten teeth. "But I like it."

With a glance at Carla's hopeful, wary face, Maggie sighed and dug through her bag until she found a piece of sugar-free gum, then handed it to the child. It certainly couldn't do her teeth any more harm.

In the early years of her career, Maggie would have driven into town and tried to buy children's toothbrushes and toothpaste, taken Carla's family bottles of kid-friendly multivitamins in colorful animal shapes, urged the mother to send her children to school. After a few years of frustration, feeling as though she were throwing

14

a teaspoon of remedy into an ocean of need, Maggie realized she could never single-handedly stop the grinding poverty, disease, and injustice that dogged so many of those she photographed. She had slowly come to understand the best thing she could offer was her camera, to turn the eyes of the world onto those who, like Carla, were ignored, forgotten, unseen.

In the past seven years, she had been gratified by the responses to many of her photos—two new schools in Kolkata, India, for girls at risk of being forced into the sex industry; an infant vaccination and health program among Roma families in the Balkans; an initiative against female circumcision in Eritrea; and a clean-water drive pairing villages in Sierra Leone with elementary schools in the United States. Her photos had been a catalyst for each one.

Maggie found tremendous satisfaction in making a difference in the world with her own two hands, but an even stronger motivation drove her to succeed. She had been raised by a single mother in a rough, inner-city neighborhood rife with poverty and violence. Her mother had worked hard, but often her earnings were barely enough to make ends meet. Some days it wasn't enough. Maggie knew firsthand the sharp pinch of deprivation felt by so many of those she now photographed. She had experienced the quiet sense of desperation, living day after day on a knife-edge, teetering between barely sufficient and not quite enough. And she had vowed never to be in that position again. She was driven by a genuine passion to help others, but also by an intrinsic need to secure her own future. She photographed the injustices of the world so she could challenge them, but also so she would never have to experience them again.

The sun was dipping low on the horizon when Maggie called it a day. Returning Carla to her mother, Maggie walked back to the shade of a spreading Spanish lime tree where her rolling camera case and the rest of her equipment lay. Sanne sat propped against the tree trunk with her laptop open. Beside her was the satellite phone Maggie carried to more remote locations for emergencies or in case the agency needed to contact her. It often provided the only internet connection in mountainous places such as this one. Sanne scrambled to her feet as Maggie approached.

"The light's going," Maggie said, pulling her camera strap over her head and handing her camera to Sanne. "I don't think I'll get any more good outdoor shots today. Let's pack up and head back to the casa. Luis wants to make some of the coffee from the plantation for us." The thought of the plantation overseer's thick, dark coffee, strong enough to make a spoon stand upright in the cup and liberally laced with Flor de Caña, Nicaragua's prized rum, was cheering after the long afternoon spent in the sun and dust. She unzipped her camera bag and checked to make sure all her equipment and lenses were in the right compartments.

Sanne carefully held the camera, a state-of-the-art digital Canon, as though it were eggshell porcelain. "And you still think we'll be done tomorrow, right?"

"Yeah. I got some great shots today, and I'll finish up whatever I still need in the morning." Maggie took the camera from Sanne and laid it in its compartment as gently as she would a sleeping baby. This was one of her favorite parts of a shoot, packing up her camera at the end of a day, the symbolic moment when she could lay an assignment to rest for the night, knowing she was free as a bird after a job well done.

"Did you manage to get an internet connection with that thing?" Maggie nodded toward the satellite phone.

Sanne grimaced. "More or less. It's slow, but it worked when I e-mailed the agency and let them know we'll be finishing up tomorrow. I'm going to see if I can get a better signal at the casa and try to book our flight."

She gathered up her laptop and the satellite phone, as well as the portable cooler and first aid kit she'd brought, and headed toward the white Toyota Land Cruiser parked by the side of the road. Their driver, Ernesto, a weathered Nicaraguan man of indeterminate age, was lounging against one of the front tires, napping.

Maggie paused for a moment under the tree, fishing through her backpack for the water bottle Sanne had given her. The branches overhead were heavily laden with clusters of small, just-ripening limes. Picking one from a low-hanging branch, she peeled an end and squeezed the juice into the half-empty water bottle. She took a few sips, enjoying the fresh sour pucker. She would miss these limes when she left.

Tomorrow or the next day she'd be on a plane back to Chicago. The thought was neutral for her, holding neither a sense of regret nor relief. Chicago was the city where she had grown up, but a place that no longer felt like her own. It was now just familiar terrain, one city among dozens of others where she could navigate the public transit and order a decent cup of coffee, well known but no longer special.

Home was an ambiguous concept for Maggie. She was never in one place for more than a month at most. She kept a studio apartment in her old stomping grounds in southwest Chicago, in the neighborhood where she was raised. It was no longer the rough, inner-city Latino community of her childhood. In recent years it had gentrified into an emergent arts community. No one she grew up with lived there now. They'd been pushed out by rent hikes and artisan coffee shops that catered to the surfeit of skinny artists with chunky glasses and side-swept bangs who now lived in the former tenements. Chicago was her landing pad and the location of the photography agency she was a part of, but it held little for her now except work assignments and memories, no real life. The truth was that Maggie felt more at home in the international terminal of an airport than she did in Chicago.

The only place that felt even remotely like home was far from where she'd grown up, in the Pacific Northwest in a cluster of remote islands north of Seattle, on San Juan Island. Every August she returned to the big yellow farmhouse perched on a bluff overlooking the sea, staying for a month with her two best friends from college, Lena and Marco, and their brood of three dark-haired children.

She wondered what they were all doing this very moment. It was early June, and they should be on the island, already enjoying the brief but golden Northwest summer before their return to New York City in the fall. She closed her eyes for a moment, picturing them— Marco with his sharp black eyes, that half smile when something amused him, his square, competent hands sketching out plans for a new library, a performing arts center. Marco Firelli was an award-winning architect who

19

hid the rough-and-tumble edges of his blue-collar upbringing in the south of Italy beneath a smooth, cultivated urbanity. He and Maggie were so alike, sharing both a remarkable artistic ability and a fierce drive to succeed. From their early college days, they had distinguished themselves, outstripping their fellow students. They had been the golden ones in those years, she and Marco. Professors' favorites, standouts.

And then there was Lena, Maggie's college roommate and now Marco's wife, who had driven up to the dormitory their freshman year in a Crown Victoria stuffed with matching powder-pink suitcases, sporting little white gloves and a dazzling smile. She'd looked like a Scandinavian Jackie Kennedy, suddenly transported to the wrong decade, all poise and guileless sophistication. Lena had ditched the white gloves long ago in favor of a gardening trowel and a cherry-print apron and the chaos of a household with three small children, but her smile was just as bright. She was a pillar of calm and order in a world that often seemed fractured beyond repair. When she hugged Maggie, the smell of butter and lemon always clinging to her hair, a sense of rightness fell once more into the world, a confirmation that at least a small part of it was still as it should be.

Maggie sighed, took a few more swallows

of water, emptied the bottle and crinkled its thin plastic, then tossed it into her backpack. A couple of months and she would be back with them again. She willed August to come more quickly. The pull of the island was an ache that felt almost visceral. August meant late nights around a bonfire, warm afternoons picking black-berries, and lazy picnics at the shore, watching for orca whales. It meant laying her head down in the red-checkered guest room, knowing she would wake up to the smell of banana pancakes. It was a little bit of heaven on earth.

"Maggie," Sanne called from the Land Cruiser. "Phone call for you." She trotted toward Maggie, holding out the satellite phone. Probably Alistair, the head of her photography agency, eager to know how the shoot was going. He liked to stay informed.

"It's a woman. She says it's urgent." Sanne offered the phone to Maggie, her brow furrowing in concern.

Maggie frowned. Not the office, then. Could it be Lena? No one else had this number. She handed her backpack to Sanne, taking the satellite phone in exchange.

"Hello?"

"Maggie?" It was Lena. The connection was terrible. It sounded like a hive full of bees buzzing angrily in the line, but even with the interference, Maggie could hear that something was wrong. It was the tone of Lena's voice, tight as a violin string with controlled panic.

"Lena?" Maggie clenched the phone, her stomach flipping over. "Lena? What's happened? Is everything okay?"

"Maggie! It's . . . Marco," she heard Lena say before her voice faded into static.

"Lena! Lena!" Maggie jiggled the phone, smacking it into the palm of her hand. It didn't help. She heard only fragments of sentences.

". . . the Strait . . . went in . . ." And then Lena's voice dissolving into sobs.

"Lena, can you hear me?" Maggie cried, desperate to know what was happening. "Is Marco okay? What's wrong?"

She hurried toward higher ground, trying to get a better signal. Nothing. A few yards away, Sanne, Ernesto, and several of the coffee pickers stood watching her, faces drawn with worry, obviously sensing something amiss. No one made a sound. She took a few more steps. The static seemed to lessen. Her heart was beating a staccato drum line, filling her with adrenaline and an icy dread.

"Lena," Maggie repeated loudly, insistently. "What happened? Is Marco okay?"

And then Lena's voice, coming through crystal clear for a brief second, just before the line went completely dead. "He drowned, Maggie. He's gone."

Maggie was vaguely aware of the phone slipping from her fingers, of kneeling in the dust as Sanne tried to help her up. Her hands were shaking uncontrollably, the shaking spreading through her whole body. Ernesto was on a walkie-talkie in the background, trying to summon help from the main house. The buzzing wasn't in the phone anymore. It was in her head. She couldn't catch her breath. She looked up at Sanne, bewildered, her mouth moving of its own accord.

"I have to go home," she said, then pressed her head against her knees as the world went dark.

In the quiet, whitewashed guest room of the casa, left alone to rest, Maggie dialed Lena's cell phone and the landline for the island house over and over. She got no answer. She left a message each time, pleading for Lena to call her back, but there was no reply.

At the insistence of the plantation overseer, Luis, they did not depart for Managua immediately as Maggie wanted to. He was adamant that traveling the mountainous roads at night was too dangerous. Maggie numbly capitulated, and Sanne booked Maggie on the first flight she could get from Managua the following day. They stayed the night at the casa, ready to leave at first light. Even after several generous shots of aged Flor de Caña pressed upon her by Luis,

Maggie didn't sleep, instead lying on the single hard bed dry-eyed and disbelieving.

At dawn, as Ernesto packed their scant luggage into the Land Cruiser, Maggie lingered in the guest room, trying Lena's cell phone again, knowing it was too early to call the island but desperate to get through. Four rings, five. It rang for so long she was surprised when someone picked up.

"Hello?"

"Lena?" She clutched the phone, overcome with a wave of relief at the familiar voice.

Perhaps she had heard wrong. The connection had been so bad. Maybe everything was just fine.

The line was quiet for a moment, and then, "Maggie?" Lena's voice, hollowed out, dulled, in an instant confirming everything Maggie had been trying to deny. It was not a mistake, then. It was true.

"Where are you?" Lena asked.

"Still in Nicaragua." Maggie gulped back the despair she felt rising in her throat. "I'm coming as soon as I can. I tried to call last night but I couldn't get through. Lena, what happened?" She hunched over the phone, staring distractedly out the window, over the dusty cement walls of the casa to a cloudless sky just blushing from gray to a vivid peach.

Lena gave a little sob. "Oh, Maggie, I don't

know. A kayaker in the Strait was in trouble. His kayak flipped. Jonah saw him and yelled, and Marco paddled out to try to help him. But then he capsized too. It was so windy, and you know how strong the currents are. I saw Marco go under, and he—" She halted for a moment. "He just didn't come back up." She sounded bewildered. "The police divers found him a few hours later. It's . . . it's all a blur."

Maggie blinked, struggling to erase the mental image Lena's words conjured up. Marco in the cold, black swirl of salt water above kelp beds hundreds of feet deep. Marco, taking one breath and going under . . .

She tried to focus on Lena instead, picturing her curled up like a little bird on the bed in their bedroom, golden hair fanned out on the quilt she'd designed for Marco, a geometric pattern to celebrate his first architectural award years before. She would be wearing her pale blue satin bathrobe, facing away from the wall of windows that overlooked Haro Strait, the spot where Marco drowned. Maggie shook her head. How could it be true? How could Marco simply be gone?

"Maggie." Lena's voice was thready, panicked. "I don't know what to do. I can't do this. I don't know what to do without him."

"I know, Lena, I know," Maggie said, trying to soothe her. "It's going to be okay. Don't worry." The desperation in Lena's voice shook her. Without thought, Maggie assumed the role she always played. Maggie, the fierce and independent one, the one who took action, always on the move, always making things happen. The one who knew no fear. "I'm on the first flight out. Just hang on. I'm coming."

Late that afternoon Maggie boarded her flight, leaving Sanne to fly back to Chicago alone the next day. She kept her camera and lenses with her. The weight of them in her hand was comforting, something familiar in a world turned suddenly wrong side out.

The plane wasn't full, and Maggie found herself with the rare luxury of two seats to herself. She stowed her camera bag in the overhead compartment and placed her leather backpack on the seat beside her as she settled in for the flight. She pulled her iPod from the front pocket. She always carried it with her. It was a little square of security in an ever-shifting world.

Whether in Paris or Kathmandu, with the push of a button, Maggie would find Bob Dylan, Bonnie Raitt, and Joan Baez unchanged. Their music was a little piece of her childhood as well, reminding her of evenings spent sitting at the kitchen table doing homework while her mother prepared dinner. Her mother, Ana, still on her feet at the end of a long shift at the hotel, would chop onions and garlic for arroz con pollo or stand at the stove stirring *asopao de gandules*, a thick gumbo with pigeon peas they often ate at the end of the month when the food stamps were running low.

The kitchen was always warm, redolent with the smell of cilantro and oregano, and in the background, playing on the crackly cassette player on top of the fridge, was the music of her mother's youth—folk singers like Pete Seeger and Peter, Paul and Mary, songs of peace and protest from the sixties. Ana had especially favored Joan Baez and Linda Ronstadt because of their Hispanic heritage. She would let Maggie rifle through the shoe box of cassettes and choose one tape after another. In those moments, in the tiny kitchen with a pot bubbling on the stove and the calls for peace and love ringing out with the strains of guitar and tambourine, it felt as though nothing could touch them, as though if they could stay there in the kitchen forever, nothing bad would ever happen.

Maggie hovered for a moment over the list of folk singers in her iPod, turning instinctively to that remembered comfort, the warmth and smell of roasted garlic, the reassurance that her mother was there beside her, that everything would turn out okay. But everything was not okay. Ana had been gone for more than seven years now. And Marco . . . Maggie felt numbed from the inside when she thought of him. Over and over Lena's words ran through her head. *"He drowned, Maggie. He's gone."*

She pressed her tongue against the sharp edge of an incisor, wanting to feel something, anything. She simply could not comprehend the loss of him, not yet. Later it would come, she knew. But for now there was a dull ache in the center of her chest, an empty space between her ribs, a proof of sorts that something fundamental had shifted in her world, that something good had vanished.

Maggie passed over the folk singers and chose a piece from her smaller collection of classical music, all compiled at Lena's recommendation. Slipping her earbuds into her ears, she chose Rachmaninoff's Symphony No. 2 in E minor, the Adagio. Fitting, since she was with Lena and Marco when she first heard it. She reclined her seat and closed her eyes, trying to sleep, trying not to remember, heading back to the woman who embraced her like a sister, back to the only man she'd ever truly loved.

Chapter Two

The first time Maggie saw Marco, she called his bluff.

It was orientation week at the Rhys Institute of Art and Design located in central Vermont, one of the premier art and design schools in the nation. Maggie was a bright-eyed freshman with coltish, long limbs and a nimbus of dark curls, canny and street-smart in a way none of her fellow classmates were. She first saw Marco when she passed him on the green. He was standing casually, one long leg clad in perfectly pressed gray trousers perched on a bench as he charmed a trio of freshman girls. He was so striking it was almost unnerving, with wavy hair as black as her own, a closely clipped black beard that gave him a rakish air, like a gentleman pirate, and a lean figure with such sharp angles he looked as though he'd been cut from a clothing ad. His eyes were so dark they were inky.

But what caught her attention were his hands. They weren't long or graceful, not the hands of a painter or artist. They were square with strong fingers, powerful hands that looked as though they could throw a mean punch. However, as he gestured, something about them was fluid too—they pulled meaning from the air as he talked, sculpting art with boxer hands.

"*Hai dei bellissimi occhi blu*," he told a pretty blonde, who giggled and pinked nicely.

"Do you know any Italian?" he asked her, brushing her fingers with his own.

She shook her head, and her friends tittered with her. Maggie rolled her eyes. Italian was close enough to Spanish that she caught the gist of his words. He was complimenting the girl on her pretty blue eyes.

"*Hai la testa vuota*," Marco crooned. *Your head is empty.*

Just about to move on, Maggie did a double take. He was still smiling in an enchanting way, but she caught the mischievous gleam in his eye. The girl sighed, gazing at him with a dreamy expression.

"I have to go to my orientation," the blonde said at last. "But maybe I'll see you around?" She sounded so hopeful.

He grinned, shrugged. "Perhaps. We shall see." He watched the girls as they walked away, heads bent together, the spell of his words still on them. Maggie narrowed her eyes, taking his measure.

"You," Maggie announced, "are so busted."

He turned, surprised, and surveyed her for a moment. Then a smile split his face. His teeth were vivid white against the olive of his skin, pointed incisors giving him a slightly wolfish expression. He looked as though he enjoyed being caught in the act.

"Indeed," he acknowledged, inclining his head. "And who are you?"

"Magdalena Henry. Who are you?"

"Marco Firelli, second-year architecture student." He held out his hand. It was strong and warm, and she tightened her grip, meeting his strength with her own. He raised his eyebrows. "I'm on the welcoming committee. I'm just making sure these new students feel welcome."

"Is that what you call it?" She dropped his hand and took a step back. "Someone should report you to the campus staff for preying on vulnerable freshman girls."

He spread his hands in a gesture of goodwill. "Preying? Such a harsh word. It is all fun and games." He shrugged. "No one gets hurt." He looked at her curiously. "What are you here to study?" Maggie hesitated, but only for a moment. "Photography. I'm on a Gilbert Scholarship."

"Ah." He cocked his head, considering her with a newfound respect. "Beautiful *and* talented."

She crossed her arms and gave him a level stare. Catching her glacial expression, he hurried on. "So, Magdalena Henry, photography student, instead of reporting me, why not have lunch with me?"

She took another look at those intriguing hands and caved.

• • •

It was the beginning of an unlikely friendship. Maggie was wary at first, expecting Marco either to mock her or try to seduce her or both. She was drawn to him in a way that frankly unnerved her. If he tried to seduce her, she wasn't entirely sure what her response would be. So she kept up her guard, trusting neither his charisma nor her own gut reaction to him.

But he surprised her. Underneath his smooth exterior, Marco Firelli was remarkably similar to Maggie. They were outsiders, neither belonging to the privileged and posh world of Rhys, where most students wore their pedigreed old money as casually as a cashmere sweater, jaunting off to Majorca for holidays and trading anecdotes about sailing clubs and polo parties.

He was from Sicily, he told her. His manner was so refined and confident, his dress so casually chic, she had assumed he hailed from a wealthy Italian family. She imagined a villa in the south of Italy, a red sports car, perhaps a vineyard with a long history of excellent wines. He laughed when she told him that one evening at dinner in the cafeteria.

"My father is a butcher. My older brother is an auto mechanic. My younger brother is still in school. Mama takes care of the men. It's how it works there. We are . . . How do you put it? Blue collar." He leaned back in his chair at the cafeteria table, away from the remains of a tasteless chicken casserole, and grinned at her, waiting for a response.

"Well, if you're blue collar, I don't know what white collar would look like," she said dryly. "You could pass for minor royalty around here."

He shrugged, looking pleased. "You mean they don't see the dirt under my fingernails?"

"They're too busy swooning over your accent and your eyes," she observed, rolling her own eyes and spearing a piece of buttered broccoli. Half the freshman girls at Rhys had fallen in was with him, wondering how she could be so lucky, what she had to offer that they did not. She knew the answer. She understood something in Marco Firelli the others couldn't. She had caught him in the act of his own charade and then found him to be a kindred spirit, and that put her in a position reserved for only a few.

"How did you end up here?" she asked. She knew Marco was at Rhys on a foreign exchange scholarship awarded to only a handful of the best and brightest art students from Europe.

"A lucky twist of fate," Marco said. "I was just a kid, stupid, full of ego." He took a sip of coffee. He drank it black and strong, anytime of the day or night. "The other boys I ran with were tough. We were always fighting, stealing just to see if we could get away with it. I got this when I was fifteen." He unbuttoned two buttons on his

33

dress shirt and pulled the collar away, showing her a thick, ropey white scar that looped across his left collarbone, collateral damage from a knifing.

He buttoned up his shirt again. "After that my parents despaired of me. They sent me to live with my aunt outside of Naples. There was nothing there, just pigs and wine. I thought my life was over."

Stuck in a sleepy agrarian community surrounded by bucolic vineyards and small farmsteads, he had been given a choice—apply himself in school or work on the farm with the pigs. He chose the former, and for the first time turned his attention to academics, revealing to everyone's amazement that he was a bright and talented student. He had a particular aptitude for mathematics. He applied himself for a year, and the next year won a scholarship to a prestigious private boys' academy. It had been hell, he told her. The son of a Sicilian butcher with metaphoric dirt under his fingernails had rubbed shoulders with the Italian elite, enduring snubs and taunts and flagrant prejudice.

"They would pretend they couldn't touch me because I was dirty. They'd go out of their way to make sure I knew how different from them I was. Once they threw all my school clothes out back in the garbage with the rotten cabbages and the spoiled meat. It was where I belonged, they said." He bared his teeth. "But it got me here." He shrugged. "So I guess in the end it was worth it." But his eyes were darkened with the memory of that stigma.

"So what now?" Maggie asked.

Marco paused, considering. "So now I will become the best architect in the world. I want them to know my name. All of them. I will be so successful that they have no choice but to respect me." And though he said it lightly, Maggie knew he meant it.

After that Maggie didn't feel she had to hide the truth of who she was from Marco. She told him without shame about the little apartment with dingy tan carpet and leaking water pipes, the long hours her mother worked while Maggie studied or stayed in afterschool activities as long as she could to avoid going back to their dark and empty home.

"She worked six or seven days a week cleaning rooms at the Marriott, and somehow we made it through each month," Maggie confessed. "Although I don't know how we did it."

She stopped, thinking of all the months they had barely made it, squeaking through till the first Friday of the following month, counting and conserving until Ana's paycheck arrived. Maggie wore clothes from Goodwill and stood in the lines at the grocery store where food stamps were accepted, feeling the burn of shame as she avoided the looks of the customers who paid with cash or credit cards.

She told him of the good things too—eating tamales on Thanksgiving and cinnamon cookies at Christmas, going house to house with her mother to deliver homemade cookies to elderly neighbors on Christmas Day, a rare day Ana didn't work. It had always been just the two of them. Ana had no contact with her family in Puerto Rico. They had disowned her after she became pregnant with Maggie. And Maggie had never known her father. Her mother refused to speak of him, saying only that he was not worth the trouble to talk about. Instead, Ana had raised Maggie on her own, and her constant, sometimes tough love had been enough to see her daughter through.

"I discovered photography my freshman year of high school," Maggie explained. The first time she looked through a viewfinder and took a series of shots, she was hooked. Later, in the darkroom at her high school, staring at the negatives she'd taken, she was amazed by the feeling of power they gave her. When she held a camera in her hands, she could tell a story, she had a voice. Maggie knew it was what she'd been born to do.

She got a job at a local fried chicken joint the next summer, waiting tables nights and weekends to save up for her own camera and equipment. "I spent the entire summer reeking of chicken skin andfrying oil, but by September I had enough to buy my first camera. After that I never looked back."

Her senior year her art teacher contacted his old mentors at Rhys and arranged for her to compete for the Gilbert Scholarship. She had been wary at first, reluctant to accept charity or a handout, but when it became clear that she would be judged on her talent alone, not on income level, she had been more than eager to compete.

She won. In a black pantsuit she'd bought at Goodwill for fifteen dollars, her curls tamed back in a severe French twist, she handled herself with poise and a steely determination that was, as one judge put it later, "verging on the intimidating." For her portfolio she chose photos from her neighborhood. Her series juxtaposed the elderly residents of her neighborhood, who clung to their Latino roots, with the rising inner-city gangs, youths who had no regard for their ethnic heritage but formed new identities as members of the Latin Kings or La Raza Nation. Although it lacked the finesse of some of the private-school entries, her work was lauded as "a breath of fresh air" and "visceral, evocative, intriguing." She was awarded the full-tuition Gilbert Scholarship. The judges were unanimous.

"Look at us," Marco said when she finished telling him her story. He shook his head in chagrin. "We have all the talent but none of their money and connections." He waved his hand around the crowded cafeteria, indicating the other students engaged in a low buzz of conversation. "You and me, we are like fish out of water."

Maggie agreed. She was amazed by her good fortune to get to study at Rhys, but she did feel out of her element. No one understood the life she had come from except Marco. She was drawn to him more than she cared to admit. There was an attraction between them to be sure; she would be a fool not to recognize that. But far more than sexual chemistry, there was an affinity for the other, an understanding between them. They recognized each other for what they were and what they were not. They understood what it meant to scrape and want and pull themselves up by their bootstraps, with nothing more than their own determination and talent. They might be fish out of water, but Maggie was comforted to know they at least had each other.

Lena was a different story entirely. She breezed into Maggie's life like the first day of May. On the Sunday of move-in weekend, she made her appearance late in the afternoon.

"Are you Maggie?" she asked breathlessly, standing in the doorway to the dorm room they were to share. Maggie stared at her in dismay.

She had been mailed a slip of paper stating

that her roommate for the year would be Lena Lindstrom from St. Paul, Minnesota. The notice had neglected to mention she would look like a dress model for Macy's circa 1950. She was wearing white gloves and a pastel blue suit. And she was beautiful. With broad cheekbones, a strong jaw, and wide-set eyes the startling blue of a cornflower, she had the type of beauty that comes not from perfection of feature but from the charms of subtle imperfections. Eyes a little too far apart, mouth a little wide, all blended to a striking whole.

"Well, I will say it is a long way from Minnesota to Vermont!" Lena exclaimed, not seeming to notice Maggie's consternation. "Now, which bed is mine?"

Lena Lindstrom was the privileged only child of an obstetrician father and a socialite mother. She had been educated in a private girls' academy and had taken a gap year between high school and college to tour Europe for a cultural music enrichment experience.

"Daddy delivers babies," Lena told her casually as she unpacked her set of powder-pink luggage.

"And what does your mother do?" Maggie asked, eyeing her new roommate in disbelief.

Lena blinked at her. "Charity work, of course."

Maggie was initially wary of Lena, expecting snobbery or elitism, on guard for even a hint of disdain. Had Lena given the slightest indication that she looked down on Maggie for their disparity in class, Maggie would have immediately distanced herself from her roommate, choosing the rest of the school year to coexist with her but not connect. What saved them was that Lena seemed perfectly unaware of any class difference between them. She seemed to take it for granted that it was routine for people to tour Europe after high school or have a baby grand piano in their bedroom in case they took a notion to practice scales in the night. Equally, she seemed unfazed by Maggie's few careful references to her own, very different background. Lena accepted Maggie without a hint of superiority.

"I wish I could speak another language," was her only comment. "Lucky you, to speak Spanish so fluently. I only know a little French and Italian I learned at school and traveling abroad. It must be so nice to dream in another language."

Maggie shook her head, finally concluding that Lena's naïveté was not put on but entirely genuine. Despite Maggie's initial chagrin, they settled into a comfortable roommate relationship, though their personalities and habits differed drastically. Lena was a piano performance major in the conservatory attached to Rhys. She filled her time with order and calm. She kept lists neatly tacked to her desk and relished crossing off items as she completed them. Maggie stayed up all hours of the night listening to music and working on her projects, encased in a solitary bubble of artistic process, but Lena was in bed by ten each night. While Maggie slept in as late as she could in the mornings, Lena did gentle stretching exercises in the middle of the room, starting at precisely 7:30 a.m.

Lena was neat as a pin, organizing her drawers by color. Maggie tended to throw her meager wardrobe into a single drawer and fish out clothes when needed. Maggie wore mostly dark colors, with lean lines and rivets and zippers, clothes pared down and angst-ridden. Lena's wardrobe shimmered with a quiet rainbow of pastels. She looked like a walking Monet.

Maggie marveled at Lena's smooth adjustment to college. She seemed to sail through, serene and poised. At least Maggie thought so until a month into the fall semester. She came back to their room after lunch to find Lena curled up on her bed, cradling her pillow and sobbing soundlessly into the satin cover. When Lena realized Maggie was there, she sat up, brushing back her hair and attempting a bright smile though her face was slick with tears.

"How was lunch?" Lena asked as though nothing in the world was wrong. Mascara was smeared in dark crescents beneath her eyes.

Maggie just looked at her.

Lena's lower lip began to tremble. "You know what? I have no friends."

That evening Maggie took her to meet Marco. As they approached the cafeteria table where he sat, Marco glanced up at them. When he saw Lena, his eyes widened. There was something so privileged and classic about her, the good breeding shining through in every gesture and smile. Marco couldn't take his eyes off her. Lena dimpled when she introduced herself, and Maggie went cold, suddenly seeing the danger in this meeting, the possibility of attraction between them, the threat of being left out. She tried to quash the sudden dart of fear that she might have written herself out of an equation meant for only two.

"So . . ." Lena sat down across from Marco, folding her hands demurely. "Maggie tells me you're Italian. I took lessons for almost a year, so don't try any funny business."

Maggie and Marco both gaped at her, and then Marco began to laugh.

That was the beginning of their little trio. From that day forward they were inseparable. Maggie soon forgot her fears. The three of them became the center of the universe, everything revolving around them. They were the sun, moon, and stars, orbiting each other, excluding all others, shining so brightly it hurt to look at them, eclipsing all else in the light they shed.

Chapter Three

In the harsh light of a SeaTac Airport women's restroom, Maggie grimaced at her reflection, noting the dark circles under her eyes. She wanted a shower and a bed. The series of flights had been grueling. On such short notice Sanne had only been able to book her on a flight with connections in Panama City and Houston. Maggie had long layovers in each city before arriving in Seattle almost forty hours after leaving Managua.

She was used to long flights, regularly jetting from Chicago to places like Cape Town, Buenos Aires, or Bangkok. She usually didn't mind the hours in the air. But this time it was different. She wasn't traveling to a new and exotic location or returning to a country she knew like an old friend. This trip was surreal—the taste of dread and sorrow like lemon bitter on her tongue.

She smoothed her hands through her hair, the long, dark tangle of curls grown obstinate and unruly through the many hours of travel. There was nothing to do but corral them. She rifled through her backpack and finally located the pair of chopsticks she always carried with her. Twisting her hair into a French knot, she secured it with the chopsticks, ignoring the few strands that sprang loose. Her travel outfit—olive-green rock-climbing pants, a brown tank top, and a white buttoned shirt with the sleeves rolled up—looked completely unruffled by hours in the air. The miracle of quick-dry gear, she reflected. Her outfit looked far fresher than she did.

Maggie hoisted her backpack onto her shoulder and grabbed her camera case, exiting the restroom and weaving her way seamlessly through the crowd to baggage claim, dodging children, strollers, and stacks of bags with practiced ease. She had learned years ago how to walk without leaving a wake, to pass quietly amid the hustle and bustle of a market or airport, completely untouched, almost invisible. She collected her suitcase and then headed to the rental car stands to pick up the car Sanne had reserved for her for the next week.

Fifteen minutes later Maggie was out on the highway, speeding north toward Seattle in a bright blue Ford Focus. Through a haze of fatigue, she barely saw the passing evergreen-ridged mountains, the shifting steel gray of water. She skirted the city, driving past the famed Space Needle, which looked like a 1960s B-movie rendering of an alien spaceship, and by Lake Union, crowded with little white sailboats. She continued north through the flatter lands with their miles of tulip fields, lying dormant now that the harvest was over. Finally, almost two hours later, she reached Anacortes, the picturesque seaside town that served as the jump-off point for the ferries to the islands. She bought a ticket and pulled her car into line for the next ferry bound for San Juan Island.

The second largest in a chain of islands that dotted the quiet waters of the Salish Sea, San Juan Island boasted two small, quaint towns, Friday Harbor and Roche Harbor, and a handful of parks. For the past seven years, it had been the summer home of the Firelli family, and a retreat for Maggie as well. She had joined them on the island the first year they took up residence. It was just after her mother's death, and Marco and Lena had only recently purchased the farmhouse and were fixing it up themselves. The combination of manual labor and their quiet compassion had been a lifesaver for her. She had returned every summer since.

The ferry ride was uneventful. Usually Maggie loved to sit on the front deck or in the long, enclosed cabin space with a cup of clam chowder, watching for seals and whales or observing the other passengers. This time, however, she simply staked a claim on an isolated back booth, ignoring the other passengers who were doing jigsaw puzzles or reading true crime novels, and hunched in a corner, trying to sleep. She roused to return to the car when the ferry reached the island.

Maggie started the Ford Focus and slowly

disembarked the ferry, winding through the postcard-perfect town of Friday Harbor. She drove down Spring Street, passing rows of brightly painted clapboard businesses—the Cask and Schooner Pub, the Kings Market grocery store, and the Palace Theater, a misnomer, as the tiny cinema had only three screens.

On the outskirts of town, she made a left turn, then a right, and followed a long stretch of coastal road bordered by tall grass and the sharp, dark outlines of evergreens. Ten minutes later she pulled into the gravel driveway and approached the familiar, sprawling yellow house.

She cut the engine and sat for a moment, surveying the scene. Everything appeared unchanged. Calm and serene, with tidy white trim and long banks of windows on every side, the house looked unmoved by tragedy, as though the bad tidings were simply a dream, nothing more. Here was reality, in the riot of brilliantly colored zinnias blooming in pots along the concrete stoop, in the red tricycle lying upturned on the clipped grass. It was a scene she had come to treasure, the time in the year when she felt as though she could simply exist, relax, and unwind and not have to produce anything of note. Except she was too early. She always came in August when the squash was ripening on Lena's garden vines and the sun spread warm over the entire island like honey on a homemade biscuit. But it was only June. The garden was a square of brown earth, newly planted and just beginning to sprout little green shoots, and the sun was watery behind a thin scrim of gray clouds, too low in the sky for this time of day. It was wrong in a dozen small ways. Maggie took a deep breath and got out of the car.

A moment later the screen door to the mudroom banged open and three children spilled out, jostling to be first, all clamoring for attention. A golden retriever squeezed out the door behind them, trying to weave in between their legs, tail wagging enthusiastically.

"Aunt Maggie, Aunt Maggie!" Gabriella reached her first, wrapping herself around Maggie's legs. Maggie bent and hugged her, marveling at the sturdy little body in her arms. She had grown so much in only nine months. There was such a difference between three and four years old. Three was still a pudgy baby in some ways, but four was a little adult. Gabby pulled back, eager to share her news. Beneath a halo of silky brown curls, her eyes were round and earnest as she looked up at Maggie. "Aunt Maggie, I got a ballerina doll for my birthday and I named her Jessica and I want to be a ballerina when I get big and I growed a lot this year and got new shoes that are pink with sparkles and, Aunt Maggie, my daddy went in the water and he didn't come back," she said all in one unpunctuated sentence, watching Maggie to see how she would react to the news.

"I know, sweetie." Maggie planted a kiss on Gabby's head. "I'm so sorry." She looked past Gabby to the two boys standing silent and solemn behind their sister. "Hey, guys."

They had grown too. Luca, the younger of the two, with Lena's cheekbones and strong jaw, tawny-haired and olive-skinned, had lost the softness of a child. At six, he was beginning to grow rangy and long-limbed, the first small signs of the man he would become. He was still enough of a little boy to be wearing the T-Rex shirt Maggie had sent him for Christmas, though. He had been obsessed with dinosaurs since before he could talk.

She turned to Jonah, stockier, husky in build, with the same close-cropped dark hair and deep brown eyes as Marco, though his were somber and watchful, as though they had seen things far beyond his almost nine years. Maggie hugged them both, inhaling the sharp dirt smell of them, kissing the tops of their heads. She knew it was only a matter of time until she wouldn't be allowed these gestures of affection, until they grew aloof and uncommunicative in the way adolescent boys often did. The golden retriever barked once, nosing in front of the boys, eager for attention too.

"Hey, Sammy." Maggie patted his head,

scratching behind his silky ears. He was still a youngster, just two years old, a Christmas present for the kids when he was a puppy. He was happiest in the center of the melee. "Have you been a good dog?" she asked rhetorically.

"He chewed up my new rubber boots that looked like frogs," Luca informed her, frowning at the dog. "And then he pooped out the plastic eyes."

"Nice, Sammy. Keeping it classy." Maggie grimaced. The dog wagged his tail and grinned. Maggie grabbed her suitcase and camera case from the back of the car and slung her backpack over one shoulder, following the children and Sammy to the house. They ran ahead, rushing through the mudroom door, eagerly calling out her arrival.

Maggie paused at the screen door for a moment, peering into the mudroom, all at once reluctant to go in. It would be so real then, the space Marco occupied in the house empty, hollowed out with loss. She stared at the tidy row of jackets on hooks, the pairs of play shoes lined up neatly beneath them. Marco's old leather bomber jacket from college hung on the farthest hook, a pair of his loafers sitting askew beneath it. She squared her shoulders, bracing herself, and opened the door.

The house was filled with the smells of butter and sugar and rosemary, the unmistakable scent of Lena's signature sugar cookie recipe. Maggie stepped into the mudroom, suitcase and camera case bumping behind her. "Hello?" she called out cautiously.

"In the kitchen!" Lena replied.

Maggie left her luggage in the mudroom and followed the sound of clattering spoons and bowls down the short hallway to the spacious kitchen. There stood Lena, clad in her familiar cherry-print apron, wooden spoon in hand, wisps of blonde hair framing her flushed face. "Maggie!" she exclaimed brightly. "How was your trip?" She ran her finger along the spoon and licked it, pausing contemplatively. "Perfect."

Maggie stared at her in consternation. She had expected tears and tomb-like silence, for the house to feel like a grave. It felt instead like she'd stepped into a "1950s" kitchen ad. In essence, it felt exactly like it always felt.

"What are you making?" she said finally, unsure how to ask what she actually wanted to know. *How is this so normal? Why hasn't time simply stopped?*

Lena looked up, eyes bright. "Sugar cookies for the library bake sale. Want a taste?"

Maggie studied her for a moment, trying to get her bearings. She noted the faint blue circles of fatigue smudging the delicate skin under Lena's eyes, the bright smile that went brittle at the edges.

"Lena." Maggie stepped forward, arms outstretched, expecting to be enveloped as always in a tight hug that smelled of lemon verbena soap and buttery, baking pastries. But all she got was a quick peck on the cheek, and Lena turned away busily, not making eye contact. And then Maggie understood. Lena wasn't coping as marvelously well as it appeared, soldiering on, making the best of things. Lena was in complete denial. Maggie hesitated, thrown off-kilter by the realization, unsure what to do.

"Can I have one?" she asked at last, eyeing the rows of golden cookies lining the newspapers spread out on the counter.

"Of course." Lena handed her a slightly misshapen one. "We eat all the ones that aren't perfect."

"I want one too." Luca poked his head around the kitchen counter that separated the open dining area and family room from the kitchen.

"Me too, me too," Gabby chimed in, joining Luca. Lena doled out three slightly elongated cookies, instructing them to give the third one to Jonah, who had disappeared, then shooed them outside to play.

"Lena." An older blonde woman appeared in the doorway that led to the seldom-used front section of the house that held a home office, half bath, and formal parlor. "The florist van is in the drive again. Should I get it?"

"I'll do it." Lena ran her hands under cold water and dried them on her apron.

The woman spied Maggie and started in surprise, putting her hand to her ample bosom. "Well, my lands, I didn't hear anyone come in."

"Maggie, this is my aunt Ellen, Ellen Foster, from St. Paul. She's my father's sister," Lena said by way of introduction. "She's come to help us since Mother and Daddy aren't able to travel right now. Mother is still unwell. Aunt Ellen, this is Maggie Henry, our oldest friend. She's like family."

"Welcome, Maggie," Ellen said warmly, coming into the kitchen and clasping Maggie's hand in her own. Her hands were strong and calloused, the hands of someone who knew hard work. She looked vaguely familiar. Perhaps Maggie had seen her at Marco and Lena's wedding among the throng of guests. "We're glad you made it here in one piece. You've come a long way."

The doorbell rang, and Lena smiled brightly at Maggie. "One minute," she called out and disappeared down the hall into the mudroom.

Ellen released Maggie's hand and pulled back, giving her a once-over. "How was your trip? Can I get you anything? Water? Are you hungry?"

Maggie shook her head. "I'm okay, thanks. Just tired. It took longer to get out of Nicaragua

52

than I thought it would. As soon as Lena called, I tried to get back."

Ellen nodded. She looked as though she was in her early sixties. Plump in a comforting, grandmotherly sort of way, she was dressed in a pink cardigan, denim skirt, and sensible leather walking shoes. She had the same broad cheekbones and hair Lena had, though her blonde hair was faded with hints of silver, and her eyes were soft and blue. She had a steady calmness about her, the sense that she would not be easily tossed about, that she was rooted to the ground in those sensible shoes.

"We're sure glad you're here now. It's a hard time for all of them, poor loves." She paused for a moment to choose a sugar cookie.

"How's she doing?" Maggie asked in a half whisper, inclining her head in Lena's direction.

"Well . . ." Ellen brushed stray crumbs from her cardigan, catching them in her hand and dumping them into the sink. She pitched her voice low, glancing at the doorway where Lena had gone. "She's baked five batches of cookies so far today, and the bake sale isn't until next Friday, if that tells you anything." She raised her eyebrows and glanced significantly at the rows of cooling cookies.

"What can we do?" Maggie asked.

Ellen considered the question. "They say people grieve in all sorts of ways, so I guess it's just best to let her get on with it in her own way. You never know how people will react to losing a loved one." She shook her head. "When my sister died, I just about went crazy with the sadness. I couldn't keep still. I knitted about every second I wasn't sleeping, just to keep myself sane. That next Christmas everyone we knew got a pair of my mittens, even the mailman. By the time I slowed down, I'd knitted more than thirty pairs. I've still got a box of them somewhere."

Maggie nodded. "So we just let her do her thing?"

Ellen nodded. "For the moment I think that's best."

Maggie hesitated, not wanting to ask her next question. "When is the . . . funeral? I forgot to ask." It felt impossible to say those words and think of them in connection with Marco.

Ellen got two glasses from the cabinet and filled them both with water from a Brita pitcher, handing one to Maggie and keeping one for herself. "Nothing's planned yet. Lena wants to have a memorial service after the cremation. I think we're just waiting on that. Maybe in a few weeks. I think they'll do something bigger later in New York in the fall, but nothing's planned for right now. We're just taking it a day at a time."

Lena reappeared in the doorway, holding a giant bouquet of dusky fuchsia lilies interspersed with spikes of greenery. "Look what the Des Moines Library sent!" she exclaimed, carrying the arrangement into the family room and setting it on a side table. "Aren't they lovely?"

Only then did Maggie notice the flower arrangements. They were crammed in every spare corner of the family room and dining room areas, covering the coffee table and end tables, the window seat, even overflowing onto an overstuffed armchair. Arrangements of every size, shape, and color, from a tasteful bunch of white narcissus to a gaudy monstrosity involving palm fronds and birds of paradise. There was even one crafted from red roses in a horseshoe shape.

"Oh wow!" Maggie exclaimed involuntarily, taken aback by the sheer number of them.

Lena nodded, surveying the room. "Isn't it wonderful? So many people have been so kind."

Maggie stared at her, brow furrowed. Surely Lena must realize these were flowers sent in response to her husband's death, that they represented loss of the most gripping and fundamental kind. She was acting as though they were some kind of gift, as though they were sent to celebrate a new baby or a birthday.

"I think we've gotten flowers from more than twenty states," Lena mused, looking at the arrangements. "I should have the children make a list . . ." Absently, she reached out and stroked the petals of a spray of yellow roses, coming back to reality a moment later. "Maggie, you must be exhausted. Do you want to rest before dinner? We're having salmon."

Maggie was at a loss for words. Surely it wasn't normal to act so normal.

"Yes," she said finally, clearing her throat. "That'd be great."

Later, seated around the long, oval dining table, they ate a dinner of grilled salmon, green beans, and salad. Through the partially open windows came a cool, damp breeze carrying the briny scent of the sea and the faint rhythmic lapping of the surf on the rocky beach below the house. The boys were quiet except to ask for butter or more milk. Lena seemed preoccupied. Only Gabby was talkative, toying with her food and keeping up a running dialogue between two My Little Ponies she'd brought to the table.

"Now, Gumdrop, you have to eat your vegetables because they're good for you," Gabby admonished one of the ponies, a fat orange one decorated with sparkles.

"But I don't want to. I don't like them," she whined in a high voice, pushing its nose into her small pile of green beans.

"Well, you have to or you can't have a cookie," Gabby reasoned with it.

"No, no. You can't make me." The pony balked

at the vegetables, pink synthetic mane falling into the beans.

Ellen glanced at Lena, who was staring into space, a fork poised in her hand. Reaching over, Ellen laid a gentle hand on Gabby's shoulder. "Let's not play ponies while we're eating, dear love. You can take them into the bath with you later."

Frowning but obedient, Gabby set the ponies by her glass of milk. The rest of dinner passed quietly. No one glanced at the empty place at the table, though Marco's absence was glaring. Ellen asked Maggie questions about her work and about the trip to Nicaragua, and she replied almost mechanically. It felt surreal, as though they were moving in slow motion through some alternative version of reality.

"Anyone for a game of Sorry?" Ellen asked as she cleared the table. They played one round. Luca and Gabby teamed up with Ellen and Maggie while Lena and Jonah played on their own. Ellen tried her best to rally enthusiasm for the game, but it was obvious no one really wanted to play. Fighting a crippling fatigue, Maggie found her mental reflexes were too slow to be of much use.

"Sorry, guys," she apologized. "Jet lag just hit. My brain feels like Swiss cheese."

"Why don't we turn in for the night?" Ellen suggested. "It's been a long day." She put the game back in its box, adding, "I've got a new Miss Marple mystery waiting for me, and I should call Ernie. That's my husband," she explained to Maggie. "He's back in St. Paul. Our daughter, Stephanie, is looking in on him, so I shouldn't worry. He'll be fine. But I don't think he can even open a can of soup if I'm not there to show him how." She smiled fondly. "I think I'll put my feet up and give Ernie a call before bed."

While Maggie was staying in her usual spot in the upstairs guest room, Ellen was sleeping in the small, rarely used office tucked behind th

front parlor. Maggie had peeked in before dinner. In the short time she'd been there, Ellen had already transformed the tiny room with only a desk and daybed into a cozy little space, complete with a hand-knit afghan and a stack of mystery novels from the San Juan Island Library.

Lena yawned, then declared, "I'm not a bit tired. Aunt Ellen, do you mind putting the children to bed? I'm going to make some peanut butter blossoms."

Ellen paused, eyeing Lena for a moment, and then nodded. "Of course. You go right ahead."

"Do you want help with the cookies?" Maggie asked Lena, secretly hoping she would say no. Her limbs were beginning to feel like they were made of lead, the emotional and physical toll of the last few days starting to overtake her.

Lena waved her away. "Go rest," she encouraged, shooing Maggie up the stairs. "We'll see you in the morning. Sweet dreams." She didn't meet Maggie's eyes.

In the soft golden light of early evening, away from the lights of the house and across the wide expanse of lawn, Daniel Wolfe crouched beneath the fringe of Douglas firs ringing the property. He sat hidden in the same spot he'd occupied for the last two evenings, dark hair and clothes blending into the shadows between the branches. He saw the women and children at the table. A whiff of supper drifted out an open window— grilled salmon. It reminded him of home, of his grandmother making salmon almost every night when the Chinook were running and the fishing was good. He remembered unwrapping the little foil tent stuffed with the bright-orange salmon steak and a sprig of dill from her garden. Sometimes there was a slice of lemon on top, but lemons were a luxury, so it had been absent more often than not.

His stomach growled, but he ignored it. He didn't deserve the warmth and the comfort of that house, let alone a full belly. When he came out of that cold, black water, he made a promise to himself, and he intended to keep it.

A new woman was at the table, tall and slender

with a mass of dark, curly hair gathered at her neck. Daniel had not seen her arrive. She ate quickly and kept glancing toward the blonde wife. At one point, when the dinner was done, she rose and went to the bank of windows, staring across the lawn. He shrank back into his hiding spot, although muffled by the thick carpet of moss and needles, hidden as he was in the shadows, she would never hear or see him. She turned away after a moment. She looked tired.

Who was she? She wore sadness like a jacket. Daniel could sense it wrapped around her. He knew that look. He had been wearing it in some way much of his life. He shifted, trying to find a comfortable position amid the roots and rocks. He was just a few years past thirty, fit and athletic, still a man firmly in his prime, but tonight he felt much older. He could feel every twig and stone beneath him.

After dinner the children and two of the women went upstairs. Only the blonde wife was left. She absently mixed something in a bowl, moving as though in a dream, then placed a tray in the oven. A few minutes later he sniffed the air, catching a faint scent wafting from an open window. Peanut butter cookies. Like Katherine used to make, long ago when they were first dating, when she was still a farm girl from Georgia, before the city transformed her.

From the open window came snatches of

music. Ella Fitzgerald, a crackly recording of a slow jazz song. It was growing dark, the shadows lengthening across the lawn. Daniel sighed, easing back against the rough trunk of a Coast Douglas fir tree and pulling his cargo jacket closer around him, settling himself in for the night. Even in summer the islands could be cold after sundown. He remembered that from when he was a boy, the chilly novelty of wearing wool socks to bed in August.

He stayed as he had for the last two nights, waiting for hours until every light in the house went dark, until the stars came out like pinpricks in the sky, a wash of them across the silky darkness. He watched while the household slumbered, until the first pale streaks of gray crept through the early morning, until the birds stirred above him and began to twitter sleepily. He watched because there was no one else to watch over them now. He kept his vigil through the darkness until he heard the first trill of a lark from the meadow nearby, signaling the dawn. Only then did he rise, muscles stiff with cold, his stomach tight with hunger, and slip away through the trees. His job for the day was done.

Chapter Four

Maggie awoke, momentarily disoriented in a bright splash of midmorning sun. She rolled over, trying to get her bearings, and stared blankly out the window framed by cheerful red-checked curtains to the side yard and fringe of firs ringing the property. She suppressed a groan as the whole exhausting trip and strange, surreal evening came back to her in an instant.

She shut her eyes and opened them again, hoping against hope that she would not see the creamy white walls of Marco and Lena's guest room but instead the palm fronds of a Honduran beach hut. She listened for a moment at the sounds coming through the slightly open window, wanting to hear a call to prayer from a minaret in Istanbul or the monotonous cry of a Moroccan fishmonger in Agadir, anything but the steady wash of waves against the cliffs and the lonely cry of gulls circling the water.

The truth was that she would rather be anywhere but here. How could she face today and tomorrow and every day after that, each of them hollowed out by a loss so fundamental she couldn't quite comprehend it? She had to approach the reality of Marco's death from the corners, with a snatch of memory, a tiny flash of recollection. She recalled the catch in Lena's voice on the telephone as she said those two words that changed the world—*"He's gone."* The image of Marco's leather jacket hanging on the hook in the mudroom, his empty loafers sitting beneath it—even those tiny slices of memory took her breath away.

Maggie rolled out of bed with a groan and hoisted her suitcase onto the quilt, rummaging for her toiletries. She could hear voices rising from the kitchen below. Everyone must be up.

In the cheery bathroom down the hall, under a stream of hot water, she lathered and rinsed, breathing in the steam and the green-tea scent of Lena's favorite guest soap, shaving her legs, mechanically performing the minor pleasures she had come to fully appreciate in her years of travel. When she was on assignment, hot water was often a luxury she did without. She was used to taking precise, minimal showers from a bucket of cold water or bathing with a bandanna and a basin. Sometimes, in arid places, water itself was so scarce her only option was to wipe herself down with a moistened bandanna to cool her skin for a moment and erase a little of the grime at the end of a sun-scorched day.

She'd learned to tolerate a fine coating of dust in her hair and a trickle of salty-white sweat dried between her breasts and behind her knees. It was part of the job. But when she had the opportunity, she relished a good hot shower and all the suds she could possibly make. Today, though, she was too preoccupied to enjoy them.

Her head was pounding, probably a combination of her long travel days and grief. She leaned against the cold tile of the shower and tried to center herself. "I'm here on the island. I'm here on the island," she repeated over and over, a mantra to secure her in time and space. Sometimes she felt so disconnected from her surroundings that she thought she might just float away and find herself in another place entirely. Brussels for instance, or Benin. Occasionally, in a neutral environment like a hotel room or airport lounge, she couldn't recall where she was. Her mind would go blank, and she would be completely unable to name the country or continent where she was standing. It was a strange sensation, floating for a few seconds in a geographical void, struggling to orient herself until some small detail clicked into place and she was once more in a budget hotel in Mexico City or in the KLM lounge in Amsterdam.

When she traveled, she dreamed of being here on the island more than any other place. Not her utilitarian apartment in Chicago with its unused musty smell, the hollow click of her shoes on the wood floors, the perpetually empty refrigerator, but here with Marco and Lena and the kids. The rest of the year she would often drift to sleep replaying their summer days together—the barbecues and game nights; picnics at Lime Kiln Point, the top whale-watching spot on the island; making homemade ice cream; sitting by a dying bonfire, watching stars wink to life.

She had always felt the pull of the island, the allure of the family who embraced her and knew her so well. But lately that pull had become even stronger. In the past few months, she had begun to notice the thrill of travel was wearing a bit thin. What would have stirred her blood a year ago had begun to seem more like repetition, familiar in a way that felt perilously close to boring. She had always laughingly insisted that the day she settled down was the day she'd die, but recently she had felt the lead-edged pull of fatigue as she disembarked from yet another international flight, laid her head on another lumpy pillow, listened to the babble of crowds speaking a language she didn't understand.

She had a new ache in her bones that she couldn't identify. She found herself sniffing apple pie–scented candles in a Heathrow Airport gift shop, ordering fried chicken and a butterscotch milkshake at an American-themed restaurant in Beijing. She tried to shake it off, muster her energy, convince herself the world was still a vast and undiscovered territory waiting for her camera lens. But she kept dreaming of her mother's voice, softly singing the words to a long-forgotten lullaby in Spanish. She woke up more than once with those words crowding onto the tip of her tongue.

She'd told no one, not even Lena and Marco, certainly not anyone at work. She was rising fast in her career. Everything she'd worked for— what she had yearned for in those long-ago nights on Chicago's southwest side, listening to the strident voices of the neighbors arguing and the boom of car stereos cranked high outside on the street—it was all within her reach. Now was not the time to turn back.

So she steeled herself, ignoring the pull of her heart toward something she couldn't quite name. "It's just a slump," she repeated again and again, forcing herself to order samosas and chicken satay, choking down the words to the lullaby that floated up in her throat at the most inopportune times. "I just need a little rest," she reassured herself, secretly wishing August could come sooner rather than later.

But now that she was here again, she wished she could turn back time, be somewhere other than this, before she learned about Marco, when she could still think of the island as a place of safety and continuity. Everything felt different now, strange and unfamiliar, as though it were another place entirely. It rattled her. Without

Marco, this place no longer felt like home.

Maggie shook her head, confused and uneasy, wiping a froth of shampoo from her cheek. If this no longer felt like home, what did? She had nowhere else to go.

She squeezed her eyes shut under the spray of hot water, trying to steel herself once again for the day ahead, forcing herself to be strong. Lena needed her. The kids needed her. She couldn't go to pieces now. With a sigh, she turned off the water and prepared to face reality.

Clean and dressed, Maggie padded down the stairs and paused at the kitchen door. Ellen was standing at the stove in Lena's cherry-print apron, making pancakes. The kitchen smelled like maple syrup, and Maggie's stomach growled. Luca and Gabby hovered at Ellen's elbows, peering at the griddle on the stove top. Jonah sat at the table with a stack of pancakes on a plate in front of him. Lena was nowhere to be seen.

"Ooh, that one looks like a bunny. I want it!" Gabby pointed to a pancake cooking on the griddle.

"Mine doesn't look like a triceratops," Luca said, peering at the pancakes doubtfully.

"It looks like a fairy!" Gabby giggled.

Luca frowned, disappointed. "But I wanted horns."

"Well," Ellen said, "let's just put a bit of batter

right here, and . . . Look at that. It's a ferocious triceratops."

"Morning," Maggie said, rounding the counter into the kitchen.

Ellen glanced up from the griddle and gave her a warm smile. "Good morning, Maggie. Sleep well?" Luca and Gabby looked up, curious for a moment, then returned their attention to the pancakes.

Maggie yawned. "Like a rock. Mind if I make some coffee?"

"Goodness no. Can you operate that thing?" Ellen motioned with the spatula toward the gleaming stainless steel espresso maker looming over one corner of the counter.

Maggie nodded. "Sure. It's not as hard as it looks." Ellen raised her eyebrows. "Well, it looks like you could fly it to the moon, all those knobs and levers. I'm afraid to touch it."

Maggie crossed to the machine and touched one of the sleek knobs. It was a top-of-the-line Italian espresso maker made in Milan. It had been Marco's splurge one Christmas. He had an identical one at their house in New York. He'd taught her how to use it when she came to the island the following summer. It was Marco who'd started Maggie's love affair with espresso, and she'd never gotten over her taste for the strong, tiny cups of coffee. It was the perfect way to start a morning.

"If you can operate that contraption, do you mind making me a cup too?" Ellen asked, expertly flipping a pancake.

"Sure." Maggie hunted in the cupboard for the coffee beans Marco ordered direct from a specialty store in Little Italy in the Bronx. In the space of a few minutes, she made two double-shot espressos and offered one to Ellen. "Oh, just leave it right there on the counter. I'm going to add a whole lot of milk. Ernie says I like my milk with just a drop of coffee." Ellen chuckled and turned another pancake. Jonah sat at the table alone, fidgeting with his silverware. Maggie slid into a chair beside him. "Hey, good morning."

He didn't look at her and didn't respond.

"How are the pancakes?" she asked before taking a sip of her espresso.

He shrugged. His hair was sticking up, still tousled from sleep. He looked like a lost little boy, even though his attitude seemed more like a teenager, drawn in on himself and generally unresponsive. Maggie turned her attention to her coffee, giving him some space. He'd just lost his father, after all.

"Aunt Maggie, what shape pancake do you want?" Gabby asked, coming to the table to take Maggie's order. "You get to pick one."

"Hmm." Maggie pretended to think for a moment. "I want one shaped like a pancake."

Puzzled for a second, Gabby gave her a look of consternation. "But it *is* a pancake," she protested. "You have to pick a real shape."

"Okay then. A cloud."

A scant five minutes later, Maggie was staring down at a stack of pancakes so light and fluffy they'd put a nimbus to shame. She slathered them with butter and real maple syrup, then took a bite, savoring it. When was the last time she'd had pancakes this good? It had been the previous August, in her first week on the island. They'd all gone blackberry picking one afternoon and lugged home fifteen pounds of them. Her remaining days had been drenched in blackberries—blackberry jam, scones, pound cake, homemade ice cream, and pancakes with blackberry sauce spiked with just a hint of vanilla. It had been a step away from paradise. Those few weeks were the last time she saw Marco. She pictured his face peering around a blackberry thicket, laughing through his dark, clipped beard at her fumbled attempts to keep up with Lena, a speed picker.

"Never race a pianist," he advised, nodding to Lena, who was intent on her task. "They've got lightning hands. You and me, we've just sketched a wall or pushed the shutter, and she's already played Schubert or Bach." He winked. "We don't stand a chance."

Recalling the moment, Maggie tried to swallow

around the lump in her throat, but the bite of pancake wouldn't budge. She sat there for a long moment, eyes burning, and finally managed to get it down. When she looked up, Jonah was staring at her. She managed a weak smile. He didn't smile in return.

"Light as a cloud," she commented. Without a word, Jonah pushed out his chair and left the table. When she looked at his plate, she saw he'd cut his stack of pancakes into perfect squares but hadn't taken a bite.

When Maggie checked her cell phone after breakfast, she saw she had a new voice mail. Probably Alistair. Maggie knew Sanne had informed the office of the situation, but her boss liked to be kept in the loop. She owed him a call to personally explain why she'd left the coffee-plantation shoot early. She had taken enough shots to satisfy the magazine's requirements. Not as many as she might have preferred, but the photos she'd taken were good enough. The series wouldn't be one of her best, but it would still be good quality. Alistair would not be too disappointed.

"I'll be back in a few minutes," Maggie called to Ellen, letting herself out the mudroom door and rounding the house, heading for the shore. The day was warming up, the sun sparkling on the dark surface of the water. She walked along a dirt-and-gravel path running along the bluff, past the steps leading down to the half circle of private rocky beach on the Firellis' property, then through a stand of tall, shadowed firs, and into the overgrown field beside the house. A bald eagle eyed her from a tall, dead tree as she passed underneath, and she gave him a salute. The tree was a favorite perch for eagles, and one was often stationed there, keeping an eye on the world below.

The San Juan Islands had the greatest concentration of bald eagles in the lower forty-eight states, Lena had told her once. Lena was a fount of information about the flora and fauna of the islands. When they were out with the children, she was forever pointing out a black oystercatcher on the shoreline or an osprey in flight or naming obscure tiny plants they found in the open prairie habitat farther inland.

Maggie stopped at a little outcropping of black rock overlooking the Strait and took out her cell phone, glancing at the display screen. Good. She had reception.

Maggie was part of Chicago Photography Incorporated, an agency whose mundane name belied the fact that it comprised some of the top photographers in the country. The agency was the brainchild of Alistair Finney, the man who brought them all together and kept them all together.

Alistair had been, in his heyday in the eighties, one of the top glamour and high-fashion photographers in the world. He regularly jetted off to Milan, Paris, and Rome. Celebrities and presidents wanted him to photograph them in their homes and with their families. Supermodels and designers demanded he oversee their shoots. And then, after almost fifteen years of stress and a bleeding ulcer, Alistair announced he was retiring to start and manage a photography agency comprised of the best and the brightest in the industry. He relocated to Chicago, bought a renovated brick townhouse in Lincoln Park with his partner of a decade, Alan, and then rented a high-end office space in the Loop and began tapping every source and contact for exceptional talent.

Within a few years CPI was a leading light in the photography field, known for cutting-edge photography and a standard of excellence few others could rival. Although the agency was composed of mostly veteran photographers with years of experience and an impressive array of credentials, Alistair had a fondness for finding diamonds in the rough and polishing them until they shone. He enjoyed the challenge. It was a hobby of sorts for him. That's how he'd found Maggie.

On her twenty-third birthday, Maggie had run into Alistair at a photo exhibit on the aftermath of war. A friend of hers had contributed a photo and invited her to the posh downtown Chicago loft for the show's private opening. As she was standing before a shot of the bombed-out shell of an office building in Baghdad, Alistair came up behind her.

"Dull, dull, dull," he pronounced in the smoothest of British accents, sipping a dirty vodka martini with three olives impaled on a toothpick. "I'm all for peace; don't get me wrong. I'm a pacifist, but do we really think another melodramatic shot of ruined architecture is going to stop a war?"

Maggie turned, surprised to find him addressing her. She knew who he was. Not someone to be taken lightly. Someone to impress.

"Alistair Finney." He offered his hand and she shook it.

"Magdalena Henry," she said, a little dazed, trying to think of something clever to say.

"Oh, I know who you are," he told her, sipping his martini. "I don't talk to strangers, you know." He studied her. "I've been told you're someone I should keep my eye on."

Maggie said nothing. He nodded sharply, as though coming to some sort of internal agreement with himself. "One o'clock Monday. Bring something nice to my office so I can see what talent you've got. And don't eat lunch; we're having sushi."

And that was that. Over salmon sashimi and yellowtail nigari, they discussed her last project, a series that followed a first-generation Mexican immigrant family as they prepared for and celebrated their eldest daughter's *quinceañera* in Chicago.

Alistair fanned out the shots she'd brought with her, studying them thoughtfully. "These are excellent." He sounded almost surprised. "Lovely technique and composition, but it's more than that." He tapped his chin thoughtfully. "You have layers of story. Anyone can take a photo of a birthday party, but you're not just telling us about a birthday party, are you? You're telling us a story about displaced people, about how they use celebration to hold on to their cultural roots."

He examined one photo more closely, musing to himself. "Hmm, interesting. I get the feeling that you're just a half step away, a pretty little voyeur looking through the front window. You're just a little removed."

Alistair stepped back from the table and pursed his lips, considering the photos and then her. "Well, my dear, you'll go as far as you want to, but you will need a helping hand. Who are you currently an intern with?"

When she told him, he scoffed. "That will never do. Here's what I'm prepared to do for you. I like you, and I don't like very many people. So I will give you a chance to prove you belong here. Six months, and we'll see if we fit."

She agreed immediately. No one in their right mind said no to Alistair Finney. Maggie started to gather her photos, but Alistair interrupted her.

"Have a care, Magdalena." He laid a warning finger over the photos on the table, not touching them, just making a point. "You are very good, but you have a flaw. You're removed from your subjects, the observer who never quite enters in. Just remember that when telling others' stories, you need to tell a little bit of your own as well." He gave her a wry smile. "We can't always live behind a camera, my dear. Life has to be touched and tasted and smelled in all its bloody, messy glory. Remember that. You have to live in the world, not just observe it."

She hadn't known what to make of his words. She could not see the flaw as he did. She gave her all to her work, and had received a steady stream of accolades and praise. She was excellent, a standout. Whatever weakness Alistair saw, it didn't seem to be holding her back professionally. She tried to put his criticism from her mind, but his words lingered, like a pebble in her shoe. She wished she could remove it but had never figured out how.

The original six-month trial period had morphed into a six-year partnership. Alistair had given her the contacts and prestige to open all the right doors, and Maggie had given the wholehearted dedication and raw talent to make an increasingly successful name for herself. She had never once been sorry she said yes.

She didn't bother to listen to the voice mail but instead dialed Alistair's cell directly.

"My little renegade star," he said without preamble when he picked up on the fourth ring. "Where are you and when are you coming home?"

"Hi to you too. Is that a jazz band I hear? Where are *you?*"

"A benefit, some sort of cancer research. Bladder cancer, I think. I can't remember. I'm representing us all, you know. And having to eat a ghastly imitation of barbecued pork. It's a picnic." He said the word *picnic* as though it were a profanity.

Maggie laughed. Alistair was a diva, but he was also loyal and shrewd. He worked hard to promote CPI anywhere he thought might be advantageous, even benefit picnics.

"I'm on the island, and I don't know when I'm coming back." She paused, listening to the muted saxophone solo in the background. It seemed worlds away from where she stood now, alone with only the rolling expanse of the sea for company. She took a deep breath. "Alistair, there's been an accident."

When she told him the details, Alistair was

silent for a moment. "Oh, my dear," he said finally, "how positively tragic. And three little children. Of course you need to be there. For as long as it takes. But, darling, you also need to be thinking about coming home as soon as possible." His voice dropped a few notches in volume, and he moved away from the music. She could hear the saxophone receding in the background. Then it was just Alistair's voice, crisp and urgent, as clear as though he were standing right next to her.

"Listen, I was going to wait until you got back from Nicaragua to tell you, but you need to be thinking about this now. I know, terrible timing, but I've put your name in for the Regent Fellowship this year, my dear. I sent in the series you did last year for that Women's Awareness Campaign, the one on mothers and daughters in prostitution in the red-light district of Kolkata. And, Magdalena, they've accepted you. You are in the running! I just received word today. Congratulations, darling. It's a marvelous accomplishment. And if you want to have a prayer of winning, we need to start strategizing about your entry straight-away."

Maggie sat down hard on the rocky outcropping. She was speechless. Alistair was still talking, but she couldn't concentrate on his words. The Regent Fellowship was the most prestigious award in the photography world. Given just once every three years to a photographer of outstanding merit, it came with a one-hundred-and-fifty-thousand-dollar cash prize and a private traveling exhibit that circled fifteen major cities across the globe. Winning the Regent vaulted the recipient into a tiny circle reserved for the best, most innovative photographers in the world. It was the golden apple, every serious photographer's dream. And now Alistair was handing her an opportunity to compete.

Maggie gripped the phone, stunned, aware that she should respond but unable to formulate a sentence. Her pulse was hammering in her ears. Alistair had submitted her name without consulting her, and her Kolkata series had won her a chance to enter, no small thing in and of itself. But now would come the real challenge. To have a prayer of winning, she would have to create a series more compelling than anything she'd ever done before.

"The entry is due by September 1," Alistair told her helpfully.

Maggie shook her head, trying to absorb the implications of his words. If she were smart, she'd be on the first plane back to Chicago to strategize with Alistair. This was the opportunity of a lifetime. But she couldn't possibly leave right now. Lena was in full-blown denial. The kids were in shock. And as for herself, she didn't even know how she felt. The spaces of her heart felt hollow and unknown. She should have been elated by this news, but it seemed so removed from her present circumstances. Alistair might as well have been promising her the moon.

"But I can't leave," she told him.

"Of course not," Alistair soothed. "You need to finish your grieving, help the family, that sort of thing. I understand. But I'd like to see you back in the office next week. Sort out what you need to, then come home."

Maggie hesitated. Would a week be enough time? If she said no, she'd be spitting in the face of the best opportunity she'd ever been given. It had been her biggest dream for as long as she could remember. It would be the culmination, the triumph of her career, the thing she had been striving for with single-minded devotion for so many years.

"I'll try," she said in the end. It was the best she could do.

Chapter Five

Maggie walked back to the house in a daze, still trying to digest the conversation with Alistair. She had a shot at the Regent, and yet she had to stay on the island, at least for the time being. Leaving was out of the question, but now staying seemed equally impossible. The tension was making her head spin.

As she rounded the front of the house toward the mudroom, she noticed a motorcycle parked beside Lena's Volvo. Curious, Maggie eyed it as she passed. Black with silver trim, it looked vintage, tough, like something Steve McQueen might have ridden. Definitely a man's bike. Whose was it?

"Lena?" she called, shucking off her shoes in the mudroom.

"Maggie, we're in here," Lena responded from the direction of the front parlor. Surprised, Maggie veered to the left, into the front room. She'd never seen Lena entertain guests there before. The room always smelled unused, like faded rose potpourri and a thin layer of dust.

Lena was sitting on a chaise lounge, ankles crossed, her posture perfect, sipping from a china teacup. She was surrounded by stiff, perfectly appointed furnishings in lemon yellows and floral-print pinks. Sitting across from her on the buttercup cotton-twill sofa was undoubtedly the owner of the motorcycle. He was handsome in a rugged, open-road kind of way, with wavy auburn hair that fell across his brow carelessly, a strong, square jaw, a cleft chin. He was about their age, maybe a few years older, early thirties. The teacup he held looked ridiculous, fragile and out of place in his large hands. Maggie got the distinct impression of broad shoulders and long legs in faded blue jeans as he leaned over, placed the cup on the coffee table, and rose to greet her. He was dressed in a dark leather café racer jacket, and as he turned toward her, she noted with shock that he was wearing a clerical collar. A priest? A motorcycle-riding priest?

"You must be Maggie," he said, sticking out his hand. She moved forward automatically, shaking it. He had quite a grip. She tightened hers instinctively. His accent surprised her, broad and open. He was Australian. What in the world was a motorcycle-riding Aussie priest doing here on the island in the middle of nowhere?

"Griffin Carter. It's a pleasure." He met her eyes with a direct, assessing look.

"Magdalena Henry." She dropped her hand and broke the gaze after a second, feeling somehow looked into, as though he could see more of her than she was prepared to offer. She took a seat in a prim chintz armchair that had been stuffed within an inch of its life. The chair made her sit up perfectly straight, as though on high alert.

"Lena's been telling me about your work," Griffin continued, resuming his seat on the sofa. "I haven't heard of you, but I feel like I should have." He grinned, displaying square, slightly crooked teeth, a deep dimple in one cheek. He was unnerving, warm and dynamic in a way that ruffled her composure. No priest had any business being that magnetic. The priests of her childhood had been dry, old men who smelled of chalky, pink wintergreen candies and had no sense of humor. She'd loathed them. Maggie stared at him wordlessly for a moment. She narrowed her eyes. Why was he here?

"Maggie, would you like some tea?" Lena offered, already filling a cup from the rose-patterned teapot on the coffee table. "It's Lemon Zinger." She added a spoonful of sugar without asking and proffered the cup.

"Where do you work?" Maggie asked Griffin, taking the tea.

"Just down the road in Friday Harbor. Church of the Blessed Redeemer."

Maggie took a sip. Tepid and too sweet. "How do you know Lena?"

"Our neighbor invited us last summer to a music program at the church," Lena answered. "When we came to the island this summer, the children wanted to go back." She shrugged delicately. "We enjoy it." She smiled at Griffin.

"It's been great having Lena and the kids with us," Griffin added. "When we heard about Marco . . . Well, of course we're all concerned about the family. I just wanted to stop in and see if there was anything I could do." He took a sip of tea and sat back, relaxed, appearing oddly comfortable in the prim surroundings.

"That's so kind." Lena looked down at her teacup. "We're fine, though. Right, Maggie? Everything's just fine."

"Right," Maggie said without much conviction, letting her gaze linger on Lena's downturned face. When she looked away, she found Griffin watching the interaction with a slight frown. He raised one eyebrow at her, nodding ever so slightly toward Lena. Maggie dropped her gaze, pretending she hadn't seen his unspoken question. No, they were not fine, but she didn't know if she wanted to admit it to the priest.

A few moments later, Griffin rose to leave. He set his cup on the coffee table and turned to Maggie. She stood, and he met her eyes squarely. His were a light brown, almost golden. She had the distinct impression that he was taking her measure just as much as she was taking his.

"It was great to meet you, Maggie." He took her hand again in that firm grip.

"You too," Maggie replied, a little wary, unsure what to think of him.

"If there's anything I can do, please call."

Maggie nodded, and he released her hand. Griffin turned to Lena, leaning down and laying his hand on her shoulder. "Lena, if you need anything at all, don't hesitate to call. We're all here for you." He squeezed her shoulder and straightened.

Lena smiled, though her lips trembled at the corners. "Thank you for everything. It means so much." She dropped her gaze.

Griffin let himself out, taking the impression of warmth and energy with him. They listened to the *vroom, vroom* of his motorcycle fading down the lane. The room seemed to exhale, falling into silence.

Lena broke the spell. "Well," she said, leaning forward to place her teacup with Griffin's empty one on the coffee table. "Well, that was lovely of him to stop by."

Maggie noted Lena's hands were trembling. Her fingernails, usually immaculate ovals lacquered with a clear polish, were bitten to the pink. Seeing Lena up close in the pale sunlight filtering through lace curtains, Maggie was struck again by how tired she looked, with dark smudges under her eyes. It didn't look as though she'd slept in quite some time.

"Lena, are you okay?" Maggie asked

gently. Lena looked up, laughing quickly, touching her collarbone with one hand, tucking a stray hair back into her French twist.

"Of course." She didn't meet Maggie's eyes.

"Really?" Maggie responded, her voice quiet but insistent. "Lena, you haven't said Marco's name since I got here. You're acting like nothing's happened, like he might walk back in the door any second. And you and I both know that's not going to happen. So when I ask you if you're okay, I'm asking because I love you and I'm worried about you, and I really want to know what's going on in your head."

Lena had gone pale at the mention of Marco. She fumbled with the tea things, gathering them into a stack, her hands shaking so that the cups and saucers clinked together alarmingly. "I'm fine," she stated, her voice reedy with strain. "I'm just fine."

She glanced up as she spoke, fixing her eyes on a point just to the left of Maggie's face, the spot she'd focused on when she told Maggie their freshman year that she'd never been drunk before. The spot Maggie had seen Lena focus on only a handful of times in their many years of friendship. The spot she focused on when she was bald-facedly lying.

Chapter Six

Later that night Maggie shut the door to the guest room softly, mindful of Gabby asleep in the next room. It was only a little past ten, but it felt like the middle of the night. Fatigue pulled at her like a lead weight, dragging down her every movement. It had been a long day. Her mind was still churning over the call with Alistair and her concern over Lena's evasive behavior, but she felt too tired to make any headway.

In the darkness she crossed the room and felt for the switch on the table lamp beside the bed, instantly suffusing the space with a soft warm glow. She hoisted her backpack onto the bed and fished around the inside for a moment. On the lower right, next to her water bottle, she found what she was looking for. She pulled out the small square leather case.

It was billed as a man's wallet in the tiny shop in Mexico, but Maggie used it to carry her most precious possessions. She fingered the case, as worn and smooth as butter from years of handling. Inside were three photos. One of her mother when she was young, smiling as she half-covered her face with her hands, embarrassed by the camera in the hands of their elderly neighbor and Maggie's occasional babysitter, Mrs. Sanchez. She was bent over the ugly avocado-colored bathtub in their first apartment in Chicago, giving three-year-old Maggie a bath. All that was visible of Maggie were a pair of dimpled knees and fat little feet. It was her mother's expression that Maggie loved—tired but happy, a soft smile lighting up the round contours of her face.

The other two were of Marco. Maggie pulled the first one out, studying it. She'd snapped it her senior year of college outside the pub where Marco worked. She had caught him leaning casually against an iron railing, smoking a clove cigarette. His hair was too long, a style he hadn't worn in the years since then, and he was wearing his old leather bomber jacket. He looked a little like James Dean. He was glancing sideways at the camera, head cocked slightly, one brow arched. It captured the essence of him, his almost feral grace and his fierce edge, the sense Maggie always had that he couldn't be contained or subdued. He was his own man.

Carefully, she slid the picture back into the wallet and took out the last photo, rubbing the edge worn soft as a scrap of flannel by her touch. It was the three of them—Marco, Lena, and Maggie, not just Marco—in the cramped kitchen of the apartment Marco rented near the Rhys campus after his graduation. He was a year ahead of them in college, and while they completed their senior year, he finished an architecture internship at a prestigious firm near Rhys.

In the photo Maggie and Lena stood on either side of him, leaning in as though pulled by the magnet of his person. Marco was bent forward over a pan of bolognaise sauce, slurping a long strand of spaghetti, testing it for doneness, looking full-on at the camera and laughing through his clipped black beard. His arm was extended, holding the camera so they could all bunch together into the frame. Both their faces turned toward him, Lena and Maggie had their mouths open like baby birds, begging for a taste. He could whip up the best pasta sauce from scratch. It seemed like magic.

They had spent many long, happy weekend evenings together, the three of them lingering for hours on Marco's tiny, weedy patio with a dish of olives, a bottle of red wine, and a citronella candle to drive away bugs. In those moments life had seemed endlessly open, laid out before them golden with promise. They were young, brilliant, on the cusp of something greater. They had used those evenings almost carelessly, secure in the abundance, sure they had all the time in the world.

Maggie slipped the photo back into the wallet and then slid the wallet under her pillow. She slept every night close to those she loved the most. They had gone with her to every country she had set foot in, lain next to her in every bed or cot or camp mat. When she slept, they were not lost to her. In her dreams her mother was alive, and Marco was not unattainable, not the husband of a woman who loved her like a sister. She didn't feel the thin filament of guilt that had run through her waking hours for so many years, the uncomfortable knowledge that she loved a man who was not hers, who could not be hers. For years Marco and Ana had traveled with her to the ends of the earth, together serving as a little beacon of love and safety. But here, in the guest room of Marco and Lena's farmhouse, sitting in a circle of warm yellow light, she was faced with the yawning blackness of their absence, the reality that those she loved most were in fact far beyond her reach.

"Why did you go?" she asked, not expecting an answer. There was never an answer. She sighed, scrubbing her hands over her face, suddenly so exhausted she felt it like an ache in her bones. She slid under the covers, acutely aware of the empty spaces on either side of her, cold pockets of loneliness, proof of her loss. She tucked the quilt around her, trying to create a little cocoon, trying to forget once again that she slept alone. She lay still, waiting for sleep as the night deepened, the taste of loss and regret familiar in her mouth— Kalamata olives and a peppery shiraz.

The first time she lost Marco, Maggie didn't see the danger until it was too late.

"Why didn't you tell me about you and Marco?" Maggie demanded of Lena, facing her roommate across the narrow dorm room they shared. It was February of their junior year at Rhys, and Maggie had just returned from a monthlong photography trip to Greece during January term. Tanned and glowing from photographing the ruins of a great civilization, she'd come back to find that Marco and Lena had formed an exclusive club of two in her absence. Suddenly she was the odd man out, the one who didn't understand the inside jokes and shared glances. It took her completely by surprise, as did the surge of jealousy that shot through her when she caught them kissing in the dorm hall. She stood rooted to the spot, mesmerized by Marco's hands on Lena's skin, the way their lips met, familiar, not awkward with the newness of love. This was not the first time they had done this, she understood. And suddenly she felt terribly alone.

"We didn't want to make you feel left out," Lena explained, trying to calm Maggie's ire. "We love you."

But even in that statement, Maggie understood it was now two and one, not three. Marco and Lena together and her separate. She isolated herself from them, refusing to acknowledge her hurt, refusing to allow them to get close enough to understand what she didn't even understand.

She stayed busy with her spring project, with the circle of photography friends she'd made on the trip to Greece.

"Maggie," Lena pleaded after a few weeks of her roommate's aloof behavior, "we miss you. We want to see you. Just because we're dating doesn't mean things have to change."

But she was wrong. Things had changed so fundamentally that Maggie couldn't see a way to make them right again. The world was off-kilter, and she was off-kilter with it. Her concentration suffered. She lost weight, becoming more solitary and brooding, consumed by angst she couldn't understand.

Lena seemed worried but helpless. Marco gave Maggie space but seemed to have no clue as to why she was avoiding him. Maggie herself couldn't pinpoint what was wrong. She couldn't neatly label her feelings like jars of spices—jealousy, envy, longing, love. Instead, she felt eaten from within by a general discontent, a feeling that the world was wrong, and she was wrongly placed in it.

One evening, restless and unable to concentrate on her project any longer, she wandered down to the pub where Marco bartended part-time. She had found a *Modern Bride* magazine in Lena's toiletry drawer that morning while hunting for tweezers. It had shocked her. The bride on the cover looked like Lena. She shut the drawer as though it contained a terrible secret and left the room. She'd avoided thinking about it all day.

The pub was crowded, and she slipped in unnoticed, taking a tiny table for two tucked into the corner opposite the bar. Half hidden by a long velvet curtain, she could watch the bar in relative anonymity. A young woman in leather boots and a mini dress took her order, a Coke, and brought it a moment later.

Maggie sipped her drink slowly, watching Marco at the bar. He fed off the energy of the place, smoothly talking to patrons as he filled their orders, laughing heartily with his head thrown back. She loved that laugh. He flirted professionally with the women, discussed sports scores with the men, all the while his quick hands moving—uncapping bottles of beer, pouring, mixing, popping maraschino cherries and olives into cocktails.

She felt a flood of warmth as she watched him with a possessive pride, proud that she knew him better than anyone in the room. He'd been hers before anyone's, before these patrons at the bar or even Lena. She felt a kind of ownership of him, as though she had a right to him, her intimacy with Marco predating anyone else's.

A fierce surge of longing swept over her as she watched him. How beautiful he was, how self-possessed and sure. She gripped her glass of Coke, unable to look away. His square hands, that low laugh, the pull of his shoulders against his dress shirt, casually rolled up at the sleeves, the deep, smooth flow of his voice with his accent like warm caramel. And right then and there Maggie realized the truth. She was in love with Marco Firelli.

At once, everything fell into place. Of course. How could she not have realized it sooner? She must have loved him for so long. The epiphany felt almost anticlimactic, so normal and so right, as though she were recalling something she'd always known but had momentarily forgotten.

She felt strangely calm as she sat there, half-empty glass in hand, suddenly enlightened. Her revelation had not set the world to rights, but somehow it had set her to rights within it. It felt like coming home. She knew what was inside herself now. She could face it head-on.

She took another sip, considering. Did Marco know? Would he still be with Lena if he did? He and Lena were opposites, not just in looks, but in personality and even in motivation. Maggie and Marco were twins, born under the same fierce star, driven to succeed. They shared a deep, instinctive understanding she was sure Lena couldn't relate to. They were kindred spirits, but Marco had never indicated that he felt more for Maggie than affection and friendship. He had been admiring and nothing more. With Lena, he had pursued. With Maggie, he had stayed a step back, never crossing the line between admiration and intent. She swirled her straw around in her glass. Should she tell him how she felt? If she did, it could ruin everything.

She glanced up at him once more. He was looking straight at her, his expression quizzical. She smiled, inclining her head in a tacit invitation for him to join her. She wouldn't say anything yet. Perhaps he and Lena would discover for themselves how mismatched they were. Perhaps he would wake up one morning and have an epiphany of his own.

Marco wiped his hands on a towel and rounded the bar, coming toward her. She steeled herself, her heartbeat quickening. Somewhere on the other side of the room, a patron slipped two quarters into the jukebox. A moment later the air was filled with the pulsing beat of Queen's "Crazy Little Thing Called Love." Maggie laughed as Marco approached her table. She felt half-drunk with self-revelation. "Now, that's what I call ironic," she called to him, knowing he wouldn't understand. She raised her glass to him in a mock salute, then took another sip.

After Maggie's epiphany, life returned to almost normal. She found she could be with Marco and Lena again, though her secret burned steadily in her rib cage. Lena seemed relieved by Maggie's apparent return to normalcy, Marco a little puzzled. Maggie was simply glad to be near him again.

Someday, she assured herself, *he'll see we're soul mates in a way he and Lena can never be. Someday he'll see we should be together.* This hope buoyed her. It was strange to see him with Lena now that Maggie knew she loved him, but she had faith that he would open his eyes one day and see the truth. She was confident all would turn out well.

Marco graduated that spring and was awarded an internship with a prestigious architecture firm nearby. It would keep him near Rhys for the next year until Lena and Maggie graduated. Lena and Maggie were both thrilled.

None of them went home for the summer, preferring to stay together. They spent long hours in each other's company, talking, picnicking, boating on the lake with a rowboat they rented by the hour.

Maggie felt like the heroine in her own novel. She was no longer the third wheel. She was the right one, not yet acknowledged. Her love heightened every sensation. She became aware of nuances, undercurrents, tiny gestures she would have overlooked before. And somewhere in those golden summer hours, Maggie discovered something astounding. Marco wasn't in love with Lena. He was the perfect boyfriend—attentive, caring, sensitive to her every wish. He brought her white lilies for no reason, took her to concerts he knew she'd love. But something was missing.

Lena, though, was head over heels in love with Marco. Every night she'd lie in bed across the room from Maggie in the utilitarian one-bedroom apartment they'd rented for their senior year, talking about him, dreamily sketching their life together. But all the while Maggie was becoming increasingly convinced Marco did not share Lena's enthusiasm. It was something in his eyes. Sometimes when he looked at Lena, Maggie caught a touch of resignation. It gave Maggie hope. She continued to believe he would yet see how wrong he and Lena were for each other, and how perfect Maggie and Marco could be together. She told herself Lena and Marco were like two puzzle pieces that didn't fit. Surely they would see that before it was too late.

She felt a sliver of guilt when she realized Marco's lack of enthusiasm. She loved Lena and wanted her to be happy, but Maggie brushed away her discomfort, reasoning that Lena would never be truly happy with Marco and vice versa, not when they were so ill-suited for one another. It would be better for everyone when Marco and Lena saw the truth.

Then two weeks before Maggie and Lena =began their senior year, Lena's grandmother collapsed while at a bridge party and was hospitalized. Lena flew home immediately. Both Maggie and Marco offered to accompany her, but she assured them it would be better for them to stay. Marco kissed her at the terminal, and they both watched her walk through the security line. Then it was just the two of them.

They spent the time together in lazy enjoyment. Long meandering hikes through the rolling meadows outside of town, a few foreign language films in either Spanish or Italian with the subtitles turned off, a gesture that made Maggie feel elite. They discussed current events, a book on early pilots Marco was reading, Maggie's current obsession with photography from the Great Depression. Sometimes in the evenings they would curl up side by side and simply read together, sharing choice tidbits aloud.

It was perfect, and Maggie wondered if Marco could see it. Once or twice she caught him looking at her with something she almost dared to call longing. It sent a jolt of awareness through her body like an electrical current. For the next few minutes every breath and movement was heightened, every moment hummed with anticipation. But then there was Lena—sweet, beautiful, naïve Lena—calling every night with updates on Grammy's condition. Marco would leave Maggie's side for a few minutes to talk to Lena, alone in the hall. He would come back from these talks heavier, silent, often curtailing the evening shortly thereafter.

The night before Lena returned, Marco cooked a Southern Italian feast for Maggie. He made homemade pasta puttanesca—rich with olives, capers, and tomatoes, accompanied by a full-bodied red wine. They finished the meal with dark, strong espresso and a rich tiramisu he'd whipped up by hand. Afterward they watched a documentary on the Mexican painter Frida Kahlo. Then Marco pulled out a book of poetry he'd been reading, Pablo Neruda in the original Spanish. He read aloud to her a poem about longing and loss, washed with moonlight and desire. He read it slowly, not taking his eyes off the page.

Maggie sat beside him, riveted by the words. Their thighs were touching. Maggie could feel the heat of him through his trouser leg. She couldn't breathe. When he finished, he abruptly closed the book. He would not meet her eyes but stared straight ahead, face as fixed as a Roman statue, brooding and stern. She sat up slowly, inching closer until she was facing him.

"Marco," she said softly, her heart pounding so hard she thought it might fly from her chest. He turned to her, so near she could feel his breath on her lips. She swallowed, gazing straight into his eyes, letting his look sear her. "I love you."

He kissed her, hard and deep. He tasted of cabernet and olives. She felt dizzy, as though he was pulling all the oxygen from her lungs. He crushed her to his chest, and she could feel his heart pounding against her breasts. When he finally pulled back, he released her quickly, as though she'd burned him. He stood abruptly and backed away.

"Marco." She put out a hand to him. Surely he would see now what they could be to each other. "Marco, wait."

He wiped his hands on his trousers and looked down, breathing heavily, as though steeling himself. When he looked up, he met her eyes with no hesitation. "I'm going to ask Lena to marry me when she gets home. I bought a ring."

Maggie stared at him, dumbfounded. Her hand dropped slowly to her side. After all this, how could he possibly still not see the truth? That they belonged together. That she, not Lena, was the one made for him.

She opened her mouth but found she couldn't speak. She didn't know what to say. He came forward, kneeling before her, cupping her face in those strong hands, running his thumbs across her cheeks, pressing against the skin of her jawline so hard that she found a faint blue bruise the size of an olive there the next morning.

"Maggie, my Maggie," he murmured. "Listen to me. I adore you. Since the first moment I laid eyes on you. But we're too much alike. Don't you see? We'd tear each other apart. I've tried to make it work in my mind a thousand times. And every time there's only one ending—one of us has to give up what we love. We are too strong for each other."

His voice was low, almost pleading, as though he were desperate for her to understand and somehow approve of his choice. "Lena . . . I love Lena, and she wants me to be happy. If I'm happy, she's happy. She's never known the . . . the crazy hunger that drives you and me. I can make a life with Lena, a good life. I need her. She's loyal and gentle and loving. But you and I . . . we're stars in different orbits. We'd burn each other out."

He stopped for a moment, looking at her with an almost tender expression on his face, a little wistful. But when he spoke his tone was determined. He had made his decision and would not be swayed. "I won't do that to you, Maggie. I won't ask you to give up who you are. So I'm going to marry Lena. Do you hear me?" He shook her a little, as though trying to shake his conviction into her bones.

She nodded, stunned, feeling numb. Somewhere inside of her a dark fissure of disbelief and shock was cracking her fragile hope in two. In the silence after his words, her heart began to keen.

Chapter Seven

Marco and Lena's wedding was a lavish affair. Lena's parents spared no expense. Ingrid, Lena's mother, an elegant woman with manicured nails and a sharp eye for detail, took the event in hand, scheduling it for late May, just two weeks after Maggie and Lena's graduation.

"It's going to be at the conservatory in St. Paul," Lena explained, glowing and toying with the princess-cut diamond solitaire on her left hand, enjoying the novelty of seeing it glittering there. "And, Maggie, Marco and I want to know if you'll stand up with us, for both of us. Just you."

Maggie, caught off guard, agreed. She could think of no alternative, no excuse good enough to say no. For the remainder of their senior year, Lena was caught up in the whirlwind of wedding planning. Maggie and Marco joined in when they were needed, which was rarely, offering opinions on petit four flavors (lemon with butter cream frosting) and the color of the invitation ribbon (pale green) but little else. Maggie numbly submitted to a barrage of details each night, drifting to sleep with Lena cataloging possible appetizers, poring over invitation fonts, and dwelling endlessly on veil designs. Maggie allowed herself to be fitted for a custom dress, a pale-green silk sheath, and submitted to a dozen different hairstyle trials. Ingrid was incensed that Maggie was the only attendant, that Marco wouldn't pick several dashing college friends and Lena wouldn't choose among her cousins. But on that point Lena was adamant.

"Only Maggie, Mother, and that's final. She's our best friend, and we want her to share the day with us. I won't discuss it anymore."

Those words were like a knife twisting in Maggie's heart. She was sharing their day, but she could not share their joy. She still couldn't believe Marco would actually go through with it. Lena was overjoyed, reveling in wedding details and planning their imminent move to New York, where Marco had landed a starting position with a prestigious architecture firm, but Maggie saw the look in Marco's eyes in unguarded moments. It was the look of a man who has resigned himself to something he knows is good for him but does not necessarily want.

Three weeks before the wedding, Maggie confronted him. Lena was at a conservatory student appreciation dinner, and Maggie had taken her rare absence as an opportunity. She'd called Marco and asked him to meet her at the lake near the edge of campus. The willows were budding new green and the air was chilly but fresh, smelling of damp earth and sprouting things. It was twilight, the sky the cobalt blue of a medicine bottle. Against it, Marco was just a dark outline, the nuances of his face replaced with bold strokes, the stark jut of a cheekbone, a square angle of brow. They walked side by side for a few minutes, the lapping of the lake water and the twitter of sparrows settling in for the night the only sounds around them.

"Why are you doing this?" Maggie demanded suddenly, rounding on him in the middle of the footpath.

He stopped, hands in his pockets. "Doing what?" He sounded surprised.

"Going through with this wedding when you and I both know it's not what you really want." She said it boldly, presumptuously, stating a fact only the two of them knew.

He shrugged. "I want it enough." His voice was calm, impassive.

"Are you serious?" She stared at him, aghast, in the near darkness. "That's not fair . . . to Lena or to you."

"Why not?"

"Well," she sputtered, "it's misleading. You don't love her like she thinks you do. At the very least you should be excited about getting married, and Lena should be getting someone who adores her. Don't you both deserve better than whatever this is?"

"Whatever this is," Marco stated calmly, "is

the fact that I love Lena and asked her to marry me. And she loves me and said yes. The end."

"That's not the whole story," Maggie accused. "Lena wouldn't want to be half-loved. And why are you so bent on marrying her when you know she's not what you really want?" On impulse she stepped forward, cupping his face in her hands. The stubble of his beard scraped her palms. She rose on tiptoe and pressed her lips to his.

Marco jumped back as though her touch were a hot coal. He raised his hands, putting distance between them.

"What are you doing?" he demanded, his voice low, a warning tone that sent chills down her spine. "I've made my decision. There is nothing to discuss. And how do you know what I want? Do I want someone like you, who shares my passion and understands what it's like to burn for something we might never achieve, to love something more than we might ever love a person? Is that what you think I want?" He made a gesture in the last glimmer of light, a denial of her presumptions. Maggie said nothing, rooted to the spot by his words.

"Do I want someone who understands me, but whom I can never make happy and who could never make me happy?" Marco continued, his tone relentless. "Hmm, is that what would be best for all of us? Because let me assure you, Maggie,

I do love Lena. I'll make a good life for her. And I asked her to marry me because I want her to be my wife and the mother of my children. Lena is loving and loyal and generous. She will work her fingers to the bone for me and for our family. That's what I want in a wife. Not this. Not you."

Maggie stood there dumbly, hands hanging at her sides, numbed by the blow of his words. She had no reply. There was nothing more to say.

Marco stepped forward, not touching her, but close enough that she could hear him. His voice softened, almost a caress. "I do love you, Maggie. But I'm not a fool. I will not destroy the very things that make you who you are. Wherever you go in life—and you will go far and soar high— remember I loved you enough to let you go. Remember that." Marco reached out and touched her cheek lightly, just the pad of his thumb tracing the curve of her cheekbone, a whisper of touch so faint she might have imagined it. "Good night, Maggie," he said simply and turned to go. She did not follow him, just watched him walk away, leaving her standing there wordless and bereft.

She moved through the remainder of time before the wedding in a daze that only intensified as the day drew closer. She was an observer of her own life, watching herself go through the motions of final exams, graduation day, and packing up, saying farewell to fellow students and teachers. She flew to Minnesota for the wedding, feeling as though with each mile she was heading toward a funeral not just for herself but for those she held dearest.

The wedding day dawned cloudless and warm, scented with the budding apple trees that lined the streets around Lena's childhood home. The hours before the ceremony were a flurry of activity as a hairstylist, a makeup artist, and all of Lena's female relatives descended on the Lindstrom home. Maggie was pulled and prodded, coiffed and spritzed to perfection. At last she slipped into the sheath dress, gazing at herself for a long moment in the mirror. A slender waif of a girl, dark curls piled high, eyes so large they almost swallowed the pale oval of her face.

"Such striking coloring," she heard one of the aunts murmur to another. "And I'd kill for that waistline." But their words were meaningless to her. Lena was stunning in a gorgeous strapless gown of creamy silk, with pearls at her ears and in her hair. Holding a bouquet of pink calla lilies, she looked like a movie star from the fifties.

"You look divine," her aunts assured her. Lena blushed, looking to Maggie for confirmation.

"Stunning. As always," Maggie affirmed, kissing Lena's cheek, trying to quell the panic she could feel fluttering and rising like a trapped sparrow in her rib cage, threatening to choke her.

Maggie climbed into the limo for the ride to the conservatory, bunched together with several of Lena's Swedish relatives all talking on fast-forward. They did not ask her questions. They seemed to forget she was there. After a quick makeup and hair touch-up in a side room, Maggie found herself standing at the back of the conservatory, facing Marco, who was calmly waiting at the front of the cavernous space. Light poured in from the glass walls and ceiling, illuminating the walkway, dazzlingly bright. The string quartet struck up the processional and she heard her cue. Then she was gracefully stepping and pausing, stepping and pausing down the aisle that seemed to stretch into infinity. How could this be happening? She kept a serene smile plastered on her lips, gripping her bouquet of calla lilies for dear life. She took her place beside Marco. The music reached a crescendo, and there was Lena, exquisite in her gown, sunlight catching the pearls in her hair, light cascading around her like a mantle. She had never looked so beautiful. Maggie darted a look at Marco, who was standing calmly watching his bride, a tender smile turning up the corners of his mouth. Maggie blinked, focusing on the flowers in her hand, their delicate mouths open and empty.

The ceremony seemed to last forever. Maggie felt her forced smile beginning to tremble and steeled herself. The trembling was spreading down her limbs. Her hands were shaking. The muscles in her neck tightened with the strain. She kept herself together by force of will alone. She would not fall apart, not now in front of all these people. Later, when she was alone, she could fall to pieces, but not here, not now. She straightened and willed every muscle and bone of her body to remain steady, to hold together just a bit longer.

Lena repeated her vows, her voice quavering a little. Marco spoke the words steadily, with not even a hint of nerves. Maggie watched in disbelief as Marco slipped the ring on Lena's finger and bent his head, kissing her softly on the mouth. And then it was over. Just like that, they were married.

The reception took place in a long, stately room overlooking the glass conservatory, a sweeping space with many windows, white tulle, and soft lighting. The wedding party and three hundred guests feasted on lobster salad, Steak Diane, and lemon wedding cake wrapped in smooth white fondant. Maggie ate mechanically and smiled automatically when spoken to, giving every appearance of poise and graciousness. Inside she felt a howl of terror swelling against her breast, a swirl of darkness sucking all thought and feeling into it. It was all wrong. Everything—the soft strains of the string quartet, the lobster and glazed heart of palm salad, her sitting alone sheathed in a dress the color of new spring buds, Lena sitting with Marco, married.

She made it through the meal and toasts, the cake cutting, and finally the dancing. She danced with various members of Lena's family and a few guests. More than one young man braved her chilly poise and asked her out as they danced, receiving a curt refusal for all their effort. She kept one eye on Lena and Marco, a dazzling couple as they turned gracefully around the dance floor. Lena was sparkling. She had never looked so happy. Marco drew her close and led flawlessly, twirling her across the floor effortlessly.

Maggie disengaged herself from her latest partner and slipped outside, needing a moment of solitude and some air. The brilliance of the day had softened into evening. Outside the reception hall the air was fresh and cool, and Maggie paused, letting the breeze flutter over her flushed skin. She closed her eyes, trying to block out the wash of light behind her and the never-ending music. Her head was pounding dully. She'd never felt so ragged or raw.

"Maggie?"

She raised her head. Marco was standing in the doorway, a dark silhouette with the lights behind him. She said nothing, and he approached her, coming to stand beside her. Together they looked at the beautiful glass dome of the conservatory, glowing softly from within.

"What a day," he said finally. It hurt to look at him, so debonair in his tuxedo, so immaculately self-possessed, now so far beyond her reach.

"I'm going away," she said abruptly. "To Brazil. I've been offered an internship for a year in São Paulo."

Marco turned and studied her for a minute. "Congratulations. We'll miss you." His voice was soft with understanding, and at that moment she hated him for it.

She did not reply. After a pause Marco held out his hand. "May I have this dance? I think the band has one more number." Maggie hesitated, then took his hand. He led her back inside, into the warmth and noise and low babble of conversation. His hand on her waist was firm, his steps unwavering as the band began to play. They danced well together. Marco led so confidently she didn't have to concentrate on the steps. After a few turns he said, "Brazil, hmm? That's very far away."

"Not far enough." She didn't look at him, couldn't look at him. She was afraid if she did, she would break wide open, crack like an eggshell and spill in a puddle at his wingtips. He turned them and turned them again, the

111

strings of white light and the tall potted ferns spinning past. "Maggie," he said, and his voice was serious, "if you ever need to come back home, you always have a place with us."

She lifted her head then, looking him straight in the eye as the band played the final triumphant strains. "Thank you," she said, knowing that wherever they were was the last place in the world she wanted to be.

She left for Brazil three weeks later, resolving to stay away until it stopped hurting, until she could look at him again without a shred of longing or regret. She suspected it might take forever. She settled into her internship in São Paulo, trying to lose herself in the whirl of the Brazilian arts scene.

Scarcely four months later, her mother called for their weekly chat, sharing tidbits about the neighborhood, asking if she was eating well. And right in the middle of the conversation, between describing how Mrs. Sanchez's toy poodle had bitten the UPS man and giving step-by-step instructions for a new almond flan recipe that was "like a little bite of heaven," Ana dropped a casual remark about another doctor's appointment. Her mammogram had detected some abnormalities. Her doctor had scheduled a biopsy. No need to worry. It was probably nothing. A benign cyst. Everyone being too cautious.

But it wasn't nothing. It was, in fact, a tumor in her breast, malignant and metastasized. Ana tried to wave it away, downplay the danger, but Maggie packed her bags and was on the next flight back. She never returned to Brazil. The next eleven months were a roller coaster of hope and heartbreak. Maggie moved back in with her mother and found a paid internship with a decent photography studio in Chicago. It was not what she had hoped for professionally, and certainly not challenging her at her potential, but it was honest work and paid the bills and kept her camera in her hand.

In the midst of rounds of chemo and radiation and medical bills and sleepless nights spent worrying, Maggie received a postcard from Marco and Lena, a birth announcement for Jonah Roberto Firelli. She mailed a blue onesie and a pack of picture books to the New York return address and taped the birth announcement to the fridge. The baby stared at her every morning with wide brown eyes. He looked like Marco.

During the final round of chemo, when Ana began to suspect her chances of remission were growing slim, she urged Maggie to call Lena. Though Maggie was unwilling to verbalize or even acknowledge that her mother might not be getting better, she began to feel the creeping ache of a world devoid of her only parent. It was unthinkable, a future too lonely to be tolerated.

She resisted for a while, but in the end Maggie broke down and called Lena. She needed her friends now more than she needed to stay away.

"Did you get the onesie?" she asked, not sure how to bridge a gap of so many months of silence. "He's beautiful, by the way."

"I'll fly over this weekend," Lena announced when she heard about the cancer. "And don't say no. No one should be alone at a time like this." She flew in from New York three days later, little Jonah in tow. She set up camp on their couch and stayed for a week, cooking and cleaning and filling the shabby little apartment with light and warmth. For his part, Jonah was a good-natured and pliable baby who spent hours in Ana's arms, watching wide-eyed as she sang him countless songs in Spanish, cooing and rocking him, her bald head bent over his fuzzy, tufted one.

Lena came twice more in those last months, brushing aside all protest, working tiny miracles during a few short days. She stocked the freezer with individually packaged servings of homemade turkey soup and mashed potatoes and beef stew. Hardy comfort foods easy for Ana to swallow. Lena talked of cheerful, normal things—Marco's new design, Jonah holding his head up far earlier than was typical, her potted flower garden in New York. Never once did she pry or question. She didn't mention

Maggie's months of silence. When she looked at Maggie, there was only compassion in her eyes, no judgment or reproach.

Maggie basked in the glow of Lena's calm and gentle presence, soaking it up like a sunflower does the light. She needed desperately to feel known and loved in such a dark and lonely hour. She had not intended to need Lena again, had not intended to be taken back into their lives. But to be alone now was unthinkable. And she had no one else to turn to.

One night during Lena's second visit, Maggie tried to broach the subject of her long months of silence. They were sitting in the cramped kitchen with mugs of coffee and slices of Lena's lemon poppy seed cake in front of them. Ana and Jonah were both sleeping. Linda Ronstadt warbled a sad love song from Ana's ancient tape player perched on the top of the refrigerator.

"I'm sorry I didn't keep in better contact," Maggie said, stumbling a little over the words. "The internship was so busy, and then when the cancer happened . . ." She gestured toward Ana's closed bedroom door. She fell silent, staring down at her plate of crumbs. Any excuse sounded weak in her ears. She couldn't possibly explain why she had needed to go away, why she had severed contact. She couldn't articulate the potent mixture of shame, longing, and guilt that churned in her gut every time she saw Lena or thought of Marco.

Lena reached across the table and gently placed her hand on Maggie's. "I know how hard it's been," she said, her tone soft but sounding a little hurt. "We love you, and we understand."

Maggie nodded, not meeting Lena's gaze. Lena couldn't possibly understand, not all of it, but she understood enough to offer grace, and that was something Maggie desperately needed.

"Now, how about another slice of cake?" Lena said, breaking the solemn mood. "Because everything in life is just a little better with cake, don't you think?"

Maggie took the slice of cake and the absolution Lena offered along with it. They never spoke of it again.

When Ana finally gave up her struggle one warm summer evening and took her last breath on earth, Lena was the first person to know. She and Marco came for the funeral. It was the first time Maggie had seen Marco since the wedding. She tensed as he walked through the door, waiting for the stilted greeting, expecting her own defenses to rise. But it was just Marco, whom she loved and had always loved and perhaps would always love. Just Marco. He wrapped his arms around her, and she sobbed against his gray pressed shirt, making a wrinkled blotch over his heart. He patted her back and murmured small endearments in Italian while Lena heated water for tea. After that there was no going back. They took her into the fabric of their lives as seamlessly as if she'd never left.

She went with them to the island for the first time later that summer. They welcomed her to the fixer-upper farmhouse they'd just purchased after visiting San Juan during a summer vacation. Lena especially had fallen in love with the slower, tranquil pace of the local culture and with the farmhouse itself. Maggie found the hard labor of wallpapering and landscaping, sanding and painting together with Marco and Lena restored her appetite and her senses.

She and Marco never spoke of what had gone before. Lena seemed oblivious to any undercurrent between her husband and her best friend. If she did suspect anything, she never gave a hint of it. And so they carried on through the ensuing years, through Maggie's far-flung travels, Marco's and Maggie's rises to success, and the births of two more babies. The Firellis were all Maggie had left, the closest thing she had to family in the world, and nothing could change that fact.

There were other men in Maggie's life. A few photographers who ran in similar circles, a handful of locals in various places around the globe. Nothing serious, nothing that held any danger of love. She was still in love with Marco. No other man could come close to that. She held her love for him before her like armor, wrapped tight against any encroaching advance. She called the shots, she decided who and where and when, and ultimately, she decided how each relationship would end.

There was a parade of them for a few years. Fernando, a Spanish chef in Barcelona; Juan Carlos, a high-end bartender in Mexico City; Michael, a nature photographer from Maine; Johan, a South African journalist covering the political situation in Zimbabwe. A few had gotten too close. Like Seamus, the Irish photographer with a dimple in one cheek, a brogue that melted her heart, and a keen understanding of human nature. He met her in a coffee shop in Prague, where they were both stationed for a series of shoots that would last for a month. They'd been together three weeks when one Saturday morning Maggie returned from the corner bakery with croissants for breakfast to find Seamus packing his suitcase.

"Where are you going?" Maggie asked, the bakery bag dangling forgotten in her hand, seeping buttery grease through the brown paper.

"Darlin', you know I think you hung the moon," Seamus stated matter-of-factly, looking up as he clicked the latch of his suitcase closed, "but sleepin' three to a bed is getting mighty crowded. If you ever let him go, you know where to find me." He placed a kiss on her brow, in blessing and in parting, and walked out the door. She never heard from him again. After a few weeks she erased all traces of him from her life. She simply could not give him what he wanted.

After Seamus she lost her taste for casual relationships, tiring of the transience, and unable and unwilling to cut herself loose from Marco. So she remained alone, in limbo, loving a man she could not have and finding all other men paled in comparison, their names and faces fading to insignificance in the long, long shadow cast by Marco Firelli.

Chapter Eight

When the first call came from the collection agency, Maggie and Lena assumed it was a mistake. It was barely a week after Marco's death. The morning was drizzly and gray, a curtain of clouds hanging low over the water. Although the outside temperature was chilly, the kitchen was warm and snug and smelled deliciously of the bacon Ellen was frying along with eggs for breakfast. Lena was on her hands and knees scrubbing out the cabinet under the kitchen sink even though it was barely seven in the morning. She was on a cleaning spree, energetically scrubbing nooks and crannies of the house that had probably lain untouched for years. Maggie was setting the table, doling out forks and napkins to the children. When the phone rang, Ellen answered it, motioning for Lena with the eggy spatula.

"For you, dearie."

Lena pulled off her rubber gloves and brushed a wisp of hair back from her face. She took the phone. "Yes, hello? Yes, this is Mrs. Firelli." She listened for a moment, and then a look of puzzlement crossed her face. "I'm sorry, I don't know what you mean," she said. "There must be some mistake."

Maggie was helping Gabby into her booster seat, but she paused when she heard Lena's tone.

Lena listened for another moment, her face the picture of growing confusion. "No, I'm sure there's been a mistake. We don't have any outstanding debts." She listened for another long moment. "Yes, my husband is . . . was," she corrected herself, flustered, "Marco Firelli. But there's been a mistake somehow. We have excellent credit."

Maggie could hear the person on the other end, his tone of voice strident and demanding. Lena raised her chin. "Well, I suggest you check your records again. This just isn't possible. Good-bye." She disconnected the call.

"What was that?" Maggie asked.

Lena put her hands on her hips and frowned. She was still holding her pink rubber gloves. "Someone claiming Marco's defaulted on debts, but there must be some mistake. We don't have any debts, other than the mortgages for this place and the New York house, of course. But I'm sure we're current on our payments." She paused, considering. "I think I'd better call our accountant to straighten this all out."

While Ellen dished up eggs and crispy strips of bacon, Lena placed a call to their accountant back in New York, but was unable to get through. She left a voice mail message explaining the situation.

The next call from creditors came barely an hour later. The third before lunch. The accountant had not yet returned Lena's call. She tried again to no avail. By the fourth call, at two in the afternoon, Lena's brisk assurance was beginning to wilt.

"I-I don't know," she stammered into the phone, shooting a helpless look at Maggie. "I'm sure there's been some mistake."

Fed up, Maggie snatched the phone from Lena's hand. "Listen," she snapped into the receiver, "you are badgering a woman who has done nothing wrong and who just lost her husband. If you call again, I will personally report you to the police for harassment. If you have a problem with Mr. Firelli's finances, I suggest you take it up with his accountant. Stop calling this number." Maggie disconnected the call and handed the phone to Lena.

"Don't answer any number you don't recognize," she said grimly. "And keep calling the accountant until you get through."

When the accountant finally returned Lena's calls midafternoon, Lena explained the situation as best she could. She listened for a few minutes, hmm-ing into the phone in agreement.

Finally she gave a sigh of relief. "Oh, thank you, George. That puts my mind at ease. I knew it must have been a mistake. But you'll check on it just to be sure? Anything to make these calls stop. They're so upsetting."

When she hung up, she turned to Maggie, who had been aimlessly flipping through one of Lena's gardening magazines while eavesdropping.

"Well, that is a relief," Lena said. "George says he knows nothing about any outstanding debts, and there must be a mistake somewhere. He says when people . . . pass, it can often cause a little chaos in their personal affairs until everything is straightened out. He's going to check everything and call me back tomorrow."

"Good," Maggie said.

"I'm sure he'll get it straightened out," Lena said with confidence.

When George called midmorning the next day, Lena and Maggie were leisurely drinking coffee at the dining table, enjoying a moment of peace. Ellen had shooed the children outside to play in the sunshine and was sitting with her knitting on the back deck where she could keep an eye on them.

Lena checked the number and picked up the phone. "It's George," she whispered to Maggie. Her expression brightened for a moment when she heard his voice, but within a few seconds her look changed to one of disbelief.

"George, what do you mean?" She sounded genuinely shocked. Without another glance, she rose and disappeared down the hall into the front parlor, leaving Maggie alone at the table, nursing the last of her espresso.

Maggie waited for Lena, but when she hadn't reappeared after twenty minutes, Maggie went to check on her. She knocked softly on the parlor door.

"Come in," Lena said. Something in her tone sent a chill through Maggie. Alarmed, she opened the door. Lena sat wilted on the chaise lounge, clutching a tissue in her hand although her eyes were dry. The phone lay on the side table nearby.

"What's happened?" Maggie asked, crossing to Lena and taking a seat on the sofa.

Lena shook her head. She looked up at Maggie in bewilderment.

"It's gone. They were right, the creditors. It's all gone."

"What's gone?" Maggie asked warily.

"Everything." Lena blinked, looking stunned. "More than everything. How could this have happened? I thought everything was fine. I left the finances to him. We hired George to make sure everything was in order. Marco made enough money. I didn't realize . . ." She lifted one hand and let it drop into her lap, a gesture of futility. She looked completely lost.

"What did George say?" Maggie prompted gently, though her mind was racing.

Lena looked down at her hands, crumpling and uncrumpling the tissue. "He said we're in debt, that Marco took out loans, as much as he could borrow. He also maxed out two credit cards I didn't know anything about. Neither did George. He found out when he looked into it."

Maggie sat back, shocked. "Marco did this?" It seemed impossible. "What did he do with the money?" she asked. A dozen sordid scenarios sprang to mind. Gambling. Drugs. A mistress. But no, not Marco. It wasn't possible.

Lena shook her head again, as though trying to clear it. "It wasn't anything terrible. It was all legitimate expenses. The children's school tuition, our family vacation last year. He used most of it for his business, to finance projects. That was the biggest chunk, George said. He financed projects I thought he was being paid for." She spread her hands. "He even charged the diamond earrings he got me last year for our anniversary." She shook her head, looking glazed. "I thought we could afford our life, but we've been living on borrowed money."

Maggie cleared her throat, trying to think logically. "How much is the debt?"

"Almost two hundred fifty thousand dollars," Lena said flatly, "not counting our mortgages, of course."

Maggie sat back, shocked by that many zeroes. How could Lena possibly dig out from a hole that deep? Her mind raced, flying through some quick mental calculations. Maggie made a good income, but she had nothing like that amount of money lying around. She knew Lena's parents had suffered financially during the economic crash of 2008 and lost most of their retirement savings, so they were not in a position to help much.

"Did Marco have life insurance?" Maggie asked, grasping at any slim possibility.

Lena made a small sound, between a moan and a whimper, and shook her head. "He told George he was going to take care of it when we got back to New York in the fall. He had a life insurance benefit when he was with the firm, but when he left the firm to go independent last year, that was gone . . . Marco was always so healthy, we didn't think . . . No one thinks this will happen."

She plucked at the tissue in her hand. "I don't know what we're going to do," she said plaintively. "I can't work and take care of the children at the same time. I've never had a real job, anyway. What would I do? But I can't lose our homes. We have to have somewhere to live. And the children . . . I don't want everything in their lives to change." She was beginning to sound panicked as the reality of the situation started to set in. "And what do I do about their school? And the debts? How can I possibly pay off the debts? Oh, I can't believe this." She buried her face in her hands.

"What do you have to pay right now?" Maggie asked, trying to get her to focus, to calm down so they could think. "How much is due now?"

"I don't know. I don't know." Lena shook her head, overwhelmed.

"What did George say?" Maggie asked gently. "Did he say what's due right now? Why were the collection agencies calling?"

Lena glanced up at her and struggled to come up with the answers. "Marco missed some of the last payments," she said finally, shakily. "George says we need nine thousand dollars just to get caught up on the loan and credit card payments."

Maggie stared at Lena in stunned silence for a moment. Lena looked back at her, the number sitting between them large and stark.

"Do you have access to any money, anything in savings?" Maggie asked.

Lena shook her head and grimaced. "I thought we did, but the account is empty. I just have the few hundred I keep in my household account for incidentals. Oh, Maggie, I trusted him to handle everything, and now it's all gone. What am I going to do?" Lena pressed her hand to her breastbone hard, holding it there as though to keep her heart from breaking out of her chest.

Maggie bit her lip, trying to come up with something reassuring to say. Lena's eyes were wide and she was breathing fast. She looked panicked. "Lena." Maggie took Lena's hand and gripped it hard, feeling the slender bones beneath her fingers. "It will be okay."

Maggie's mind was whirling, trying to grapple

with the problem. It seemed massive. What had Marco been thinking, to put his family in this predicament? Obviously he hadn't anticipated dying so soon and leaving behind a gaping financial black hole, but Lena and the children could lose everything. They could lose this house. The thought stopped Maggie in her tracks. The idea of losing this place, more of a home than anything else she had, felt like a sucker punch to the gut. She couldn't let it happen. They had to think of something.

Maggie sat for a moment, trying to formulate a plan, but her mind was a blank, white slate. No grand plan occurred to her.

"I'll lend you the nine thousand dollars," she said finally. "I'll have it wire transferred to your account today."

Lena glanced up, doubt on her face. Her mouth trembled. "I can't let you do that, Maggie."

"Of course you can," Maggie said briskly. "You would do the same for me. You know you would. So call George back and we'll tell him the money is on its way. Let's take it one step at a time. First we'll handle the back payments and then we'll worry about the rest of it later." It was a sound plan, a sensible first step, but Maggie felt a cold, sinking dread deep in her stomach. How could they possibly make this all come out okay?

Lena just looked at her with wide, frightened

eyes as the magnitude of the predicament sunk in. "Oh, Maggie, I can't do this," she whispered. Her pupils were large and unfocused. *Shock*, Maggie thought. *She's in shock.* She'd seen it before in her line of work. She gripped Lena's hand hard, trying to communicate a strength and confidence she didn't feel. Instead, she sat across from Lena in the prim floral parlor, fighting to maintain her equilibrium, to not feel overwhelmed by this new, disastrous revelation. Their lives felt suddenly more precarious than ever before.

"We'll think of something," Maggie said, trying to sound strong and reassuring. "You don't have to do this alone." She squeezed Lena's hand, but Lena didn't respond. Already Maggie could feel Lena shutting down, slipping away to some far, solitary place.

Lena looked away, out the front bay window to the wide green sweep of lawn. Her expression was so lost. "It makes so much sense now," she murmured. "If he had just told me . . ." She shook herself slightly, for a moment coming back to the present. "Maybe it wouldn't have changed anything," she said with a slight, wistful smile, "but at least I would have known."

Puzzled, Maggie opened her mouth to ask what Lena was talking about, but Lena had already moved on, her eyes on the far horizon and her thoughts a million miles away.

Chapter Nine

Maggie woke late the next morning to the rattling of jars. Blearily, she sat up in a wash of midmorning sun, trying to get her bearings. She'd fallen asleep well after midnight, kept awake by the financial problem, turning various ideas over in her head. Earlier she'd talked to George, transferred the necessary funds, then sat Ellen down and outlined the extent of the problem as well. "Oh dear," Ellen sighed. "What a pickle. We'd love to help, but even with Ernie's pension and both our Social Security checks, we're just making ends meet."

The financial disaster was held at bay, at least for a few weeks. It would give them breathing room, a bit of time to work out a good solution—if they could come up with a good solution. Otherwise. . . it did not bear thinking about. They would just have to make something work.

Maggie yawned and squinted at the bedside alarm clock. Almost ten. Sifting up through the floorboards came the muted tones of a cartoon on the TV in the family room and an unholy racket coming from the kitchen. What was going on down there? After a quick trip to the bathroom, she hastily pulled on her clothes from the day before, tugged her hair into a messy ponytail, and went to investigate.

At the foot of the stairs, Maggie stopped short, staring at the scene before her in the kitchen. She felt as though she'd just wandered into a beehive, buzzing with energy. Lena was at the stove stirring a vat of bubbling fruit. Ellen was elbow-deep in a sink full of bobbing red strawberries. Canning jars were stacked in cardboard boxes on the floor, and rows of full jars gleamed like jewels on trays on the counter. The air was thick with sugar and steam. Lena's favorite Doris Day CD was playing in the background, Doris's voice as bright and happy as sunshine.

"What's going on?" Maggie asked, going into the kitchen.

"Good morning, Maggie. We're canning," Ellen informed her, rolling her eyes toward Lena, who was peering into the pot of fruit and stirring vigorously.

"Canning strawberries?" Maggie yawned, trying to get her brain to function. She needed an espresso, maybe two, strong enough to feel like a kick in the teeth. She wasn't ready for this level of activity so soon after waking.

"Strawberries, and whatever we can get our hands on, apparently," Ellen said, adding in a low voice, "These are strawberries from all three markets. She had me buy every pint on the island."

Maggie looked around, trying to gauge the mood in the room. It felt as though the events of the previous day had never happened, as though all the worry and fear of financial ruin had been swept under the rug, replaced by a current of high energy and productivity. It was eerie, as though she had awakened in an alternative universe where nothing bad could touch this level of domesticity. Maggie had seen Lena behave like this before, throwing herself wholeheartedly into a project, completely unrelated to whatever personal crisis was looming in her life. Maggie remembered the last time.

Faced with the reality of her beloved Grammy's failing health, Lena had organized a campus-wide hat-and-mitten drive at Rhys the fall of their senior year, collecting over two hundred sets of cold-weather hats and mittens for the local homeless shelter. It was a good cause but completely unrelated to the real crisis Lena was facing. Hats and mittens had not slowed Grammy's decline.

The doorbell rang just then, and Lena nodded toward the mudroom. "Could you get that please, Maggie?"

Maggie opened the mudroom door to find a rotund man in a John Deere baseball cap and overalls standing on the step. He touched the bill of his cap by way of greeting. "Paul Young from down the road. I got the load of plums I promised Miz Firelli. They're not real ripe, but she said she wanted them now." He shrugged, indicating that it was not his problem if they should turn out to be less than satisfactory. "So where do you want 'em?"

Maggie followed him to the driveway and peered into the bed of his Ford pickup. "All of these?" she exclaimed, staring at the round fruits, some dusky purple but most tinged with pink and green. "There must be a hundred pounds here!"

"Yup," he agreed complacently. "So where do you want 'em?"

"The garage?" Maggie guessed, feeling at a loss to make an intelligent decision. She didn't really understand what was going on.

Paul nodded. "Right-o."

The canning continued unabated throughout the morning. Apron firmly tied around her waist, face flushed from the fragrant steam, Lena canned with a zeal that bordered on mania. She seemed almost unaware of her surroundings, entirely focused on the task at hand. The children stayed in their pajamas and watched cartoons until lunch. Lena never let them watch cartoons more than a half hour a day, but she was concentrating so fully on canning that she forgot to feed them, let alone monitor their television consumption. At noon Ellen made peanut butter and jelly sandwiches and carrot sticks and apple slices and fed the kids at the table on the back deck, the only flat surface untouched by the canning.

Maggie was roped into helping with several batches of jam, but she began to feel claustrophobic in the confines of the kitchen. She was smothered in equal parts by the steamy fruit vapors that had turned the kitchen into a sauna and by Lena's refusal to engage reality. Lena's forced cheer and manic productivity grated on Maggie's nerves. At some point Lena would crack—Maggie had seen it before and knew it was only a matter of time—but until she did, it was like living with a robot, a Stepford wife, her mask of perfection firmly in place.

Maggie lasted until early afternoon, but after the third repetition of Doris Day's upbeat crooning of "Dream a Little Dream of Me," she was done. Catching a glimpse of the children, who were wearing similar looks of worry as they peered through the French doors from the deck, she decided enough was enough. She had to get out. She grabbed her camera on impulse and told Ellen they were leaving. Taking car keys from a hook in the mudroom, she loaded the kids and Sammy into Lena's Volvo and drove to Friday Harbor.

"Okay," she said, pulling into a space at the Dairy Dee-lite, a small, red wooden shed with a giant rotating plastic ice cream cone attached to the roof. Tucked away on a side street near the ferry dock, the ice cream stand was often crowded with tourists in the height of summer, though there was usually a picnic table free if you knew to come between ferry arrivals. She'd been bringing the kids here since they were each old enough to walk, spoiling their suppers with hot fudge sundaes covered in sprinkles or with butterscotch-dipped cones.

Sometimes Marco would accompany them, but often Maggie would bring the children by herself, sneaking out with them once or twice during her monthlong visit while Lena was busy with something else. Normally Lena strictly limited their sugar consumption, and Maggie liked the feeling of being the naughty aunt, the one who broke the rules and indulged the kids' desire for marshmallow fluff or gummy bears on their scoops of Superman or Rocky Road. Lena turned a blind eye to the illicit visits, clucking her tongue when they returned sticky and wired with sugar. She'd be waiting at the door with a wet washcloth to clean their smudged faces and fingers.

But today was different. This wasn't an illicit sugar adventure. It felt more like damage control. Maggie wasn't even sure Lena was aware they had left. Maggie turned to the children in the backseat. They looked at her solemnly, three faces so alike and so like Marco. She swallowed hard. What was she thinking, trying to single-handedly mend something this broken? The death of a parent couldn't be fixed with a Butterfinger Tornado or a banana split. Maybe she had made a mistake. What did she know about helping kids through something like this? Her exposure to children, besides the month each year with these three, was solely through the lens of a camera, as subjects for photos. She knew much more about highlighting the problems of the world than solving them, especially when it came to matters of the heart. But it was too late to turn back now. She just needed to do the best she could.

"Okay," she said again, taking a deep breath, mustering her courage. "This is not just our usual ice cream adventure. This is a challenge. I have prizes, so listen closely. Jonah, I want you to find the ice cream treat that reminds you of Africa. Luca, you find the one that seems most like America. And, Gabby, you find the ice cream treat you think fairies would like. Okay? And if I agree with you, you get a prize I brought back from one of my trips. And we'll take a picture so we can show your mom your prize-winning ice cream creations." She paused expectantly, looking at their blank expressions. Maybe this hadn't been such a good idea after all.

"What do you have to find?" Luca asked finally.

"Um, the weirdest combination of ice cream possible," Maggie said, improvising.

That seemed to satisfy them, and they piled

out of the car. It was overcast and cool but not raining. Maggie clipped a leash to Sammy's collar, and he pulled her over to the kids as they stood at the order window, looking at the menu. They were the only ones ordering ice cream at this hour of the afternoon between ferry arrivals. An hour later and the place would be swarmed with tourists just off the boat.

A man puttered into the parking lot on a moped, the stutter of the engine loud on the quiet street. He cut the engine, and when Maggie looked up, she saw he'd stayed seated. He was also staring at them. He looked about her age or a few years older, with tanned skin and straight black hair pulled back in a ponytail. She would have guessed he was Native American, maybe from one of the reservations on the mainland. He didn't move, and Maggie turned her attention back to the kids.

Jonah stood back slightly, hands in his pockets, reading the menu options silently. Luca pressed his face close to the glass, sounding out the flavors and toppings aloud. "But . . . ter . . . scotch . . . pray . . . leen . . . marsh . . . mallow."

Gabby stuck her thumb in her mouth, looking doubtful. "But I can't read the words," she protested, taking her thumb out of her mouth just long enough to speak before popping it back in. She'd stopped sucking her thumb before she was two years old, but had taken it up again.

Maggie squatted down beside her and read the list aloud, pointing to the various options.

"But what if fairies don't eat ice cream?" Gabby asked.

"Oh, they do. Fairies love ice cream. It's their favorite," Maggie assured her.

They all ordered, including a vanilla ice cream cone for Sammy, who would try to steal people's if he didn't have his own treat. Maggie led them to a concrete picnic table in a weedy, graveled area near the parking lot, noting that the stranger had finally gotten off the moped and was placing an order at the window. A minute later he took a seat at one of the other tables, the one farthest from them.

Maggie put Sammy's vanilla cone on a napkin on the ground and wound his leash around the leg of the table. The dog immediately set to work, downing ice cream, cone, and napkin together with abandon. He licked his jowls and eyed the treats on the table. A bit of soggy paper napkin stuck to his nose.

"Is that bad for him to eat the napkin?" Maggie asked.

Jonah shook his head. "It won't hurt him. He eats paper stuff all the time." He took a spoonful of his sundae.

Maggie glanced over at the man sitting at the far table. He had ordered a Coke but wasn't drinking it. He was just watching them. She met his eyes, and he looked down quickly. He wasn't a threat; she sensed that. After so many years of travel in foreign places, Maggie had a finely honed intuition about danger. His stare wasn't sinister in any way, but it was puzzling. She felt as though she was missing something. Had they met before? Should she recognize him from somewhere? There was something about him . . .

She squinted at his bowed head, trying to pinpoint what it was that intrigued her. His features, with high cheekbones and dark eyes, were striking, but there was something else compelling about him. With his faded camouflage pants and black T-shirt, he looked like just another normal island resident, a mechanic or a construction worker, but there was something incongruous Maggie couldn't put her finger on. There was more to him than met the eye.

"Auntie Maggie, my ice cream is melting." Gabby's voice drew her attention back to the children.

Maggie turned away from the man, dismissing him from her mind. "Okay, let's see who got what. Jonah, how'd yours turn out?"

Jonah shrugged. "I got coconut with bananas and marshmallow 'cause coconuts and bananas grow in Africa, and 'cause I like marshmallows." He looked down at his shoes, not meeting her eyes. He had always been the most serious of the children, introverted and thoughtful, while

139

Luca and Gabby tended to be far more animated and chatty. His introversion had become more pronounced since her last visit, now bordering on the sullen. She wondered what was going on inside his head. His shoulders were slumped, as though bearing a weight far too heavy for his age. He was growing up too soon. She wanted to say something more, reassure him in some way that things would be okay, but she couldn't find the words. How could she guarantee something she wasn't sure of herself?

"That's great," Maggie affirmed. "Very tropical. Here, let me take a picture of you." She took her camera from the bag, adjusted the focus, and snapped a few shots of Jonah with his ice cream. It made her feel better to have her camera in her hands. Life made more sense when she could see it through a viewfinder.

Jonah didn't smile, just stuck his spoon into his ice cream and took a big bite.

"I got a sundae with vanilla ice cream and strawberries and blueberries on top," Luca volunteered. "See? Red, white, and blue, like the flag. And peanuts. We learned in school that peanuts grow in America." He tucked into his bowl with the plastic spoon, taking a gigantic bite.

"Wow!" Maggie surveyed his creation, impressed. "Very nice. Let's document this very patriotic ice cream sundae." She snapped a few photos of him, smiling at his cute face mugging for the camera, mouth already rimmed with vanilla ice cream. "And how about you, Gabby?"

"I got strawberry with sprinkles 'cause it's pretty, and fairies like pretty," Gabby said decidedly, then stuck her thumb back in her mouth.

"Very pretty," Maggie agreed. "Do you want me to take a picture of it?"

Gabby nodded, and Maggie took a photo of the little girl and her pink ice cream.

"What'd you get, Aunt Maggie?" Luca asked, his mouth full.

"Well, I thought the weirdest thing I could get would be Rocky Road with pineapple and pecans."

The three eyed her creation doubtfully. "That's not weird," Jonah said, expressing what they all seemed to be thinking. The other two nodded.

"Oh, come on," Maggie protested. "Chocolate, marshmallow, peanuts, pineapple, and pecans? That's weird."

Luca shook his head. "Not weird enough." He pulled two small plastic dinosaurs out of the pocket of his jeans and engaged them in mortal combat over the melting ice cream in his bowl.

"You don't get a prize," Gabby announced, eating a spoonful of her ice cream.

"Oh, fine. Well, I'll just have to give you your

141

prizes, then." Maggie put her camera away and fished around in its bag, pulling out three small packages wrapped in newspaper and tied with twine. She'd brought them back from a photo shoot in Kenya earlier in the year and had mailed them to Lena from Chicago, asking that they be left in the guest room until August when she could give them to the children. She'd found them in the top dresser drawer the night before. Now seemed like a good time to give them out. Maggie glanced up at the far table, but the stranger was gone. She turned her attention back to the children and the presents in her hands.

"These came all the way from Kenya in Africa." She handed each a package. After a minute of fumbling with twine and paper, they pulled out their presents. For Jonah a curved wooden knife in a leather sheath decorated with geometric patterns. For Luca a small drum made of wood and goatskin. And for Gabby a baby hippo made of colorful knit yarn and stuffed with rags.

"Cool!" Luca set down his dinosaurs and thumped the drum experimentally. Jonah didn't say anything, but he slid the knife in and out of its sheath several times, the corner of his mouth turned up in a small smile. He stuck it in the pocket of his cargo pants and turned back to his ice cream.

"No sticking people with that thing," Maggie admonished him.

"Why'd I get a hippo?" Gabby piped up, examining her gift.

"Well, they love the water just like you, and they even make their own sunscreen on their skin. How cool is that?"

"Do daddy and mommy hippos love their baby hippos?" Gabby asked.

"Absolutely," Maggie declared. "And they keep their baby hippos safe from crocodiles and all sorts of bad things."

"But sometimes bad things still happen," Gabby countered, stroking the hippo's head. "Sometimes bad things happen to the daddy or mommy hippo."

Maggie hesitated, unsure how to answer. She was fairly certain Gabby wasn't talking about hippos anymore.

"That's true," she said carefully. "Sometimes bad things do happen. But the big hippos do whatever they can to keep the baby hippos safe. They love the baby hippos and try to protect them."

"Are you going to eat your ice cream?" Jonah interrupted abruptly. "It's melting."

They all turned back to their treats. "Don't worry, little hippo," Gabby said, wedging the small animal into the pocket of her dress as she scooped up a spoonful of pink ice cream. "I'll keep you safe. You'll see."

When they returned at sundown, Ellen had dinner waiting. Mashed potatoes, peas, and baked chicken casserole. Lena didn't eat with them and continued canning.

With unwavering cheer, Doris Day was still singing "Love Me or Leave Me" in the background as they ate a silent supper. No matter the songs she sang it with the same peppy goodwill.

After dinner Gabby begged to play Candy Land. For an hour Maggie refereed fights between Luca and Gabby because Gabby refused to play cards in colors she didn't like. Jonah didn't join them. He read a comic book on the couch. At last it was bedtime. Ellen shooed the three kids upstairs and followed to oversee baths and story time. Maggie put the game away, then reluctantly ventured into the kitchen. She glanced around. All the counter space was covered in orderly rows of pint glass jars glinting in a rainbow of colors.

"What are those?" Maggie asked, pointing to ones that shimmered translucent green, like emeralds in Mason jars.

"Oh, don't touch those. They aren't set yet. That's mint jelly," Lena answered without looking up from the stove.

"But you don't like mint," Maggie said, surprised.

Lena frowned. "Some people love it."

Marco had loved it, served with a leg of lamb. His chosen birthday meal every year.

"Want some help?" Maggie offered.

"Yes." Lena nodded, stirring the contents of the pot vigorously. "Next I was thinking another batch of spiced plum."

A half hour later Maggie peered dubiously into a pot of rock-solid plum segments. The plums were mostly unripe, just starting to tinge purple, difficult to get off the pit and mouth-puckeringly sour. The jam had every likelihood of being completely inedible, but as Maggie watched Lena bustle about the kitchen, she acknowledged that the quality of the canning was not the point.

"*Que sera, sera,*" Doris belted out heartily in the background. Maggie rolled her eyes. She didn't know how much more of Doris she could handle.

"Are you stirring?" Lena asked her, back turned as she stood in front of the sink. It was like she had eyes in the back of her head, a trait she'd perfected as a mother.

"I'm stirring," Maggie assured her, giving the jam a cursory pass with the spoon. The pieces of plum sat like little lumps of granite, unmoved. "Maybe it needs more heat," Maggie suggested.

Lena shook her head. "It will be fine. It will all be fine. Just keep stirring."

So Maggie stirred. It was a bizarre scene, and one she couldn't wrap her mind around. Just a few days before, she'd been traveling in the high, lush mountains of Nicaragua, eating oranges so ripe the juice ran down her arms to her elbows, free as a bird. And now here she was in a kitchen watching her best friend preserve anything she could get her hands on in a mad attempt to stave off the reality of her husband's death and the subsequent financial unraveling of their entire life. It was horrible. It was surreal. She kept stirring.

They finished at almost eleven that night. Lena had not stopped for hours, insisting she had to keep canning. She hadn't eaten and seemed to be subsisting on Earl Grey tea laced with a spoonful of sugar. Maggie saw the glint in Lena's eyes and the set of her jaw and didn't cross her. They didn't talk much, working in a silence punctuated only by Doris's voice, the sounds of the wooden spoon against the pot, and the occasional happy *pop* as a full jar sealed itself on the counter.

Soon Lena would break. She was strung as tightly as a violin bow, resonating with suppressed emotion, taut and completely self-contained. Her jaw was clenched, her back straight. The atmosphere was thick with sugary steam and denial. Maggie just hoped she could be with Lena when she snapped. And then, just when Maggie was about to call it quits and head for bed, Lena dropped a tray of jam. It was another batch made with plums from the seemingly inexhaustible supply in the garage. She was transferring the still-hot jars to a little space she'd cleared by the sink when the tray nosed forward. They both watched in horror as the jars slid in orderly lines down the tray, falling one by one onto the tile floor and shattering.

"Oh no. No!" Lena dropped to her knees and began scooping the entire mess, glass fragments and steaming jam, onto the tray. Maggie grabbed for her wrists.

"Lena, you'll cut yourself. Stop!" She squatted across the debris from Lena, gripping her forearms. Scalding jam ran down Lena's wrists and between Maggie's fingers.

Doris crooned gently above them, her voice warbling about dreams and saying good-bye.

"But it will be ruined. I can't let it be ruined." Maggie could hear the panic in Lena's voice as she struggled to extricate herself from Maggie's grasp.

"Lena, listen to me." Maggie shook her gently, keeping a firm hold on her arms. Lena twisted in her grasp, but Maggie held on, waiting until finally Lena looked up and met her eyes. Her pupils were dilated; she had never looked so lost.

"It was ruined before we even started," Maggie said softly. Lena looked at her for a long moment and then slowly sank back on her heels. She covered her face with her hands, sticky with inedible jam, and then she began to cry.

Chapter Ten

The next morning, when Maggie tiptoed into the master bedroom with a cup of tea and a pancake in the shape of a hot-air balloon, Lena was awake, curled up as Maggie had left her the night before, staring out at the water. She didn't look up when Maggie entered. Maggie set the plate on the nightstand, lingering for a moment in the hope that Lena might acknowledge her presence. Gaining no response, she turned to go.

"I didn't know it was good-bye," Lena whispered, her voice hoarse.

"What?" Maggie turned back to face her.

"I didn't know, when it happened . . . I didn't know it was good-bye. I wasn't prepared. If I had known . . ." Lena twisted the corner of the quilt in her hands. Her face was pale and tear-streaked. "Instead, I just asked him if he wanted squash or green beans. The pie was in the oven, and I was running late. I went up to his studio to ask if he wanted squash or green beans with dinner. He said squash, and I left. I knew the timer was going off and the pie was getting overdone. But I could have taken a moment to tell him I loved him. It would have been so simple." She drew a deep, shuddery breath. "But I was angry with him. We'd been having an argument. I went back to the kitchen and took the pie out, and then I heard Jonah on the back deck yelling that there was a man in the water. Marco heard him and ran past me, telling me to call the police. I did, and by the time I got to the beach, Marco had his kayak in the water and was paddling out. We could see the man was in trouble. He couldn't get righted, and the currents were so strong . . ."

She stared out the window as though seeing the scene replaying before her. Her voice was distant, her eyes unfocused as she recounted the events of that day. "It was windy. I remember that. There were whitecaps on the water. Marco got to the man and was trying to help him up. They were both struggling, but then Marco's kayak capsized too. I don't know what happened. They weren't that far out. And Marco was such a strong swimmer. The other man managed to hold on to his kayak, but Marco went under. The police told us he hit his head when his kayak flipped over. The man was trying to pull him up but couldn't. Marco went under . . . and then he didn't come back up . . ." Her voice trailed off into a little gasp of a sob.

Maggie sat down on the bed and put her hand on Lena's foot, staring out at the Strait. The water was dark and calm, lapping gently against the weathered rocks speckled white with barnacles. But it was deep, she knew, dropping off sheer just a few feet from shore, plunging down hundreds of feet with wicked currents swirling through the kelp beds. The water was cold, even in the summer, frigid to the touch. She looked away, unable to bear the mental images of what had happened there just a few days before.

"I'm so sorry, Lena. I'm so, so sorry." She squeezed Lena's foot, feeling the fragile bones and long toes beneath her fingers.

Lena was silent for a moment. When she spoke, her voice was flat.

"I don't know if I can do it, Maggie. I don't know if I can do this without him. He's gone and I'm left with all this mess. I don't know how to do it all myself. I don't think I can." She stared unseeingly out at the water. She looked so helpless.

Maggie nodded. "I know. But you're not alone. I'm here too." She said no more, offered no platitudes, no assurances this time that it would be all right. She wasn't sure how it would be.

After a few moments, Lena roused and drank a sip of tea. Maggie watched her, noting the tousled blonde hair usually so carefully smoothed and the hollowness of her gaze, as though someone had scooped all meaning from the world in one fell swoop.

Lena lay back down, curling once more around the pillow that must still smell of Marco. He'd smelled like licorice and cloves, a dark, spicy scent Maggie had wanted to bury her face in.

They hadn't touched, except for brief hugs of greeting or farewell, since her mother's death when Marco had held her as she sobbed. It seemed so long ago, but she still remembered his scent. She squeezed Lena's foot once more, and together they sat, sharing a grief too deep for words as the reality of all they had lost slowly seeped into the marrow of their bones.

Lena was still in bed three days later. She'd been silent and inert, hardly eating, just staring out at the water and crying in harsh, choked sobs that hurt to hear. Ellen had put her head down and carried on, cooking and cleaning as though she were keeping their bodies and souls together by the power of pot roasts and Pine-Sol. Maggie did what she could to keep the kids occupied. She organized a nature scavenger hunt, a movie marathon with Disney movies, games of tag and hide-and-seek.

Now, late on Sunday afternoon, Maggie couldn't bear for them to be around the house any longer. In desperation, she piled them into the car and drove to Friday Harbor in search of some entertainment. Most of the shops had closed already, and none of the movie theater's few offerings were suitable for young children. She crisscrossed the town looking for anything that might entertain them for an hour. It was spitting rain, so outdoor activities seemed unappealing. She drove past the Island History Museum, noting the Open sign, but dismissed it. How interesting could it be? But after traversing Friday Harbor in its entirety twice over, she opted for the museum. They could always leave if it was too boring.

Located in a staid, clapboard, Victorian-style house on a side street, the museum was open until six o'clock, but the parking lot was empty at a little after five. The children complained, but Maggie cajoled them through the creaking wooden doors with promises of Popsicles after supper.

They stopped at a long wooden counter inside, bare except for a round silver bell and a stack of brochures for whale-watching cruises on a historic schooner. At Maggie's nod, Jonah pressed the bell once. It pinged and they waited for a response. A moment later a brief "Halloo?" echoed from somewhere down a narrow corridor behind the counter, and a second later a tiny, bright-eyed lady with hair like white spun sugar popped out of the doorway.

"Well now!" She looked astounded to see them. "Good afternoon! How nice to have young guests." She peered at them over the top of her spectacles and cleared her throat. "A full guided museum tour, including if you want to see the film, is three dollars per adult and a dollar fifty per child." The kids perked up at the mention of a film, so Maggie dutifully handed over a ten-dollar bill, telling her to keep the change. Business didn't seem to be booming for the museum. They could probably use the extra money.

'Well then." The lady smoothed her tailored brown serge skirt and delivered her speech. "I'm Verna Hawkins, and let's travel back in time to a period when there were no cars, no electricity, no movies, and not even no toilets inside houses. Why, sometimes children didn't even have shoes!"

Gabby's eyes were wide as quarters, taking all this in. "No movies? Not even on their birthdays?"

"That's right, young lady." Verna nodded solemnly. "Not even on their birthdays. Now, come along and watch the film."

Seated in a row on an uncomfortable wooden bench, they watched a short film about the history of San Juan Island, learning about the earliest inhabitants, members of the Lummi Nation, who fished for salmon along the shores. The film breezed through the island's history, from the famous Pig War between the American and British armies to the period during Prohibition when the island was a popular smuggling spot for liquor.

At the end of the ten-minute presentation, Verna reappeared and led them to a line of glass display cases. She showed them various artifacts and drawings pertaining to the film.

"What's that?" Luca piped up, interrupting her explanation of the lime mining industry on the island. He pointed to a small display case in the corner.

"Oh, well, that is a very interesting and little-known part of the island's history," Verna said, leading the way over to the case.

"See now, here's a picture of the first German farmer to live on the island." She pointed to a dour-looking man wearing a tall black hat and holding a hoe. "His name was Gunther Schroder, and he brought his entire family over from Germany when he realized what a good life they could make for themselves here." She pointed to another photo, this one of a large cluster of people standing stiffly and unsmilingly for the camera, the women all heavy-bosomed, the men frowning behind their mustaches. "They, in turn, brought other people to live on the island too," Verna continued, pointing to more sepia-toned photos of people building houses, driving wagons, and standing rigidly for formal portraits. "They started their own small community on the north side of the island and called it Schroderberg."

"Inventive," Maggie murmured wryly.

Verna continued, "Now, there was something different about the group of people who lived in Schroderberg. They weren't like the other settlers on the island. They were part of the Lutheran church of Germany, but after living on the island for a few years, they began to develop some peculiar ideas."

The boys were staring at the photos, but Gabby had lost interest. She wandered over to a display of clothing from the turn of the century and stared in fascination at the petticoats and feather-trimmed hats. Maggie turned her attention back to Verna, deciding that Gabby was behaving herself.

"You see," Verna said, dropping her voice, "in all other ways, the Schroderberg community was strictly Lutheran, but they had some unusual ideas about dying." She leaned closer to the three of them. Her cardigan smelled faintly of lavender, a little musty. "They believed when a person died, their soul was flung free of the body, up and out into the world. It had to make its way back home to be at peace. This meant everyone who loved the dead person wanted to do whatever they could to help the soul return home so it could go on to heaven. So they began a practice they called 'beckoning.'" She motioned them onward, to another display of photos. One of them showed the body of an old woman in a casket.

Maggie drew in her breath, glancing sharply at Jonah and Luca, but they were examining the photo with interest, seemingly undisturbed by the depiction of death.

Verna continued her explanation. "The people who had been closest to the deceased, both family and friends, would stay in the dead person's home until the soul found its way back. Sometimes they'd build a shrine with the person's favorite possessions on it. They'd burn candles, make the person's favorite foods, sing their favorite songs, whatever they thought would help the dead find their way home again." She pointed to a photo of a group of people seated in a circle in a kitchen. One man was asleep. The women were knitting or sewing. In one corner sat a small pile of stones in the rough shape of an altar. A few items sat on top of the stones— worn black shoes, a book, a pair of wire-rimmed spectacles.

"What were they waiting for?" Jonah asked, eyeing the picture curiously.

Verna beamed at this show of interest. "Well, they were waiting for a sign, you see. They needed to know the soul had come back home and could now rest peacefully. The sign could be anything—a strange bird flying by the window, a whistle of wind that sounded like the deceased person's voice. They just had to believe it was the sign they had been waiting for. Then they could go on about their lives, assured that their loved one was safely on his or her way to heaven."

Jonah peered down at the photos. "What if the sign didn't come?"

"Oh, it always came." Verna smoothed her skirt again. "You see"—she leaned in confidentially—"the island is full of surprises. Strange and wonderful things can happen here, things you can't explain, things that don't happen anywhere else. The people of Schroderberg knew that for themselves. They believed it."

"But what if they didn't wait for the dead person?" Luca asked.

Verna smiled brightly, enjoying such an interested audience. "Well, they felt that the person who had died would simply roam the earth until they eventually found their way home, but it could take a long time. Not a very appealing prospect for people who wanted to know their loved ones were safe and sound in heaven. So they beckoned them to speed up the process. Now"—she motioned them onward—"over here is a wonderful model re-creation of an early settler's home, set up just as it would have been over a hundred years ago."

At that point Luca lost interest. He pulled his two small plastic dinosaurs from his pocket and began an epic battle between them. The remainder of the tour consisted of Maggie running crowd control, trying to keep Gabby from touching everything she could reach and Luca from falling behind or wandering off. Only

Jonah continued to show even vague interest, and soon his attention span grew short.

"Thank you so much, Verna, for such a great tour. Very informative," Maggie said, cutting the tour short. She poked the kids, who echoed a trio of faint thanks, then ushered them out the door. Gabby and Luca bounded toward the car, already planning their Popsicle flavors, but Jonah was even more silent than usual.

"What did you think of the museum?" Maggie asked, trying to draw him out, a little worried that it had been too much talk of death. He shrugged but said nothing. She didn't press him.

When they arrived home, the kids piled out of the car, racing to be the first inside, out of the rain that pattered gently but relentlessly from a steel-gray sky. They stopped abruptly at the mudroom door, Jonah's hand on the knob. They were all three examining something on the concrete stoop.

"Are they for us?" Luca asked. Maggie peered over their bent heads, trying to see what they were looking at. Three small, carved wooden animals stood in a row. A dolphin, an owl, and a fox. They were well crafted. Whoever had carved them was skilled. The fox glanced over its shoulder, wary. The owl looked solemnly ahead, eyes wide, and the dolphin's back was arched as if it were leaping from water.

"I want this one." Gabby picked up the fox. Luca chose the dolphin, and after a second Jonah slipped the owl into the pocket of his cargo shorts.

"Guys, we don't know who those are from," Maggie said. "Or if they're for you."

"But there are three of them and three of us," Luca interjected logically.

"Mom and Aunt Ellen won't want them," Jonah muttered, opening the door.

"Well, let's just ask them about it," Maggie said. The three kids filed inside to show the animals to Ellen.

"Now, aren't those the cutest things?" Maggie heard her say from the kitchen. "Who do you think left them? I wish they'd rung the bell so we could have said thank you."

Maggie started to follow the children but stopped. The carved animals were sweet gifts, but it seemed strange that they had just been left on the stoop. No note. No one had rung the doorbell. She glanced back down the drive and across the sweep of lawn. She had a faint niggling sensation of being watched. There was no sound or movement, just the steady *shush, shush* of the rain and the tide. She didn't see anything, and after a moment she dismissed the sensation. But still she wondered. Who had left the carvings on the stoop, and why had they chosen to remain anonymous?

● ● ●

From the shelter of the fir trees, Daniel watched the children each choose one of the animals he'd carved for them and go inside. He saw the woman glance in his direction and shrank back farther into the damp gloom. He had meant for the children to find the animals and was pleased they had. He'd seen their faces light up. It was a strange feeling to bring happiness to someone again. It seemed so long since he'd done it. In reality it had not been so very long, a little more than six months according to the calendar. But out here on the island, alone with the keening wind and the ever-rolling sea, he was losing perspective on time. It seemed to stretch longer and longer, spooling out like a white thread stretching to the horizon on the endless gray of the water, empty of human interaction.

Daniel couldn't remember the last time someone had touched him on purpose. The clerk at the grocery store had brushed his hand a few days earlier when he'd given her change for apples, but that was it. How had it come to this, that his life was so empty he cherished the brush of fingertips on his palm from a stranger as she handed him a nickel?

He watched the dark-haired woman as she turned and went into the house. He felt an affinity with her. She seemed lost somehow, as though she were searching for something she couldn't name. Perhaps he would carve an animal for her too—a skylark. Their call was a song for travelers and weary pilgrims, for those who had lost their way or were longing for a place to rest. Something in the dark-haired woman was seeking. She was a traveler, he sensed, like himself, weary with the searching. Perhaps it would help her find her way home.

The children came outside again just after dinner. The rain had stopped, bringing the sweet scent of the dark earth and a gray mist that hung low over the ground. Daniel watched from his place in the trees, melting back into the shadows, dark eyes and dark hair and muted clothes making him almost invisible. He was a shadow, felt like a shadow, as though someone might look right through him and see only the criss-cross of boughs at his back.

He had been coming here daily. He couldn't keep away. He had promised himself he'd look after them, but it was more than that, he knew. He was drawn to them, to the life and warmth in that house. He felt his loneliness acutely when he watched them. They were grieving but still had each other. He was alone now.

He hunkered down, boots sinking into the needles and the soft earth, and watched the woman as she shooed the children together for a game of freeze tag. Rainwater dripped off the fir boughs, dropping cold onto his tanned hands and down the back of his neck.

"Aunt Maggie!" the younger boy called out, gesturing for her to come to him.

"Maggie," Daniel murmured. The name fit her, all flyaway dark curls and lithe energy. The children loved her; he could tell by the way they wanted to touch her, especially the little girl. Small wonder, with what they had lost, that they gravitated to someone so alive. She darted to and fro, avoiding the grasp of little hands. The oldest boy hung back, though, keeping apart even as they played the game. He carried a burden too heavy for his young shoulders, equal parts anger and guilt. He wore it like an overcoat too big for him. The boy had been the first to the water that day. He had seen everything. Perhaps he blamed himself. He shouldn't. The blame lay elsewhere entirely.

Daniel's attention shifted back to the woman, Maggie. He couldn't look away from her. She was beautiful, but it wasn't just that. Again and again he felt his gaze turn to her, drawn by some intangible quality. She was laughing as the younger boy finally succeeded in catching her.

"I got you!" the boy crowed. "You're frozen!"

"Jonah, Gabby, help me!" Maggie cried, stretching out her arms to the others. Giggling, the little girl darted past her brother, only to be tagged a second later when she slipped on the wet grass and fell.

"Jonah," Maggie called out, "you're our only hope. Help us!"

And grudgingly Jonah turned, evading his younger brother, tagging both frozen players as he barreled by.

Daniel shifted his weight from one foot to the other, intent on the little scene. It seemed so normal, like a thousand other summer evenings, nothing extraordinary, but he felt as though he were watching a scene from another world entirely, something he remembered only from long ago. Once he had stood in the sunlight, head thrown back, laughing with baby Eli and Kate, swinging Eli so high he looked as though he could almost touch the sun. But that was before they knew about Eli. Before Katie's love turned to cold disdain. That was before everything changed.

Now Daniel was a thing of shadow and silence, the brightness as foreign to him as the children's laughter, a sound so sharp and high, he felt it might cut his skin. To stand in the light, you had to be able to see yourself clearly. To laugh, you had to hear your own voice. And he was resigned to remain in the shadows, silent and unseen, carrying the burden of solitude and guilt for a thousand bad decisions, carrying the fault for all that had happened in his own two hands.

Chapter Eleven

Maggie let herself out the mudroom door, closing it softly behind her. She bent on the stoop to tie her tennis shoes, then straightened and headed down the driveway at a brisk trot, elated by the feeling of freedom. It had been too long since she'd pounded the pavement. She'd taken up running when she moved back to Chicago to help her mother during chemo treatments. It had served as a release valve for her. Since then she ran as often as she could wherever she was. When she ran, she never felt trapped or worried or alone. She simply felt free.

The road was empty of cars, a ribbon of asphalt winding through wide, rolling meadows and stands of dark evergreens dripping with water from the late-afternoon rain. She turned away from the direction of Friday Harbor and ran fast, eating up the ground with a feeling almost like flying. Maggie had taken the opportunity to slip away while Lena was still in her room and the children were watching a movie before bed as Ellen cleaned up from dinner. It was just before sundown, the hushed and golden hour when the island seemed to hold its breath before the light slowly faded into shadows. The air was sweet and heavy with moisture and the smell of green growing things—spicy firs and ferns in the woods, hay from the meadows. And, as always, with the salt tang of the sea.

As Maggie ran, she let her mind wander, but she kept coming back to the problem at hand—the enormous debt and how she could help Lena and the children and save the island house. It was all she'd been thinking about the past few days, and only one solution seemed feasible after all her hours of contemplation, turning the problem this way and that. The Regent Fellowship. She had to win the Regent Fellowship. It awarded a cash prize of a hundred and fifty thousand dollars, which wouldn't cover the debt but would take a substantial bite out of it. It offered more money by far than any other idea she'd had.

As her feet pounded out a steady rhythm on the pavement, she pictured what winning the Regent would mean. The image hung suspended in her mind, glittering like a crystal chandelier, alluring, promising all she so fiercely desired. If she won, it would be the pinnacle of her career, the dream she had worked and hoped and yearned for since she was sixteen, the stellar success she craved above all else. She had lived day by day with the burning of that ambition in her chest. It had pushed her to Rhys, to Alistair, to all the lonely places she had been for the last seven years. She had chosen it above a home and family, above a feeling of place or belonging.

The pursuit of that dream had been her place, her belonging. And finally it was within her reach. To compete, to win . . . The thought brought a longing so sharp it felt almost like pain.

When Maggie finally stopped by a tumbledown mailbox a few miles from the farmhouse, she put her hands on her knees and took a moment to catch her breath. The light was fading from sepia to gray. She needed to head back soon before it got too dark to see the road. A deer stepped hesitantly from the undergrowth, saw Maggie and froze, then darted back the way it had come. Birds were twittering in the trees, getting ready for the night. Maggie straightened, walking in a circle, stretching her muscles gently. Trying to win the Regent seemed like the best solution any way she looked at it. That amount of money would surely save the island house and stave off creditors until everything could be made right. Nothing would bring Marco back, but at least her plan could help Lena and still allow Maggie to pursue the chance of a lifetime. She took a deep breath, wanting it to work, willing it to work. It was the best shot they all had.

Mind made up, Maggie looped back toward the farmhouse, feeling lighter than she had since she'd first heard about Marco's accident. That had been only a handful of days ago, but it felt like forever. She would tell Lena about her decision as soon as she had the chance, break the news that she had to head back to Chicago, but explain her plan. She thought Lena would be supportive. Maggie was doing this for all of them. Now she just had to win.

The smell of burning eggs was really quite vile, Maggie reflected as she swiped at the blaring smoke alarm with a kitchen towel. Eyes smarting from the acrid smoke rolling over the lip of a frying pan, Maggie waved the towel back and forth like a flag of surrender. No luck. "Fine!" She pulled over a kitchen chair, hastily balanced on it, and smacked the hush button on the smoke alarm. A sweet silence descended on the kitchen. Now for the eggs.

"Who knew scrambled eggs could burn that fast?" she muttered, staring at the scorched mess of brown and yellow. She'd turned off the gas burner when the smoke alarm first sounded, but the eggs were still sitting there accusingly. With a sigh, she dumped them into the trash and turned to find Jonah, Luca, and Gabby peering over the kitchen counter.

"Is that our lunch?" Jonah asked, all three eying her dubiously. Ellen was running errands in town, and Maggie had glibly volunteered to take care of feeding the kids. Lena was still in bed. Maggie had not yet had an opportunity to tell Lena about the plan she had decided on the evening before, but she was going to buy a ticket back to Chicago just as soon as she had a chance to talk to her.

"Well, not anymore." Maggie put her hands on her hips and pursed her lips. She had never really learned to cook. Her eating habits fit her transient life—airplane food, meals cooked by other people, hole-in-the-wall restaurant fare, and exotic street food. She loved food, loved the taste and texture of so many diverse flavors. Spicy yellow curry, bratwurst and mustard, papaya salad with shrimp and chilies, hunks of succulent grilled goat dripping with grease— all of it. But she was incapable of translating those flavors into meals made with her own hands. Her mother had tried to pass on traditional recipes from her childhood in Puerto Rico, but Maggie had never been interested in the kitchen. She'd rather eat food than learn how to make it.

She opened the fridge and assessed the contents, trying to put a meal together in her head. Alfalfa sprouts. Greek yogurt. A package of bacon. She was stymied.

"We have waffles in the freezer that you cook in the toaster," Luca offered helpfully.

Maggie turned to the trio. "Do you all like waffles?" Three nods of affirmation.

"With butter and syrup," Gabby amended.

"And powdered sugar," Jonah added.

"Great." With a sigh, Maggie opened the freezer.

A scant ten minutes later all four were sitting at the table eating waffles successfully toasted, not burned, along with yogurt and a half carton of strawberries that had somehow escaped being turned into jam. Maggie had found them in the back of the refrigerator, hidden behind the yogurt.

"These taste funny." Gabby wrinkled her nose and poked at a slice of strawberry. Maggie speared a segment of the fruit and chewed it. It was a little rubbery but edible.

"Anyone want more waffles?" she asked.

"Did I hear someone say waffles?" Lena asked, suddenly appearing at the foot of the stairs.

"Mommy!" Gabby flung herself at Lena, wrapping her arms around her mother's legs. Lena laughed, hugging her close. "Go finish your waffles." She shooed her back to the table.

Maggie surveyed Lena in amazement. Dressed in a soft, short-sleeved, dove-gray sweater and jeans, her hair smoothed back into a casually elegant chignon, she looked for all the world like she'd just stepped out of the pages of a *Good Housekeeping* magazine. No hint of fatigue or sorrow. She even wore her pearl studs, the ones Marco gave her when Jonah was born, and a touch of pale-pink lipstick. She dug through her purse, finally producing her keys.

"Are you going out?" Maggie asked, wondering if she should broach the topic of the Regent Fellowship now. Lena looked up, nodding, her gaze flickering to Maggie's and then away. Maggie felt a tiny dart of unease somewhere in the pit of her stomach. Lena was not as well as she looked.

Lena cleared her throat. "I'm just going to run down to the quilting shop. I have some squares I've been trying to finish for Gabby's quilt and I've run out of the pink fabric. I won't be gone long." She rounded the table to each of her children, hugging them tightly and kissing their foreheads.

"Be good for Aunt Maggie while I'm out, okay? No getting into trouble." She smoothed Gabby's hair, then turned to Maggie. "Take care of them while I'm gone, will you, Maggie?"

Maggie nodded. "Sure. Of course." She'd talk with Lena about the Regency when she returned.

"Good. I don't know what we would do without you." Lena met her eyes for an instant, her own cornflower-blue gaze flicking away from Maggie's. Then she slipped her purse onto her shoulder and walked out the door.

After Lena left, the mood in the house quickly soured. No sooner had Maggie cleared the lunch dishes than the sky turned brooding, with thick, iron-gray clouds rolling in and blotting out the sun. Within a few minutes it began to spit rain. Stuck inside, the children's tempers flared, and the afternoon progressed in fits and starts, punctuated by spats over which cartoon to watch, who was sitting in who's seat, and all manner of other minor disagreements.

By two thirty Maggie was ready to pull out her hair. Where was Ellen? Where was Lena, for that matter? And why in the world had she volunteered to babysit? Why hadn't she volunteered for the grocery run? At least she could tell the difference between a good cucumber and a bad one, but she had no idea how to referee fights over programs she'd never heard of and quell sibling rivalries and grievances that seemed endless.

"Okay!" she announced loudly, cutting Gabby off midwhine. She held out her hand for the TV remote, which Jonah was purposefully sitting on. "Right here, right now, the pity party is over. I am the crabby police. You!" She pointed to Gabby. "I can't hear you when you whine. You!" This one to Jonah. "Stop trying to control your sister. And, Luca . . ." She looked around for Luca, who was at that moment in the kitchen trying to sneak fruit snacks out of the cupboard. "Stop eating sugar!"

She strode resolutely to the cabinet of DVDs and pulled out *Mary Poppins* at random. "Now, we are all going to sit here and watch this together, without fighting, and in silence. Got it?" She turned a gimlet eye on the room.

Gabby nodded. Jonah looked mutinous but shrugged finally, resigned. Luca rejoined them, undeterred, piping up, "Can we make popcorn?"

Armed with bowls of microwave popcorn, they started the film. *They're probably wishing I was a little more like Mary Poppins*, Maggie thought grimly as Julie Andrews took the children to a magical world through a chalk drawing. Gabby snuggled up to her, resting her head on Maggie's chest, and Maggie hugged her close, reveling in the calm.

A few minutes later she heard a car crunch down the lane, and a second after that, the door to the mudroom slam. She craned her neck, expecting either Lena, fabric in hand, or Ellen with a load of groceries. It was Ellen, but her hands were empty. She stopped dead in the doorway, her face drained of color. Maggie sat up, a sudden feeling of dread blooming in her chest. Ellen looked at Maggie, clasped her trembling hands tightly in front of her, and said very calmly, "It's Lena. There's been an accident."

Chapter Twelve

Lena lay pale and silent in a hospital bed, an IV and heart monitor snaking from her arm and chest. She was unconscious. She had been airlifted from San Juan to the nearest hospital trauma center on the mainland in Bellingham. Maggie sat beside her, alone and in shock. She had caught the tiny San Juan Airlines' four-thirty flight from Friday Harbor to Bellingham and arrived at the hospital just as Lena was being wheeled into her room after a round of tests. Ellen had stayed at home with the children and was waiting to hear any news from Maggie.

So far no one had told Maggie anything other than a nurse who assured her brusquely that a doctor would arrive shortly to give her an update. Lena's medical insurance card had been in her purse the EMTs had brought with her, the nurse informed her, and all her personal belongings, including her jewelry, were in a secure place. Maggie could pick them up after she talked with the doctor. All Maggie had to do was sit there and wait.

Maggie crouched forward on a hard chair as though to protect herself, waiting for someone to tell her exactly what had happened and why Lena wouldn't wake up. She watched the heart-rate monitor, finding reassurance in the steady *beep, beep, beep* of Lena's heart. Lena looked untouched except for a cut across the bridge of her nose, bandaged with a bit of gauze, and an ugly bump on her forehead. She lay still, eyes closed, as pale as though she'd been carved from marble. Maggie pressed her hand to her own heart, trying to force away the dull ache spreading there. She felt adrift, with no information, no assurance that Lena would be okay. How could something like this happen? First Marco and now this. It was too much to take in.

She shifted uncomfortably in the hard chair. She hated hospitals. She had spent so much time in the hospital during her mother's battle with breast cancer. She knew the blanched smell of them, the metallic clatters and whirs and beeps. They were so impersonal, filled with hearts and bodies and voices, but all of it smothered under a layer of institutional practice. The scrubs and clipboards, the covered trays and sealed plastic packages of medical equipment. They bore no relation to real life, to people who wept and worried over loved ones—many of whom lived, but many who died. She hated it all.

She clenched her hands together, keeping herself in the chair by force of will. She would not bolt. She had to stay put and find out what was happening, not just for Ellen, but also for the kids and for Lena herself. She knew the medical jargon more than most people. She knew how to ask questions and how to make sure medical personnel were taking enough time, paying enough attention. She glanced again at the figure on the bed, biting her lip, filled with worry and more than a little in shock. Lena looked so still and serene, in direct contrast to Maggie's agitated state. Lying there, Lena looked almost peaceful, no sorrow pinching the corners of her lax mouth, her hands still, face placid, the only one at ease in a world gone so very wrong.

"Mrs. Firelli has sustained a brain injury from the forceful blow to the head she received upon impact in a car collision," Dr. Yamamoto, Lena's attending physician, explained to Maggie more than two hours later when he finally arrived for a consultation. With soft brown eyes and thinning hair, he had a world-weary, responsible look about him, as though constantly aware he held people's lives in his hands on a daily basis.

He scanned Lena's chart slowly.

"Mrs. Firelli was very fortunate that she sustained no other major injuries, but initial tests indicate she has an acute subdural hematoma, which has resulted in a coma. There's some bleeding on the brain accompanied by swelling, but we're monitoring the situation and feel there is no need to intervene yet to reduce swelling. She is stable but unconscious."

"Is there any way to know when she'll come out of the coma?" Maggie asked, pretty sure of the answer but hoping she was wrong. She'd faithfully watched *ER* every week through high school and knew a lot about comas, though she was the first to admit watching *ER* wasn't the most accurate way to learn medical information.

"I'm sorry, no. There is no way to tell. Sometimes it's a matter of hours or days, even weeks or months." He did not say what they both knew to be true, that sometimes the person never regained consciousness at all.

"Is there any way to tell whether she has any . . . brain damage?" Maggie asked, steeling herself for the answer. How could she be sitting here so calmly, discussing Lena, her best friend and college roommate? It seemed surreal. Perhaps it was the sense of unreality that made her able to talk so clearly, ask the right questions, gather what information she could, which, as it turned out, was precious little.

"Until Mrs. Firelli wakes up, we can't tell if there's been any permanent damage to the brain or assess the extent of it. In some cases there is no permanent damage." And again the unspoken fact, weighty between them, that in many cases the patient was not nearly so fortunate.

"Okay," Maggie said, scrubbing her hands on her jeans, taking a deep breath, trying to think. What more should she ask? "Is there anything we can do?" She looked at Dr. Yamamoto, feeling helpless.

"I'm sorry," he said again, looking sympathetic. "There really isn't. All we can do is wait and see. The brain will either repair itself or . . . Well, we hope this condition will resolve itself quickly. Until then, you can be assured we will make every effort to keep Mrs. Firelli comfortable. She is in excellent hands."

"And you'll let me know if there's any change in her condition?" Maggie asked.

"Of course," Dr. Yamamoto assured her.

Maggie left Lena's room and walked outside to the front entrance of the hospital, calling Ellen with an update. Ellen listened with concern as Maggie briefed her.

"Oh dear heavens," she said. "Poor Lena. I know they're doing all they can, but it's just such a shock."

"I know." Maggie ran a hand over her weary eyes, feeling the strain of the last few hours.

"I'll stay here tonight and call you tomorrow—or sooner if I hear anything new. How are the kids?"

"I told them you're with their mama and she's hit her head, but the doctors are going to take good care of her. They're pretty scared."

The thought of the three children, their world already shaken with the loss of their father, made Maggie's heart ache. "I'll call you tomorrow,"

Maggie repeated. There didn't seem to be anything more to say.

She spent a fitful night in Lena's room, waking early the next morning with a sore neck from sleeping in a hard chair. There was no change. Lena looked the same. Dr. Yamamoto confirmed it when he paid a visit around lunchtime.

"There's really no telling how long Mrs. Firelli could be unconscious. Go home," he urged her. "Get some rest and have a good meal. We'll call you if anything changes."

Maggie was reluctant to leave Lena, but the thought of the children spurred her to return to the island. She needed to see them, needed to explain what had happened to their mother. She couldn't reassure them that Lena would be okay, but she could be there with them in the midst of the uncertainty.

She caught the three o'clock flight back to the island. The San Juan Airlines planes were tiny, the ride over in a matter of minutes, and Maggie was glad to pay for the convenience of being able to go back and forth with ease. What would have taken several hours with the ferry and a commute on the mainland took just minutes by air.

She was dropped off at the house by Bob's Taxi and Tours. Ellen and the children were out. Slightly relieved, Maggie took the opportunity to shower and change her clothes. She was making an espresso when the doorbell rang. Surprised by the unexpected visitor, Maggie answered it.

A giant of a man stood on the stoop. He was young, early twenties, Maggie guessed, and dressed in a policeman's uniform. A shock of bright-red hair stood up from his head, giving him a startled look.

"Can I help you?" Maggie asked through the screen door, and he blushed a fiery red, matching his hair.

"Yes, ma'am. Sorry, ma'am. Officer Benjamin Burns of the San Juan County Sheriff's Office. Is this the home of Lena Firelli?"

"Yes," Maggie answered cautiously. "What is this about?" She tensed, every nerve on high alert for whatever came next. They could not handle any more bad news or drama.

Officer Burns cleared his throat. "I'm just finishing up some paperwork on the case"—his eyes drifted to the notepad in his hand—"and I wonder if I could ask you some questions about Mrs. Firelli." He held up the notepad by way of explanation.

"The case?" Maggie asked, puzzled.

He nodded. "Mrs. Firelli's car crash yesterday. Just filling out the forms. It's standard procedure," he explained, peering at her through the screen door. Maggie relaxed a little, reassured there was no new crisis. She opened the door and motioned him in, pointing toward the front parlor.

"Can I get you some coffee?" she offered.

"Oh, thank you, ma'am. That's mighty nice of you, but I'm okay. I just have a few questions for you." He perched awkwardly on the edge of the sofa, focusing hard for a moment on his notepad. He cleared his throat, darting a look at Maggie.

"Are you, uh, a relative of Mrs. Firelli's?" He fished a pen from his pocket and clicked it open.

"No, a close friend. She's like . . ." Maggie paused, swallowing hard, steadying her voice. "She's like a sister to me." She sat down on the foot of the chaise lounge, waiting for his next question.

He nodded and made a notation. "I was, uh, the one who responded to the call about the crash," he said after a moment.

"Oh," Maggie said, suddenly realizing she'd never thought to ask about the other people involved in the accident. "Was anyone else hurt? How is the other driver?"

"Other driver, ma'am?" Officer Burns asked quizzically, shifting uncomfortably on the sofa. "Mrs. Firelli was the only driver involved in the incident. She hit a concrete retaining wall going fifty miles an hour. If it hadn't been for her airbag deploying . . ."

Maggie was shocked. She had just assumed the accident was caused by another driver swerving across the center line or pulling out carelessly and T-boning Lena's Volvo. Lena was a cautious driver. She stopped twice at stop signs, once at the line and once where she could actually see oncoming traffic. Lena going fifty miles an hour on the island roads and losing control of her car was a bizarre and incongruous thought.

"What caused the accident? Do you know?" Maggie asked. Perhaps it had been the rain. Or an animal crossing the road. The island was teeming with wildlife, from black-tailed deer to red foxes, not to mention the usual array of raccoons, birds, and other small creatures.

"Well, ma'am, that's the strange thing. There isn't any sign of a cause. No obvious debris in the road, no dead critters, no curves where she hit the wall. The pavement was a little wet but nothing unusual. It's just a long, straight stretch of road alongside the water. And, ma'am"— Officer Burns glanced quickly around the room, lowering his voice although they were alone— "the thing is, there weren't any tire marks."

Seeing Maggie's look of incomprehension, he explained, "She didn't even hit her brakes."

Maggie stared at him, a sudden suspicion making her skin prickle with gooseflesh. It couldn't be. She darted a glance at the officer as he scribbled notes, the suspicion crystallizing into a coherent thought. Could Lena have done it on purpose? Had the strain been too much for her, first Marco and then the truth about their financial situation causing her to finally snap?

Maggie shook her head. How could she even think such a thing about Lena, who loved her children more than life itself? But she remembered Lena's voice, flat and final, in the bedroom the morning after she had broken the jam jars. *"I don't know if I can do it, Maggie. I don't know if I can live without him. I don't think I want to."*

"Ma'am." Officer Burns cleared his throat and peered at her earnestly. "I know Mrs. Firelli lost her husband recently. Do you know if she was taking any medication at the time of the crash? Did she seem to be in her right mind the last time you saw her?" He asked the final question hesitantly. "Do you think Mrs. Firelli might have wanted to . . . to end her own life?"

Maggie didn't answer for a moment, staring past the young officer out the window to the wide expanse of front lawn, trying to collect her thoughts. Had Lena been taking any medication? Maggie had no idea. She would need to check the medicine cabinet in Lena's bathroom. Was it possible that she had intended to end her life? What should she say? She didn't know anything for sure, certainly not the truth.

"I don't know about any medications," she said finally. "But no," she said, shaking her head, speaking with more conviction than she felt. "No, Lena wouldn't have done this on purpose. She wouldn't have left her children. It must have been an accident."

Officer Burns nodded and clicked his pen closed. "Well, then I'll be filling out the report, assuming she was going too fast, lost control of the vehicle, and didn't have time to apply the brakes. I do wish Mrs. Firelli a speedy recovery."

Maggie nodded. "Thank you, Officer."

After he left, Maggie stood at the door watching the taillights of the police cruiser wink down the drive. Officer Burns's visit had left her feeling distinctly unsettled. She turned and went up the stairs to Lena and Marco's bedroom. As she rifled through Lena's nightstand drawer, at first glance it contained nothing of interest, just a crumpled handkerchief, a lemon verbena–scented hand lotion from L'Occitane, and the newest issue of *Real Simple* magazine. Maggie almost shut the drawer, intending to try the bathroom medicine cabinet, but at the last moment she swiped her hand across the back of the drawer.

A plastic bottle was in one corner. She pulled it out, frowning as she read the label. It was a prescription for an antianxiety medication in Lena's name, filled the day after Marco died. She opened the container and counted out the little white pills. Five were missing. Maggie stared at the pills in her hand. Was this part of the puzzle? Maggie knew sometimes medication like this could have the opposite of its intended effect. Had Lena been under the influence of some medication that had altered her behavior? There was no way of knowing when Lena had taken the pills or how many she had taken. Perhaps they had contributed to the crash, perhaps not. Lena's accident could easily have been just that, an accident, caused by a moment's lapse in concentration, a slip of the wheel at the exact wrong time.

But still, as Maggie slid the pills back into their container and stored them on the highest shelf in the bathroom medicine cabinet, well out of reach of the children, she couldn't help but wonder. Had Lena deliberately caused this catastrophic event? In the depths of sorrow, faced with the enormity of loss, with the prospect of crushing debt and a life devoid of Marco, under the influence of medication and in a moment of desperation, had Lena turned the steering wheel, put her foot on the gas, and hoped never to wake up?

Over a hasty late dinner of boxed macaroni and cheese, Maggie and Ellen explained to the children as gently as they could about Lena's condition, trying to be both honest and reassuring. It didn't go well. Gabby burst into tears and ran to her room. Jonah got up from the table without a word and disappeared outside, leaving his dinner almost untouched. Only Luca stayed at the table, methodically finishing both his plate of macaroni and Jonah's with a determined look on his face.

Ellen went to check on Gabby. Maggie thought about going after Jonah but decided against it. He could probably use some space. When he was done eating, Luca followed Gabby and Ellen up the stairs. Maggie ate a few more bites but found her appetite was gone. So she busied herself clearing the table and washing the dishes, routine tasks that lent a veneer of normalcy to the evening.

A half hour after she'd gone upstairs, Ellen returned. "I've given Gabby a bath and put her in her pajamas, poor mite. She's looking at books in her bed, and I told her I'd be up to tuck her in after a minute. Luca's brushed his teeth and he's in bed now too." Ellen looked exhausted.

"Let me tuck her in," Maggie urged. "You take a rest. It's been a hard day."

"Well, it hasn't been a picnic for you either," Ellen protested.

"Yes, but I spent the morning waiting at the hospital, not taking care of the kids. Let me do this," Maggie urged her.

185

Ellen wavered, looking tempted. "I should call Ernie and give him an update," she admitted. She had called her husband after Lena's accident but had not yet had a chance to tell him what the doctor had said that morning.

It took only a moment more of persuasion before she was convinced. Maggie sent her off to her room. "But come get me when you're through with the children so we can have a chat. I'll call Ernie and then put my feet up for a minute," Ellen said as she left, cell phone in one hand.

Maggie wiped down the counters and put the kitchen in order. She was about to head upstairs when the French doors leading to the back deck opened and Jonah slipped inside. He went up the stairs without a word. A minute later she heard water running in the bathroom.

In Gabby's room, Maggie knelt beside the small white bed. Gabby handed her the book she'd been looking at, a story of a piglet who dreamed of being a ballerina. Maggie put the book on top of a stack by the bed.

"Aunt Maggie, Aunt Ellen said Mommy hit her head and her brain went to sleep so it could get better." Her little mouth was pinched with worry. Maggie tucked the Disney princess sheets and appliquéd, petal-pink bedspread around Gabby and snuggled her stuffed rabbit, Bun Bun, close to her pillow.

"Yes, sweetie, that's exactly what happened. We don't know how long your mommy has to sleep, but her brain is resting so it can get better and help her wake up."

Gabby considered this for a moment, then nodded. "Okay, Aunt Maggie." She stroked Bun Bun's worn head. "Maybe tomorrow Mommy will wake up."

"I hope so," Maggie murmured, pressing a kiss onto the soft spiral curls at the crown of Gabby's head. Her hair smelled like bubble gum–scented shampoo. Maggie switched on the Beauty and the Beast nightlight and crept from the room, heading down the hall to the room the boys shared.

Jonah was lying in bed, awash in a faint green light from the Superman nightlight in the corner. Head pillowed on his arms, he stared unseeingly at the ceiling. Luca wheezed gently in the bed across the room, already asleep.

"Hey," Maggie whispered, kneeling by Jonah's bed. He turned. In the faint light his eyes looked so grave, too old and burdened for someone his age. She smiled tentatively, but he simply looked at her, his face expressionless.

"Is my mom going to die?" he asked finally, softly.

Maggie glanced over at Luca's slumbering form, a small mound beneath dinosaurs-of-the-world cotton sheets, and pitched her voice low. "I don't think so," she answered honestly.

"But you don't know for sure?" he asked, giving her an assessing look.

"Not for sure, but most people wake up from comas. She's in a coma because her brain has been hurt, and a coma is like a nap to give the brain rest and a chance to heal. Your mom's brain is trying to get better."

"I know. I sneaked into Aunt Ellen's room and looked it up on the internet. But Mom could still wake up and not remember anything, right? She could not remember how to walk and stuff. She could wake up and not remember us." His voice was tight.

He was scared, she realized. Of course he was scared. He'd lost one parent while he watched, and now this was happening so soon after. It was too awful to believe. She remembered what it felt like to lose her mother, the sensation of being adrift in the world, the hollow ache that throbbed in the soft space between her collarbones, right below her throat.

"Oh, Jonah." She squeezed his arm, trying to comfort him but feeling clumsy in the gesture. He didn't respond. "The doctors are doing everything they can, and we are too. We'll get through this. It'll be okay."

"But you have to go back to your job," he said, his voice quavering just a little. He sounded so young. "I mean, you can't stay here forever.

You only come for a month, and then you have to go back to work. What happens if Mom isn't awake by then?" She could hear the uncertainty in his tone, the fear that everything familiar was suddenly being taken away.

Maggie winced, thinking of the Regent Fellowship. She hadn't had a chance to talk with Lena, and she knew now there was no way she could jaunt off to Chicago right away and start preparing her entry. The Regent would have to wait. Everything would have to wait until they saw what happened with Lena. She swallowed hard, tamping down the bitter taste of disappointment. There was still time. She would just have to delay a little longer. She couldn't allow herself to think about less hopeful outcomes, not yet. It was too painful to contemplate. She could do only what lay in front of her, what she knew she needed to do at this moment.

"I'll take care of you. I'm not going anywhere until your mom is okay," she whispered, her voice calm and sure, hoping against hope that she hadn't just made a promise she wouldn't be able to keep.

"Well, this is a fine kettle of fish," Ellen said wearily, settling into a chair opposite Maggie at the dining room table. An open bottle of red wine sat between them, a half-full glass in front of each woman. It was a good vintage—a five-year-old Cave de Tain Hermitage Syrah. Marco had been an avid wine connoisseur and had kept a well-stocked wine cave in New York. Here on the island the options were more limited, but he had still managed to keep a small but selective collection on hand. Maggie moved her goblet in a slow circle, watching the wine swirl against the glass, so deep a red it looked black. She sniffed it as Marco had taught her to do so many years before, then tasted it. Oak aged. Peppery notes over ripe fruit. She had known nothing about wine until Marco taught her.

Maggie set down her glass and leaned back in the dining room chair. She took a deep breath and scrubbed her hands over her hair, smoothing back a few flyaway curls, trying to order her thoughts, unsure how to proceed. She felt as though she were in some alternative reality where the world had tipped on its axis, spilling all the good and predictable patterns of life out into the vast nothing of the universe, leaving only chaos and destruction in its wake. Surely she would awaken tomorrow somewhere sane and normal—Jamaica or Jakarta or even Chicago—and realize the world was as she had left it, moving along at a predictable speed, everything still as it should be. Anything but this. This was madness. She took another large swallow of wine, trying to brace herself. "So what do we do now?" she asked.

"Well, goodness. I don't know. We just have to keep going. What else can we do?" Ellen sighed heavily, brushing a strand of silvery-blonde hair back from her brow. A cool, moist breeze was trickling through the open windows, and she pulled her cardigan closer, buttoning the middle button. "We've got three scared children up there. Somebody's got to take care of them until we see what happens." She picked up her wine glass, sniffed the contents, and set it back down.

Maggie didn't ask the obvious question that followed that train of thought. What would happen if Lena didn't wake up? She couldn't bring herself to go there, not yet.

Ellen met Maggie's eyes as though discerning her thoughts. "Let's take it one step at a time," she said, her practicality comforting. "How long before you have to be back at your job?"

Maggie hesitated. "I've taken an indefinite leave of absence, but I have to get back at some point soon." She didn't mention the Regent Fellowship, although she was now on borrowed time. She needed to get back as soon as possible, but she couldn't leave immediately. It was unthinkable. Perhaps if Lena woke up soon, if there was no brain damage. But she couldn't dwell on all the possibilities, not tonight. They just had to put one foot in front of the other.

"I called Ernie and told him I'll be staying longer than we thought." Ellen sighed again and straightened her shoulders. "After thirty-nine years of marriage, that man still cannot use the clothes dryer or the stove top, but he'll be fine for a few more weeks. I keep the freezer stocked with homemade meals for us anyway, so he can just heat those up in the microwave. And Stephanie will keep an eye on him."

Maggie looked at Ellen, vaguely surprised, realizing for the first time that the older woman would have to sacrifice to stay here too. She sometimes forgot Ellen had not always been there on the island, washing dishes and making meals and keeping the household running smoothly. "Are you really okay to stay longer?" Maggie asked. She had simply assumed Ellen would stay, but it felt presumptuous now not to at least ask. If she didn't stay . . . Maggie could not imagine doing all that needed to be done by herself. She was ill-equipped to handle a household and the children without help.

"Of course," Ellen said. "They're family." She frowned. "I know my brother, Dick, and Ingrid can't help. Ever since Ingrid had her back surgery, she can't travel. And Dick is too tied up with his practice to come out. Besides, truth be told, neither of them is exactly comforting or practical anyway. They're about as helpful as poodles in a pigsty. What Lena knows about running a household, canning, cooking, baking, and sewing, she learned from me. I used to spend quite a bit of time at their house when Lena was younger. Her mother's health was always a little poor, and I helped out when I could."

Maggie nodded, thinking of Lena's parents. They had been terribly shaken by Marco's death, of course—devastated, they'd said. In his last call, Dick had confided that Ingrid was confined to bed with prescription tranquilizers for the shock. Maggie and Ellen had been fielding their frequent calls so as not to burden Lena, giving Dick updates on how Lena and the children were handling everything.

"They know about Lena's accident?" Maggie asked.

Ellen nodded. "I called them last night and told them everything I knew. I need to call them again. I told them I'd let them know when I heard anything more. I'll give them the hospital's number so Dick can call and ask all the questions he'll ask us. They're worried sick about her." She took a sip of wine and grimaced, whether from the taste or the thought of Lena's parents, Maggie couldn't tell. "Sometimes I can't believe what life throws at you." Ellen shook her head. "Poor Lena. And those dear little ones." She looked tired, the bags under her eyes pronounced in the overhead lighting.

"I can stay for a while," Maggie said. She winced, remembering the promise she'd made to Jonah. She couldn't keep it indefinitely, but she could keep it for now. She still needed to enter the Regent competition. If she didn't, how would Lena manage to keep afloat financially? Lena and the children needed to be secure, to not lose their home. They needed a safe and familiar place now more than ever.

And you don't want to lose the best opportunity of your career, a little voice whispered in the back of her mind. Maggie pushed it away, refusing to acknowledge it, although she knew it spoke the truth. Now was the time for altruism, not personal gain. "I'll stay at least until things are more settled and we see how Lena is recovering. At least a week or so, maybe more."

She would call the agency in the morning and let them know her change in plans. Alistair was not going to be happy. Not at all. She put the thought of his reaction from her mind. She'd deal with it tomorrow.

Ellen nodded, her face slackening in relief. "Well, that's a blessing, make no mistake." She folded her hands in front of her and straightened her shoulders again, as though preparing to face what had to be done. "We'll just take it one day at a time," Ellen said, then added with an assurance neither of them believed, "It will be okay."

Chapter Thirteen

Maggie caught the ten o'clock morning flight to Bellingham and arrived at the hospital with a dull, pounding headache. She hadn't slept well, again dozing fitfully, this time waking with every creak and whistle of the wind, sure she heard the phone, one of the children calling out, Lena's voice, Marco's laughter. She'd had two Tylenol and a double espresso for breakfast, thrown her hair into a messy ponytail, and gone to catch her flight.

When the taxi from the airport dropped her off at the hospital, all Maggie wanted was a few moments alone, some space to try to come to grips with what was happening. If she could just have a couple of minutes of peace and quiet, perhaps she could clear her head.

Lena had a visitor. Father Griffin Carter was sitting in the chair by her bed, leaning forward with his arms on his knees and his head turned toward Lena. He didn't see Maggie.

"Oh great," Maggie muttered, taken aback by the sight of him, clerical collar and cleft chin. What was he doing here? She watched him from the doorway for a minute, hoping he would leave. He didn't seem to be in any hurry. An orderly rushed by, throwing her a brief, uninterested look as he passed. From the nurses' station at the corner, she heard someone paging Dr. Morrison to the OR.

Giving up, she stepped into the room. Griffin glanced up and caught sight of her, his face breaking into a pleased grin. "Maggie." He rose, instantly sobering as she came into the room and stood beside him at Lena's bedside.

"I heard this morning," he said. "I caught the first ferry I could. I was going to stop by the house when I got back to the island to see if you needed anything." He searched her face, his expression concerned.

"We're fine." Maggie stepped back, wishing he would leave so she could be alone. She leaned over the bed, assessing Lena. She looked the same. Skin as pale as milk in the glare of the overheard lights, a blonde fan of lashes over closed eyes, she seemed like a modern-day Sleeping Beauty. Griffin joined her at the bedside.

"What do the doctors say?" he asked, gazing at Lena. He smelled like pine soap, a clean, manly scent, and just a hint of exhaust fumes. He must have ridden his motorcycle onto the ferry and up to Bellingham.

"They said we won't know anything until she wakes up. If she wakes up. They can't tell now if there's been any damage." Maggie reached out, touching Lena's arm, the skin warm and smooth. She traced the smattering of freckles on Lena's wrist. Lena hated her freckles, complaining that truly beautiful women had flawless skin. Maggie, who didn't have a freckle on her body, had always found the visual texture of them intriguing.

Griffin shook his head, stuffing his hands into his pockets. He looked visibly shaken. "I couldn't believe it when I heard the news. First Marco and now this . . . It's unbelievable. How are the kids?"

"Scared." Maggie gripped the metal rail of the bed, wishing he would leave, wishing he weren't just standing there looking at her, his eyes full of pity. There was nothing he could do, nothing any of them could do. She felt so helpless in the face of this newest tragedy. It burned her from the inside, the senselessness of it all.

She inhaled deeply, trying to calm herself, drawing in a lungful of air that smelled like hospital disinfectant. The scent was so horribly familiar, reminding her of her mother's illness, of the long nights waiting for the inevitable while Ana counted out the seconds on her well-worn rosary, the click of the glass beads measuring the slow slide into an irreversible loss.

Standing there next to yet another hospital bed, Maggie was again overwhelmed by a sense of futility and by the injustice of it all. First her mother, then Marco, and now Lena lying there on the pillow, another line in a litany of wrongs.

She bit her lip and shut her eyes, turning slightly away from Griffin, trying to get herself under control. She didn't want to unravel in front of him. She focused on the steady *beep, beep, beep* of Lena's heart monitor, trying to center herself. When she looked up, Griffin was watching her, his face creased in sympathy.

"Maggie," he said gently. "I know it seems dark right now, but we can't lose hope."

"Why not? Do you have some kind of guarantee that Lena's going to be okay?" Maggie asked sharply.

"No," Griffin answered truthfully, resting his arms on the bed railing. "No guarantee. This is one of the hardest parts of life, the waiting and the uncertainty in the face of a possible great loss." He looked down at Lena's still face, his expression open and honest. "But I believe things will turn out well in the end."

"How can you possibly know?" Maggie asked bluntly.

"Have you ever heard of Julian of Norwich?"

Maggie shook her head.

"She's one of my heroes. An English mystic from the fourteenth century. When she was about thirty, Julian got sick and everyone thought she was going to die. On her sickbed, she had a divine vision, and when she recovered she

198

summed up all she'd seen in one sentence. She said that, in the end, 'All shall be well, and all shall be well and all manner of thing shall be well.'" Griffin glanced down at Lena's face as he spoke, his tone steady with assurance. "I think Julian was right. I don't know how, but I believe in the end everything is going to be okay."

For a moment Maggie felt herself sway toward the pull of his words, spoken with such quiet surety, toward the comfort they offered. But then she glanced at Lena and reality came crashing down again.

She shook her head. "No," she said finally.

Griffin looked up, surprised, but said nothing, just watched her. She straightened and turned to him, meeting those golden eyes fiercely.

"Lena and the children are the only family I have left now. I've lost everyone else I've loved," she said, biting the words off individually. "So you can say anything you want about hope and everything turning out well, but I don't believe it." She stared him down, her chin raised in challenge. "Not in my life, not in the world I've seen."

He gazed at her for a long moment, face unreadable. At last he said, "I'm sorry, Maggie." He didn't say anything else.

After a minute Maggie nodded wearily. "So am I," she said simply. She took a last look at Lena's still face, as pale as pure-white marble. Then she picked up her bag and left.

Maggie waited in the lobby until Griffin left, then stayed the night at the hospital again, returning to the island the next day on the midmorning flight.

"No change, but she's stable," Maggie reported to Ellen when she arrived home. She didn't mention her encounter with Father Griffin the day before. As she stood in the kitchen, sniffing the tantalizing odor of fresh biscuits baking in the oven, it took her a moment to realize what was missing. The incessant noise. It was too quiet.

"Where are the kids?" she asked.

"They're in the backyard building something." Ellen opened the oven and pulled out a baking sheet filled with perfectly round buttermilk biscuits. "They said it was a secret and a surprise. They've been at it all morning and won't let me see what they're up to. I've been keeping an eye on them as best I can, but they won't let me near them." She raised her eyebrows skeptically.

Curious, Maggie headed out the French doors onto the deck. The lawn was empty. She crossed the yard and leaned over the white picket fence that separated the lawn from the sheer drop-off to the stony beach below. Nothing. They weren't playing on the stairs that hugged the side of the bluff and meandered down to the beach. There was no sign of them. A little alarmed, she circled the property, keeping an ear tuned for them. Partway around, she caught a flash of red in one of the small stands of firs that bordered the yard. Luca's hoodie. She changed course and approached quietly. All three children were crouched in a bare spot ringed by the dark, fragrant arms of fir trees, a protected place of soft dirt and patches of moss. They didn't hear her coming.

"We need one here," Jonah directed Luca, who obediently picked up a stone about the size of a baseball from a small pile.

"Hey, guys, what's up?" Maggie asked. Startled, Luca dropped the rock. Gabby let out a small cry and promptly stuck her thumb in her mouth. Maggie stepped forward, and Jonah moved to block her, then seemed to change his mind at the last second and stepped aside.

They'd built something. Maggie stared at the lopsided edifice. Constructed of beach stones worn smooth by the tide and leaning precariously to one side, it stood about two feet high. They had driven small fir branches into the dirt to make a frame for it. On top of the stones they had placed a wedding photo of Marco and Lena in a silver frame, a single black woven loafer of Marco's, a few of his drafting pencils, and some small bits of sea glass. Maggie crouched down and touched the frame of the wedding picture with one finger.

"What's this for?" she asked softly. Luca and Jonah shifted uncomfortably. Gabby sucked her thumb. Finally Jonah answered, "We thought Dad might need help getting back. You know, like those people in the museum."

Puzzled, Maggie surveyed the assorted items. It took a moment before she put the pieces together. They had built an altar, a shrine. "You mean the exhibit we saw at the museum? About the settlers who helped people get back home after they died so they could go to heaven? The beckoners?"

Jonah nodded, and Luca piped up, "We got Dad's favorite stuff so he'd be able to find us easier."

"I gived up all my sea glass that Daddy helped me find," Gabby volunteered, taking her thumb out of her mouth to speak and then replacing it again.

"And you did all this to help your dad find his way home?" Maggie asked, amazed by their dedication. They had spent all morning building the altar in the hopes that it would help Marco.

Jonah nodded. "And we thought maybe . . ." He stopped and stubbed his toe in the dirt, not looking at her. "Maybe we could put some of Mom's stuff out here too."

"In case she needs help getting back," Maggie guessed. They nodded.

"Well." Maggie rose, brushing off the pine needles from her pants, biting her lip hard to keep back the prickle of tears behind her eyelids. Their hopeful faces broke her heart. She cleared her throat. "I think that's a great idea," she said. "What else should we put on here?"

Gabby shyly took her hand. Her thumb was wet, but Maggie didn't care.

"Do you have anything to put on it?" Gabby asked. Maggie studied the items on the altar, then nodded, thinking of her precious photographs in the wallet upstairs. She would give them one, the photo that showed the three of them—Maggie, Lena, and Marco. Her small sacrifice to add to theirs. Who knew, maybe it would help somehow. She recalled Verna's words during the tour, about how the island was special, that strange and wonderful things could happen here. Of course Maggie didn't really believe that, but still, what could it hurt to go along with the children?

"I think I do," she said slowly. "I'll get it." She returned a few minutes later with the photo and her camera in her hand. She wanted to document the children's efforts. When she woke up, Lena would be touched to see their desire to help her. Maggie set her precious photo on the altar and snapped a few shots of the scene. One with the three children clustered around the altar, another a close-up of the objects they'd collected. She felt that by taking photos, she could honor the moment, preserve Jonah, Luca, and Gabby's creativity and sacrifice.

Later, after the kids were tucked into bed for the night, Maggie took Ellen out and showed her the altar. She explained about the beckoning ceremony and how the children had gotten the idea to build an altar in the first place.

"Well, that sounds just plain pagan." Ellen frowned, looking down at the ramshackle structure. She was a staunch Lutheran, Maggie had discovered in their time together, and was suspicious of anything that smacked of aberration.

"But it makes them feel like they can do something to help their parents," Maggie explained. "It helps them not feel so powerless. Besides, they got the idea from Lutherans right here on the island."

"Hmm." Ellen didn't look convinced, but she didn't argue further. "You say Lutherans thought this up?" she asked finally. At Maggie's nod she sighed and threw her hands in the air. "Well, if you're going to have a proper altar, you're going to need candles. We just can't let the children light them by themselves. Come on, I know where Lena keeps the ones for power outages."

Something was wrong. Daniel could sense it. He could see a new tension in the set of Maggie's shoulders. He had heard the little girl crying last night through an open window. The house was enveloped in a lingering air of sadness, but now it was undercut with a sharp frisson of fear. What had happened? He'd seen the children working all morning, the boys hauling stones up the stairs from the beach and into the trees. He'd stayed far past his usual time, curious to see what they were doing. And where was the blonde wife, the beautiful one who had lost her husband? Where had she gone?

He left before lunch, returning a little after twilight. It was late, after ten o'clock, but the light was still fading. The summer days were long so far north. He crept as near to the edge of the trees as he dared, staring at the house, trying to see anyone inside, but the windows remained empty. The TV was on in the family room. He could hear the faint canned laughter, but nothing stirred. He took a deep breath, smelling sadness and the sea. On the western horizon, far out on the water, a black bank of clouds rolled ponderously across the sky. It would be a full moon tonight, but not for long. Rain was coming.

He waited until it was almost full dark before crossing the lawn. He did so silently. His grandmother told him her ancestors could walk through these forests without making a sound. Her own grandfather had been able to do so, she claimed. It had seemed like just another tall tale, one of the many his grandmother kept in her pocket like the cherry cough drops she liked to suck. As a child he had never been able to perfect the skill of walking silently, though he had spent hours trying. And he hadn't had the means or the desire to practice in New York, a world of cement and rushing pedestrians. But here, his steps covered by the sound of the ocean, his dark clothes blending into the long shadows of the night, he could almost imagine his great-grandfather, an elder of the Lummi Nation, keeping pace with him, step by soundless step.

He found the children's building project easily enough and bent low to examine it. An altar, he noted in surprise. Clumsily made, it would topple over at the first careless push. A lit votive candle in a glass holder sat before a silver picture frame, flickering and guttering in its own wax. It was almost burnt out. He crouched before the photo, studying it. The couple smiled out at him, the man's eyes dark, a little brooding, the woman glowing as though she were lit up from inside. For some reason it made a lump rise in the back of his throat.

There was another photo as well. He picked this one up, tilting it to see better in the candlelight. It was Maggie, the blonde woman, and her dead husband, all leaning over a pot of sauce. They were all three beautiful—young, carefree, exuberant, with the possibilities of life just beginning to spread before them. He saw how the women both leaned in, pulled by the polarity of the man's body. Marco Firelli. Who had he been, to have drawn both women to him so completely?

Reluctantly he set down the photo. He glanced back at the house, but all was still. Carefully, he placed the wedding picture, the shoe, the drafting pencils, the flickering votive, and the bits of sea glass on the soft dirt, looking over his shoulder every few moments as he did so. Nothing stirred. He paused for a long minute, considering his next move. Then stone by stone, he began to rebuild.

Chapter Fourteen

The next day Maggie did not go to the hospital, instead staying home with the children so Ellen could run errands in town. She came in from a rousing morning of playing pirate ship with the kids to find five new messages on her phone. Her heart skipped a beat. If someone had called five times, surely there must be an emergency. What if it was the hospital? She had just punched the button to listen to the first message when the phone rang again. She picked it up without looking at the screen.

"Aha, I knew my little scheme would work," Alistair said triumphantly. "Good day, my bright star."

"What little scheme?" Maggie asked, moving back outside to stand on the deck where she could see the kids. Luca was wearing a scarf tied over one eye like a patch. Jonah, the pirate captain, had collected several sticks to use as swords. Gabby had insisted on being a mermaid and was wearing all her shiny plastic bead necklaces over her two-piece bathing suit, although it was too cool to be in swimwear. She refused to put on anything warmer because it would look less mermaid-like.

"Oh, I just decided I'd call you every fifteen

minutes for as long as it took for you to answer. Persistence, you know, is the child of necessity."

"I thought that was invention," Maggie interposed. "Isn't invention the child of necessity?"

"Both. Both are the child of necessity, and speaking of necessity, when are you coming home? I'd so hoped to see you in my office, oh, say, last week."

"I left you a message about that—" Maggie began, watching Luca do battle against an invisible opponent with the stick sword Jonah had given him.

"Yes," Alistair said, interrupting her. "And I'm ignoring it. Forgotten, done, gone forever."

"Alistair." Maggie sighed, exasperated. "I can't come home right now."

There was a measured silence on the other end of the line. "I'm going to pretend I didn't hear you say that and give you a moment to reconsider," he said, his voice still light. She heard the warning in it, though. She moved to the other end of the deck, away from the children, and dropped her voice so they couldn't hear her.

"Alistair, I'm not leaving. I can't leave. I explained this already. Lena's still in a coma. Gabby's having nightmares about drowning almost every night. Luca's begun wetting the bed, although he thinks we don't know it. And Jonah . . . Jonah has just closed himself off from the world. I can't leave. Not yet."

A long pause this time, and then Alistair's voice, biting each word off with perfect British enunciation. "Magdalena, are you mad? You have been given the opportunity of a lifetime, worth all the blood, sweat, toil, and tears of an entire career, and you are just throwing it away without hesitation!"

"Without hesitation . . . Alistair," Maggie retorted indignantly, "you have no idea how hard this is for me!" She was speechless for a moment, trying to grasp the right words to make him understand what her decision was costing her.

"I lie awake and fantasize about taking off from here, about just getting up and packing my bag and hopping on a plane, showing up at the office and starting my project for the Regent. You have no idea how much I want to be back there working on my entry. How much I need to win. Everything is riding on this." She ran a hand through her tousled curls, searching for the best way to convey the position she was in.

"This opportunity is more important to me than it is to you," she said flatly. "I have given my life for my career. I know what I'm risking by staying on the island right now. I know I'm weakening my chances every day I stay here. I understand that, Alistair, but I cannot—*cannot*— leave right now. Period. End of story. I made a promise, and I can't leave yet. Not now."

She clutched the phone tighter and glanced at the children. Gabby was trying to fasten seashells to her hair with bobby pins. Jonah and Luca were fencing against one another now, Jonah with the decided upper hand.

Alistair sighed, his tone resigned. "Oh, Magdalena, why must you adhere to such cursed notions of loyalty and honor? Why can't you just be heartless and conniving like the rest of us?"

"You're not heartless and conniving." Maggie smiled despite herself. She had just bought a little more time, but at what cost? She hoped she wasn't making a serious error. She had a feeling she was. "You've got a heart of gold no matter how you try to hide it."

"Yes, well, bully for me." Alistair's voice became serious. "Listen, my dear, I know I don't tell you this nearly often enough, but you're one of the brightest I've ever seen, and you know that's saying something. I understand you think you have to stay. I know I can't change your mind. But think very carefully about the choice you're making. Every day you stay is a day less you will have to prepare. Your competitors aren't taking breaks, you know. You only get one Regent invitation. No repeats. You know that. You have a chance to win, especially if you can somehow manage to tap into that part of yourself you've never known how to access. If you can do that, really connect with your subjects and let yourself be part of the story, I think you stand as good a chance as any of the rest of them, maybe better. So think about what you're doing by delaying your return. I want you to be sure."

Maggie gripped the phone hard as his words sank in. She knew he was speaking the truth. She was silent for a long moment, feeling torn. She had been trying to think up ideas for her Regent entry, to at least start mentally preparing for the competition even if she was geographically constrained to the island, but her attention was completely preoccupied by stress, uncertainty, and grief. It was a disastrous combination for her creative process. She knew she needed to be making headway on her project, but she just couldn't seem to get into the right frame of mind. When she determined to make some headway, there was always some interruption, something else that demanded her time and attention. She felt blocked in all directions. It felt impossible to leave the children now, but equally impossible to watch the Regent slip away forever. What she needed was time away from the island and mental space where she could think and breathe and dream again.

Alistair's call was swaying her resolve. Perhaps some compromise could be made if Lena didn't wake up soon. Ellen was doing a fine job with the children. Perhaps Maggie could make a trip back to Chicago, work like crazy for a couple of months, and then come back. Maybe it would be enough. Maybe she could keep her promise *and* enter the Regent. It wasn't ideal, but it just might be possible.

"I'll think about it," she said. "I can't do more than that right now."

Alistair sighed deeply. "Remember, Magdalena, you're my brightest star. Don't forget that, no matter how dark it seems right now."

She nodded even though Alistair couldn't see her, blinking hard against the tears that unexpectedly filled her eyes. The yard blurred, the children dissolving into bright dots of color. "I will," she promised. There was nothing more to say.

"Ellen, I'm going for a run," Maggie called out, lacing up her tennis shoes. The morning had been gray and overcast, threatening rain, but after lunch it had cleared suddenly. Maggie seized the opportunity to get out of the house. It had been more than a week since Lena's accident, and their lives were settling into a routine. Maggie visited Lena at the hospital every other day, flying home the next afternoon to spend the evening with the kids. The following day she would stay at home to help Ellen with the household and the children.

It was a grueling schedule, but one that was

beginning to feel familiar. Maggie and Ellen had discussed allowing the children to see Lena but had decided it would be too upsetting for them. Better to wait until she woke up. They didn't discuss what would happen if she didn't. They would face that later if need be.

"Have fun," Ellen said, bustling about the kitchen with the radio on, listening to Neil Diamond. The strains of "Sweet Caroline" filled the house. The kids were seated at the table, eating a snack of celery sticks filled with peanut butter and dotted with raisins.

"Aunt Maggie, somebody rebuilded our altar!" Gabby blurted around a mouthful of peanut butter and celery. "Today we looked and somebody made it better. I think it was a fairy."

"That's nice, sweetie," Maggie said, not really concentrating. She declined a smeary celery stick, grabbing a glass of water instead.

"Your phone rang," Ellen informed her, nodding to her cell phone perched on the table.

"Thanks." Maggie grabbed the phone and checked the number to make sure it wasn't the hospital. It wasn't, so Maggie ignored the call, tucking the phone in the pocket of her running shorts and slipping out the French doors to the deck. She stretched for a few moments and then loped across the lawn. The grass was growing tall around her ankles. Almost time for another visit from the landscaping crew Marco and Lena employed to keep the property looking beautiful. Maggie made a mental note to check with the company about how Marco and Lena handled payments. She needed to start figuring out how the recurring bills worked for the household, the mundane but necessary tasks that kept a home running smoothly. It wouldn't do for the electricity or water to be turned off for lack of payment.

And she hadn't even begun to figure out how to handle the details of the Firellis' New York house, what the expenses were and how to manage them. She assumed Marco and Lena had set up a system to take care of the house over the summer while they were gone, but she had no idea how it worked. She would need to sort it all out soon. But she wouldn't worry about that now, not in her few brief moments of freedom.

It was a relief to be out, to be released from the demands of the children and the house. The truth was that she had begun to feel very trapped indeed. The sensation prickled along her skin like a heat rash, making her irritable. She was familiar with the feeling. It happened whenever she stayed in a place too long. After a few weeks or a month she'd get the almost uncontrollable urge to move on. It rarely happened on assignment. There was always something to do, something interesting and new to focus on. And her assignments almost never lasted long enough to make her itch to go. But the infrequent times she'd been in Chicago for more than a few weeks, she'd found herself eaten alive with the sensation. Sometimes it even happened on the island when she visited Marco and Lena. A month was a long time to stay with one family, live one life. Usually when she began to feel this way she could just leave, jetting off to someplace new and exciting. But not here, not now. She was stuck.

Maggie headed for the bluff path that ran along the water's edge, winding along the black rugged cliffs high above the water. She needed the wide-open sky above her head and the rolling expanse of the sea below. She ran fast, feet pounding the packed dirt, the steady *thud, thud, thud* of her pace beginning to clear her head. A fox, black with a white-tipped tail, darted across the path and disappeared into a tangle of brush under a red Madrona tree.

Maggie ran harder than usual, longer than she realized, and when she finally began to tire she was miles from home. She looped back, taking the return at a leisurely pace. When she was close to the house again, she stopped for a break. She still had an hour before dinner, and so she headed toward the bluffs, enjoying the moment of peace.

The sun was bright, warming the chilly breeze blowing in over the water. Above her, gulls circled and cried, looking for a meal. She sat down on her favorite little promontory, a knuckle of coarse black rock speckled with grayish-green lichen jutting out from the shore, and pulled out her phone to listen to her messages. The first was from the rental car company, wondering when she would like to return the car. She guiltily pressed the Save Message button, reminding herself to call them. She'd contacted them the day after Lena's accident to extend her rental time and put Ellen on the rental contract so she could also drive the car. Lena's Volvo had been totaled. But Maggie hadn't told the car company how long she would keep the car. In truth, she still didn't know.

All the rest of the messages were old ones from Alistair. Of course. She sighed, deleting all of them. She didn't want to listen to them again. His words hit too close to the bone, not because he was being callous or mean, but because he was brutally honest. She slipped her cell phone back into the pocket of her running shorts and stood, stretching out her muscles after the run, using a series of simple yoga poses she'd learned years ago in India.

Slowly raising her arms into the Mountain pose, Maggie thought about her last conversation with Alistair. Every day she felt as though she was sliding one step closer to an inevitable conclusion, but she was stymied. She didn't know what to do, not yet. So she simply tried to avoid both Alistair's calls and thinking about the deadline fast approaching. She knew that with her lack of action she was making a decision, albeit a passive one. Soon she would have to make a choice.

Maggie lifted one arm high in the air and spread her legs, stretching into the Triangle pose, holding her body still, breathing slowly and trying to release tension. It was impossible. She thought of Lena, so silent and pale in the hospital bed, of Marco, gone forever. And of the children. She pictured their three small, worried faces. They desperately needed stability, someone to hold Gabby when she woke screaming, choking on salt water in her recurring nightmares. Someone to keep an eye on Jonah as he slipped further and further into an aloof silence. But there were other pressing issues too. A mountain of debt that couldn't be erased with the flick of a magic wand, as well as the career opportunity of a lifetime slipping further away each day she stayed. She touched the cell phone in her pocket but did not draw it out. Alistair's words had been haunting her since their last conversation. She could not push them from her mind. She squatted on the rocky ground, bringing her palms together in front of her in the Garland pose, trying to breathe in and out slowly, peacefully, struggling to find serenity in the whirl of her thoughts.

"You only get one Regent invitation. No repeats," Alistair had told her. This was it, her one chance. There would not be another. Yet could she really leave now? What was stopping her?

"Think very carefully about the choice you're making," Alistair's voice in her head reminded her. *"Every day you stay is a day less you will have to prepare. Your competitors are not taking breaks, you know."*

Maggie exhaled sharply, frustrated, the feeling of being trapped returning in a rush. "What do I do?" she asked aloud. Far out in the water, two porpoises arced from the swells, the graceful curve of their dull-gray backs showing for a moment. It was the only answer she received. She stood, determined to calm her scattered thoughts by force of will. Raising both arms and tucking one leg up like a flamingo, she held the Tree pose, concentrating on not toppling over.

More than a week, and there was still no change in Lena's condition. This was a waiting game, an exhausting one, and Maggie felt more drained than she'd ever been in her life. Partly it was the strain of worry for Lena and the transit back and forth between the island and the hospital, but more than that it was the sheer domestic bustle of raising children. It all seemed second nature for Ellen, who cooked and did laundry as though she'd been doing it all her life. Maggie supposed she had. She even refereed the children's arguments with ease. But Maggie was more often than not at a loss for the right words or techniques for dealing with three children whose worries and insecurities came out in myriad ways. When it came right down to it, the only thing she did better than Ellen was reading stories at bedtime. Ellen did all the characters in the same voice, which was boring.

Maggie let her hands drop, abandoning the yoga poses, too preoccupied with her current dilemma to find inner peace. What if she did return to Chicago? She considered the idea, turning it over in her mind, testing its mettle.

Ellen can handle the household while I'm gone, Maggie assured herself, pacing the rocky bluff path as her thoughts churned. *It's not like I'm really contributing a whole lot anyway.*

Maggie stopped and put her hands on her hips, staring out to sea. Maybe it was best if she used the time well, not just waiting on the island, but doing something productive to help them all out. Whether or not Lena awoke, someone had to tackle the pressing financial problem. If Lena woke up, she would be grateful to have at least some of the debt taken care of. And if she didn't . . . well, that was another issue entirely, but either way, the debt was not going to magically resolve itself, and time was ticking away day by day. It was up to Maggie to take care of Lena and the children, to provide a way for them to keep their home. It was her responsibility.

"So I need to go back to work," Maggie said aloud, a little uncertainly. A bald eagle soared overhead, wings motionless as he banked and turned. "I need to go back to Chicago and try to win the Regent." The words felt wrong in her mouth, as though she were spitting out stones as she spoke them, but it was the option that made the most sense. She could see no other way.

"I'm doing this for all of us," Maggie said finally, trying to convince herself. She would head back to Chicago, work hard for as long as Ellen could cope with her being away, finish her entry for the Regent before the deadline, and return to the island once her entry was complete. It still might not be enough time to really give the Regent her best shot, but it was the best she could do. She straightened her shoulders and strengthened her resolve, shrugging off her twinge of guilt and unease. This was the best thing for everyone. Decision made, she headed back to the house to buy a one-way ticket to O'Hare.

On her way back to the house, Maggie stopped at the altar on impulse. It was cooler in the shadow of the Douglas fir trees, light filtering dimly through the branches, illuminating mossy rocks and gnarled roots rising from the soil. She inhaled deeply, filling her lungs with the fecund scent, dampness and decay and the sweet spice of fir needles. Her steps were silent on the springy earth. It felt like a holy place somehow, although just a few days before it had been nothing but a patch of bare ground.

She stopped in front of the altar in surprise. Gabby was right. It had been rebuilt. All the objects were arranged in the correct place, but the bits of sea glass were now set in even rows, the stones fitted with care, forming an even, uniform structure. Maggie examined the construction more closely. It was a far cry from the children's lopsided efforts. Maggie felt a prickle go down her spine. Who had done this? Who knew the altar was here, and who would care enough to build it again, this time so it would last? She shivered once, suddenly feeling eyes upon her.

Don't be ridiculous, Magdalena, she scolded herself, turning toward the house.

He was standing right in front of her. She uttered a small scream and stepped back, instinctively curling her hands into fists. He didn't move. She recognized him immediately. The stranger from the ice cream stand in Friday Harbor—the one who'd been watching them. And now here he was in the Firellis' yard. What was he doing here?

He had wanted her to see him, she understood. Dressed in the same faded camouflage pants and black T-shirt, he blended well with the shifting shadows of the trees. He could have taken a few steps and she might never have noticed him in the dimness of the tree line. He watched her calmly. Face-to-face, he was only a few inches taller than she was, broad-shouldered but with the lean physique of a runner. His long, straight black hair fell loose almost to his shoulders. His eyes, black as jet, never left hers.

"Who are you?" she demanded, taking another step back, bumping against the altar. His gaze never left hers. He didn't seem to blink.

"Daniel." His voice was a little raspy, as though he was unused to talking.

Maggie had regained a little of her composure, though her heart was racing with adrenaline. She darted a look toward the back door, gauging the distance if she had to make a run for it. She wouldn't make it. He stood between her and the house, and though he didn't seem aggressive, he was not relaxed. He balanced on the balls of his feet, muscles coiled beneath the stillness of his body. And yet his presence did not seem threatening. He didn't mean her harm, she could have sworn it. She took a deep breath, collecting herself. She was struck again by his enigmatic air. There was more beneath the surface than she could see, something strangely compelling about him.

"What do you want?" Maggie challenged, lifting her chin.

He smiled a little sadly. "To give you this." He held out his hand. Cautiously, she stepped forward. "Here," he prompted.

She offered her hand hesitantly, and he placed the object in her palm. It was small but weighty. A porpoise, carved from wood mottled dark and light. It had a gouge above one fin, on the shoulder, a scar across the wood, as though the knife had slipped.

"What is this for?" Maggie asked, touching the delicate detailing. Except for the gouge, it was beautifully made.

"For the altar," he said, almost shyly.

Maggie examined the animal. The craftsmanship looked familiar. "Did you make the animals we found last week?" Maggie asked. Daniel hesitated for a moment, then nodded. "And did you do this?" She gestured to the rebuilt altar. He nodded again.

"Why?" she asked him.

He shrugged, looking at the ground, then

gazed past her, out at the water. "It's the least I could do."

"Why do you need to do anything?" she asked guardedly, a suspicion flitting through her mind. "Who are you?"

He glanced up at her then, meeting her eyes. She couldn't look away. There was something so raw there, sorrow and a terrible guilt.

"It was an accident," he said quietly. "I didn't mean to hurt anyone."

Maggie inhaled sharply, recalling in one instant that Marco had not been alone when he died. He had been trying to rescue someone else. She had never asked about the other man, had forgotten that anyone else had been involved in the tragedy that took Marco's life. She took a step back, feeling as though she'd been punched. "Marco." It was not a question.

He nodded. "It was an accident," he said again. He scuffed his feet in the dirt, waiting for her response. "I think you need to leave," she said stiffly. He nodded and turned, lithe and silent as a shadow. Only when he'd gone did she realize she was still holding the porpoise.

Chapter Fifteen

"Ellen, I need to head back to Chicago for a few weeks." Maggie toyed with her dessert fork, not meeting the other woman's eyes. The children were tucked into bed and she and Ellen were sitting on the deck in the chill evening twilight, enjoying a slice of Ellen's strawberry pie and the novelty of a few moments of quiet.

She had not mentioned her encounter with the mysterious Daniel that afternoon in the woods. It had shaken her, and she was still puzzled by it. She didn't quite know what to do, if anything. The little carved porpoise was tucked in her nightstand drawer, safely out of sight.

After supper, while Ellen corralled the children for baths and teeth brushing, Maggie had put her new plan into action. She'd bought a ticket back to Chicago, leaving in three days, and left a message for Alistair letting him know when she would arrive. Once she stepped onto the plane, she'd be back to Chicago in less than four hours, back to her normal life. Then she'd begin preparations for the Regent. She figured there was just time enough left to do so if she was both very diligent and very lucky.

"I'll come back as soon as I can," she continued, staring at the strawberries spilling from their flaky golden crust on her plate. "But I can't wait any longer." She glanced over at Ellen, who was listening calmly, a bite of pie balanced on her fork. "I think I have a chance to help Lena out of this financial mess, but I don't have much time."

She explained about the Regent Fellowship, about what it would take to win and the cash involved if she did.

Ellen listened closely. "Well, then, you have to go, don't you?" she said, accepting the news as she seemed to accept everything else, with a stoicism that would have done the ancient Spartans proud.

"We'll miss you for sure, but you do what you have to do," Ellen told her, "and, my lands, it would be good to know that terrible debt was taken care of." She sighed heavily. "I think it's a real generous thing for you to help Lena out of this mess." Maggie didn't mention what winning the Regent would do for her career as well. Her motivation was not entirely self-sacrificing.

"When do you head out?" Ellen asked.

"Saturday morning. I'll come back as soon as I can. It might be awhile, though," she said honestly, feeling a twinge of misgiving. She could see no other way, but she couldn't rid herself of the niggling feeling in the pit of her stomach that she was making a mistake. "If anything changes with Lena, you'll let me know immediately? I can be back here in a few hours if I need to be."

Ellen nodded. "Of course. Don't worry about us. We'll make do. You focus on winning that award." She ate her last bite of pie before continuing. "It would be a blessing for Lena and these children, make no mistake. Besides, I've been thinking about asking Ernie to come out here for a spell anyhow. I don't like to be away from him for so long, and he could help with things around the house." She put her fork down on her plate. "You go ahead and catch your flight. We'll handle things on this end."

"Good," Maggie agreed. It was a relief knowing she wasn't abandoning Ellen to cope alone. She ate the last of her pie without tasting it, tamping down a twinge of guilt and savoring the taste of freedom, sweeter than strawberry pie filling, lighter than air.

Late Friday morning the doorbell rang. It had rained all morning, and Maggie and the kids were in the family room watching a nature documentary about dolphins. Ellen was mixing up blueberry muffins at the kitchen counter and listening to Elvis's greatest hits turned down low. Maggie was stretched out on the sofa, Gabby draped over her legs, watching as a marine biologist took a boat up the Amazon in search of the elusive pink river dolphin.

Maggie's bags were already packed. She was leaving on the earliest ferry the next morning and returning the rental car at the airport. Ellen had already reserved a car from a local company and would pick it up that afternoon. All the details for Maggie's departure were in place.

At the sound of the doorbell, Ellen looked up. "Are we expecting anybody?"

Maggie shook her head. "I'll get it."

She slid out from under Gabby's warm little body and went to the mudroom door. On the step stood a small, neatly dressed woman in a business suit, clutching a clipboard.

"Is this the . . . Firelli residence?" the woman asked, consulting her clipboard when Maggie opened the door.

"Yes," Maggie said, waiting. There was something about the woman, a tightness that set Maggie's teeth on edge.

The woman looked her up and down. Maggie had the distinct impression she was being weighed in the balance and found wanting somehow.

"My name is Jane Bigelow, and I'm from Child Protective Services," the woman said, introducing herself. She did not offer her hand. "I'm here about the children of Lena and Marco Firelli."

Ellen came up behind Maggie, drying her

229

hands on a dish towel. She had flour scattered down the front of her blouse. She looked at Maggie, then at the woman on the step who was watching them in a cool, analyzing way. Maggie stood there for a moment, not sure how to proceed. Her instinct was to back up and close the door. She didn't want this woman in the house.

"Of course," Ellen said finally, around Maggie. "Please come in."

In the front parlor, over a plate of day-old oatmeal cookies and some freshly made coffee, Ms. Bigelow wrote down their names and explained the nature of her visit.

"It has come to our attention that Mr. Firelli is recently deceased and that Mrs. Firelli has sustained a life-threatening injury and is currently hospitalized and unresponsive on the mainland. Is this the case?"

"Yes," Ellen affirmed, shooting a questioning glance at Maggie as if to ask if she should elaborate. Maggie shook her head slightly, unwilling to give this small, starched woman any more information than was absolutely necessary. She knew all about Child Protective Services from her days in Chicago. Once they had taken away Gloria Gomez's two girls for nine months and placed them in a foster home. When the girls came back, the little one, Elena, had stopped talking and was eating her own hair. In Maggie's neighborhood government agencies were not your friends.

"Where are the children now?" Ms. Bigelow asked, peering around as though she might find them hiding beneath the furniture.

"They're watching a nature show in the family room," Ellen said. "About pink dolphins."

"I will need to see them before I leave," Ms. Bigelow stated. It was not a request. "Now, Mrs. Foster, what is the exact nature of your relationship to Mr. and Mrs. Firelli?" Ms. Bigelow turned to Ellen, her pen poised over her clipboard.

"I'm Lena's aunt," Ellen replied. "Her father's sister."

"And you, Ms. Henry?"

"I'm a . . . close family friend," Maggie said, for the first time realizing how flimsy that sounded. "The children have grown up with me. I'm like family."

"But you are not in fact a biological relation," Ms. Bigelow clarified.

At Maggie's reluctant assent the woman marked something down on her paper. She did not touch her coffee or the cookie on her plate. "Do the Firellis have any closer family members who could have an interest in the welfare of the children?" she asked. "Grandparents? Or Mr. or Mrs. Firelli's siblings, perhaps?"

Maggie answered briefly but truthfully.

"Marco's family is all in Sicily except for his youngest brother, Anthony, who lives in Miami. He and Marco weren't close. Marco's parents are in poor health. They don't travel now. Lena is an only child, her mother is unwell, and her father wouldn't be able to care for the children on his own."

"I see." More markings on the clipboard. "Now, Mrs. Foster, were you given or are you aware of the existence of any legal forms or specific written instructions from either Mr. or Mrs. Firelli regarding their wishes for you to care for their children?"

"Well, no, but of course it isn't as though they planned for this to happen," Ellen pointed out. "No one thought they'd both have accidents so close together."

Maggie shifted uneasily at Ellen's words. Marco hadn't planned for this to happen. She wasn't so sure about Lena.

"Ms. Henry, did Mr. or Mrs. Firelli give you or anyone else any specific instructions regarding the care of their children?" Ms. Bigelow was watching her closely.

Maggie swallowed hard. She had a sinking feeling in her stomach. "Lena told me to take care of them, right before the accident," she replied.

"Did she put that in writing?" Ms. Bigelow asked.

"No. She told me to take care of them, and then she walked out the door. Not long after, she had the car crash," Maggie said.

"I see." More markings. Ms. Bigelow looked up, examining them through her glasses.

"Ms. Henry, Mrs. Foster, I will be blunt. What you have done by taking care of these children during an uncertain and tragic time is admirable. However, it is not the practice of the State of Washington to allow minors to be cared for by people other than close relatives without direct parental instructions unless the court has determined that the individuals in question are the best possible caregivers for the children . . ."

Ms. Bigelow continued talking but Maggie couldn't hear her. A whole hive of yellow jackets was suddenly buzzing angrily in her head. She had a mental image of the littlest Gomez girl with her wide, blank eyes, chewing a strand of hair always coated with spittle at the corner of her mouth. This could not be happening. The State had no business interfering here. She wouldn't let them. When she focused on the conversation again, Ellen was asking a question.

"But what happens if there are no written instructions?"

"We will be following up with all the next of kin. I believe you said Mr. Firelli had a brother in Miami? We will contact him immediately."

"He and Marco didn't get along," Maggie

blurted out. She had never liked Anthony. He and Marco had fallen out years ago over some family matter. He was an attorney in Miami, handling divorce cases. She had met him only once, but the impression he left on her was decidedly negative. His eyes had been so cold, his handshake firmer than necessary. Lena had always said he made her uneasy and that she preferred to imagine he wasn't part of the family.

Ms. Bigelow peered through her glasses at Maggie. "Be that as it may, he is next of kin, unlike you, Ms. Henry. And we will be contacting him as well as the children's grandparents to determine their interest in the children's future. We will allow a reasonable amount of time for the next of kin to respond, and then we will proceed with what the State feels is in the best interest of the children. I would like to see them now."

Ellen led her into the family room while Maggie stayed in the front parlor, seething with outrage and struggling to get her emotions under control. Who did this social worker think she was, marching into their house and ordering the children's lives when she knew nothing about them? It was ludicrous. But Maggie felt helpless to change anything. She knew how futile it was to fight the system. No one ever won.

Ellen and Ms. Bigelow returned in a few moments. Ms. Bigelow finished making notes and then turned to Ellen, ignoring Maggie.

"It is my opinion that the best thing for the children now is to remain here in the home with you, Mrs. Foster, until such time as other arrangements can be made for them to be put under the guardianship of a closer relative. Are you willing to allow the children to remain under your care until we have investigated this matter? I will need your verbal and written consent."

Ellen consented immediately.

Ms. Bigelow turned to Maggie. "Ms. Henry, as you are in no way related to the children, I am afraid we are not able to put them under your care, even on a short-term basis."

Maggie did not respond. She clenched her hands together hard to avoid throttling the woman. She should have felt relieved. She had no more responsibility here. Ellen was in charge of them now, and perhaps in a few weeks it would be Marco's parents or brother. She was free to catch her plane to Chicago. Instead, she felt exactly the opposite.

The children's lives were suddenly being decided by people who understood the letter of the law but knew nothing about them, not who they were and certainly not what was truly in their best interest. They didn't know Gabby would fall asleep only if Bun Bun's head was tucked under her chin, or that you had to keep sweet snacks hidden behind the bins of beans and flour in the cupboard so Luca couldn't sneak them. And Jonah . . . She winced when she thought of Jonah, those dark, somber eyes and the downward slope of his young shoulders. He was a little boy carrying a misplaced guilt so heavy it was slowly crushing him.

"We will notify you as soon as possible when we are in contact with the next of kin," Ms. Bigelow said to Ellen. "The children's provisional placement with you should last no longer than thirty days."

"What happens after thirty days?" Maggie asked, tuning back in to the conversation.

Ms. Bigelow cleared her throat. "If no suitable next of kin have come forward by that time, the court will determine the best placement for the children in a long-term care environment. That could be a family member such as Mrs. Foster, or it could be a situation such as a group home or foster family. It varies from case to case."

"Are you serious? You can't do that to them," Maggie protested, trying to keep her voice calm and reasonable, although she wanted nothing more than to grab the social worker by the arm and shake her until her teeth rattled. "They've been through hell recently. This is the most stable and loving environment for them, at home with people who've known them all their lives in a place that's familiar to them."

Ms. Bigelow smiled, as polite and icy as a glass of frozen lemonade. "Then I suggest you find out if Mr. and Mrs. Firelli documented their wishes to that effect, Ms. Henry. Otherwise it will be up to the court to determine the best caregivers and environment for the children."

Ms. Bigelow rose, tucking her pen into the clipboard. "The State prefers to know the wishes of the parents in matters pertaining to children. If that information is provided, the court will in most cases honor the parents' request. Quite simply, if you are able to locate any documentation whatsoever stating Mr. and Mrs. Firelli's choice for the guardianship of their children, it would be in the children's best interest that you do so immediately." She gave them both another tight smile, signaling that the interview was over.

While Ellen saw Ms. Bigelow out, Maggie excused herself, taking the dirty dishes and coffee cups to the kitchen. She bent over the sink and ran hot water on full blast to mask her outrage as she swore silently and repeatedly, pounding her closed fist against the cold ceramic of the sink until she calmed down. She looked at the back of the children's heads as they watched the nature program. How small and vulnerable they looked, completely unaware of just how precarious their lives had become.

Maggie straightened, shutting off the flow

of water. She couldn't leave them like this, not until she knew they were safe. It's what Lena had asked of her. It's what Marco would have wanted. At the very least she had to see if Marco and Lena had thought to make any provision for their children's future. If there was paperwork naming a legal guardian, she and Ellen had to find it. Maggie sighed heavily, dreading what this new turn of events might cost her. If nothing else, it would certainly cost her more time. And time was the one thing she did not have to spare.

When she heard the mudroom door slam, she went back into the parlor. Ellen was sitting in the prim floral armchair, looking dazed.

"Well, that does beat all," Ellen said slowly. "How do you think they found out?"

Maggie crossed her arms and shrugged, too agitated to sit. "Probably someone at the hospital. Or the police. Maybe they have to report anything involving minors."

"I just don't think it's right, making the children have to up and move somewhere else when they've lost so much already." Ellen shook her head. "But I guess what we think doesn't matter since we're not next of kin. But to think of them having to go to that man in Florida. Have they even met him before?"

Maggie stood by the sofa at the front window, looking out at the long sweep of lawn. "The boys did once when they all went to Italy to visit

Marco's family. I think Anthony was there too. He and Marco didn't get along at all, though. They haven't spoken in years. Lena and Marco wouldn't want him to have any say in their kids' lives."

"Well, maybe Anthony won't want to take them," Ellen said comfortingly. "It's a big responsibility, after all."

Maggie set her jaw and shook her head. It felt like too big of a risk to take.

"Is there anything we can do?" Ellen asked.

"We can start looking for documents," Maggie said grimly, "and hope Marco and Lena wrote down what they wanted for the kids."

"Well, all right, let's get to it." Ellen sighed and started to rise but stopped as a thought struck her. "But you're leaving in the morning."

Maggie shook her head. "Not now. Not until I know the kids are safe. I'll stay until we get things sorted out."

"But what about your competition?" Ellen asked. "Don't you have to get back?"

Maggie nodded, feeling the tension in every muscle of her body. The truth was that, yes, she did have to get back. Every second she delayed was costing her, possibly more than she could calculate. But she couldn't leave Ellen and the children in such a precarious situation. It was unthinkable. She had no other choice. "A couple more days won't make much difference," she lied. "Now, let's get to work."

Chapter Sixteen

They started the search as soon as the children were in bed.

"What if the papers are in New York?" Ellen asked, voicing a concern Maggie had considered as well.

"I don't know. I don't know who their lawyers are. I don't know how we would even find any of that information. I don't even know how to get into their house in Brooklyn," Maggie confessed. In truth, she was surprised to realize how little she knew about their life eleven months out of the year. "I'll call Marco's old firm on Monday and see if they can give me any information, although I'm guessing they won't know much about this situation. Maybe they'd know the name of the attorney he used, though."

"I'll look through all the cards people sent with the flowers," Ellen offered, "just to see if a law office sent anything."

Maggie nodded. "Good idea. Let's do anything we can think of and see what turns up. Hopefully we'll find something helpful."

"Let's look here first and worry about New York on Monday if we haven't found what we need by then," Ellen said practically. "Maybe the documents are right under our noses."

Maggie made them both a double-shot espresso and then they split up. Ellen began in the small office where she was sleeping. It seemed like a likely spot. Maggie volunteered to search Marco's third-floor studio. Besides a drafting table, it had a filing cabinet and a desk with several deep drawers. She liked spending time in the studio. She felt Marco's presence in that room.

Maggie had forgotten the sheer amount of time required to look through personal papers. It had taken her weeks to sort through her mother's. Lena said Marco, along with George, managed their finances, so Maggie wasn't surprised to find the filing cabinet filled with copies of utility bills, magazine subscription renewal forms, and credit card statements, as well as a stack of newspaper clippings for Marco's designs and assorted files and folders pertaining to his work. But no legal documents.

Maggie sat back on her heels, discouraged. She still had a drawer of the filing cabinet and the desk drawers left to go through, but so far had found nothing of use. At a quarter to one, she looked in on Ellen and they called a halt for the night.

"Let's get some sleep," Ellen suggested, yawning. "We'll start again in the morning. I've found household and medical records, quilting patterns, and about a hundred recipes in this desk. Lena is very organized, but so far she doesn't seem to have any legal documents."

The next day, as soon as they could, they set the kids down in front of a Disney movie and resumed the search. Still nothing. They ate lunch in discouraged silence as the children chattered on about the movie, a modern-day *Swiss Family Robinson.*

"They made clothes out of coconuts and leaves, and they made traps for pirates, and they had a pet monkey," Luca said, summarizing the entire plot in one sentence. Maggie looked at each of them—Jonah silently eating a turkey sandwich, Luca picking all the grapes off the stem one by one, Gabby asking if they could get a monkey to keep Sammy company. Maggie was trying to be stoic, but she was worried. What if no papers existed? What then?

We'll just keep looking, she told herself, gulping the last bites of her sandwich. Surely Lena and Marco wouldn't have left something this important to chance? But then she remembered the misstep with the life insurance and didn't feel so confident. They hadn't expected Marco to die so young or Lena to have her accident, one tragedy on the heels of another. Maybe Lena and Marco had been careless with the issue of guardianship for their children as well, banking on their youth, health, and good fortune. Maggie sincerely hoped not.

● ● ●

Late in the afternoon Maggie found it. She was alone in the house, sifting through the last desk drawer in Marco's studio. Ellen had finished her search and taken the children into Friday Harbor to buy some groceries and pay a visit to the harbor to watch the ferry come in.

Maggie had just stopped for a quick break and stretch, going through a couple of yoga positions. She eased into Downward Dog and then the Cobra pose, trying to lessen the tension in her shoulders and soothe her frustration at their search turning up nothing useful. She made another espresso and kept looking. There had to be something there. She refused to give up until she'd turned over every scrap of paper.

Halfway through the final desk drawer, Maggie found a folder labeled "Winters & Cline." Her heart skipped a beat. That sounded like the name of a law firm.

"Oh, please be something good," she murmured, leaning forward in Marco's black leather office chair and opening the folder. It was filled with copies of legal documents. She flipped through the pages, barely registering them, glancing only long enough to assure herself they were not about guardianship for the kids. And then she found them, two documents. "Last Will and Testament of Marco Firelli" and "Last Will and Testament of Lena Irene

Lindstrom Firelli." And within those documents a paragraph naming a guardian for the children.

She skimmed Lena's will quickly, mouthing the words, elated by the discovery. "If it should be necessary to appoint a guardian of a child of mine, I designate the following persons, in order of preference and succession, to serve as guardian of the estates and persons of such child, if the child's other parent cannot so serve: (i) my dear friend, Magdalena Margaret Henry."

Maggie stared at her own name for a moment in shock. *My dear friend, Magdalena Margaret Henry.* Lena had given Maggie her children. Somehow, even though she had hoped to find this document, she had not considered what it would mean if her own name were on it. She bit her lip, rereading the paragraph a third time, stunned by the discovery. She flipped through Marco's will, but the paragraph was the same. He had also named her guardian. What had they been thinking, giving her care of their three children, she who barely saw her own bed more than two nights in a row? There had to be people far more qualified. Ellen, for instance

Maggie shrank back in the chair, holding the paper away from her as though it contained some dangerous secret. It did. She closed her eyes for a moment, feeling a rush of relief that the children would not be taken from their home, that they would be safe, that they wouldn't have to live with ill-suited relatives or strangers. But on the heels of that relief came panic at the thought of becoming a mother to three children all at once. It was terrifying.

She dropped the will, rubbing her forehead, suddenly aware of the weight of those few sentences. Lena's and Marco's last wishes had just effectively sealed her fate. She was not going anywhere, not for a long time.

Numbly, Maggie called Ellen with the news.

"Oh my lands, what a relief," Ellen confessed. "I was getting so worried."

Maggie agreed, although she couldn't summon the older woman's enthusiasm. "I'll call Jane Bigelow and let her know we've found the wills," she promised Ellen. After hanging up, she read the paragraph once more. She touched her name on the paper, trying to make it real. What did it mean for her future? She dared not think about it, not yet.

Carefully laying the documents on Marco's desk, making sure all the pages were together, she quickly flipped through the rest of the documents in the legal file. If she were to be the children's guardian, she reasoned, it was probably good for her to know as much as she could about Lena and Marco's life from a legal perspective. It didn't feel like prying now. They had named her as guardian for their children. They trusted her with what they loved most in life. Surely that gave her the right to know as much as possible about their circumstances.

Toward the bottom of the stack she came across a letter addressed to the same law office. She unfolded the single sheet of paper. It was a copy of a letter sent from Marco and Lena to their lawyer, a Mr. Calvin Winters. She scanned it quickly. A line partway down jumped out at her.

It is still our desire to continue with the course of action we spoke with you about in New York at our last meeting in May. Mr. Winters, we are instructing you to please proceed with the legal separation of Marco Firelli and Lena Irene Lindstrom Firelli.

Maggie stared at the words for a long moment. Legal separation? There must be some mistake. She read it again, starting from the beginning this time. It was dated the third of June, just before Marco's accident. She scanned the few lines that seemed most pertinent.

As you know, Mr. Winters, we recently approached you regarding our decision to obtain a legal separation. It is still our desire to continue with the course of action we spoke with you about in New

York at our last meeting in May. Mr. Winters, we are instructing you to please proceed with the legal separation of Marco Firelli and Lena Irene Lindstrom Firelli. We wish to proceed with this legal separation as a matter of irreconcilable differences. Please verify that you have received these instructions. We will await further correspondence from you about how to proceed with this matter.

And then both of their signatures. She recognized the handwriting—Lena's feminine, looping script and Marco's bold, unintelligible scrawl. Maggie set the paper down very carefully, as though it could explode in her hand. She didn't want to touch it. She stared at the single sheet of paper uncomprehendingly. What did it mean? ". . . *We are instructing you to please proceed with the legal separation of Marco Firelli and Lena Irene Lindstrom Firelli. We wish to proceed with this legal separation as a matter of irreconcilable differences.*"

Maggie stared at the words hard, willing the single sheet of paper to reveal more, to somehow prove that those few lines did not mean what they seemed to say. It had to be a mistake. It simply could not be what it seemed to be. It was impossible. She pressed her hand to her chest, trying and failing to draw a full breath. It felt as though the world were falling completely apart, the pieces settling one by one on top of her, crushing her. There had to be some explanation for the letter, but there were only two people in the world who knew the truth, and neither of them could give an answer.

"That's done," Maggie said on Monday, disconnecting the call. She had scanned and e-mailed the wills to Ms. Bigelow and had just received the confirmation call from Child Protective Services. "She said they will be in touch about the process of having the guardianship legally approved, but there shouldn't be any problem. And the children are to stay here with us while they walk me through the paperwork process."

Ellen stood at the sink, rinsing lettuce for Cobb salad. She looked relieved. "I don't know what would have happened if you hadn't found those papers."

"Me neither," Maggie said grimly. She hadn't mentioned Marco and Lena's letter to their attorney to anyone, not even to Ellen. She had hidden it back in the folder, afraid to take it out again. It felt like a shameful secret. She couldn't concentrate on it now. Too many other things were pressing first. Like Alistair, and what the guardianship meant for her entry into the Regent competition. There was no way she could enter now, not if she had to stay on the island and shoulder the care of the children. She was their legal guardian. She couldn't simply jet off to Chicago for several months. It was unthinkable. And there was no way she could manage to create a strong and compelling entry with the myriad of responsibilities and questions clamoring for her time and attention. She had no time or space to do what she needed to do for the competition.

"I have to make a call," she said reluctantly, picking up her cell phone and heading for the bluffs, dreading the conversation she was about to have. She was supposed to be in Chicago right now.

Alistair was not amused.

"Have you lost your mind?" he demanded, his clipped tone sharper than she could ever remember it. "Magdalena, this will not do. You must be on a plane tomorrow, today if you can manage it. Have you forgotten the opportunity I've given you? You can't simply waltz in and out of this profession whenever you feel like it!"

"Waltz?" Maggie was speechless. "Waltz, Alistair? That's ridiculous. I work harder than anyone in the office except you. How many times have you said it yourself? And not just for a few weeks or months. For years. I've been doing it for years. So don't make it sound like I don't care. And don't think for one second I don't understand what giving up this opportunity means for my career."

She took a deep breath, the words bubbling up from some deep place of frustration. "I can't get on a plane and leave three children I've been asked to protect. I'm their legal guardian, Alistair. I didn't ask for it or sign up for it. Lena and Marco never even asked me, but I'm not going to refuse it. What's the alternative? For Child Protective Services to put them in State care? I saw a lot of that growing up. I know you might not understand what that means, with your Swedish au pairs and your prep school, but I do. And I will not let that happen. Not when there's someone who knows them and loves them. Not when they can stay in their home. So no, I'm not waltzing anywhere. I am very conscious of what this is costing me." She dropped her voice, trying to deescalate, to reason with him so he would understand.

"Alistair, I know I'll never have this chance again. I know exactly what I'm giving up. And I have no choice." Saying the words felt like someone was stabbing her in the heart. She gritted her teeth against the pain and disappointment, willing herself not to give in, not to just pack up and leave. It was so very tempting.

A long pause, and then Alistair's voice,

measured and calm. "There is always a choice, my dear. And you have made yours." And then a moment later, a click. He was gone.

Maggie stood for a long moment, staring out at the water, not thinking, just letting the weight of what she had done sink in slowly. She had just given up the greatest opportunity of her life. And there was no going back. She slipped the phone into the pocket of her jacket and sat down on a nearby rocky promontory, wrapping her arms around herself, trying by force of will to keep from falling to pieces. But it was no use. She could hear her heart beginning to rip in two, the threads of hard work and ambition and opportunity giving way to the inexorable pull of necessity and loss. It was a rending that felt like the end of the world.

Chapter Seventeen

Maggie silently crept up the spiral staircase that wound from Lena and Marco's master bedroom into Marco's drafting studio. She paused at the top, trying to steady herself. Her hands were trembling. She couldn't hear any noise from the rest of the house although she knew the kids were watching a nature program on TV two floors below while Ellen scrubbed the kitchen floor. Maggie just needed a quiet place to hide after her disastrous call with Alistair.

The room felt like a sanctuary of quiet, an open, airy space awash in light and solitude. Late-afternoon sunshine streamed in from huge picture windows looking out over the Strait. The room was spacious and bare except for the enormous drafting table, the filing cabinet, and Marco's desk piled high with books and sketches. Maggie stood at the table, reverently touching the papers and pencils scattered there. In his office in New York, Marco used the most cutting-edge architectural computer programs on the market, but here on the island he reverted to the old-fashioned methods, preferring to put pen and pencil to paper and draw the buildings he dreamed of.

The black rolling stool was pushed away

from the drafting table, and with a sharp pang, Maggie realized Marco had probably been sitting here in the last moments of his life. She had been too preoccupied with finding the legal documents when she'd been up here before. She hadn't noticed these details or understood their significance.

In all likelihood Marco had pushed the stool away when he heard Jonah's yell and saw the kayaker in trouble in the water below. These were some of the last things his hands had touched. Maggie brushed her fingers across the black pencils, the whisper-thin sheet where a half-finished sketch rose from the blank space. It was an impressive design, arresting even in the gray and white of graphite and paper. It would have been remarkable in real life. Tears pricked her eyes, and she bit her lip, careful not to let them fall on the sketch. Daniel's words echoed in her head. *"It was an accident. I didn't mean to hurt anyone."*

And yet the truth was that the accident had hurt a great many people. Marco had risen from this stool, set down his pencil, and never picked it up again.

Maggie sat down hard on the stool. Marco was gone. The reality hit her in the stomach like a low punch. Marco was truly gone. She blinked and blinked again. Hot tears welled up in her eyes, spilling over. She didn't wipe them away. She hadn't really cried until this moment, though she'd felt the pressure building inside her since she'd heard about Marco's death. Now she let it out. She cried silently, tears streaming down her face, teeth clenched around a sob.

As she cried, she realized she wasn't mourning only the loss of Marco. She was crying also for her own mother, dead for more than seven years now, and for the deep loneliness that lay in the pit of her stomach, slick and black as a spill of oil. And not least of all she was crying for the Regent, for the opportunity now lost to her, for all the years she had worked and sacrificed and dreamed of what she had just given up. It cut her deeply, as deeply as any death. All her grief blended together into a silent keening wail.

She doubled over on the stool, her body curling in upon itself, willing Marco back, willing Lena to wake up, willing her mother not to have left her so early, willing things to have turned out so very differently. She cried until her ribs ached with the strain and her throat was raw with salt.

After a long while she calmed, wiping her face on the sleeve of her shirt. She felt exhausted and emptied out. She took a long, slow breath, once, twice, again. All was silent around her. It was peaceful in this space, almost reverent. Quieted, she closed her eyes and then opened them.

Her gaze fell on a series of newspaper clippings in frames hung across the far wall. All were glowing articles lauding Marco's designs or publicity pieces about architecture awards he'd received. Marco had been justifiably proud of his success. Before his death he'd been accomplishing what he set out to do, achieving the goal he shared with her when they were at Rhys together.

A few years after graduating from Rhys, Marco had become the youngest partner at one of the top architecture firms in the country, and in the following years his designs quickly gained recognition. He developed a name for himself by blending classic and modern forms, designing remarkable buildings powerful in structure and startlingly unique in their aesthetic. At just twenty-eight years old, he'd been recognized with a prestigious American Architecture Award for a new public library design in Des Moines, Iowa.

"Amazing," one reviewer stated in the national design magazine *Blueprint*. "From the cornfields of humble Iowa bursts an edifice of such power and audacity that those who see it find it hard to look away."

Another praised, "A potent concoction of whimsy and brooding intent."

By the time he was thirty, Marco Firelli was a power player in the architecture scene, and just a year ago he'd stepped away from the firm to work independently under the prestige of his own name. In a way his success felt inevitable. It was what he had always wanted, and he had the raw talent and the opportunity to achieve his ambitions. But it was not without a price. Marco put in long hours on weekdays and then mingled with the movers and shakers of the design world nights and weekends. On the infrequent occasions when Maggie called them, she would more often than not find Marco still working at ten o'clock in the evening, or Lena would lament that they had to attend yet another black-tie affair, talking to Maggie as she gave instructions to the babysitter and applied her mascara.

Only on the island did they seem to find a measure of peace and calm, for three months inhabiting a world where nothing was more urgent than deciding what to make for dinner. When Maggie arrived each August, she'd find the family relaxed, carefree, and a little tan from the long, golden days. Marco still worked on his designs in his studio above the master bedroom, but he kept shorter hours. They spent weekends with the children on the rocky beaches and evenings playing board games. Lena and the kids loved the island, but the months of slower activity were harder on Marco.

"This place makes me feel crazy sometimes,"

Marco had admitted to Maggie last summer. They were sitting together by the embers of a bonfire while Lena put the kids to bed. Side by side they watched the light fade on the distant horizon in easy companionship. Marco was smoking a clove cigarette, something he still did now and then. He gestured around him.

"There's nothing here but air and water, but I can't breathe. Not like in New York." He took a deep draw on the cigarette. "I'm addicted to the city. It's in my blood—the lights, the energy, the opportunity. I've had a taste and now I want more." He slowly exhaled a thin stream of smoke. The sweet scent of the cloves hung low in the air. "Here, I feel out of the game, like the world is passing me by and I'm just standing still." He shook his head and muttered something in Italian.

"You can take a rest, Marco," Maggie reminded him, leaning back in her Adirondack chair. "Your career is made. You're where you've always wanted to be."

Marco nodded. In the darkness she could see only the outline of his face, like a charcoal sketch in broad strokes. "Yes, but for how long? You always have to keep it up. When I go back, I have to produce something more brilliant than before. And now that I'm on my own, it's all on my shoulders. I don't have the firm to fall back on. Each time I design something, I make or break my own career. I'm only as good as my last design." He sounded tired.

"That's a lot of pressure," she observed.

He grinned, a flash of white in the near darkness. "You don't feel the same way? Come on, admit it's true. But we thrive on it, don't we? What would we do without the thrill of the chase?"

"I don't know," Maggie said slowly. An owl hooted in the trees, a lonely sound. "But I'm beginning to wonder if I want to find out." She said the words aloud for the first time, voicing what was only a sliver of discontent, a faint glimmer of longing for something more.

"What do you mean?" Marco asked, turning to her in astonishment, the glow of his cigarette a tiny orange ember in the darkness. "You're at the top of your game. Outstanding New Photographer of the Year last year from the American Photographer's Association and two major magazine feature stories in the last twelve months. What more could you want?"

Maggie said nothing, staring out at the shimmer of the rising moon on the water. After a moment she admitted, "I don't know. You're right. I have what I've always wanted. But I'm starting to wonder if I'm missing something."

"Like what?" Marco tapped his cigarette, the glowing ash falling in a trail of sparks to the ground. "You're doing what you've always said you wanted. And you're doing it extremely well."

"I know, and I love it," Maggie assured him. "I do. I wouldn't trade my life for anything. But sometimes . . ." She paused. "When I come back from a trip to a closed-up apartment and a month of junk mail, I just wonder if I'm missing something. I can't even put a name to it. Just . . . something. You have Lena and the kids. I have my work, nothing else. I love the freedom, but it can be a lonely life. All those single beds, hopping countries every few weeks. I'm always a stranger, even in my own life. Maybe I just want to be known."

Marco was quiet for a moment, and then he said contemplatively, "Do you know how much I envy you, Maggie? I love my wife and my kids, but when you call and you're in Zambia or Iceland or some other place I've never been, sometimes I want more than anything to be there with you."

Maggie let his words hang in the air, feeling as though she were suddenly standing on dangerous ground. She thought of the wallet with his two photos tucked in her backpack upstairs in the guest room. In a way, he was always with her, even if he didn't know it.

"And I envy you for having all this," she responded lightly, choosing to deflect his words.

Any other response she could give felt too loaded, an emotional land mine. "Ironic, isn't it? So maybe the moral of the story is that we don't get everything we want."

Marco shrugged, grinding out his cigarette on the ground. "Maybe," he said. "Or maybe the moral is that we figure out what we really want, and we get that instead."

In the studio so many months later, Maggie thought back to those words, eerie in the light of what had happened. She turned to the drafting table, to that unfinished building, forever caught in limbo. Marco would never pick up his pencil and bring it to life. The ending for his design, like the ending of so many things, had come too early, with a rush of icy water and a final gasp of air.

"Maybe we were both wrong," she murmured to herself, staring at the place where his pencil had left the paper. There was a little smudge, as though he'd been abruptly interrupted midstroke. She put her finger on the smudge, lightly, in remembrance. "Maybe the moral is just this—in the end we don't get to decide anything at all."

Chapter Eighteen

Three . . . what's that word? Kiwis? Maggie frowned, pushing a cart through the grocery store on the outskirts of Friday Harbor and trying to decipher the handwritten list Ellen sent with her. The store was busy around lunchtime, filled with locals who avoided the high prices of the downtown Kings Market and shopped at this more remote and reasonably priced location on the edge of town. She picked out three kiwis and half a dozen local Golden Delicious apples, maneuvering around two gray-haired women in hiking gear. They were standing by the bananas, chatting about the weather and the resident pods of orca whales spotted heading south that morning. Maggie grabbed a gallon of whole milk and a tub of yogurt, crossing items off the list as she went.

It was good to be out and about, doing something normal. As she navigated the store, Maggie felt a little of the tension of the last days melt away. She sensed they were in the quiet place in the eye of a storm. The storm was by no means over, but she could at least catch her breath in this brief lull.

The children were safe for now with Maggie named as their legal guardian. The thought brought both a profound relief and paralyzing terror. She couldn't consider her guardianship in permanent terms yet. She could take it only a day at a time. Lena was still in the hospital, unresponsive. There was no telling when, or if, she would wake.

Maggie browsed the canned-goods aisle, scanning rows of creamed corn and sliced mushrooms. She thought uneasily of Marco and Lena's letter to their attorney about a legal separation. What did that mean? There was no way of knowing any more, not unless Lena woke up. Her mind drifted once more to the Regent Fellowship and she winced, feeling the sharp sting of loss all over again. The Regent Fellowship was gone. She had to face the facts. Even if Lena woke up tomorrow, Maggie wouldn't have time to put together an entry that stood a chance of winning. That door was closed to her now, but it pained her every time she thought of it.

In the bread aisle Maggie surveyed the selection of wheat loaves, finally choosing one with honey. She added two bags of bagels to her cart and headed to the deli meats.

Two big problems were yet unresolved. First the debt. They were safe for a few more weeks, but Maggie's wire transfer of funds had bought them only a little time. It was not a permanent solution. And the only permanent solution she'd been able to come up with was gone now, leaving a mountain of debt and no clear way out.

"We can't lose the house," Maggie murmured vehemently, resolved but unsure how to secure its future. She felt the weight of it on her shoulders, a pressing problem with no easy answer. She tossed a package of oven-roasted turkey breast and one of ham into the cart alongside a brick of Tillamook Medium Cheddar Cheese. Just a few more items to go.

The second problem was Daniel. Maggie stopped in the cereal aisle, empty at this time of day, and slipped the little carving out of her bag, staring at the porpoise in her hand. She had been carrying it around for days. In the drama with Child Protective Services and the ensuing search for guardianship papers, Maggie had pushed her encounter with Daniel to the back of her mind, but now that things were calmer she'd been thinking of it again.

"It was an accident," he'd said, facing her in the cool dimness of the firs. His eyes had looked so sad.

Maggie turned the porpoise over in her hand, noting the smoothness of the wood. It had been carved with skill. Who was he? Why was he lurking in their woods, doing penance? What exactly had happened on the water that day, and why did Daniel seem to take such responsibility for it when it was an accident?

It wasn't so much Daniel himself she was interested in. It was the simple fact that he was the other half of the tragedy that had claimed Marco's life. She wanted to know so much more. She felt helpless to make sense of it. She had no information and therefore nothing with which to comfort herself or to bring any sort of closure. If she could just understand what happened, why Daniel felt such responsibility, perhaps it would be easier to lay Marco to rest. Perhaps she could begin to make sense of his death.

Maggie slipped the carving back in her bag and scanned the shelves, taken aback by the endless varieties of cereal. Traveling abroad so much, she tended to forget the number of choices available at American supermarkets. She found the variety both dazzling and a little overwhelming. Ellen's list said Cheerios, but she saw several varieties on the shelf. Maggie grabbed a box of plain Cheerios and stuck it in the cart, hoping plain was the right one.

She consulted the list again but couldn't concentrate on the remaining items. She kept picturing Daniel. She needed to talk to him, to ask him the questions no one else could answer. But how could she even find him? Presumably he'd stopped lurking around in the woods, but she had no idea where he might be. Maybe he didn't even live on the island. She could ask the police, but she was hesitant to approach them.

She had no good excuse for asking for more information about Daniel. She didn't think Ellen knew anything about Daniel. She had never mentioned him. Maybe Father Griffin would know something, but she was reluctant to bring the priest into what felt like such a personal matter. That left her with few options.

Maggie grabbed a large package of toilet paper, the last item on the list, and headed toward the checkout. As she waited in line, she watched the customers in front of her. The cashier, a round, grandmotherly woman wearing a bright-pink zippered fleece the exact color of a piece of Dubble Bubble gum, greeted many of them by name, asking about one woman's bike trip, another man's dog. Maggie narrowed her eyes, considering. If Daniel did live on the island, someone was bound to know him. San Juan was a small, tight-knit community. What she needed was an informant, a local person who had access to a lot of information and liked to share it.

Standing behind a woman in running gear, Maggie eyed the cashier speculatively, unobtrusively eavesdropping on the conversation between the two women. The cashier leaned forward over the register, sharing a bit of gossip with her customer. "So, what do you know, but Janet says she isn't going to have chickens wandering through her garden anymore and she set cage traps out. Well, you can imagine what Walt thought of that! So now they've taken it to the local authorities . . ."

Maggie smiled, tuning out the rest of the conversation. She'd found her informant.

The customer in front of her paid and took her leave with a "See you around, Becky," and then it was Maggie's turn. Maggie made eye contact and smiled in a friendly way, inviting conversation.

"You new to Friday Harbor?" Becky asked, eyeing Maggie curiously as she started to scan the groceries on the belt. "Here on vacation?"

"No, I'm a good friend of the Firellis, Marco and Lena. I came to help out after Marco's accident," Maggie told her casually, putting the milk on the belt. Though usually very reserved about personal information, Maggie knew she had to prime the pump of their conversation. If she wanted to know anything about Daniel, she'd have to provide some juicy tidbits of her own.

"Oh, you don't say." Becky clicked her tongue, looking at Maggie with a sudden compassion as she weighed and scanned the apples. "Such a tragedy. And then that terrible car crash so soon after. Now, how is Mrs. Firelli doing? I heard there's been no change?"

Maggie shook her head. "Not yet. The doctors are doing all they can."

"Oh goodness, and those three little ones. Such a beautiful family." Becky shook her head, scooting the yogurt across the beeping scanner and into a bag.

"It's been tough for all of us. But we aren't giving up hope. And at least one person survived the first accident," Maggie observed, setting the bait.

Becky looked up sharply, taking the hook. "You mean that fella, Daniel Wolfe?"

"The kayaker?" Maggie asked innocently.

"Well . . ." The cashier pursed her lips and nodded once. "You know what I keep asking myself?" She lowered her voice and glanced from side to side, then leaned confidentially toward Maggie. "Why was he on the water anyway? He should have known better, if you ask me. It's not like he doesn't know the currents. They can be mighty dangerous. Everyone knows that." She shook her head again, resuming a normal tone of voice and ringing up the deli meat. "If it'd been a tourist, I'd have understood it. But a local? He's been here long enough to know better." She pursed her lips in disapproval and swooshed the bread and bagels across the scanner, then soundly punched the button for Maggie's total.

"Oh, is he from around here?" Maggie asked casually, sliding her credit card through the machine.

Becky began putting the rest of the groceries into a second bag. "Well, I suppose you could

267

say so. Moved to the island not long ago, though. He lives just a couple of miles up the road from the Firelli place, just a bit farther on West Side Road. It's hardly a house, if you ask me. Doesn't even have plumbing, just a little cabin by the water. He's a strange one." She handed Maggie a receipt. "'Course, folks say he got into some sort of trouble in New York. He's a writer or something, I guess, some sort of hotshot. He's from around here, though, on the mainland. Comes from one of the reservations." She shook her head again. "If you ask me, local folks should have more sense."

Maggie left a few moments later, bags of groceries and useful information firmly in hand.

Maggie waited until the kids had gone to bed before she put her new information to good use. She kept the routine they'd established over the past week—a chapter from *Peter Pan*, the book Lena had been reading to the kids before her accident, then a tuck-in and hug for Gabby and a quick check on the boys to see if Jonah was reading under his covers with a flashlight and if Luca had brushed his teeth.

It took longer than usual. The children begged for another chapter, and when Maggie refused, Gabby pouted and Luca thought up a half-dozen requests to keep from going to bed. After getting him a glass of water, a tissue, and a cough drop, Maggie put her foot down and sternly bid them all good night. Finally all was quiet from their rooms. She tiptoed down the stairs. Ellen was snoring softly on the couch, mouth open a little. The TV was turned to a crime drama. Maggie slipped into the home office, now Ellen's room, and sat down in front of the antique French writing desk that held Lena's MacBook Air and printer. Quickly she googled "Daniel Wolfe writer," half expecting to find nothing there.

To her surprise the screen was instantly filled with a long list of links. American Society of Poets, New York University staff page, schedules for poetry readings. One listing showed thumb-nails of several photos, and on impulse Maggie clicked on one. The image sprang to full size, and there was Daniel, the same sharp cheek-bones, same dark eyes, but clean-shaven, and in a tuxedo, accepting an award from former mayor Rudy Giuliani.

She stared at the photo in amazement. Although Daniel was a good-looking man, even with long hair and camouflage pants, the picture revealed another side of him. She squinted, studying him. He looked like a young Johnny Depp, or maybe a more mature Orlando Bloom. Either way, in his tuxedo he was downright handsome. In another photo, Daniel was holding the award in one hand while his other curved around the waist of a beautiful redhead who looked demurely away from the camera. The caption read, "Poet Daniel Wolfe is joined by his wife, attorney Katherine Kernshaw, at the NYC Artist Vision Award ceremony." A third photo showed Daniel clutching the award, head thrown back, sharing a laugh with former U.S. poet laureate Billy Collins. Maggie blinked, staring at the picture again. Billy had his hand on Daniel's shoulder in a fraternal way. Maggie sat back for a moment, stunned. "Who are you?" she murmured, shaking her head in disbelief. "And what were you doing in our yard?"

She clicked on link after link. She found Daniel's two books of poetry on Amazon, *The Keening Water* and *Salmon Song*, half price if she bought them used. On impulse, she purchased them, choosing the fastest method of shipping.

After scanning through a dozen more links, she was even more puzzled than before. What was Daniel Wolfe doing here on the island? Halfway down the Google search page a news article from an online New York arts gossip column caught her eye. "Where in the World Is Daniel Wolfe?" read the title. She clicked on it. There was only a short blurb.

Award-winning New York City poet Daniel Wolfe was a no-show last Friday at the Poetry Circle critic's award dinner, where he was to receive a special commendation for his work focusing on First Peoples. He also failed to make an appearance on the radio show *Good Morning, Big Apple* the next day. His agent could not be reached for comment. Mr. Wolfe, New York is asking, where are you?

The article was dated January 5.

"Hmm, that's interesting," Maggie murmured, scanning the few lines again, looking for clues. She looked again at the photo of Daniel with the beautiful redhead. On impulse, she typed in the name Katherine Kernshaw, coming up with fewer links, but still an impressive array. She browsed Katherine's legal profile on the website of Brauer, McKinsey & Scott. Graduate of Stanford, a junior partner with the firm, specializing in litigation. In the accompanying photo she looked beautifully collected, wide bow mouth and fall of fiery hair softening the determined set of her jaw and the steel in those big green eyes. Maggie clicked out of Katherine's legal profile page and went back to the list of search results. And then in the next link down on the Google page was a single sentence that sent a chill spiraling down Maggie's spine.

Up-and-coming New York City attorney Katherine Kernshaw filed for divorce from her husband of eight years, poet Daniel Wolfe, on Monday, citing irreconcilable differences.

It was from the same online gossip column. There was no more information. It was dated two days before he failed to show up to receive his award.

Maggie stared at the screen until the words blurred. So that was it. He had simply disappeared, walked out of New York and disappeared. He was hiding here on the island. She recalled the haunted look in his eyes, the depth of sadness she sensed in him, the resignation creasing the corners of his mouth. He was not the same man in the photo, grinning as he shook Rudy Giuliani's hand, handsome and successful and on top of the world. She knew the look he had now, for she saw it when she looked in the mirror, when she thought of her mother or of Marco or of the Regent. Daniel Wolfe was a man who had lost what he held most dear.

Becky had been right, Maggie thought grimly, surveying the tumbledown little wood cabin nestled on a bluff overlooking the water. It had an isolated air of neglect, a shutter hanging at an odd angle from a curtainless window, the yard a jumble of ferns and weeds overgrown and creeping up against the foundation. Since the day before when Maggie had googled Daniel

Wolfe, she had been plagued by thoughts of him. The information she found about Daniel had not answered anything for her. Instead, it had only added to her questions. Again and again her mind returned to the accident that had claimed Marco's life and the questions that still surrounded it.

She'd slipped away late in the afternoon, claiming an errand in town, but had turned the car in the opposite direction of Friday Harbor, following the curve of the road as it hugged the shoreline. The island was sparsely populated here, with long stretches of trees and grassland between the houses. She found the cabin after driving the same stretch of road twice. It was almost hidden by a stand of evergreens that screened it from view. Parking along the soft shoulder, she approached on foot, picking her way carefully down the ribbon of dirt path that led around the cabin to the front door facing the water. Daniel's old Honda moped leaned against the side of the cabin. When she saw it, she knew she had found him. The trees opened up on this side of the cabin, and the view was spectacular, the late-afternoon sun making the sea glitter like a bed of diamonds. Maggie raised her hand to knock, but the door opened before she touched the wood.

He was dressed as before, same black T-shirt and camo pants. He didn't look surprised to see her, nor did he say anything. He just stood there, watching her with those dark, inscrutable eyes.

Why am I doing this? she thought. *I should just walk away now.* Instead, she raised her chin and met his gaze.

"I'm Magdalena Henry."

"I know who you are," he said.

She stopped, thrown off-kilter by his response. When she'd pictured confronting him, she'd only imagined asking the questions. She had never dreamed he'd know who she was.

"I've followed some of your work," he said, seeing her confused expression. "Your series on farmers fighting for their land in Brazil was very good."

Maggie stared at him, taken aback, feeling suddenly exposed. She glanced away, trying to regroup for a moment, aware of his eyes on her. She set her jaw, determined not to be dissuaded from asking the question that had been plaguing her since their encounter at the altar.

"Why were you on the water the day Marco died?" She raised her chin and met his gaze, demanding the truth.

"Why are you asking?" he answered evenly. His eyes were hooded, cautious. He was protecting something; she could sense it. She swallowed hard. He was protecting something, and Marco was dead because of him.

"What happened?" she asked, ignoring his question. "How did you survive and Marco didn't? Why were you out on the water that day?"

Daniel watched her carefully. "Which do you want to know? Why your friend died or why I was on the water?"

Maggie paused. "Both. All of it."

Daniel stepped back and inclined his head, a tacit invitation. She followed him. The cabin was small and dim. Square four-paned windows let in a little light. It was sparsely furnished—a twin bed with a wool blanket, a small wood-stove, a table, and one chair. Underneath the far window sat a workbench with a set of carving tools and a block of half-carved wood on it. The room smelled like cold coffee and fir shavings, sharp and pungent, for a moment reminding her of Christmas. Maggie let her eyes adjust to the dimness. Daniel offered her the lone chair, taking a seat on the workbench. He picked up the half-formed carving, a salmon just beginning to emerge from the wood, and turned it over in his hands carefully. He had beautiful hands, she noticed, well-shaped with long fingers and neatly trimmed nails.

"I know the currents," he said finally. "I knew it was dangerous to be on the water with that wind."

"Then what happened? Why did you go?" Maggie spread her hands, seeking an explanation.

He met her eyes. "I didn't intend to come back."

She inhaled sharply. "You went out there on purpose," she said, understanding dawning. She felt sick.

He nodded, his face impassive. "I was desperate. I wasn't thinking clearly. At the time I felt I had nothing to lose. I knew it was dangerous, and I didn't care. I got into trouble near the Firellis' house. I'm a novice with a kayak, and I capsized it. You know how strong the currents are there. And then all of a sudden he was paddling out to me, trying to save me, pulling me up. I kept shouting to him to let me go, that I didn't want to be saved, but he kept saying, 'Hold on, I've got you—'" Daniel dropped his head, his voice breaking off suddenly at the memory. He turned away from her, looking out the window, as though seeing the scene replaying through the glass. Just as Lena had the day she told Maggie how Marco hadn't come back.

"When my head went under the water, I panicked. Suddenly taking another breath on this earth seemed like the best idea in the world. Marco was trying to help me, but then his kayak capsized. I think he hit his head as he went under. It was all a blur. I just know I tried . . ." His voice cracked, and he ducked his head again, going silent for a moment. "When I

276

realized he was sinking, that he wasn't conscious, I tried to hold him up," he said softly. "But he was dead weight, and when he went under, I couldn't hold him anymore."

Maggie touched her cheek, trying to reassure herself that she was still sitting there in the cabin, not in some terrible dream. She was surprised to find it wet.

"I didn't mean for it to happen," Daniel said at last. He turned toward Maggie, his face open and desolate. He spread his empty hands, a gesture of helplessness. "I tried to save him. It was supposed to be me."

Maggie had braced herself for anger, expected to lay blame and feel hatred toward the man whose carelessness or ignorance had cost Marco his life. She had readied herself for it. But now, faced with the reality of Daniel, penitent, a man broken with remorse, she was surprised to find she felt only a great swell of sadness tinged with pity. How tragic that the man who wanted to die had in fact been saved, while the man who had everything to live for had lost his life. They sat together in silence for a long moment. A fly buzzed frantically against the windowpane. Far out on the water, a freighter honked its deep bass horn.

"I'm so sorry," Daniel said simply.

Without another word, Maggie got up and left.

Chapter Nineteen

"Aunt Maggie, Aunt Maggie, I got one through the hole!" Gabby yelled excitedly as Maggie climbed from the car, still shaken from her trip to Daniel's cabin. Curls bouncing, Gabby swung a croquet mallet almost as tall as she was, running over to Maggie's side to demonstrate. Maggie had seen the motorcycle parked by the mudroom door as she'd driven in, and she now spied Griffin in the side yard, which had been transformed in her absence into a croquet court. Griffin raised a hand in greeting and then went back to showing Luca how to line up a shot through a wicket.

Ellen had told her the priest stopped by the house several times. But he'd always come on the days Maggie was at the hospital, so Maggie hadn't seen him since their confrontation at the hospital right after Lena's accident.

Sammy was barking, chasing every shot, prancing and pouncing on the balls as they rolled toward the wickets. Jonah swiped at the dog with his mallet, trying to shoo him away as a ball missed the wicket and came to a stop in the grass beside it.

"Come on, Aunt Maggie." Gabby took her arm

and led her to the remaining mallets. "You can be red. I'm yellow," she announced. Maggie allowed herself to be pulled to the court, intending to put in an appearance and then excuse herself.

"But, sweetie, I don't think I'm going to play." She tried to disentangle herself from the little girl's grasp. Gabby stuck out her lower lip.

"Please?" she entreated.

Maggie took a look at her expectant little face and caved. "Okay, but just one game."

Satisfied, Gabby raced ahead. Maggie lingered for a moment at the edge of the court. The others were all intent on their game, making a ring around Griffin as he explained a technique. Maggie glanced out at the Strait, at the swirling dark water, the long strands of bull kelp waving gently under the surface. She shuddered, closing her eyes and trying not to imagine Marco and Daniel in the water, Marco being pulled under the surface by another man's folly. The ache was too much to bear. She took a deep breath and then another, steadying herself with the croquet mallet, trying to banish the images from her mind.

"Maggie!"

Maggie opened her eyes. Griffin was looking at her curiously across the court. "You okay?" he called.

She nodded, pasting a smile on her face.

"Great," she called back, although her voice wavered just a little. She didn't trust herself to say more. She took her time gathering up her croquet balls, buying a few seconds to regain her composure. She didn't want Griffin or the children to sense anything was amiss. She felt as though every fiber of nerve had been stripped raw. She wanted nothing more than a long run and a hot shower, a little solitude to try to recover her equilibrium.

"Come on, Aunt Maggie, your turn," Luca called to her.

With a sigh, Maggie put all thoughts of long runs, hot showers, and the Strait's dark, cold currents from her mind and joined the group. She pointed her red mallet at Gabby, who giggled. "You're going to regret this," she announced ominously. "I've got a wicked curveball."

Griffin glanced over his shoulder at her and then sent his ball through two wickets. "Nice to see you join us," he said cheerfully. "I should warn you. I never lose this game."

"Well, there's always a first time," Maggie retorted, hitting her ball crooked and sending it spinning into the grass far to the left of the wicket.

"Want to make a bet?" Griffin grinned. "Just to keep it exciting."

Sammy chased Maggie's ball, bounding around it joyfully.

"Are priests allowed to gamble? Isn't that against the rules?" Maggie asked as Luca took a turn, tapping his ball and getting it halfway through the first wicket before it stopped.

"Not if it's a bet for something good," Griffin said. He tapped his chin in mock contemplation. "Ellen's making cookies for us right now. Let's say if I win I get your cookies."

Maggie considered his offer. "Okay," she agreed finally, "but if I win I want something more than cookies."

"Like what?" Griffin asked.

Maggie thought immediately of Lena, then the number of zeroes needed to pay off the debt and keep the house. "A miracle. Can you deliver that?"

Griffin cocked his head and grinned. "Not sure if I have that much clout with the Almighty, but I can ask for sure. That good enough?"

Maggie thought for a moment and agreed.

Three games later Griffin was declared the champion and Maggie grudgingly handed over her share of the cookies.

"I'll still ask for your miracle," Griffin offered generously around a mouthful of gingersnaps. He offered her a cookie from his now sizable pile. "Want to tell me exactly what you're hoping for, though I'm betting I can guess?"

Maggie opened her mouth to tell him that in fact they needed two miracles, but caught sight of Jonah watching them, close enough to hear her reply.

"Some other time," she said, inclining her head slightly toward the children.

Griffin caught her meaning and nodded. "Well, anytime you want to tell me, I'll be happy to keep my end of the bargain."

"Thanks." Maggie wasn't entirely sure she wanted to tell the priest about the debt anyway. At the end of the day, what could he do? Quote another dead mystic? Tell her that even this would turn out okay? She thought of Daniel paddling out in the kayak, intent on not returning, of Lena lying in the hospital far away, of the huge amount of money they had to come up with if they were to keep the island house. They needed far more than simple optimism or offhanded petitions won by croquet matches. They needed a genuine miracle. Problem was, Maggie had no idea how to find one.

Two days later Maggie returned from yet another fruitless visit to the hospital. Lena remained unresponsive, and every day Maggie's hope dimmed just a little more. She paid the taxi driver and had him drop her at the mouth of the driveway, giving herself a precious few seconds of solitude before she went into the house with its bustle and energy, the smell of something good bubbling on the stove, the barrage of words from the children.

She trudged up to the house, giving in for a brief moment to the overwhelming sensation of frustration and despair. She would do anything to help Lena, but the truth of the matter was that she was doing all that could be done—taking care of the children, keeping Lena's world running as well as possible while her life hung in the balance. Lena's fate would be determined by something entirely out of any of their control. It seemed as though they could do so little.

Maggie spotted Griffin's black motorcycle parked by the door for the second time that week. She sighed. She didn't feel up to a visit from Father Griffin, not now, not when her spirits were so low. Her initial wariness about him was softening, but he could still rub her the wrong way with his optimism, his perceptive gaze that saw more than she wanted to share. Perhaps she could sneak upstairs if he was occupied with the kids.

As she walked up to the house, Griffin appeared, backing out of the mudroom door, talking to Ellen, who nodded at his every word. It was clear she thought Father Griffin Carter hung the moon. Maggie straightened her shoulders and forced a polite smile as she approached.

"So you'll talk with Maggie about letting the

kids come?" he said to Ellen. He turned and caught sight of Maggie behind him.

"Maggie, we were just talking about you." He gave Ellen a cheerful wave. "No worries, I'll ask her myself." He latched the screen door, and Ellen disappeared back into the house. Maggie waited, expecting him to ply her with whatever request he'd come to make. He approached her, opened his mouth, but then stopped. He studied her for a long moment. "Ellen said you were at the hospital," he said gently.

Maggie nodded. "No change." She couldn't keep the tinge of bitterness from her voice or stop the catch at the end of her words. She felt like she might start crying and blinked fast and hard, trying to gain control of her emotions. Griffin waited for a moment, his expression warm and sympathetic. Maggie glanced down, irritated by her show of weakness. She braced herself for whatever words of encouragement were sure to come, but Griffin surprised her.

"Want to go for a ride?" he offered, nodding toward the motorcycle. Maggie, caught off guard, didn't reply. He took her silence as assent and handed her his helmet, clambering aboard the bike.

"Come on, it will do you good. Fresh air, a little freedom. You don't even have to talk to me. You just have to hold on."

Maggie hesitated. What she really wanted was to be alone and have a good cry, but that was unlikely to happen now that she was home. She would be mobbed by children and the dog the minute she opened the door. At least going with Griffin meant getting away for a while from the routine of the house. It would feel good to be on the move again, even if it was just circling the island.

"Let me just text Ellen to let her know." She sent the text and then put on the helmet. Griffin revved the engine and waited as she climbed up behind him. She settled in, a little self-conscious as she grabbed his waist for balance. It felt a little wrong to hold so tightly to a priest. And then with a roar they were off.

Griffin Carter liked to go fast. Luckily, so did Maggie. They couldn't talk over the noise of the engine, and Maggie relished the enforced solitude, the feeling of the wind rushing past her body, the sense of freedom that came with the open air and the pavement rolling away beneath the tires. She took a few deep, gasping breaths that smelled of warm plastic from the helmet. The frustration and tensions of the past few days seemed to slip from her, thin and brittle as a snakeskin, fluttering away behind them. Her heart lifted. She had missed this, the feeling of being a bird on the wing, able to change direction without a second's hesitation. As they roared down the road, she felt the cares and responsibilities of her current life lift from her shoulders, leaving her with an exhilarating lightness. She hadn't felt this free in weeks, not since Nicaragua, before the call from Lena. She drank it in like oxygen, feeling it bubble through her veins. She grinned inside the helmet. Oh, how she had missed it! The thrill of flying high and free.

They slowed all too soon, cruising into Roche Harbor, the tiny, picture-perfect resort town on the north end of the island. It boasted a café selling overpriced Northwestern-style food and homemade donuts, a historic white clapboard hotel, a gift shop or two, a fresh-seafood stand, and a tiny craft market. At the mouth of the expansive marina stood a little store selling fresh produce and grocery essentials to the upscale boating community that crowded the harbor in the summertime.

Griffin pulled to a stop before the store. Reluctantly, Maggie took off the helmet, shaking out curls flattened from the ride.

"You keen for an ice cream?" Griffin asked casually. Maggie eyed him for a moment.

"Is this a date?" she asked lightly, trying to match his casual tone. "Isn't there a special circle of hell reserved for people who tempt priests?"

Griffin laughed, ruffling his hand through

his windblown hair. "Maybe for Catholics. But since I'm Anglican, all bets are off. We Anglicans are allowed to date, get married, have kids, the whole nine yards."

Maggie gaped at him, surprised. "You're not Catholic?"

"Nope." Griffin stretched, unkinking his back. "Anglican to the bone. And as such, very datable. But don't worry," he reassured her. "This isn't a date. If it was, you'd know."

"So you just take women for rides and buy them ice cream as . . . what? Part of your work as a priest? Am I a charity case?" Maggie asked, balancing her helmet on the seat of the bike.

Griffin laughed again. "That's a cheering thought, taking beautiful women out for dessert as part of my parish duties." He shook his head. "Take it as a gesture of friendship. That's all. Besides, you're not my type," he tossed back over his shoulder as he headed into the market. Bemused, Maggie followed.

The store was deserted this time of the afternoon. Its narrow aisles were lined with shelves neatly arranged, holding a mishmash of objects— cake mixes, trail mix and beef jerky, boxes of cereal, fishing nets and bobbers, travel-sized toiletries, and tiny containers of laundry powder.

"Ice cream's back here." Griffin wove his way through the aisles until he found the freezer case stocked with treats.

"Looks like they're out of Butterfinger bars." He sounded mildly disappointed as he browsed the selection. Maggie peered into the case, scanning the options.

"Can I have an ice cream sandwich?" she asked.

"Great choice. I'm going with the Snickers ice cream bar, king-sized." Griffin fished both selections from the case.

"So what is your type?" Maggie asked, a little nettled by his previous statement.

"Oh, you know, sweet, demure, a girl who doesn't instantly get her back up at the sight of me." He shrugged and handed Maggie her bar. Maggie looked down at her treat, feeling uncomfortable. Had her irritation with him really been so obvious? Griffin seemed unaware of her discomfort. He peeled back the wrapper on his bar, took a bite, and went to pay for them both at the register. Maggie unwrapped the white paper covering her ice cream sandwich. A dribble of vanilla ice cream was beginning to seep through the seam of the wrapper. She wiped it up, licking it off her finger, delaying walking to the front of the store where Griffin was.

He was right. She had been unfriendly to him, but she thought he hadn't noticed, or that perhaps he didn't care. As though being a priest made him immune to her prickly demeanor. And why had she treated him that way? Why did he get under her skin? He had shown only kindness to Lena and the kids. He'd gone out of his way to be supportive.

She thought it over as she retraced her steps to the front of the store. She didn't have a concrete reason. It was pure instinct. Their confrontation at the hospital when Lena had first been injured highlighted an underlying truth. Maggie didn't trust the goodness Griffin projected, afraid that behind it was something else entirely. She was worried that sooner or later the truth would win out and she would find ulterior motives. She couldn't quite bring herself to trust his openhanded goodwill. Experience had taught her there was likely something hiding behind it. She was on guard until she figured out just what it was. She joined him outside by the motorcycle.

"Thanks for the ice cream." She took a big bite, her tongue going numb with the cold.

"Sure," he said around a mouthful of his ice cream bar. After a moment he added, "I'm guessing you might need to get out once in a while. Someone like you who travels so much, the change in lifestyle must be hard."

"Yeah, you can say that again." Maggie gazed out at the marina filled with rows of expensive white yachts and sleek sailboats. She licked the line of ice cream between the two chocolate cookie halves, then bit deeply into one end. They ate in silence for a few minutes. Out in the harbor a seal barked. One of the boats started its engine and slowly glided out of its slip, leaving an empty space between a row of boats, like a missing tooth in a smile.

"Want to head down to the south side of the island?" Griffin offered, and Maggie agreed, not yet ready for the sensation of freedom to end. She climbed onto the back of the motorcycle, sucking the last of the soft chocolate cookie from her fingertips.

They hugged the wide, gray ribbon of road through rolling hills, passing an alpaca farm, a small winery with a picturesque white chapel, and homesteads with hand-lettered signs advertising jams, pies, dyed yarn, and all manner of other handmade goods for sale. The air smelled of baking asphalt and cut grass. Maggie took it all in, letting the rush of the breeze and the peaceful, bucolic scenes soothe her. They approached a farm stand by the side of the road, its folding table loaded with cartons of ripe cherries. Griffin slowed down and pulled up beside the stand in a spray of gravel. A Mason jar sat beside the cherries with a sign that said, "$8 a carton. Be honest. Keep your good karma."

"Hold on," he instructed, returning after a moment with a carton full of ripe Rainier cherries. Wordlessly he put them in the side saddlebag on his bike and then returned to the stand to stuff a ten-dollar bill into the Mason jar.

They continued south, not stopping until they reached San Juan Island National Historic Park and wound their way to the long stretch of shore that comprised South Beach. They parked in the deserted lot, then picked their way to the beach down a narrow whisper of a trail through high, dry grass. It was empty, with huge stacks of driftwood piled haphazardly like a giant game of pick-up sticks. Waves rolled in slowly and pulled out across the smooth stones, making them clatter together with a sound like rain on a tin roof.

Griffin found a giant bleached driftwood log and settled down, carton of cherries in hand. Maggie perched next to him on the same log, putting a little distance between them. They sat in companionable silence, looking out across the Strait of Juan de Fuca to the distant Olympic Mountains. The sun scuttled behind clouds, cooling the air, only to reappear again a moment later in a blaze of warmth. Maggie turned her face to it, breathing in the salt tang.

"So, have you figured it out yet?" Griffin asked after a few minutes.

"What?" Maggie turned to look at him.

"Why you don't like me. You've been worrying

that question like a dog with a bone ever since we left the store." Griffin scooped a handful of cherries from the carton and offered them to her. Maggie smiled ruefully at his intuition, opening her hand for the fruit. She didn't answer for a moment. She looked down at the cherries in her palm. They were plump and vividly colored, the translucent, sunny-yellow flesh blushed bright with pink. She chose one that was mostly yellow. They were the sweetest.

"It's not a question of not liking you," she said finally, honestly. "I don't know if I can trust you." She bit into a cherry, savoring the burst of flavor.

Griffin spit a cherry pit far out into the sand. "Why is that? The motorcycle? The accent? My rakish good looks?" He gave her a wry smile.

"The collar," Maggie said quietly.

Griffin turned, surveying her. "So that's it, is it? Raised Catholic?"

Maggie winced and nodded, turning away from his gaze, again thinking he saw more than she wanted him to. "Yeah, that's it." She stared hard at the cherries in her hands.

"That bad?" Griffin asked gently.

Maggie laughed, a short, harsh sound. "You could say that. My mom was as devout as they come—Mass twice a week, fish on Fridays. She wore a little white-lace cap to church, and she said the rosary every night before bed. I was raised on the saints and angels."

She stopped. Just speaking the words dredged up so many painful memories, the sting of them still sharp after more than a dozen years. Griffin said nothing, but she could sense him waiting beside her. "My mother was a good little Catholic girl with only one problem—me. She wasn't married when she had me. She moved from Puerto Rico to Chicago right after high school to work and got pregnant just a couple of years later. I grew up without a father. I have his last name but nothing else. I never met him or knew anything about him. And a single unwed mother wasn't okay with the church. When our parish priest in Chicago found out, he told my mother she was no longer in good standing. She was disgraced. He refused to baptize me, and he refused to give her communion. But she just kept going back, every week, sitting in the last pew with her little white cap on. Every week, going forward and crossing her hands to receive the blessing the priests give to anyone not worthy enough to take the Eucharist."

Maggie stopped and leaned forward, hands cupped around her cherries. She couldn't continue. The memories were still raw. She ate a cherry, pursing her lips and spitting out the pit. It landed a good three feet shy of the water.

After a moment she said, "I think she was hoping for absolution, but she never got it. All we ever got were sideways glances and half-hearted blessings for the fallen." Her mouth twisted around the words, the image of her mother's face, raised in hope beneath the priest's outstretched hand, enough to squeeze her heart with equal parts fury and pity, a mix that still wrenched her gut.

Again, Griffin said nothing, just looked at her for a long moment. "I'm so sorry, Maggie." His voice was kind. She thought he might defend the priests, but he didn't. It took her by surprise, and she brushed off his words.

"It was a long time ago."

"That still doesn't make it right."

"Yeah, well, they thought it was right. They used every possible opportunity to make me feel bad about myself," Maggie countered.

Like an old movie, jerky and slightly off-kilter, she saw Father Flanagan leaning down, his dry lips forming a perfect O of contempt as he said, *"Do you know where your name comes from, Magdalena? Mary Magdalene was a woman of ill repute, known for her sins. Your mother named you very rightly. Magdalene, the fruit of sin."* And then he smiled, his voice frigid with righteousness. *"You remember that now, you hear? Be a good*

girl and don't repeat your mother's mistake."
Mistake . . . He had meant her.

"They even told me my name was sinful. Magdalena. That I was the fruit of sin, branded from birth like I was already bad." She threw a half-rotten cherry into the foam of the surf, livid all over again with the remembered shame.

Griffin shook his head, his brow furrowed. "They were wrong," he said firmly. "Faith is an open door for everyone. It's not closed to you just because of how you were born." He paused, searching for the words to explain. "A German mystic named Meister Eckhart describes it like this. He said, 'God is at home. It's we who have gone out for a walk.'" Griffin threw a mushy cherry in a long overhand, and a seagull swooped down and caught it midair. "I think Eckhart was on to something. I imagine God standing at the door, inviting us to come back. And the door is wide open for us if we want to come in. It's as simple as that."

Maggie said nothing, just watched him. She wanted to believe his words were true. They felt like a soothing balm on a wound that still ached so many years later. Griffin continued to surprise her. He was a puzzle. He got under her skin, but if she were honest with herself, she'd have to admit she was drawn to him. Not in a romantic way, but in a more fundamental sense, drawn by all in him that seemed right and true.

And Griffin Carter certainly seemed true. Perhaps she had misjudged him after all.

"What are you doing here on the island?" she asked finally. She'd been curious since she first met him. What was an Australian, motorcycle-riding priest doing tucked away in this remote little corner of the world?

He shrugged. "Oh, you know, the oldest story in the book. A girl." He took another handful of cherries from the carton, offering them to Maggie. She accepted a few but waved off the rest.

"On San Juan?" Maggie asked.

"No." He laughed. "Slim pickings for girls here. No, back home, in Perth." He picked out a rotten cherry from his hand and launched it out to sea with a languid overhand toss. "Her name was Lucy. We were high school sweethearts, and we planned to get married after college. But after a while, she realized she didn't have the same calling I did." He paused. "She saw what it meant to live as a priest's wife—the late-night telephone calls, the hospital visits, how committed you have to be to the people you serve. It wasn't a life she wanted. She broke off our engagement three months before the wedding."

"Ouch," Maggie murmured.

Griffin nodded. "Yeah, you got that right. She told me I had a choice—her or the collar. And

I couldn't choose her. I couldn't give up what I knew I was meant to do with my life. And then she got a job at the local news station. I got tired of seeing her face on a billboard every time I went out for coffee, so I looked for a parish somewhere far away. And this is what opened up." He spit a cherry pit toward the water. A lick of wave caught it and sent it spinning wildly out with the current.

"Do you ever regret it?" Maggie asked.

"Coming here or becoming a priest?"

Maggie shrugged. "Both. Either."

Griffin shook his head. "I've never regretted becoming a priest. Coming here . . . Sometimes I wonder if I could have stuck it out in Perth to be closer to my father and sister." He paused, considering. "But I've learned to love the island and the community here."

They sat together in companionable silence, finishing their cherries. Maggie glanced sideways at Griffin, his clean profile turned away from her, gazing out at the water. She was beginning to believe she had indeed misjudged him, that there was far more to Griffin Carter than a collar and a cleft chin.

"That miracle you need," he said, interrupting her thoughts. "Want to tell me about it?"

She hesitated but found that she did. In a long string of words the truth tumbled out—about Marco's death and the enormous debt, about Jane

Bigelow and the wills naming her guardian, about giving up the Regent Fellowship and the very real threat of losing the yellow house. She described her feeling of helplessness to do anything for Lena, who was still unresponsive, lying as pale and inert as a warm marble statue day after day. She spoke so fast the sentences were tripping over each other. It was a relief to speak them out, as though her tongue were a release valve on a pressure cooker. Once more Griffin said nothing, just listened to her. She talked and talked, the words finally slowing to a trickle and then stopping completely. She felt emptied out but strangely relieved. *No wonder people go to confession*, she thought.

Griffin studied her carefully. "I think you may need more than one miracle," he said finally.

She laughed, a bleak sound. "You got that right. Got any bright ideas?"

He was silent for a long moment. Before them the surf washed over the rocky shore, the rhythm almost hypnotizing in its calm monotony. Everything felt peaceful here, unhurried and in its proper place. Gazing out at the water, Maggie could almost believe that everything would be okay. Almost, but not quite.

"I don't know how to fix things," Griffin said finally, "but I know no sacrifice goes unrewarded. Keep doing the right thing even though it isn't easy."

"Still think everything's going to turn out all right in the end?" Maggie asked, an edge to her voice. She was thinking of the conversation they'd had in Lena's hospital room. Of the beatific Julian of Norwich and her assurance that in the end all would be well. She still couldn't bring herself to believe it.

Griffin turned to her and nodded. "I do, yes," he said mildly. "I don't know how, but I think it will be okay in the end."

Maggie shook her head, thinking of Ellen waiting at home with the children, of Lena lying still in the hospital bed, of the mysterious, guilt-ridden Daniel Wolfe, of Marco. The sensation of calm evaporated in an instant.

"Well, at least that makes one of us." She got to her feet, brushing sand from her jeans. "I think I'd better get back."

Griffin stood, empty carton in hand. Together they wound their way up the path from the beach to the parking lot.

Griffin handed her the helmet. "One more thing," he said, as though it were an afterthought. "What the priests said about your name, they were wrong. Mary Magdalene was one of the greatest women in history. She's been branded in history as a harlot, but there's not a shred of evidence for that. Mary Magdalene's legacy is one of sacrifice and devotion toward those she loved. You should be proud to share her name." He straddled the motorcycle and gave her a lopsided smile. "Ready?"

On the ride back Maggie gripped Griffin tightly around the middle. They wound through the island, down long, looping curves of road that cut through yellow prairie lands and thick stands of fir, hemlock, and cedar pressing tall and close to the berm, the ground beneath them thickly furred with salal and sword ferns. Ahead of them a small black-tailed deer peered from the forest and froze, nose twitching as they roared past.

Over and over Griffin's explanation of her name ran through her head. Mary Magdalene, a woman known not for her scandalous past as the priests had always said, but for her devotion and sacrifice. For those she loved, Griffin had told her. For the first time Maggie felt an affinity for the woman whose name she bore. Perhaps they shared more than a name. Perhaps that was not such a bad thing after all.

Chapter Twenty

When Maggie got back from her ride with Griffin, she found two packages waiting for her. Daniel's volumes of poetry. She made herself wait until the children were in bed, then hastily put on her pajamas and crawled under the covers, tearing the shipping envelope off the first one. It had a picture of a salmon on the front, struggling up a rocky outcropping against a strong freshwater current. She hesitated, wondering if she should even read these books. Her conversation with Daniel in his cabin had been deeply unsettling. But a powerful curiosity overcame her qualms. She clicked on the bedside lamp, opened *Salmon Song* to the first page, and began to read.

She had planned to approach his poems clinically, as pieces of research to help her better understand the tragedy of Marco's death. She hoped Daniel's writing would give her a glimpse into the inner workings of his troubled mind, bring some meaning to his attempted self-destruction. But his words did something else entirely.

His poems were a love song to his fractured family and his childhood, at times heartbreaking in the vivid, frank way they portrayed his years growing up on the reservation with an alcoholic father and a grandmother who held the family together by stubborn force of will. He described the brokenness and poverty of his upbringing, the shame that encompassed even the simple act of buying a loaf of bread. One poem in particular caught her attention. It was an elegy for himself, the little boy lost to the man he had become with his tuxedo and, as he put it,

a glass case of wine
stored
at precisely 54
degrees,
a bottle
would have paid
the rent,
meant
the roof was safe
over
our heads.

Maggie ran her fingers over the lines, caught by an unexpected emotional response. His words resonated with her. She understood his conflict, coming from a life of deprivation to one of almost extravagant refinement. She'd felt the same way more than once, holding a glass of Dom Perignon at an awards dinner, thinking briefly that the bottle cost more than her mother's entire monthly food budget. It was a contradiction she carried within herself, sometimes less easily than others. Daniel's style was spare but not simple, with an undercurrent of sorrow, the tone quietly heartbreaking even if the words were not. He was very, very good.

Reading the poems, she'd begun to draw a sketch in her mind—not of Daniel's face, the dark swoop of hair across his brow, those deep, sorrowful eyes, but of his spirit, an artist's sharp eye for the raw moments of beauty and pain. His was a soul that saw the world as broken, and both loved it and longed for it to be transformed.

Finishing the first volume, Maggie pulled the covers tighter and opened the second one. It was past one in the morning but she couldn't stop. In the cabin Daniel had been a stranger, a quiet man turtled inside a shell of silence and guilt. But here, on these pages, he was not hidden, he was not unknown. Reading the lines he'd written, she felt as though he was laying himself open to her, showing her the inner workings of his soul. And to her surprise, she found she understood him very well.

It was not a simple realization. She was conflicted, both intrigued and repelled. He was to blame for Marco's death, and for that she should hate him, pure and simple. His careless action had taken the life of the only man she'd ever loved. But something about Daniel drew her despite the role he had played in Marco's death. She didn't want to like him, did not want to identify with him through his poems on those pages. But she did.

When she finished the second volume of poetry, Maggie set it down, clicking off the light, trying to sleep. It was no use. She lay awake for more than an hour, feeling torn and disconcerted. Finally giving up on sleep, she put Daniel's books in the nightstand drawer and pulled on her running clothes. She tiptoed down the stairs and through the darkened house. The clock on the stove read 4:05. Sammy heard her footsteps and rose from his bed in the mudroom, tail wagging, eager to go along. She patted his head but left him inside as she let herself out, determined to run until her emotions were more under control. She opted for the road this time and used a headlamp to light her way in the dark. All was still around her as she ran. No cars passed her, no lights broke the darkness.

When she returned an hour later, she was winded but clearer-headed and calm. She rounded the house and circled the back lawn a few times to catch her breath and cool down. She was sweating, even in the chilly gray of the morning. It was getting light, almost sunrise, although she guessed it was only a little past five. Sunrise came early here during the summer, the days stretching long this far north of the equator. It looked as though it might rain, with clouds mounding on the horizon, the rising sun showing as only a faint pink tinge around their edges. She knew she would regret her sleepless night later, but at the moment she felt refreshed and calm, enjoying the silence as night gave way to day.

Maggie paused at the fence overlooking the Firellis' private half-circle beach, letting the cool salt breeze fan her flushed face. In the growing light she noticed a figure sitting on a driftwood log on the beach below, motionless and staring out to sea. Her heart lurched as she took in the camo pants and black hair pulled back in a ponytail, the broad shoulders clad in an old blue fleece. Daniel. His head was bowed, and he was hunched in upon himself. He looked desolate, sitting there alone.

She took a step back, not wanting to be seen. Her heart was pounding. She thought of the two books in the nightstand upstairs, feeling guilty somehow, as though she had been caught spying on him. She turned to go inside but hesitated. Something drew her, an impulse she couldn't pinpoint. She wanted to see him again. Maggie wavered for a long moment, caught in indecision. Then without giving herself time to think, she clambered down the steps to the rocky beach.

He glanced up when he heard the crunch of her footsteps on the pebbles. He didn't say anything, but she saw a flicker of surprise cross his face as she approached. Perhaps he had thought she wouldn't want to see him again. She sat down without invitation at the other end of the log, facing the water, not looking at him. He didn't say anything and neither did she. Together they stared out at the tide, the only sound the steady wash of the water over the stones, a lulling, lonely cadence.

After a long silence Maggie spoke. "I've been thinking," she said slowly. "About Marco." Her voice caught a little, and she swallowed before continuing. "He chose to save your life." She stopped, suddenly unsure of how to go on. "I know you feel responsible for his death, but it was an accident that he drowned." She bit her lip, weighing her words. "If he hadn't gone into the water to help you, he'd still be here and you . . . you'd be drifting five hundred feet down there in the kelp right now. And that might be what you wanted, but it isn't what happened."

Daniel was watching her intently with those dark, sad eyes. He said nothing. She drew a deep breath, steeling herself, and then continued. "Marco's dead. Nothing can change that now, but he gave his life to save yours. That's the biggest gift anyone can give another person. So don't treat it lightly, don't throw it away. If you do, you'll waste the life he gave for you."

The words spilled out of her, both a challenge and an absolution. She was surprised to find she meant them. She didn't look at him as she said them, but she could feel his eyes on her, assessing.

"You loved him," he said. It was not a question.

"More than I should have," she answered honestly, voicing a truth she had never spoken to anyone before. She stared straight ahead, surprised by her own admission. It began to drizzle lightly, tiny pinpricks of water dotting her face and hands. She folded her hands between her thighs, letting the rain bead on her hair, her forehead and cheekbones. It felt cold and lonely out here, a little wild with a distant storm blowing in over the sea. The clouds had turned from pearly pink to a somber steel gray.

"At some point we all love someone like that," he said gently.

She turned and looked at him then, the sharp planes of his face, the understanding in his eyes. For a moment she saw him as he'd been in New York—smiling, so debonair and handsome, on top of the world.

"I know who you are," she said suddenly. "I saw the pictures, the awards, you with Rudy Giuliani. Why are you here?"

He flinched as though her words were a lash. He didn't answer for several long minutes, so long she thought he would not reply at all. It began to rain a little harder, still just a heavy, spitting mist. Neither of them moved.

"I loved someone," he said finally. "Same as you. Too much and not enough." He gazed out at the water. "And when I lost her, I lost everything."

Maggie bit her lip, fighting back a sudden rush of grief. They sat together, not speaking, as the rain sifted gently down on them, their silence grown suddenly easier with a shared sorrow, letting grief and memory ebb and flow with the steady wash of the sea.

"This can't be happening," Maggie murmured in stunned disbelief. "Not now." Still holding the phone to her ear although the call had already been disconnected, she wandered into the kitchen. Her head was pounding and she felt fuzzy, no doubt a product of her sleepless night.

Ellen glanced up, her fingers poised over the piecrust she was crimping. "Bad news?" She gave Maggie a worried frown. "Is it the hos-pital?"

"No." Maggie shook her head, setting the phone down on the counter gently, as though it might explode in her hand. "No, it isn't anything about Lena. That was George." She stared at the phone, still shocked by what the accountant had told her. "One of the banks called the loan."

Ellen brushed a strand of silver-blonde hair away from her cheek, leaving a streak of flour. "What do you mean, 'called the loan'?"

Maggie glanced out toward the deck, checking to make sure the children couldn't hear. They were sitting at the picnic table with sheets of construction paper, gluing on objects they'd found on their nature hunt that morning. Jonah was affixing the bones of some small mammal to his. Gabby had a fistful of leaves and was trying to glue them on all at once, but the breeze kept catching them and one by one they were fluttering away. She lowered her voice anyway.

"George said with the kind of loan Marco took out the bank can demand payment at any time. Usually they don't. You just repay monthly with interest, but one of them must have gotten worried that Lena was going to declare bankruptcy after Marco's death. They called the loan. We have thirty days to pay it in full."

Ellen wiped her hands on her apron, nodding slowly, taking stock of the situation. "How much is it?"

"Ninety thousand dollars," Maggie said bluntly, too shaken by the bad news to cushion the blow.

"Oh good heavens." Ellen looked shocked. "That much?"

Maggie winced and nodded. "And that isn't the worst part." She braced herself to deliver the next spate of ill fortune. It seemed impossible that there could be more. There had been so much already.

"What's the worst part?" Ellen asked. She braced herself against the counter and waited for the blow.

"Marco put this house up as collateral. So if we don't pay the loan in full, the bank takes the property."

As she spoke the words, Maggie felt their full impact for the first time. Ninety thousand dollars. It was an impossible amount to scrape together in thirty days. They were going to lose the house. The inevitable truth dropped like a lead weight in her stomach. *We can't lose this place*, Maggie argued with herself. *We need it too much.* The children needed the stability of a familiar space, and Lena would need a home to come back to if and when she woke up.

And Maggie—it was the only home she had left. She couldn't lose it. She swallowed hard, trying to force down the panic she could feel ballooning in her throat. She forced herself to breathe in and out through her nose, trying to be calm and strong, trying to think. She could not afford to crumble. There was no one to pick up the pieces.

"What are we going to do?" Ellen asked quietly.

Maggie shook her head. "I don't know." She

needed coffee, at least a double espresso. Maybe that would clear her head.

Ellen looked down at the piecrust, thinking hard. "That's a lot of money."

"Yeah, it is."

"Did George say anything that might help us?" Ellen asked, hopeful.

Maggie shook her head. George's advice had been to file bankruptcy, a move Maggie was fairly certain Lena wanted to avoid. It wouldn't solve their problems even if they did.

"Hope for the best and plan for the worst," George had told Maggie at the end of their call. It was not helpful advice. It was too little too late. The worst had already happened, and Maggie had no idea how to make things right.

Chapter Twenty-One

"Why are you here?" Maggie muttered to herself, rounding the corner of Daniel's shabby cabin later that evening. She had no real excuse to see him, but that hadn't stopped her from coming. Her shock over the disastrous news from George had faded to a low-grade agitation. She was buzzing with it. The truth was that she was completely and totally stuck. At whatever angle she looked at the problem, she could find no clear way to make any of it come out right.

Turn around and go home and come up with a plan, she told herself sternly as she came in sight of the front door. She kept walking. She'd brought her camera with her, although she wasn't exactly sure why. But as always, it made her feel better to have it in her hand. It gave her a small sense of control, even as the world seemed to be spinning completely into chaos.

The door to the cabin was open, so she knocked on the doorframe and poked her head in. The single room was empty. *See, he's not even here.* She felt a little nudge of disappointment at Daniel's absence. She turned to go but spotted him a hundred yards away, perched on a shelf of rock jutting out over the Strait. His back was to her. She hesitated.

He hadn't seen her yet. She could just go. Instead, she walked out on the point to join him.

He didn't turn as she approached. She gave no greeting, just dropped down beside him on the ridged black rock. He glanced up, seemingly unsurprised by her abrupt appearance. "I heard you drive up," he said. He was wearing a clean white T-shirt and jeans but no shoes. He was whittling, the pitted rock around him covered with little golden whorls and spirals of wood. It was a deer this time, eyes wide, one foot raised as though ready to dart away.

Maggie lifted her camera to her eye, watching the sunset over the water through the viewfinder as the last touches of light gilded the clouds a pearly pink and gold. There was nothing like a sunset over the Pacific Ocean. She'd seen a lot of sunsets in her life, in the Himalayas, over the Danube River, in the desert where darkness blotted out the light almost in an instant. But nothing compared to these Pacific sunsets, the fiery orange coal of the sun sinking into an endless blue sea.

She snapped a photo, knowing it would never do justice to the actual beauty of the event. Although she knew all hope of entering the Regent was gone now, she was determined to keep taking photos. She had to keep believing she would one day return to doing what she loved. She needed something to hope for. There was no guarantee that it would be soon, but she wanted to keep fresh, to continue to practice her craft, to keep moving forward even though the future seemed impossibly muddled and uncertain.

"Everything in my life is conflicting, and I can't see how to make it come out right," she said, lowering her camera, a little surprised that she'd voiced the quandary out loud. She was usually so guarded with her thoughts, but it was different with Daniel. They had skipped all the small talk from the beginning, diving into deep water from the start.

Daniel concentrated on his carving for a moment before answering. Carefully, he made several small divots in the deer's hindquarters. Now it was a fawn, speckled on the haunches. "What's the most important thing to you?" he asked at last. He cleaved the tiny raised hoof with a careful slice of the knife.

She sighed. "All of it." It was the truth. She could not make a hierarchy out of the things she held dearest in life. "It feels impossible."

"Is it?" he asked mildly.

"I don't know. It feels like it is." In a few sentences Maggie outlined the problem, stating the conundrum baldly. The situation looked even uglier when she spoke it out, a convoluted maze.

Daniel didn't say anything. He began sanding the fawn with a small square of sandpaper, rasping it over the hindquarters in a rhythmic motion. Maggie watched him for a moment, intrigued by the motion of his hands. She raised her camera, focusing on the deer. "Do you mind?" she asked. He shrugged his assent, and she took two shots, one of the deer and one of him, head bent over his work in concentration.

A light breeze was blowing in over the water, tossing Maggie's curls about her face, bringing with it the salty sweet odor of rotting kelp. She lowered her camera and inhaled deeply, taking in the scent of the sunbaked rock, the dust and dry pine needles mixed with the brine of the ocean, trying to inhale strength and wisdom and a peace that was proving increasingly elusive. They sat in silence for a few moments, the rasp of the sandpaper the only sound between them.

"Have you ever had to make a choice like this?" she asked at last, thinking of the beautiful red-haired woman who had been his wife, of the list of awards and accolades beside his name when she'd googled him, wondering if he had somehow already faced a similar dilemma.

"I didn't get to make that choice," he said, his voice sober. "It was made for me."

He didn't offer any further information, just began rubbing the fawn's head with a small ball of beeswax. Maggie watched him for a moment, then turned back to the water. They sat in silence for a while, Daniel methodically rubbing the carving with wax while Maggie mulled over the problem at hand.

"What did you give up?" she asked finally. "Your marriage? Your career?" She knew she was prying, but she was curious to know more about him, about what had happened in New York to bring him to the island.

Daniel snorted. "My career wasn't hard to give up."

Maggie was surprised, taken aback by the casual dismissal of his work. The very real probability that she was going to have to sacrifice her own career felt catastrophic to her. Why did it not seem to matter to Daniel?

Daniel said nothing more for several minutes, concentrating on his carving and the ball of beeswax. She thought he might not answer, but then he surprised her.

"His name is Eli," he said finally. "He's four, and he's my son."

Maggie's eyes widened. A son? This was news to her. None of the articles had mentioned a child. Daniel set down the ball of beeswax and turned the carved deer over in his hands. The deer wore a look of startlement, as though caught unawares.

"We knew something was different by the time he was two. He didn't like to be touched anymore. He'd play in a corner all day and scream if anyone came near him. When he was three the doctors told us he was autistic. We immediately started therapy and put him in a special preschool. We did everything we could to help him. But he couldn't bond with us. He didn't want us to be close to him. Especially me. He'd let Kate hold him sometimes. When he cried, he wanted her. But never me."

Daniel swallowed hard, bending his head over the carving. A long hank of hair fell over his cheek, almost hiding his expression. "We handled it so differently. Kate threw herself into helping Eli like he was one of her court cases. Books and articles and support groups and case studies. And me . . ." He shook his head. "I just grieved for my son. I loved him so much, and he felt so far from me." His mouth twisted with sorrow. "I loved him, and I felt such loss at the same time. But Kate didn't understand that. She thought I couldn't accept him. There wasn't room in her mind for regret, only for action. My grieving seemed pointless to her. She accused me of rejecting him. My own son."

He looked down at his hands, the pain etched on his face. "And I couldn't just pretend I didn't feel the loss of things that would never be. I stopped writing, and I started drinking some, not all the time, but too much and too often. One night I got a DUI. It was so stupid. And finally Kate had had enough.

"On Eli's fourth birthday she served me with

divorce papers. She said—" His voice cracked, and he cleared his throat before continuing. "She said our son didn't need me in his life if I couldn't accept him the way he was. She said I couldn't support either of them anymore, and so I didn't deserve to have them. She wanted full custody." He ran his finger over the smooth head of the fawn, between the tiny pricked ears, over the slope of the nose.

"Did you fight her for him?" Maggie asked, leaning forward intently.

He laughed, a short, bitter sound, and shook his head. "Kate's an attorney with one of the top firms in the state of New York. They could make Mother Teresa look like a hard-time felon if they wanted to. There was no way I was going to win, not with the DUI, not against her."

"So what did you do?" Maggie already had an idea of his answer.

He shrugged. "I left. Packed a bag and just left. I didn't tell anybody where I was going. And I came here. My grandmother used to bring me here when I was a kid to watch the whales in the summer. I knew the island. I knew I could hide out here until I figured out what to do next."

"And what did you figure out?" Maggie asked.

Daniel gave her a look of chagrin. "How to screw up even more people's lives."

They said nothing for a few minutes. Far out on the sea a group of kayakers rounded the shoreline, heading south, their paddles dipping into water that looked like molten gold in the sunset.

"And yet here you are," Maggie observed finally.

"Here I am," Daniel agreed, sounding resigned. He set down the fawn beside the knife and ball of beeswax and stared out to sea. The air was chilly now, the light seeping from the clouds, leaving only shades of gray. They watched a sleek, black cormorant dive into the water with a spray of white, reemerging a few seconds later with a fish in its beak.

"Do you think we ever get what we really want in life?" Maggie asked.

"Do you know what you really want?" Daniel responded.

"What I can't have now. What I never could have," Maggie answered cryptically.

Daniel nodded. "I had everything once. And then I lost it all."

They said nothing more. There was nothing more to say. After a few moments Maggie rose, brushing bits of lichen and moss off her pants. "I should go."

Daniel stood, slipping his knife and the carving into the pocket of his jeans. "I'll walk with you."

As they headed for the cabin, two small birds with wings fringed in white swooped low, passing just a few feet from their faces, then wheeled upward sharply into the graying pink of the sky. Maggie stopped, glancing up after them. "What are those?"

Daniel followed her line of sight. "Skylarks. They have a nest over here. Come on, I'll show you." He headed toward a patch of knee-high grass away from the water, and she followed.

"They're rare on the island now," Daniel said. "There used to be a lot more of them. Here it is." He squatted down and moved aside a tuft of grass, motioning her over. She knelt next to him, peering down at the nest, suddenly aware of his proximity to her. She could smell him, a warm scent of roasted coffee and cedar shavings mixed with the sweet dry grass where they knelt. She shifted, putting a few inches between them, concentrating on what he was showing her, flustered and feeling like a teenage girl at her reaction to him. Concealed in the tuft was a little nest made of the same strands of pale-gold grass. Inside were four creamy-brown speckled eggs.

"I found them this morning." He leaned back, letting her inspect them.

"Where's the mother?" asked Maggie, careful to keep her distance from the nest, fearful that if she got too close she'd damage the eggs somehow. She took her camera and focused on them, taking one shot and then another.

"Up there somewhere." Daniel pointed above them, where the birds soared in spirals higher and higher in the sky. "Hear that?" He cocked his head. Maggie looked up, straining to listen. From high above them came a liquid trilling cascade of notes. It reminded her of a stream burbling over rocks.

"Skylarks are famous for their song," Daniel told her. "They're not native to the island. German settlers brought them when they emigrated from Europe. The birds reminded them of home, of working in the fields and heading in at suppertime with the song of larks at their backs." He watched the birds for a moment, then added, "My grandmother told me skylarks are a friend of travelers. She said they help people find their way home."

Maggie craned her neck, watching the graceful spiral of a lark as it swooped and dove in the evening air. "Do you think that's true?"

Daniel rose, brushing bits of grass from his pants. He offered her his hand, and she took it. His palm was dry and warm as he hoisted her to her feet. He released her hand and tipped his head back, watching the larks in their flight. "I hope so," he said quietly.

"Me too." Maggie watched the birds' flight path, wishing they would point the way, give her some clue about which way to go. Daniel turned and Maggie fell into step with him. They walked in silence to her car, the trill of the larks following them in the evening stillness, singing of things lost and found. Singing of a future that felt more uncertain than ever.

"Aunt Maggie, Jonah says we need to do something at the altar," Luca told her at breakfast the next day. Gabby nodded in agreement. Maggie looked at their earnest faces and set down her forkful of scrambled eggs.

"What kind of something?" she asked. The younger two looked at Jonah expectantly. He shrugged, avoiding her eyes. "Like a ceremony," he said. "Like those old people did at the museum. To bring back something we lost so we can find it again."

"And what are we finding?" she asked carefully, taking a sip of orange juice.

"We're finding Mommy," Gabby piped up. "Her brain is sleeping, and we need to wake it up."

"And we're helping Dad so he can find us again," Luca interjected.

"And how do you think we do that?" Maggie asked. The kids looked at one another. Jonah shrugged again. "We don't know," he said. "We thought you'd know what to do."

"Do you, Aunt Maggie?" Gabby asked.

Maggie thought for a moment. "I don't," she said, then seeing their crestfallen expressions, she added quickly, "but I think I know someone who will."

"I can't." Daniel turned away from Maggie in the dim confines of the cabin, clearly agitated by her request.

"Why not?" She faced him across the narrow table.

"I'm not . . . I'm not good with kids," he muttered, avoiding looking at her.

"Look, I'm not asking you to babysit," Maggie reasoned with him. "I just need your help. They want to have a ceremony to try to help their mom and dad. I know you know something about this. I read one of your poems about losing something and finding it again. You talked about a ceremony in that."

He looked surprised at the mention of her reading his poems but then shook his head. He wouldn't look at her, just kept picking up objects and putting them down—a bowl, his carving tools, the enamel coffeepot. "I can't," he said again.

"Daniel." Maggie considered her next words carefully. "Lena's in a coma because of a car crash. She hit a concrete retaining wall going fifty miles an hour. The officer at the scene said she didn't even hit the brakes." She let her words sink in for a moment. Daniel glanced sharply at her. He said nothing.

She continued, "You know the situation. I told you everything that's at stake. I don't believe any ceremony is going to bring Lena back or make everything turn out okay, but right now three ery scared, very sad children have lost both parents in the last few weeks. Marco's gone and there's nothing we can do about that, but Lena might still come back to us. At the very least we can help the kids feel like they're doing something to help. Please," she asked gently. "They've lost so much. Give them something to hope for."

He considered her words for a moment, then nodded unhappily, looking trapped. "Okay, I'll figure something out."

They gathered just after sunset around the altar. Jonah, Luca, and Gabby were solemn and silent. Daniel paced, nervous and on edge, and Ellen stood with her arms crossed, frowning in staunch Lutheran disapproval. Gabby was wearing her fairy princess outfit, pink tulle skirt and sparkly wings and a tiara tilted on her curls. The boys shot furtive glances at Daniel, who was wearing a white T-shirt and dark-navy cargo pants. His hair was combed but loose, hanging down around his face, and he wore a tooled leather belt with a hunting knife fastened to it. Jonah eyed the knife enviously.

Maggie had brought her camera along to document the ritual. When Lena awoke, she would want to see what they had been doing to help her in her absence. Maggie raised her camera and focused, taking a couple of shots of the altar and the children gathered around it. She captured an image of Ellen in profile, arms still crossed, watching Daniel suspiciously. She took one or two of Daniel, crouched down and hovering over the objects they'd collected for the ceremony.

Even when she wasn't looking at Daniel, she was aware of his presence. As she snapped photos of Ellen and the children, she could feel him crouched to her left. Her heightened awareness flustered her. She didn't know what to do with it. When Daniel looked at her, she felt as though he really saw her—not as the globe-trotting photographer or the bereaved best friend, but as herself, simply Maggie. It had been a long time since someone had looked at her that way. Maggie turned her attention away from Daniel by force of will, making herself concentrate on the task at hand.

Using small white pebbles, Daniel outlined a large circle around the altar. In the center of the circle he placed a few new objects—a black crow feather, a bottle of gardenia perfume Lena wore for special occasions, a few pinecones gathered by Gabby, and half a dozen more candles Ellen retrieved from the mudroom for the ceremony.

Maggie lowered her camera. "So where do we start?" She looked to Daniel for direction.

He cleared his throat. "First, we light the candles." He drew a small box of matches from his pocket and handed it to Jonah and Luca, who looked impressed at the task assigned them. "Don't play with those in the house," Daniel instructed them quickly, seeing Ellen's alarmed expression.

It took them several tries, but Jonah lit the candles one by one while Luca held them, then handed them to Daniel, who placed the lit votive candles around the edge of the clearing, making a rough ring of light.

"Okay," Daniel said, coming back to the center and taking the matchbox from Luca, who was attempting to ignite a pinecone. He slipped it into his pocket and faced them, balancing on the balls of his feet. He was clearly nervous. "Okay," he said again. The evening was beginning to chill as dusk crept across the horizon. Maggie shivered in the damp coolness under the trees. All was still except for the sleepy chirping of birds settling in for the night and the ever-present sounds of the sea below them. It felt as though the very air were holding its breath, waiting for something.

"Now what do we do?" Luca asked, clearly in awe of this stranger who allowed him to light matches and who wore a real knife.

"Now we do the beckoning ceremony," Daniel said. Maggie glanced at him, curious. He knew about the old rituals of the island?

"From the German settlers?" she asked.

Daniel shrugged. "Partly."

"Humph," Ellen interjected. "I've been Lutheran all my life, and I'd never heard of this before Maggie told me about it. Are you sure it's a Lutheran ceremony?"

"It's a lot of things," Daniel said.

Ellen raised her eyebrows, skeptical.

"Come on," Gabby urged, pulling at Maggie's shirt, her pink net fairy wings bouncing against her back. "We got to call to Mommy so she can find us."

Daniel picked up four pinecones and handed them to the children and Ellen, who took hers grudgingly. "Now put these at the four corners, north, south, east, and west." He gave the perfume bottle to Maggie, instructing her to spritz the perfume at each compass point as well. She did. As the familiar scent of gardenias filled the air, Maggie felt a shiver brush across her skin. The scent evoked such a strong sensation of Lena's presence, as though Lena were standing right behind her, close enough to touch.

"Come back to us," Maggie whispered softly, feeling a little self-conscious.

Daniel placed Marco's drafting pencils in the middle of the clearing, then took the crow feather and dipped it into the flame of a candle.

It smoldered, adding the stench of burnt feather to the sweetness of the perfume. He stood in the center of the ring by the altar as the feather smoked and sputtered. He blew on it, coaxing the sparks to life. The children watched him, wide-eyed, hanging on his every move.

Daniel raised the feather high above his head, waving it slightly, watching the smoke drift upward into the deepening dusk until it disappeared. He muttered a few sentences in a language Maggie didn't recognize, then paused, looking around as though at a loss for how to proceed. Maggie suspected he was improvising, making things up as he went along. Ellen clearly thought so too. She waited until he was done, then picked up one of the candles and stepped into the ring of pebbles. Daniel made room for her, looking a little relieved at the interruption. Ellen cupped her hand around the flame, keeping it from any stray breeze.

"Dear heavenly Father," she intoned, "you who know all things. Please grant our lovely Lena life and health again. Wake her from her sleep and bring her back to us. And for Marco, who is gone now, please take him in your arms and grant him peace. And send us a sign that he is in your good and loving care, amen."

Maggie and Daniel exchanged a glance, impressed by Ellen's sudden burst of eloquence. Ellen bowed her head for a moment, the graying gold in her hair illuminated in the small flame. She set the candle in the very center of the circle. "There," she said, smoothing back her hair, looking a little self-conscious. "They can find their way home now."

They watched the candle flicker for a moment. Maggie was aware of something different in the air, in the hush of early night, a sense that they might indeed be standing on sacred ground. On impulse, she crossed herself, muttering a quick prayer, memorized as a child and long forgotten, a request for blessing and protection and the benefaction of grace. She hadn't prayed in years, scorning such things as merely superstition and repetition and foolish belief. But now she found she was not praying as her mother had, with penance and candles and pleas that never seemed quite good enough to earn an answer. Instead, she echoed the words of Julian of Norwich, asking for all things to be turned to good. She said the words without faith—the future looked too impossible for that—but as she spoke she mustered the tiniest glimmer of hope.

She did not feel foolish. She was too desperate for that. Here, faced with such sorrow, with the scent of gardenias still soft in the air, she would do anything if it would bring back what was lost, if it would grant them all a measure of peace in the face of Marco's death, if it would save their home, if it would bring Lena back.

Chapter Twenty-Two

Arriving at the hospital the next morning, Maggie peered around the corner of Lena's room, her heart fluttering in her throat with a tiny, absurd hope. Perhaps, perhaps . . . But there was no change. She set her camera bag at Lena's bedside, trying to shake off her discouragement. The ceremony had not worked, not that she had expected it to. Still, in the slow passage of minutes and hours and days of waiting since Lena's accident, Maggie was beginning to realize how easy it was to cling to anything—an omen, a premonition, a beckoning, a prayer, anything that gave hope.

She sat down in the hard chair, resting her head against the wall. She was exhausted, and a headache was pounding across the back of her skull. She'd had trouble going to sleep after the ceremony and then been awakened at three in the morning by Gabby crawling into bed with her, trembling from another nightmare about drowning. Maggie had held her until her little body slackened into sleep again, but Maggie had lain awake until dawn, thinking about the future, trying not to give in to panic and despair.

Lena lay unmoving. Maggie scooted her chair to the side of the bed, picking up Lena's limp hand. It was cool and slim, with long fingers and prominent knuckles, a pianist's hand. Maggie pictured Lena's engagement ring, a beautiful princess-cut diamond in a delicate white gold filigree setting. Maggie had retrieved it from the hospital along with Lena's other belongings after the accident, and now it was safely stored in Lena's bureau at the house. Lena adored the ring. She never took it off. She had adored her family. There'd never been any question of that. She had always wanted a family, and she loved her husband and children more than anything.

Maggie ran her fingers over Lena's, feeling the strength in those hands. Lena was a talented pianist, but she had sacrificed a career to be a wife and mother. She possessed the technical skill to be successful, but she had none of Maggie's and Marco's drive for success. She had always been a puzzle to Maggie and Marco alike, who were stymied by her lack of ambition, her priorities so different from their own.

Maggie smiled sadly, thinking of the last time she'd heard Lena perform. It had been the spring of their junior year of college. Lena and Marco had been dating for a few months already. Maggie and Marco decided to stay at Rhys and work through the summer months. Marco continued bartending and Maggie found employment doing freelance photography—family portraits and engagement photos, mostly. Lena was unsure of her summer plans, but she was auditioning for a summer European touring ensemble. It was a good opportunity with a prestigious group. Many who had joined before had gone on to successful careers in musical performance. Lena's advisor had secured her an audition spot without telling her first, insisting that she at least consider the option. With both Marco's and Maggie's persuasion, she'd reluctantly agreed.

The night of the auditions, Maggie and Marco filed into the small concert hall and took seats three rows back. The lights were dimmed, a single spotlight illuminating the Steinway grand piano in the center of the stage. The three judges who would decide the winning pianist were seated in the front row, their pens poised over their clipboards. A freckled girl from Louisiana went first. Her hands shook as she readied herself, and although she played with technical brilliance, she lacked passion. Next a dark-haired young man from Romania auditioned, playing with such zeal that it felt like watching a caricature of a pianist, sweat gleaming on his brow and fingers flying as he swayed dramatically with the music.

"It's like watching a young Liberace," Maggie murmured to Marco, who gave her a sardonic smile. And then it was Lena's turn—beautiful, serene Lena. In her black concert dress, hair pinned up and shining in the spotlight, she looked as poised and perfect as an ice sculpture.

She took her place, waited a moment, and then plunged into her piece. She played remarkably well, transcending perfect form with a passion that surprised Maggie. Lena, usually so calm, displayed a depth of emotion in music that she rarely displayed elsewhere. She was the best performer by far. Maggie watched her, amazed. She was sure to win.

And then, as her piece reached a crescendo, Lena looked up, straight at Marco, and hit a wrong note. It was jarring, ringing out clearly in the concert hall. And then she hit another and another. An entire measure of missteps, sharps and flats flying in all directions. One of the judges turned to the other, mouth pursed as though tasting something sour, and made a mark on his paper. Lena turned back to the music and played the remainder of the piece with cool precision, flawlessly, without a moment's hesitation.

"You did that on purpose," Maggie accused Lena later when they were alone in their dorm room. Lena shrugged out of the black dress, letting it puddle to the floor. She didn't deny Maggie's claim.

"I don't understand. Why would you do that?" Maggie followed her into the bathroom as Lena unpinned her hair. "You had the competition in one hand. You could be touring in Europe all summer. Instead, that freckled girl won. She wasn't half as good as you are."

"Maybe I don't want to tour in Europe," Lena suggested, wiping off her lipstick. Maggie stared, uncomprehending, as Lena slipped into her peach silk robe.

"But you could have won!" she finally protested. "You know you could have. You're talented. You could go far."

Lena shrugged. "Some things are more important than that to me." She smoothed lemon-scented cream onto her face, rubbing it into her throat and across her wide cheekbones.

"Like what?" Maggie challenged. "Isn't that why we're all here? So we can perfect what we have and hopefully make something of ourselves?"

"You don't have to be famous to make something of yourself," Lena countered.

Maggie stared again, mouth open, aghast. "Oh really? Well, what do you want, then? You want to bake the best banana bread in the PTA? Sew a straight seam? Is that what you want?"

Lena whirled on her, nostrils flaring a little, indignant. "No, but what about being a good wife to someone? What about being a good mother? So I don't want to be a performer and have a life on the road and see my name in bright lights. So what? I know I could, Maggie. I know I could. I'm good enough that I could make a career of it if I wanted to. But I don't want it. I don't want the pressure and the long nights in strange places and the loneliness . . . I don't want it. I want a home and a family and a warm, safe place for my children. And yes, maybe I do want to make the best banana bread at the PTA. Is that so wrong?" She brushed past Maggie and went back into their room. Maggie followed, baffled, unable to comprehend Lena's point of view.

Lena turned to her. "I want different things than you and Marco do," she said gently. "You both are so driven. And I'm just not like that. Maybe one day I'll wake up and want to make a name for myself. But not today. I want other things more." She took the hairpins from her updo and carefully placed them in a small silver box on her dresser, combing her fingers through her hair so that it fell around her shoulders in golden waves. She glanced at Maggie. "And maybe one day you'll wake up and want other things too. Maybe one day being famous won't seem like the greatest thing in the world."

Maggie could not have imagined such a thing at the time. She still wasn't entirely sure she could. But Lena had made her choice, and she seemed happy with her life.

"You gave up everything for love, for Marco, for all of us, didn't you?" Maggie murmured, leaning over the hospital bed, remembering the shimmer of the stage lights on Lena's hair, her slender hands flying over the keyboard, the moment when her fingers deliberately slipped from the keys in a cascade of discordant notes. She had wanted only one thing. And she had gotten it, the life she wanted—Marco, a home, children. Her whole world centered on family.

"So what happened?" Maggie asked, thinking again of the letter to the lawyer. "Did something go wrong between you? If it did, why didn't you tell me? I had no idea. I still have no idea. Maybe it's just a mistake." She sighed and laid Lena's hand down at her side, then sat for a few moments, chewing over the conundrum, but she had no flash of inspiration.

On impulse, she laid Lena's hand over her heart, adjusting it so it made a cradle. She snapped off the head of a dark-pink rose shot through with pale streaks, part of an arrangement sent by the ladies' society quilting group, and placed it in Lena's palm. It bloomed over her chest, directly where her heart beat slow and steady. The streaks of white made the bloom look broken into a dozen pieces. Maggie pulled her camera from her bag, adjusted it, and took a shot, then another and another. It felt good to do something, even if it was just taking a few practice shots. She focused on Lena's still face, so beautiful and serene, a real-life Sleeping Beauty.

Maggie slipped into the rhythm of her work, taking shots from several different angles, catching the light and shadow in the hollows

336

of Lena's face. She broke off suddenly, feeling exposed by her own camera. She couldn't treat Lena as though she were any other subject. It felt too close somehow, both to Lena and to herself. She felt as though she were opening up a corner of her own heart and placing her camera inside. In photographing Lena, Maggie was photographing her own life as well. She stowed the camera carefully away and sat down, taking Lena's hand again.

"We never appreciated you enough," she admitted, thinking of all the years of Lena's quiet sacrifice, devotion, and care since Maggie had known her. "Me included. You gave more than we saw, and I never realized it, not until now."

Lena had never complained, never demanded. She had just given of herself thoughtfully, gently, focusing on those she loved. And what had Maggie given Lena? Not enough. Never her whole friendship, her unreserved love. She had kept herself always a half step away from Lena. Marco was always between them.

"I should have given you more," Maggie whispered, feeling ashamed. "You deserve better."

She looked down at Lena's face, pale and peaceful in the glare of the overhead lights, realizing with a pang of remorse that it might be too late. There might not be a chance for her to make it right.

"The swelling has gone down," Dr. Yamamoto told Maggie when he stopped in a short time later. He scanned Lena's chart. "There's no obvious reason for her not to wake up. It's up to the brain to decide what to do next. It could be an hour. It could be a year."

"Can anything help her?" Maggie asked, although she knew the answer.

"All we can do is wait," he said. "And remain hopeful for the best." The doctor hesitated, then added gently, "If there continues to be no change, we need to start considering moving Mrs. Firelli to a long-term care facility." He gave Maggie a sympathetic look when he saw her stricken expression. "Not yet," he assured her. "But if there is no change, then soon."

After his departure Maggie sat silently for a long time, trying to remain calm in the face of the doctor's words. A long-term care facility? She glanced at Lena and shuddered. It was a horrible thought. And with the debt repayment looming closer every day, how would they cope with the expense of a long-term care facility? She had to force herself not to panic, not to take Lena by the shoulders and shake her, insist that she wake up. Maggie and Ellen were doing the best they could, but they couldn't continue in this state of limbo forever. The clock was ticking. Maggie reached out and clasped Lena's hand. It was cool, as though Lena were already halfway gone.

"We're doing all we can," she whispered. "But it isn't enough. Your children need their mother. We need you to come back to us." She squeezed Lena's hand. "We're running out of time."

"Aunt Maggie, Luca found a starfish." Gabby pranced on tiptoe, pointing to the shallows where Luca was crouching, peering under the edge of a half-submerged rock.

"It's purple," Luca added.

"Don't fall in," Maggie called from the dusty path that ran along the cliffs of Lime Kiln Point, above where the children were exploring the tide pools. She set the picnic basket on an empty picnic table, hung her camera by its strap around her neck, and began to navigate her way down to the children, carefully descending from rock to rock, avoiding colonies of mussels attached to the sides of rocks and slick spots covered in kelp. Sammy followed her happily, tail waving like a silky banner. She'd taken him off his leash, assured by the children that he liked to wade in the water and would not go far.

"Jonah, are you finding anything?" she called. Jonah was farther out on a neighboring penin-sula of rocks exposed during low tide.

"Yeah, just some crabs," he yelled back.

It had been Maggie's idea to spend the sunny

Saturday at Lime Kiln Point State Park. After a long, full week, Ellen was looking frazzled and needed a break. She had gratefully taken Maggie up on the offer of a free day. "I'm going to start that new knitting pattern I got in Friday Harbor and call Ernie for a nice long chat. I do miss that man," she said, sighing. "And then maybe if there's time I'll have a bath, a good long soak."

After the guardianship question was resolved, Ellen had decided against having Ernie come out to the island. She and Maggie determined that if Lena was not awake in the next few weeks, Ellen would fly home to Minnesota for a visit, and they would reassess the situation after that. Neither of them liked to think too far ahead. A future without Lena was a frightening prospect, but the reality was that Ellen could not stay on the island forever and that Maggie was, at least until Lena awoke, responsible for the children.

It had taken almost two hours to leave the house. Maggie had loaded up the kids, her camera, the picnic basket Ellen packed with peanut butter and jelly sandwiches, apples, and marshmallow treats, and Sammy with his leash and doggie bowl for water. She'd looked at the rental car, stuffed to the gills with kids, dog, and supplies, and sighed ruefully. Gone were the days of slipping through crowds in solitary, compact precision. There was nothing small or simple about life with children, she was quickly discovering.

They'd arrived at the park at low tide. For most of the morning they explored the tide pools at the base of the craggy black cliffs, the kids scrambling down to the water's edge to find treasures in each new crevice and eddy. Sammy followed at their heels while Maggie lagged a little behind, photographing their joy and excitement. Even Jonah seemed to be enjoying himself, smiling when a crab, threatened by Luca's stick, brandished his claw, grabbed the end of the stick, and wouldn't let go.

Eventually the children tired of the exploration and settled on a rock promontory jutting out into the water, hungry and ready for lunch. Maggie retrieved the picnic basket and doled out the sandwiches, boxes of organic grape juice, and apples. Sammy flopped down beside Maggie, tail wagging, his long tongue lolling out of his mouth. She gave him a couple of dog treats Ellen had stashed in with their lunch, and he happily crunched them, licking the crumbs off the rock.

The day was cool and sunny, with a breeze off the ocean. Maggie sat on a flat rock and munched her crisp apple, enjoying the moment of peace. No one else ventured down onto the rocks. Above them the cliff path was littered with little clumps of people, tourists and islanders alike. Some snapped photos in front of the picturesque white-and-red lighthouse on the point to the north, while others sat at picnic tables, watching for the resident pods of orca whales that often visited to feast on salmon in the deep kelp beds near the shore.

Two kayakers maneuvered their kayaks around the lighthouse and silently glided by a few minutes later, waving at the children as they passed. The sea was calm, lapping gently against the black rocks speckled with barnacles and algae. With low tide came the smell of rotting kelp baking in the sun. A harbor seal popped its head from the water, looked around for a moment, and glided back under the surface. Taking the opportunity of a few minutes of calm, Maggie set aside her apple core and assumed the Lotus pose, centering herself, breathing slowly and relaxing. For now, for this moment, she felt peaceful. She closed her eyes, enjoying the warmth of the sun on her eyelids.

"Hey, look!" Luca cried excitedly. Maggie blinked, following the direction of his finger. A black fin broke the surface of the water a hundred yards out. They waited, and a few seconds later the creature appeared again. This time it arced from the water, and they could see more of it.

"Is that an orca?" Maggie got to her feet, shading her eyes with her hand, trying to see better. It had the same black-and-white coloring, but the fin was short. The creature was far smaller than the orcas that frequented these waters. It was bigger than a human, certainly, but would be dwarfed by the huge orcas.

"No, it's just a Dall's porpoise," Jonah corrected her, shrugging. "We see them all the time. That one looks like a boy porpoise. Boys are bigger and thicker." He looked bored and took a bite of his sandwich.

"Look, it's coming to see us," Gabby called excitedly.

The porpoise was rapidly closing the distance between them. It seemed headed straight for the rocks where they stood. Luca and Gabby scrambled to their feet, watching as the porpoise dove out away from the rocks and then doubled back again. He was fast and agile, cutting a swath through the water like a speedboat.

"He's saying hello." Gabby giggled, waving at the creature. It doubled back again, swimming closer to them. Maggie had never seen anything like the creature's behavior. It was common to see whales and seals and porpoises in the waters around the island, but she'd never seen one come so close. Sammy, on high alert, ran to the edge of the rocks, barking and growling.

"Look, it's hurt." Gabby pointed. When the porpoise surfaced again, even closer this time, Maggie caught a glimpse of its left side above its flipper, the shining black flesh crossed with a thick white scar, probably the result of a long-ago run-in with a boat propeller.

Luca tentatively called to it. "Hi, porpoise. Want an apple?" He tossed his apple core into the water.

"They don't eat apples, just fish and stuff like that," Jonah said scornfully. With a sigh, he got to his feet and joined them. He crossed his arms, but his eyes never left the porpoise as it veered back and forth around their pile of rocks, the fan of its tail making a V of white in the dark-blue water.

"That's funny." Gabby laughed as the creature dove and then arced out of the water again and again. "I think he likes us."

Maggie joined the children, and together they watched the porpoise's antics. Maggie was puzzled by its proximity. Was there something wrong with the animal?

"Aunt Maggie." Jonah turned to her, his voice low. His eyes were solemn. "Do you think it's the sign?"

Maggie looked at him blankly for a moment, trying to follow his train of thought. "The sign?"

"You know," he prompted, keeping his voice down and his eye on the porpoise. "From the ceremony."

"The beckoning ceremony," Maggie said, understanding dawning. "The sign that your dad has found his way home?"

He shrugged. "Yeah, I guess." He scuffed at the rock with the toe of his tennis shoe.

Maggie was at a loss for how to answer. "I don't know. What do you think?" she asked finally.

He shrugged again. He squinted at the creature as though trying to determine its motives. It played in the water for a few more minutes, then suddenly leapt high from the surf, its body sleek and shining as spray flew from its path. Then it dove down below the surface and cut a straight path out to sea. It did not return. They watched it until it was just a speck against the horizon.

"It's probably just a stupid idea," Jonah said.

Gabby bounded over to them, grinning widely. "He wanted to be friends," she cried excitedly.

"It sure looked like that, didn't it, sweetheart?" Maggie ruffled Gabby's curls. "Everybody ready to pack up? Or do we have room for marshmallow treats first?"

"Marshmallow treats," a chorus of voices affirmed. She doled out the sticky bars. Sammy patrolled along the water's edge, on guard for any more wildlife.

The children sat down again on the rocks, devouring their treats, the porpoise seemingly forgotten, but Maggie kept glancing out to sea. The conversation with Jonah had made her oddly uneasy. The notion was ludicrous. There was no rational way to explain how a burnt feather and some perfume had summoned a sea creature from the ocean. But she thought of the early occupants of San Juan Island, those hardy Germans who had traveled so far from their homeland. She thought of them gathering in houses with smoking fires, rain drizzling outside as they waited patiently for a sign, any sign, that those they loved could now rest in peace. She thought of the skylarks they'd brought to the island, birds whose special purpose was to help travelers find their way home.

Maybe it wasn't so ludicrous after all, just unexplainable. She glanced up. Jonah sat with his marshmallow treat half eaten in his hand, staring out to sea with an unreadable expression. She followed his gaze but saw nothing. The surface of the water was empty now. What had been there was gone.

Sunday afternoon Maggie was helping the kids construct a fort in the side yard when Ellen delivered the news. She appeared at the entrance to the fortification, a hodgepodge composed of blankets, lawn chairs, and an old pup tent, looking for Maggie.

"Maggie?"

Hearing her name, Maggie scrambled to the front of the fort, poking her head out in time to see Ellen being challenged by the fort guard, Luca, and his trusty guard dog, played by

Sammy wearing an old bandanna tied around his neck.

"Do you know the secret password?" Luca asked Ellen, barring entrance to the fort. Ellen put her hand on her chest. She was out of breath. It looked like she'd run from the house.

"Please?" she said, peering around Luca to try to spot Maggie.

"Nope." Luca shook his head. As if by magic, Gabby appeared, taking Ellen's hand. "It's kangaroo," she confided.

"Kangaroo. Now let me through," Ellen said firmly.

Jonah poked his head out of the other side of the tent, eyeing Gabby with disgust. "You can't go giving the password to everybody," he admonished her. "That's why we have a password, to keep people out."

Ellen glanced at the children, who were arguing over who would guard the gate next. "Kids, there're lemonade and fresh oatmeal cookies on the back deck," she called. As if by magic, all bickering ceased immediately as the children abandoned their posts in favor of snacks.

"Maggie?" Ellen called again as Maggie struggled out of the fort and stood, brushing grass from her clothes. "What is it?" Maggie asked, sobering at the look on Ellen's face.

Ellen glanced toward the deck, but the children were well out of earshot.

"The hospital called," Ellen said, taking a deep breath. "Lena's awake."

Lena's eyelids fluttered, and Maggie leaned forward in the hard hospital chair, heart in her throat. This was it. What if Lena opened her eyes and didn't recognize her? What if she'd suffered brain damage? Would she have to learn to walk and talk again, relearn the names of her children, rediscover that her husband was dead? It was a terrible thought. What if Lena didn't remember Marco's accident?

Maggie had caught the next flight to Bellingham as soon as Ellen delivered the news. She and Ellen had agreed to say nothing to the children until they knew more about Lena's condition.

Maggie carefully took Lena's hand, eyes fixed on her face. For a few long minutes nothing happened. Lena lay as still as stone. And then, very gently, Maggie felt Lena's fingers curl around her own and squeeze for a second. She stared at their joined hands, at those long, pale pianist's fingers curved over her own slender brown ones. When Maggie looked up, Lena's eyes were open; Lena was looking at her.

"Hey," Maggie said softly. Lena smiled, closed her eyes, and slipped back into sleep. Maggie waited a few moments, then went into the hall to call Ellen with the little bit of news. She peeked back into the room. Still sleeping. She checked in with the nurse on duty, listened to the report that said nothing more than what she already knew. Lena was awake. No details on her condition. They were waiting for some test results, and Dr. Yamamoto would be by to talk with her later. Maggie grabbed a cup of terrible coffee and a newspaper, and went back to Lena's room to settle in for the long haul.

She was antsy, unable to concentrate on anything for more than a few minutes. She got up and sat back down, trying to read the world news, then got up again and paced the hall. The wait was excruciating. Two hours later Lena woke again. Maggie was sitting in the chair, staring out the window, the newspaper open in her lap.

"Maggie?" Lena croaked, bringing Maggie out of her reverie with a start. She turned to find Lena's eyes on her, clear and calm.

She knows my name, Maggie thought, reassured by that one word.

Lena tried to clear her throat and winced. "Thirsty," she said hoarsely.

Maggie called the nurse, who gave Lena a few chips of ice. "I'll let Dr. Yamamoto know Mrs. Firelli is awake," the nurse said, keeping her voice low and darting a look at Lena. "Try not to excite or agitate her." And then she whisked from the room. Maggie sank back in the chair by Lena's bed. Lena's mouth turned down in frustration as she clumsily tried to scoop an ice chip from the little bowl on her tray. "My fingers don't work," she complained. "What happened?"

"Here, let me help you." Maggie scooped up a few chips, and Lena opened her mouth obediently, like a baby bird. "You had a car accident," Maggie said, choosing her words carefully. "And you hit your head. You've been unconscious for a while."

Lena stared at her, digesting the information. "How long?"

"About three weeks. A little more." Those weeks had felt like a lifetime.

Lena gasped as though suddenly recollecting something and struggled to raise herself up on her elbows. "Where are my children?" She looked around the room, panicked.

"They're fine. They're fine," Maggie assured her hastily, putting her hand on Lena's shoulder, trying to calm her. The bones beneath her fingers were slight and sharp. Lena had lost weight. "They're with Ellen right now, using all the patio furniture to build a fort in the yard."

"They're okay? Are you sure?" Lena looked worried.

"They're just fine," Maggie assured her again. "They weren't in the car with you. They were at home watching *Mary Poppins* with me."

Lena frowned, her forehead creased in concentration. "So . . . what happened?"

"You crashed the Volvo and hit your head. You're at St. Joseph's in Bellingham."

Lena processed the information for a long moment, then nodded and sank back into her pillow. She closed her eyes again. Maggie carefully set the bowl on the bed tray, thinking Lena had fallen back to sleep. Suddenly Lena's eyes flew open. She grabbed Maggie's wrist in a surprisingly firm hold. "I want to see them," she demanded. "I want to see my children."

"Of course." Maggie gently extricated herself and tucked Lena's hand back under the blanket. "But first we have to talk to your doctor. I promise I'll bring them as soon as he gives the okay."

"Are you sure they're all right?" Lena asked again, an edge of panic in her voice.

"They're fine. Absolutely fine. They miss you, but we've taken good care of them. Here, look. This is what we did yesterday." Maggie quickly grabbed her camera from her bag and flipped through a few photos of the children at the beach.

Lena studied the screen intently, then nodded, satisfied, and closed her eyes. A moment later she had drifted back to sleep. Maggie rubbed her wrist, feeling the imprint of those strong fingers. Lena had not asked about Marco. How much did she remember?

Chapter Twenty-Three

The reunion the next morning was a joyous one. Ellen packed the kids into the rental car and took the ferry to the mainland, arriving at the hospital before lunch. The children bunched together in the doorway, hanging back, a little shy. Lena sat up eagerly when she heard her children's voices.

"It's okay," Maggie encouraged them. "Your mom's awake, see?"

When Gabby saw her mother, she clambered onto Lena's bed and wrapped her arms around her neck. Luca and Jonah held back, their faces suffused with a heartbreaking mixture of fear and hope.

"Come here, come here, my boys." Lena motioned them to her side. "Jonah, Luca, come here." Hearing their names, the boys' faces brightened and they eagerly crowded around the bed. Lena gathered the boys close with one arm while she cradled Gabby with the other.

"Your brain waked up," Gabby murmured, touching her mother's forehead. "It waked up for real, right? It's not gonna go back to sleep?"

Lena pressed her closer and stroked her hair. "No, my brain isn't going to go back to sleep.

It just had to rest for a while, but it's fine now. Everything's going to be okay."

Maggie saw Jonah's shoulders slump with relief. What a weight he had been carrying. It wasn't gone, but it had eased markedly when his mother called his name.

Ellen moved to the side of the bed and embraced Lena, pressing her niece against her chest.

"It's good to have you back, dear," she said, her voice suddenly clogged with emotion. Stoic Ellen, who had held them all together with her practical, competent care and homemade baked goods, looked vastly relieved to see Lena awake and coherent. She wiped her eyes hastily and stepped back.

"I expect you might be hungry," she said. "I brought real food, not that swill they give you in hospitals." She sniffed contemptuously at the congealing bowl of oatmeal lying on the bedside tray. It looked as though Lena had barely touched it.

From a paper grocery bag, Ellen pulled three Tupperware containers and began laying out their contents on the tray. Fresh fruit salad with red raspberries and blueberries, a pecan streusel coffee cake, and a little tub of whipped cream. "We need to fatten you up. You're all skin and bones," Ellen clucked, eyeing the knobs of Lena's wrists, the delicate wings of her collarbone as they rose above the neck of her thin hospital gown.

Maggie watched the family with a profound sense of relief. It was going to be all right. She could sense it. Lena and the kids still had each other, though the grim fact of Marco's death lurked in the corners of the room, a dark absence, a space hollowed out by loss. That wouldn't change. She had a feeling they would sense that hollowed space for the rest of their lives. For the moment, however, all their other troubles paled in the light of Lena's recovery.

Pulling her camera from her bag, Maggie stepped back and focused, taking a few shots of the reunion. Ellen was selecting tasty bits from the containers of food and popping them into Lena's mouth. Lena laughed as a forkful of berries and whipped cream collided with her nose. Gabby snuggled against her mother's chest, her little face serene with satisfaction. Luca was sneaking bits of streusel cake when Ellen's back was turned, and Jonah looked out the window, his young profile both heavy and relieved.

A few minutes later Dr. Yamamoto peered into the room, taking in the scene. He smiled, for a second erasing the tired lines around his mouth. He motioned to Maggie, who cast one last glance at the group around the bed and stepped into the hall, knowing she would not be missed.

Dr. Yamamoto led the way to a small waiting lounge around the corner. Maggie stood next to him near the lone window as he consulted Lena's chart, shaking his head in amazement. "Most remarkable," he murmured, flipping through pages of charts, test results, and doctors' notes. "It appears Mrs. Firelli has sustained no major damage to the brain. She is exhibiting some short-term memory lapses, which are to be expected, but her motor functioning is not impaired, and she shows every sign of being able to make a rapid and full recovery." He met Maggie's eyes. "She is very, very lucky," he said quietly. "I was not expecting such a positive outcome." He consulted the charts again for a moment, then nodded decisively and made a few nota-tions. "I want to run several more tests and keep her here for a few days of observation, just to make sure we haven't missed anything. If everything looks clear, you can take her home after that."

Maggie felt her legs give way beneath her. She sat down in the nearest chair. She had not even realized the tension she'd been holding, the adrenaline that must have been keeping her going all these weeks. Her hands were shaking and she wanted to burst into tears. It must be the relief, she thought, the letdown now that she did not have to be strong and stoic.

"Thank you," Maggie said. She closed her

eyes, feeling the knowledge seep slowly through her body, sweet as honey. Lena was coming home. They would have to face other hurdles in the next days, but at least they could face them all together.

Later that day, when Ellen had driven the children home and Lena had fallen asleep again, Maggie wandered down to the cafeteria for a cup of coffee and a sandwich. When she returned, Lena was awake, staring out the window with a far-off look in her eyes. She turned when Maggie entered the room, watching as Maggie settled herself in the chair by the head of the bed. Maggie proffered the sandwich. "Want a bite? It's not very good."

Lena shook her head, her eyes never leaving Maggie's face. "Maggie," she said finally, a little hesitantly. "What happened while I was asleep?"

Maggie's heart skipped a beat. Lena hadn't mentioned Marco at all, and Maggie hadn't known quite how to broach the topic. She thought briefly of the phone call from George about the loan and the letter to the lawyer, but decided they would have to wait awhile longer. Lena couldn't handle all the bad news at once. Maggie set the sandwich on the bedside tray and took a deep breath. She couldn't keep something like Marco's death a secret from Lena, even if she was still fragile. Lena deserved to know.

"Lena," Maggie said slowly, "do you remember Marco's accident?"

Lena's gaze was searching, her answer clear. "I remember the water. I know Marco's dead."

"Oh." Maggie sat back, relieved. "I thought you might not remember. I didn't know how to tell you."

Lena turned her face away. "I remember everything about that day," she said, her voice catching on the last word. She paused for a long moment, composing herself. "And I remember about the phone call from George and about Marco's debts. Is there anything I should know about what happened after the accident?" She studied Maggie's face.

Maggie hesitated. "Nothing that won't wait," she said finally, honestly. She would break the news about the bank calling the loan later, when Lena was stronger. And she would wait to ask Lena about the letter she and Marco wrote to the lawyer as well. But she did ask the other question that had been bothering her since the visit from Officer Burns.

"Lena." Maggie leaned forward and took Lena's hand. Lena looked at her, blue eyes wide and trusting. "Do you remember anything about the car crash?" Maggie asked.

Lena shook her head. "No. Is there something I should remember? What happened?" A new thought dawned on her, and she weakly gripped

Maggie's hand, suddenly alarmed. "Was anyone else hurt?"

"No, it was just your car. You hit a retaining wall going fifty miles an hour. But, Lena . . ." Maggie paused for a long moment. Lena looked at her questioningly. "It doesn't look like you touched the brakes before you crashed."

Lena furrowed her brow. "What do you mean?"

"It means," Maggie said very gently, "it looks like it might not have been an accident. Do you remember what you were thinking before you crashed? Had you taken any medication before you went out? I found some antianxiety pills in your nightstand. Did you take any of them that day?"

Lena shook her head. "Maybe. I don't know. They make me feel funny, so I don't like to take them."

Maggie nodded. She had not really expected Lena to be able to answer her questions, but she had to ask them all the same. "Lena," she said, "did you mean to crash the car?"

Lena looked confused for a moment, puzzled by the question. "I don't know," she said at last. "I don't have any idea. I can't remember."

A few days later Maggie drove the rental car onto the ferry and went alone to pick up Lena from the hospital. Ellen had opted to stay home with the children, who were busy making a giant welcome-home banner out of construction paper and yards of tape. Maggie waited quietly in the room as the nurse bustled in and out, checking last-minute details, making final notations. At Lena's instruction, Maggie helped Lena into the outfit Maggie had brought with her—a linen sundress the pale, translucent green of sea glass and a cream-colored cardigan sweater. The ferry ride could be chilly.

Lena brushed her hair, freshly washed with the help of a nurse, and with shaking hands tried to pull it back in a French braid. After a few moments she looked beseechingly at Maggie. "I'm so weak," she admitted. "Can youhelp me?"

Maggie sat on the bed behind her, braiding the strands of hair until they lay neatly, if a little lopsidedly, in a plait against Lena's neck.

"It's not exactly straight, but it'll do," Maggie said, eyeing her work critically.

"It's fine." Lena smoothed a strand of hair from her temple and tucked it into the braid. "Thank you."

The nurse popped her head into the room. "We're just finishing up the discharge papers. You should be ready to go in a few minutes," she assured them before hurrying away.

"I'll bring the car around." Maggie made a move for the door, but Lena grabbed her arm, her grip surprisingly strong.

"Maggie, wait. I need to tell you something before we go." Her face was grave.

Maggie sank down in the chair, and Lena released her arm. "What is it?"

Lena took a deep breath, not looking at her but staring fixedly at the foot of the bed.

"I need to tell you something," Lena repeated. She glanced sideways at Maggie and then dropped her eyes. "Maggie, Marco was leaving us at the end of the summer. He'd requested a legal separation, and our lawyer was working on it when the accident happened."

Maggie went very still. So it was true. The letter had not been a mistake. "Why?" she asked, still stunned by the admission even if she had already seen the letter.

Lena sighed, brushing a few crumbs off the blanket on her lap. "I've asked myself that a thousand times. I don't know. I didn't want it. I fought it every step of the way. But Marco said he was sure. He said he didn't want this life anymore, our life. He wasn't even going to come to the island this year, but I begged him to. He said he couldn't afford to take the time off work. I reminded him this was part of our arrangement. Nine months in New York and then the summer here. And he came, but as soon as we got here, he sat me down and told me he couldn't do it anymore."

"Couldn't do what?" Maggie asked. She didn't

understand. "Couldn't you have made some sort of compromise? A month on the island, something like that?" She heard the desperation in her own voice, trying to fix the situation although it was far too late for that.

Lena met her eyes, her own sorrowful and resigned. "I tried, Maggie. I offered him everything. And at the end of the day, he said he was done, that he'd made his decision. He said our life was pulling him away from his work, from his designs. He said he couldn't think with the noise; he couldn't plan with the kids always in the background. He wanted a clean slate, a blank space for a while, to see if he could get his inspiration back. He planned on supporting us financially and seeing the kids regularly, but he just didn't want a life with us anymore. I tried everything, I really did. But he chose his work over us. He always chose it over us."

Lena blinked hard, two tears rolling down her cheeks. She didn't wipe them away, just bowed her head and let them come, her shoulders shaking. "I think he felt so much pressure being out on his own and not with the firm anymore. He was desperate for his next project to be a success, desperate enough that he used our money and the money that he borrowed to fund it. George told me a lot of our debt is because of that. It was an experimental project in Chicago, developing sustainable office spaces around shared green space. It was a completely new direction for him, and Marco hoped it would be recognized and give him the boost he needed. I think he must have felt the pressure to perform and thought we were holding him back somehow."

Maggie was furious. How could he? How could he abandon them like that? But in the depths of her heart, she knew. She'd almost done it a few weeks ago when Alistair told her about the Regent. She understood more than she cared to admit. As much as Marco had loved Lena and the kids, he'd desired something else more.

Maggie scooted her chair closer and wrapped her arm awkwardly around Lena's shoulders. "I'm so sorry, Lena," she murmured. "I'm so sorry."

Lena covered her face with her hands and leaned into the embrace, tears dripping from between her fingers onto Maggie's shirt. She smelled like lemon verbena and the clinical hospital shampoo.

"I wanted to tell you so much," Lena cried, her voice muffled, "but I didn't want to worry you when you were so far away. So I decided to wait and tell you face-to-face. Except then Marco's accident happened, and it was too late." Lena looked up at Maggie, her face streaked with tears, not red or swollen, but pale and mournful, like a glazed porcelain bust of some conquered Greek goddess. "I know we're all the family you have, and I didn't want you to feel like we were coming apart at the seams when you were away."

"But maybe I could have helped," Maggie protested, appalled that Marco had been planning to leave his family. "I could have talked to him, made him see reason. Lena, maybe I could have changed his mind."

Lena sniffled, reaching for a tissue on the bedside cart and blotting her nose. She sat up straight and folded her hands, gazing calmly at Maggie. "You of all people should know that's not true," she said gently. "You know nothing gets between an artist and his art. You understood Marco in a way I never could, but I don't think that understanding would have helped us." She met Maggie's eyes, and in that bright-blue gaze, Maggie suddenly saw how much Lena really did know. Maggie had underestimated her, assuming that because she didn't give voice to certain things, she didn't see them. Lena held her gaze, and Maggie flinched, wanting to look away from the knowledge there.

She dropped her eyes, suddenly ashamed. For too long her feelings for Marco had created a distance from Lena. She had felt a little scornful of her best friend, who would never understand Marco as Maggie did, who would never know what had transpired between them, the words he had spoken that long-ago night. But perhaps Lena had sensed these things all along. Perhaps she had known and had chosen to love them both anyway.

"I'm sorry," she said finally, not looking at Lena. Her words encompassed so many things she regretted. At least now she had a chance to start to make things right.

After a moment Lena reached out and took Maggie's hand. "I loved you both," she said softly. "And I knew you loved me. I always trusted that." She said no more, but when Maggie raised her head, she found only a calm acceptance in Lena's gaze.

Chapter Twenty-Four

"How could you do it, Marco?" Maggie demanded. "What were you thinking, planning to leave Lena and the kids like that?" She sat in the chilly darkness on the half circle of private beach below the house, on the same log she'd shared with Daniel that early morning. It seemed so long ago now. The night was quiet around her, the only sound the rhythmic lapping of the water. Hunched down into the warmth of her old fleece, she stared out across the black expanse of sea.

Above her the household slept, peaceful now that Lena was back with them. The moment Lena had stepped through the doorway there had been a sense of rightness about the house again, as though things were falling once more into their proper place. But Maggie could not rest.

Although the beach was deserted, she didn't feel alone. Marco felt strangely close to her tonight, as though she had summoned his presence with her words. She didn't believe in ghosts, but more than once after her mother's death she could have sworn she felt Ana's hand on her head, soothing her, comforting her. She'd turn suddenly, and though the room was empty, the air was warmer, redolent of oregano and a whiff of her mother's Charlie perfume. It felt the same tonight. Marco was so close she half expected to turn and see him sitting where Daniel had sat. She could almost smell him, his clove cigarettes and the spicy scent of his skin.

"How could you?" Maggie demanded again, staring at the empty space on the log as though he were sitting there beside her. She shook her head, outraged by his actions. They seemed so callous, so selfish. How could he want to trade his family for a pile of drawings, for something made of steel and glass?

"It isn't worth it. Nothing is worth that," she said with conviction.

She pictured him on the log, leaning away from her, long legs crossed, casually lighting a clove cigarette, cupping his hand around the flame to shield it from the breeze blowing in off the water. He smiled, that knowing half smile that was part of his charm but could irk her so.

"What are you really angry about, Maggie girl?" she heard him say, his tone light. *"Would you still say that if I had left them and come to you?"*

And there it was, the traitorous thought she'd been dodging ever since Lena told her about the separation. She had not allowed herself to voice it, but she could not avoid it. Marco had pinpointed it exactly. The ugly, painful, tantalizing truth.

If Marco had left Lena, he could have been hers.

Maggie felt for the pocket of her travel pants, her fingers brushing the familiar shape of the leather wallet holding her photos. It could have been real. She could have had Marco. The thought made her heart race. For so long she had wanted him, ached for him, dreamed about what their life together could be.

She closed her eyes, riveted by an image—she and Marco rolled up together in a Bedouin tent in North Africa, keeping each other warm in the cold desert air, laughing with the sheer adventure and improbability of their lives spent together in this way. In an instant she saw it all, their days together spinning out before her like threads of brightly colored silk, a vivid jumble of ruby and canary yellow and turquoise—the future they might have had. She saw them standing wind-burnt and carefree in the thin air on the high salt flats of Bolivia, the glistening salt stretching away before them like a vast, solid ocean. In the jungle in Fiji, balancing in an overloaded canoe on a rain-swollen river, soaked through from a summer rainstorm. Cross-legged at a low wooden table in a tent in Turkey, drinking alma chai and eating gözleme as the smoke from a wood-burning oven stung their eyes. Together, always together, traveling the world, living the life they should have shared all along. The images felt so real that she was rooted to the spot, struck with a longing so intense she couldn't move.

"It could have been real," she murmured. "I could have had him." She tried to draw a breath around the terrible longing choking her, the truth lodged like a stone in her throat. It would never happen now. Marco was gone for good. His life had ended that day in the cold, black water. In those few bleak moments, all her hope had ended too.

A sharp breeze whipped in off the ocean, chilling her face. She touched her cheek, expecting to find tears, but it was only the salt spray from the water. She sat for a long while, thinking of Marco, whose life was over too soon, and the tragedy of what he had left behind, the mess and puzzle and sheer loss of him. He would never be hers. He had never been hers. It felt like such a waste of life, an irrevocable waste.

"Why did it have to happen like this?" she demanded, half expecting an answer. "When we finally could have been together."

She stared at the spot beside her, willing Marco to answer, conjuring him with her despair.

She saw him there, arms crossed, listening to her. His hair was longer than it had been for years, and he was wearing the old bomber jacket he'd had since Rhys, the leather so broken in it felt like butter to the touch. She wondered briefly, if she went into the house, where the jacket would be. Would it still be hanging empty over Marco's loafers in the mudroom? She wanted so badly for it not to be so, for Marco really to be here beside her tonight.

Marco cocked his head and looked at her, curious. *"Would you have wanted me, if I had left them and come to you?"* he asked.

"Of course," she answered him immediately. "You're the only one I ever wanted."

The words rolled off the tip of her tongue by instinct. She accepted them as true. They had always been true.

"Really?" He raised an eyebrow, challenging her reflexive response. He tapped the glowing end of his cigarette, ash falling to the stones below. She glanced down, opening her mouth to repeat her affirmation. When she inhaled, she could taste cloves. She looked up, but the space where Marco had been was empty. All was still around her. There was only the soft *shush, shush* of the waves in the darkness and the chill breeze that tossed her curls across her face. She wrapped her arms around herself, cold to the core.

She had always wanted Marco. Her longing for him had defined her life for so many years. It had not changed or lessened with the passage of time. It was the hunger never satisfied, the ache never eased. Her longing was removed from the reality of her day-to-day life, existing alone and unabated. From the moment she'd lost him to Lena, her deepest wish had been to have him again. It was an irrefutable fact, one she didn't question, had not questioned in all those years they'd been apart. Of course she wanted him.

But Lena's revelation at the hospital had changed something, Maggie realized as she sat there on the beach. If Marco had not drowned, he might have been hers, not in the abstract, but in flesh and blood. The possibility felt startlingly visceral, earthy, and immediate in a way it had never been before. Staring out across the water, she thought about his question again in the light of this reality.

"Would you really have wanted me, if I had left them and come to you?"

"Of course," she'd said without hesitation. And it was true in the abstract. But as she reflected on his question, she realized she'd only answered the first half of it.

If I had left them and come to you. Those last words echoed in her head. They highlighted an aspect she had never considered before, a kernel that held within itself the reality of their lives now. They could not turn back time, could not make different choices in retrospect and reclaim a decade of decisions. What would it really have meant for Marco to come to her after he ended his marriage to Lena and left their three children, after a divorce? He and Maggie could not rewind time, could not start fresh from the point where their paths had begun to diverge so many years before when Marco had chosen Lena over her. They could not reclaim a decade of decisions.

So what would Maggie have gained and what would she have lost if Marco had left Lena and come to her now, after so many years of other choices?

She had never considered the concrete reality before. She did so now, playing out the scenario in her mind. She would have lost Lena, the children, the big yellow house. The thought made her heart constrict with a sudden sorrow.

The island house had been her home more than anywhere else after her mother's death, but Maggie had never felt quite settled there, the longing for Marco an impossible barrier to wholly accepting the love and sense of family it embodied. For years she had been uneasy in her relationship with Lena and Marco. Her longing for a different reality had kept her a half step removed, never able to fully embrace what the Firellis could offer her. But to lose Lena and the children . . . The thought made her a little breathless. It was unimaginable.

A series of images sprang to her mind, snapshots of her life with Lena and the children. Gabby curled up with her head against Maggie's chest, her little fingers coiled in strands of Maggie's hair. Lena's expression at the hospital, the understanding and absolution in her calm blue eyes when she'd spoken to Maggie of Marco's planned desertion. Maggie waking up in the familiar red-checkered guest room, the smell of banana pancakes drifting down the hall, bringing with it the warm contentment of knowing she was safe and loved.

Maggie put her hand to her heart, pressing the spot where a dull ache had begun to throb. She could not imagine losing all that. But she would have gotten Marco in exchange, all she ever wanted. Wouldn't it have been a fair trade?

"It would have been enough," Maggie said aloud. "We could have made it enough." But even as she spoke the words she wondered if they were true.

Her relationship with Marco had never been easy. Her longing for him had been simple and elemental, but the reality of their lives had been anything but straightforward. Their relationship had been defined by things unspoken, by the complexity of the past and by the different paths they had taken since that single point in time when Marco chose Lena over her.

Maggie's life had been held in stasis for years by the question "What if?" What if Marco had realized they belonged together before he proposed to Lena? What if he had chosen Maggie instead? She had been trapped in the longing for the path not taken, the choice unmade. But Marco was a different story entirely. He had not been trapped. He had made his choices and acted as he saw fit. He had never voiced a doubt or regret. Maggie caught her breath, seeing for the first time what she had never seen before. The truth shocked her.

"It wouldn't have been enough, not even if we were together," she said in surprise, "because it was never about me, was it? It was only ever about you."

She pictured him sitting beside her, dark eyes sardonic, languid and sure. He ground out his cigarette and glanced away from her, out over the sea, his movements restive, his expression a little pensive.

"I thought you wanted me as much as I wanted you," she confessed. "Because I understood you, understood the burning need to succeed and make a name and be the best. I thought that put me on the inside, closer than anyone else, even Lena, even your own family. But it didn't matter how close I was, how much I understood you, did it? It never would have been enough. Nothing was ever enough for you."

The words were a revelation, not an accusation. She understood it clearly now. Marco had loved no one as much as he loved himself. And he was willing to sacrifice them all on the altar of his ambition. She thought of what he had said to her so many years before when she confronted him about his impending wedding to Lena.

"There's not enough oxygen in a room for the both of us, Maggie. We'd burn each other out." His voice had dropped, almost a caress. She shivered now to think of it. *"I do love you, Maggie. But I'm not a fool. I won't destroy the very thing that makes you who you are. Wherever you go in life—and you will go far and soar high—remember I loved you enough to let you go."*

She did remember. He had loved her. She was sure of that. And he had been smart enough to understand that their future together would have been doomed. Not for lack of passion or talent, but because somewhere deep within himself, Marco Firelli was more dedicated to his own brilliant arc than to anyone on earth. His desire to succeed obliterated all else. No one could stand in the way of his one, grand ambition. Not even his wife and children. Not even Maggie.

She stared out at the dark water, stunned by the truth. They couldn't have made each other happy. No one could have made Marco happy. Perhaps they might have tried once, so many years ago. If he had chosen Maggie over Lena, their life together would have been a shooting star, arcing brilliantly across the night, burning so brightly before it burned out. Even then it ultimately would not have succeeded.

Certainly it would not have been successful if they had tried now. Not after all these years, a thousand days spent building separate lives, a million disparate decisions. Not with the life Marco had chosen to create, with Lena and the children and so many years of history already made. Marco had chosen his path. Maggie had chosen hers. They were never meant to be together. They would have destroyed each other in the process, and Maggie would have lost everything she now held dear.

Maggie sat there in the darkness, speechless. She could see it all so clearly now, what she had never seen before. It was strangely liberating. She took a full breath of salt air, bracing and sweet, drawing it deep into her lungs, marveling as the cold rushed through her. With each breath she peeled away a layer of illusion she'd carried for so long. She had not even noticed the weight of them. But they fluttered away one by one. Gone were the regret and disappointment, the secret, bitter longing that had been like an ache in the marrow of her bones. Underneath them was a sensation of lightness she could hardly comprehend. Who was she without Marco Firelli? She had wanted him for so long that she didn't recognize herself now that she was set free. She was a stranger on the inside.

She stood abruptly, feeling at a loss. Where did she go from here? She walked down to the water's edge, her shoes crunching over shells and stones rolled smooth by the water. The tide was out, dark rocks and long strands of bull kelp making mounded shadows and twisted black ropes in the light of a half-moon. An owl hooted from somewhere far away; another answered it close by. Far out in the water, on one of the islands across the Strait, tiny lights pierced the darkness from houses perched high above the sea. Maggie wrapped her arms around herself, staring out across the black expanse.

The reality was this: Marco was dead. She would never have him now. And even if he stood before her, she would not choose him now. She had lost too much already. She wanted no more regrets. Maggie stood straighter, filled with a new, true resolve. It was time for her to stop living in a fantasy, longing for something that would never come true. Her life was before her, with Lena as she recovered and with the three children who needed stability and care. It was also in the work she loved so well and in the lives of those she had the power to affect with the click of her camera. Home was the big yellow house and the hearts of those who loved her still, had always loved her, would continue to love her.

This life was not perfect, and until now she had not even known she wanted it. But as she stood there on the beach, free and unencumbered after so many years of blindness, she realized how much she treasured it. Nothing was as important as those now in her care. They were her family. This was her home. It was not what she thought she had wanted for so long, but it was what she had been given, and she was grateful for it.

She thought suddenly of Daniel, of their conversation that day on the rocks, when they heard the skylarks' song in flight. Daniel told her he lost everything when he lost his family. She had not understood him then, but she understood now. He had known the value of what had been taken from him, while Marco had been preparing to carelessly throw it all away. She had almost done the same. But it was not too late. She had seen the truth while there was still time. She had come back to the island thinking her life was over, only to discover it had been here all along.

Chapter Twenty-Five

A few days after Lena's return from the hospital, Ellen drove slowly up to the house in a gently used Volvo, almost identical to the one Lena had totaled, though this one was green, not silver.

"Figured we needed to get things settled a bit around here," Ellen said, laying the keys on the table. She had seen it parked at the Ace Hardware store with a For Sale sign in the window that morning and called Lena, who agreed to buy it on the spot. The insurance settlement for the wrecked Volvo would just cover the cost. "Now you can return your rental car if you want to. No sense giving them any more money," Ellen told Maggie.

Maggie jumped at the chance to return the car to Seattle. She was being driven mad by the sheer domesticity of the house now that it was back in some semblance of order. The routines were making her feel claustrophobic, hemmed in by lunchtime and snack time and bath time and story time. She felt regulated by a giant clock called childhood, bound to a schedule not of herchoosing. She had endured it for the weeks Lenawas lying in the hospital because she had to. There had been little choice. But now that Lena was recovering rapidly, Maggie could sense a return to normal life. She was on the verge of no longer being needed. And she had never been more relieved.

"I'll return the car at SeaTac Airport in the morning and take the shuttle back to the ferry terminal in Anacortes. I'll get a taxi from Friday Harbor and be home late afternoon or early evening," Maggie told Ellen.

Early the next morning Maggie sped toward the ferry line in the rental car, feeling giddy and a little nervous at the thought of returning to her old life. So much had changed, not least of all her revelation about Marco. It was so new that she had no idea what exactly it meant. She knew she wanted to see Lena and the children more than only one month in August. She wanted to be more a part of their lives but had no idea what would happen next. The future felt wide open and uncertain. The matter of the debt still loomed, closer day by day. She had not yet told Lena about the called loan, reasoning that she was still recovering and too fragile to bear such a heavy burden. Maggie knew she would have to tell Lena soon, but she was savoring the sweet moments before she had to break the latest bad news.

While she waited for the ferry, she snapped a few shots of Friday Harbor—the quaint clapboard storefronts, the boats bobbing in the harbor. She'd decided to develop a few of the photos she'd taken in the past weeks and give them to Lena as a going-away present. She just had to choose which ones to use.

On the ferry ride back to the mainland, Maggie took more photos, leaning over the railing, enjoying the rush of the seawater the motor churned up behind it, milky and green as Chinese jade. She bought a bowl of Ivar's clam chowder and ate it on the deck, spotting dozens of translucent jellyfish floating calmly beside the ferry. She couldn't stop grinning. She felt as though she'd been holding her breath underwater for ages, concentrating on survival and keeping afloat. Now she'd finally come up for air. With Lena recovering and Maggie no longer guardian for the children, she had the internal space and freedom to dream and create again. She could feel the creativity beginning to bubble up in her blood with each passing minute, the thrill of new and exciting vistas just waiting around the next bend.

After returning the rental car at the airport, Maggie rode the Link light rail into Seattle and walked to Storyville Coffee, her favorite coffee shop in Seattle, nestled near the iconic Pike Place Market. She sat in one of the comfortable leather chairs by a window and sipped an espresso, Lena's borrowed MacBook Air open on her lap. She flipped through the shots she'd taken while Lena was in the hospital, choosing the best ones to print out. Closing her eyes for a moment, she took a sip of the espresso, savoring the moment and the rich caramel and chocolate taste of the roast. This was her world—coffee shops, espresso, anonymity, and photos that told a story about people and places across the globe. It was exhilarating to be back.

She continued browsing through the images, smiling at the antics of the children, flipping quickly past the few photos of Daniel but then returning to them, studying them with an avid, almost voyeuristic interest. She had not told Lena about the beckoning ceremony, and she didn't think the children had either. Maggie wondered what Lena would think when she saw the shots, if she would be touched to know her children had taken such care to call her back. Who knew? Maybe it had actually worked.

"Not soon enough," she murmured, thinking regretfully of the Regent. Even if she flew back to Chicago tomorrow, there was no hope of creating a winning series on such short notice. She needed all the time she'd lost on the island to create a series good enough to enter. And even then it might not have been enough.

The Regent wasn't only about technical brilliance; it was most of all about the personal perspective of the artist, about the story being told through the photos, about the connection between photographer and subject. And as Alistair had reminded her more than once, that was Maggie's area of weakness. She had never been able to spot it herself, never been able to put her finger on the flaw and figure out how to change it. So far it had not affected her success. Her photos' beautiful compositions and the poignancy of their subject matter covered any flaws, her strengths masking her weakness. But the Regent . . . that was a different story entirely.

Maybe the lost time doesn't matter, Maggie admitted to herself. *I don't know if I could have won, even if I'd had all the time in the world.* But the lost opportunity still felt bitter. She finished her espresso and flipped through the rest of the photos. Lena with the kids at her hospital bedside, Luca sneaking bits of coffee cake, Jonah's profile as he turned away from the happy scene, his grave face lightened with relief.

As she looked at the shots, documenting so many moments of joy and sorrow, despair and isolation, Maggie was struck by something about them, something different, an aspect of her work she'd never glimpsed before. She slowed her perusal, studying the photos, beginning to see a theme to the images, a narrative arc she hadn't seen when she'd taken them. Her photos told a story about a family, about loss and hope and bittersweet endings.

But it was more than that. The intimacy of some of the shots startled her, exhibiting an emotional aspect she had never seen in her work before. She could feel herself in every shot. The results were warm, resonating with emotion, touching in their empathy.

Maggie sat back, surprised. *Maybe this is what Alistair's been trying to tell me is missing,* she thought, studying the photos with a growing awareness. The pictures were somehow different from anything she'd done so far, closer to her heart, more vulnerable. *It's just because you know and love these people,* she argued with herself, drumming her fingers on the tabletop. *These are no better than your other shots.* But she couldn't shake the sense that these photos were something special. She had a feeling Alistair might agree.

She studied several of the shots—Lena's still face, hands cupping the rose at her heart, tubes snaking from her wrists; a candid snapshot she'd taken of Daniel as he lit the feather for the beckoning ceremony, his profile sharp in the glow of the candles; and one of Gabby, hands raised as if in prayer, holding a piece of sea glass over the makeshift altar, her eyes shining with hope.

Maggie stared and stared at them, a faint anticipation stirring in her breast. It was probably nothing, false hope or desperation. But what if it wasn't? What if they really were as good as she suspected? What if she had somehow finally managed to put herself in her photos? She sat for a moment more, caught in indecision, and then she e-mailed them to Alistair.

"You," Alistair said without preamble when he called a few hours later as Maggie was speeding north toward the ferry dock in the back of the shuttle bus. "My dear, you are absolutely insane. Absolutely insane. I've just seen the photos you e-mailed me. Magdalena Henry, what in heaven's name makes you think you can just click, click a few photos and enter the most prestigious and highly competitive photography competition in the world? No planning, no forethought, just point-and-shoot photography if I've ever seen it. Really, Magdalena, have you lost your mind?"

Maggie winced, her hopes plummeting in disappointment. She should have known it was too good to be true. She must be losing her edge. She was too close to the subjects, and it had compromised her objectivity.

"I'm sorry," she said, her tone resigned. "I just thought—"

"Ah, ah, I'm not quite finished," Alistair said, interrupting her. She imagined him sitting back in his leather Eames chair in his office, finger raised as though lecturing a naughty child.

"Now, the really mad thing is—and I've checked with a few others at the agency, just to see if we all agreed—the really mad thing is those little point-and-shoot photos are brilliant! You've done it, Magdalena. No glass walls this time. You are right in there with the blood and guts and viscera of this family. And that's what makes it work."

"Because they're my family," Maggie murmured, her heart swelling like a helium balloon. Alistair wasn't listening.

"Now, of course, the series needs work. Some of the shots aren't nearly strong enough, but honestly, Magdalena, I've never seen anything quite like it, not from you. They're certainly not your most polished photos, but I've been following the Regent competition for years, and in my opinion, with this madcap little exhibition, you might just have an outside shot. You can at least hold your head up and not be ashamed to enter. And considering that a few hours ago we all thought you had bloody nothing, well, that's pretty near miraculous."

Maggie disconnected the call and sat for a moment, stunned. She could still enter the Regent. She still had a chance to win. She spent the remainder of the shuttle ride and the ferry crossing to Friday Harbor in a euphoric daze. How was it possible? Just days ago she'd felt as though she'd lost everything in the world. And now she felt as though she'd been given it back again.

When the taxi dropped her off at the house after dinnertime, she didn't tell anyone about the call with Alistair. She would need Lena's permission to use the photos for the competition, but at that moment there was only one person she wanted to share the good news with, someone who could understand. Maggie had not seen Daniel since the night of the beckoning ceremony. Lena's awakening and recovery had occupied the last week completely. But she had been thinking of him.

After checking on Lena and the children, who were all curled up together on the couch in the family room watching a Disney movie, Maggie invented an errand in Roche Harbor and borrowed the Volvo.

"I'll be back before dark," Maggie told Ellen as she went out the door. She slid into the driver's seat, feeling a thrill of anticipation at the thought of seeing Daniel.

When she told him the good news, he didn't react as she'd expected. He was sitting on the single bed, facing her as she sat in the one hard chair. He watched her, his expression oddly wistful. He looked disheveled, unshaven, his hair hanging around his face. Was he eating? He looked thinner, more depressed.

"That's great," he said a little flatly. "You deserve the chance. You're very talented."

Maggie shook her head. He was missing the point. "It's not just about that," she said, trying to put it into words. "A week ago I thought I'd lost everything. It felt like the end of the world. I thought my life was over." She spread her hands in surprise. "But now look. Lena's going to make a full recovery. I still have a shot at the Regent. And Marco, well, I lost Marco a long time ago. It just took me awhile to realize it. I think everything's going to be okay." She looked at Daniel, her eyes bright with the unexpected turn of events.

Daniel nodded, staring at the floor. "I'm happy for you."

Maggie sat back, disappointed. "I thought you'd be encouraged."

Daniel looked up, meeting her eyes. "Why? What does it have to do with me?"

Maggie hesitated, grasping for the right words. She thought of Griffin, sitting on the driftwood log spitting cherry pits into the surf, of what he'd said when she told him why she needed a miracle. "A friend told me once that no sacrifice goes unrewarded, that we have to keep doing the right thing, even though it isn't easy. He said in the end all will be well. He told me not to lose hope. I didn't believe him at the time."

"And do you now?" Daniel asked, his tone skeptical.

"I think I'm starting to," Maggie said slowly, thinking of the past week. She could not have imagined how things would take a turn for the better. Not everything, but it was a start.

"Daniel, this isn't just about me," Maggie insisted. "That's what I'm trying to tell you. We all have a choice. When the hard things happen in life, we can choose to curl up and die, or we can choose to do the best we can, take the next step forward, and hope for the best. Do you see what I'm saying?" She leaned forward, trying to press her meaning home to him with every word, trying to show him that in the midst of his own struggle he still could choose. "Daniel, maybe it's not too late. Maybe you can still set things right." She stared at him, willing him to grasp her meaning.

"I can't fix what I've done," he said, sounding final. He didn't look at her.

"Have you tried?" she asked in exasperation, glancing around the sparsely furnished room. "You're an amazingly talented poet, but you don't even own a pen. I know you grieve for Kate and Eli every day, but have you tried to make things better? Have you even called them?"

Daniel didn't respond. Maggie leaned forward, on impulse laying her hand on his knee. She could feel the muscles of his thigh tense under her fingers in surprise. "Don't give up," she urged, trying to get him to understand, to see there might be hope in even the darkest hour. "You have to at least try."

Daniel's head snapped up at her words, his eyes fierce. Snatching her hand away, Maggie shrank back in the chair, startled by his sudden anger. He jumped to his feet, moving away from her, putting distance between them. He stood at the window, staring out at the sea. His voice was harsh when he spoke.

"You think buying a pen will make up for all the mistakes I've made? You come in here with your good news and your little morality tale. What do you want me to do, run back to New York and see if I can put all the pieces back together?" He whirled on her, his expression dark. "Well, I can't. Maybe you forgot the details. There was a divorce and a little boy locked away inside himself and too much alcohol and a lot of pain. I ran away from all of it, Maggie. I didn't make the right decisions, any of them. And then, after I'd run as far as I could, I tried to kill myself, and another man died instead because of me." He stared at her for a long moment, eyes burning. "That's why my story will never turn out like yours, Maggie. Because even when things were darkest, even when it cost you everything, you chose to do the right thing. I didn't, not once."

When he spoke again his voice was heavy with self-loathing. "I tried to run away from everything, even my own life, and now I'm paying the price. All I've done in the past year is screw up everything I've touched. It's too late for me." He dropped his head, his dark hair falling in a curtain around his face, all the fight going out of him in an instant.

"Marco's drowning was an accident," Maggie said, wincing at the trite sound of her words, knowing as she spoke that he would not listen. She didn't know how to make him see what she could see, the possibility of a better ending for him.

"It was my fault," Daniel said, his tone low and determined. "It's all my fault, every single mistake that hurt Katherine and Eli and Marco, especially Marco. I was trying to end my own life, and I cost another man his life instead. I can't forgive myself for that." He looked up at Maggie helplessly. "Do you know what it's like to watch a man drown?" he asked.

Maggie stared at him for a long moment. "Yes," she replied simply, with a mixture of pity and regret. "I'm watching one right now."

Chapter Twenty-Six

Life quickly settled into a comfortable routine. Lena was recovering rapidly but was still weak and sometimes forgot the most basic things—how to operate the hair dryer, the name of a classical piece on the radio. She spent most of each day on the deck in a cushioned, reclining Adirondack lounge chair, an afghan over her legs to ward off the chill from the water.

Gabby and Luca bounded about like puppies, giddy with the joy of having their mother back. Even Jonah began to emerge from his shell. He smiled more often and even entered into conversations voluntarily at times. The children spent hours at one of the island parks or on their own rocky beach with either Maggie or Ellen, racing home to proudly show Lena their treasures—a colored stone, an empty snail shell, bits of dried kelp, or a lozenge of sea glass. Once Jonah found an abandoned skylark's nest, the little woven basket empty. He brought back the nest and shyly presented it to Lena, who kept it on the side table by her chair on the deck. The nest reminded Maggie of Daniel. She had not heard from him or seen him since leaving the cabin after their last conversation. She ran her fingers lightly over the rim of the nest, recalling what he told her about skylarks and trying not to think about their last, disastrous encounter.

Maggie still had not told Lena about the call from George or about the Regent and her imminent return to Chicago. She'd wheedled another week from Alistair, who was far more amiable now that Maggie had such a good start on a promising entry. Every day Maggie found a reason to wait to tell Lena. Lena was still so weak, Maggie reasoned. It wasn't fair to burden her just yet. Maggie knew she would have to speak to her soon. The deadline for both the loan and the Regent entry loomed larger every day, but still she procrastinated, not wanting to shatter the peace and joy of Lena's return. Instead, she savored each day, the hours slipping by soft and sweet, knowing they wouldn't last.

Lena and Maggie didn't speak again about Marco and Lena's intended separation. What Lena had confided to Maggie at the hospital had fundamentally changed the shape of Maggie's world. It had toppled Marco from the golden pillar she had put him on. She'd held on to an illusion for so long that it was a strange sensation to see clearly now. She found her senses sharper, brighter, more in tune with the world around her. She noticed things she wouldn't have before. The way Lena would absently touch the empty place where her wedding band had been, then draw her hand back quickly as though the skin burned her fingers. How in quiet moments her gaze would drift out to the Strait, and for a brief second her face would be etched with a mixture of sadness and regret, and her mouth would soften with a bittersweet memory.

Griffin visited more frequently now, dropping by almost daily. Maggie noticed a delicate flush in Lena's cheeks when he was near. She saw how Griffin leaned forward beside Lena's deck chair, elbows on his knees, playing with the kids or drinking coffee with Ellen, but always tilted a little bit toward Lena, the very polarity of his body drawn to her.

Maggie watched their growing intimacy with a mix of bittersweet feelings. Lena was her best friend, and Maggie wanted her to be happy, but so much had changed so quickly. It was hard to imagine Lena with anyone other than Marco, but Maggie understood now that though Marco and Lena had shared a life together and borne three wonderful children, in the end it had not been enough. The parts of Marco's soul no one could touch had been the hollow spaces of longing and ambition, of solitude and desire, the places that spoke most loudly, beckoned with an irresistible siren song that drowned out the face of his wife, the voices of his children. He'd been no monster, but neither had he been the paragon she'd always imagined him to be. He'd been a brilliant and conflicted and ultimately selfish soul, torn by what he wanted and could never quite attain—peace, triumph, a rest from the fire in his belly that drove him to succeed.

He and Maggie had shared a bond, one she had clung to for far too long and believed to be stronger than anything else, even his love for Lena. She could not say whether that was true, but true or not, it no longer mattered. What mattered now was what Marco left behind—a handful of brilliant structures, his mark on the world, and a beautiful wife and family. They were his legacy too. In the end he thought he didn't want them, but whether or not he realized it, they were his greatest contribution to the world.

Maggie watched as Griffin performed a silly magic trick for Gabby, whistling a tune as he pulled a quarter from behind her ear. Gabby giggled, and Lena laughed as well, her face serene as she turned to Griffin.

Enjoy this while you can, Maggie thought, taking a mental snapshot of the scene, knowing she'd be leaving soon. *This cannot last.* It made her feel wistful and a little sad, watching them. How many evenings had she sat with Lena and Marco in this very place, watching the light fade over the water and simply enjoying being together? Too many to remember. So many she couldn't single one out from all the others. What had they done the last night they'd been together? Eaten Lena's blackberry cobbler or sipped hot cocoa? Played Texas Hold'em or listened to music on the radio while they watched the stars wink to life in the night sky? Whatever they had done, it must have been easy and comfortable. She knew they had enjoyed those long, last golden moments, oblivious to the fact that they had run out of time.

Maggie swallowed hard against the tiny flutter of panic deep in her stomach when she thought of the future. It seemed almost inevitable that they would lose the yellow house; even if she won the Regent, the cash prize would come too late for the ninety-thousand-dollar loan payment due soon. The thought brought such a sense of loss. Maggie wasn't ready to say good-bye to the place that had been her refuge and security. If they lost the island house, where would she find a home? Was there room for Maggie in Lena and the children's New York life? What if Lena married again? Would there still be a place for an old friend like Maggie, such a vivid reminder of a past that had offered such sorrow?

Maggie could not imagine a future without Lena and the children in it. They were her family, her home. She had been willing to give up everything for them, and she would again if she needed to. But so much seemed uncertain now. She had no idea what would happen next. It was out of her control. Maggie tried not to dwell on thoughts of the future. Her mother had always told her worrying was like trying to run a race while sitting in a chair. It was useless. But she felt the cold little fingers of worry creeping up her spine at the most unexpected moments.

When the box came, they were not expecting it. Lena was upstairs napping. The kids were with Griffin at a children's day camp at Blessed Redeemer in Friday Harbor, and Ellen was up to her elbows in bread dough. When the doorbell rang, Maggie answered it. The postman handed her a square Priority Mail Express cardboard box. It was surprisingly heavy.

"Package for Lena Firelli. Sign here, please." Maggie signed for the package and carried it into the kitchen, setting it on the counter without paying much attention to it. She'd give it to Lena when she woke from her nap.

Ellen paused from her kneading and cocked her head. "What's that?"

Maggie shrugged. "The postman said it's for Lena."

"Oh, I bet it's that Pyrex mixing bowl I asked Ernie to send to me, but he probably addressed it to Lena instead of me. I had an extra one in a nice blue color and I thought I'd give it to Lena as a get-well present." Ellen nodded to the package. "Go ahead and open it. I want to wrap it up nice and give it to her."

Armed with a pair of scissors, Maggie had the package open in a matter of seconds. She pulled out the bubble wrap, then lifted a silver jar |with a lid.

"It's not a mixing bowl," she said slowly.

Ellen put her hands on her hips and surveyed the jar, puzzled. "Well now, what do you think it is?"

Maggie lifted the lid and stared at the contents for a moment. The jar was filled with a fine, gritty, gray dust. Ashes.

She checked the outside of the box, immediately spotting what she had missed before— the black sticker to the side of the address slip that stated "Cremated Remains" in bold white letters. The return address label was for a crematorium on the mainland.

She looked up at Ellen, eyes widening in sudden comprehension. "It's Marco."

"Auntie Maggie, Auntie Maggie, there's a letter on the altar and it's for you," Gabby shouted, barreling onto the deck where Maggie and Lena were sitting, enjoying the late-afternoon sunshine. Luca and Jonah followed close at her heels.

"It's got your name on it," Luca told her breathlessly, skidding to a halt by her chair and holding out a brown envelope.

Maggie reached for it. Made from a brown

paper grocery bag, the envelope felt light, almost empty. She immediately knew who it was from.

"What is it?" Luca asked. The children ringed her, avid with curiosity.

"I'm not going to open it right now," Maggie said, stalling. She had no idea what was in the envelope and wanted to be alone when she opened it. "Maybe later."

They protested loudly but she wouldn't budge. At last they gave up and filed off the deck, grumbling.

Lena eyed the envelope. "How mysterious. I wonder what it is."

Maggie shrugged. Lena didn't know anything about Daniel, and Maggie intended to keep it that way. She told herself she was protecting Lena, that finding out about Daniel might be upsetting because of the part he played in Marco's death. This was partly Maggie's motivation, but the other part was something she didn't examine closely. She wanted to keep Daniel hidden until she figured out what her feelings were about him. He was a puzzle she wanted to decode privately.

A few minutes later she excused herself from the deck and slipped upstairs to her bedroom, shutting the door behind her and locking it. She slid her finger under the flap of the envelope. A single thin slip of paper was inside. She pulled it out and froze in astonishment. It was a check made out to Lena Firelli for ninety thousand dollars. And it was signed by Daniel C. Wolfe.

Maggie pulled the Volvo onto the shoulder of the road in front of Daniel's cabin in a spray of gravel, the brown envelope with the check inside clutched in one hand. She'd been having an imaginary conversation with him all the way to the cabin.

"This is insane," she muttered, waving the check in the air. "You can't just give someone ninety thousand dollars. What are you thinking?"

She was both immensely pleased and very irritated with him, and she could not even say why. Maggie slammed the car door and picked her way toward the cabin. It was silent, curtains drawn, door closed. She knocked. No answer. She glanced around. No figure on the rock outcropping. No sign of life at all. She knocked again.

"Daniel?"

Silence. Fighting a twinge of unease, she turned the handle, hoping against hope that he had not done something rash. What if he had left the check as penance and then paddled out into the Strait, determined this time to finish what he'd started? She shoved hard against the door, suddenly afraid of what she might find.

He was gone. The bed was made. His coffeepot

and single plate were stacked on the stove. But he was gone. He'd taken his carving tools and the row of little animals that usually lined the window. With a sinking feeling in her stomach, Maggie surveyed the room. All his personal effects and his rucksack were gone too.

On the table by the window lay a single sheet of lined paper, ragged along one edge where it had been torn from a notebook. On one corner of the paper sat a delicate carved bird, its wings outstretched. She picked it up. A skylark. She rubbed her finger over its smooth head, somehow knowing the little bird was meant for her before she even saw her name. She looked down and read the few scrawled lines.

Maggie,
You are finding your way home.
I have not yet found mine.
As you can see, I bought a pen.
—Daniel

"He's not coming back," she whispered. To her surprise she felt tears spring to her eyes. She sat down in the lone chair, clutching the little bird and the brown envelope, overcome with an unexpected hollow sense of loss.

Chapter Twenty-Seven

The next morning Maggie confessed everything to Lena. She told Lena about George's phone call and the loan that needed to be paid in full or they would lose the island house. She told Lena about the Regent, about her unexpected opportunity for entry, and what winning would mean for Maggie's future and the Firellis' finances. She had already purchased a plane ticket back to Chicago, with Ellen's assurance she would stay as long as Lena needed her. The flight left in six days. And finally she laid the check in Lena's lap and told her about Daniel, about his role in Marco's death, about the guilt he wore like a hair shirt, and about his unexpected act of generosity.

Lena listened wordlessly as Maggie poured out the entire tale. When Maggie finally ground to a halt, Lena still said nothing. She sat in her deck chair, looking out at the water, roiling silver beneath a bright, cloud-riddled sky.

"My goodness," she said finally, drawing a deep breath. "That is extraordinary." The check from Daniel lay in her lap, the quantity of zeroes, Maggie knew, both unnerving and reassuring. "Of course you can use the photos of us in the competition," Lena said at last. "What a wonderful opportunity, Maggie. And it's selfless

of you to want to help us this way. Thank you."
She looked down at the check from Daniel.
"I'm not even sure what to say about this. What
do you think I should do?"

Maggie considered. "What do you want to do?"

Lena thought for a long moment. "I don't
know," she answered, looking surprised. "I think
I need a little time to figure that out."

The next couple of days passed swiftly. Maggie
readied herself to return to Chicago, taking more
photos to round out her entry, preparing to return
to her old life. She had wanted to leave for so
long, but now that she was free to do so, she
found herself oddly reluctant to go.

Alistair was calling her daily, giving her little
pep talks and reminding her to hurry home.
He was almost jovial, a strange and vaguely
disturbing mood compared to his usual droll
irony. She had managed to talk him into allowing
her to stay almost an extra week by pointing out
that she needed additional shots for her Regent
submission. He had readily agreed, but warned
her not to tarry too long. They had work to do
on her submission as soon as she returned to
Chicago.

A few days before Maggie was to leave, Lena
broached the topic of the future.

"I've been thinking," she said, shifting in the
Adirondack chair and tucking her feet under a
thin crocheted throw. The day was cloudy, the

sun peeping fitfully through the gray. It was chilly in the shadow of the deck. Maggie laid the book she'd been reading in her lap.

"About what?"

"What comes next for us." Lena picked at a loose stitch on the throw, tucking it under another to cover the flaw. She glanced over to the side yard where the children were playing Wild Wild West. Gabby and Luca wore bandannas over their faces and were pretending to be outlaws. Jonah was the deputy and carried a shiny silver cap gun in a fake leather holster. They were holed up in their respective forts, preparing for a showdown.

"I'm going to cash the check from Daniel Wolfe and pay off the loan. And then I've decided we're going to stay on the island." Lena looked up at Maggie, her expression frank. "I can't go back to New York. Not now, not alone. It was never my life. I can't face the house in Brooklyn and the friends there, everything that was Marco's world. My life was always here. I'm going to try to keep the house and enroll the kids in school in Friday Harbor. We'll stay through the next school year at least."

She looked down at her hands. "Colleagues of Marco's who were based in Dubai are moving to New York next month. They're interested in buying our house there. I spoke with George yesterday. If I use Daniel's money and combine it with the equity we have in the New York house,

I'll be able to pay off most of the debts. The rest we can handle a little at a time. And I will pay you back for the money you lent us when we first discovered this whole mess. Don't think I've forgotten about that."

Maggie shook her head. "Forget it. Consider it unpaid rent for all the summers I've been coming here and freeloading."

Lena made a sound of protest, but Maggie waved her objection away. She looked down at the book in her lap, surprised by the feeling of relief that swept over her. Lena was keeping the house and staying on the island. Maggie would still have a home to come back to.

"Can you afford to do this?" she asked. "What will you live on?"

Lena brushed the question aside with a wave of her long, pale fingers. "I've been thinking about that. Marco had some retirement money in an account through his old firm. I'd forgotten about that until George reminded me. It's not a lot, but we'll cash that out. My parents want to help us out as well, as much as they can, anyway. If we're careful and frugal, I think we could have enough to live on for a couple of years. It isn't a perfect solution, but it should give me enough time to figure out our next steps."

"If you need anything . . ." Maggie didn't look at her, just left the offer open. She fully intended to make a generous contribution to

Lena's finances if she won the Regent. Even if she didn't, she could still help ease the financial strain a bit. Her income was generous for a single woman with few financial obligations.

"I know." Lena leaned over impulsively and rested her hand on Maggie's, squeezing gently. "I've never doubted that."

Maggie didn't answer, just let Lena hold her hand. The fear that had been constricting her heart for so many weeks loosened a little. She took a deep breath, then another. She had a fleeting impression that everything was somehow being set right, though she couldn't say how.

"And what about you?" Lena asked. "Are you excited to be heading back to Chicago?"

Maggie nodded. "If you and Ellen can manage, I'd like to work for a couple of months and then come back in the fall. I think I can get away then for a few weeks. After I turn in my submission for the Regent." Maggie glanced quickly at Lena, as though assessing her strength.

"Of course we can manage." Lena brushed off her concern. "Ernie's flying in next week, and he and Ellen are going to stay for at least a month. They'll be a big help." Lena squeezed her hand and let go. "We'll miss you. I know you need to get back to work, but come back when you can, and don't worry about us. We have a community here now. If we needed anything, Griffin would be here in a few minutes." She flushed a little. "He's a great support."

Maggie did not pursue the subject of Griffin, though she was tempted to probe a little. She sensed it was an area too new and tender to bring up just yet. Best to leave it for now so it could take shape quietly, away from the spotlight.

"I'm glad," she said simply, letting the matter drop.

Lena nodded. "I am too."

Maggie picked up her book again but didn't start reading. She watched the children playing in the yard. Jonah discharged his cap gun and Luca fell to the ground dramatically, arms and legs splayed out.

"Maggie," Lena said after a moment. "Thank you, for everything. I know it wasn't easy, and I know you made difficult sacrifices for us. I just want you to know how much it means to me."

"You would do the same for me," Maggie responded. "You always have. When my mom died, you were the one who got me through." She glanced up at Lena, meeting her calm, blue gaze squarely. "I was tempted to leave," she admitted. "I didn't know if I could really do what I had to after your accident. But I learned something through all this. Remember what you said to me the night of your piano audition, the one you botched on purpose? We were having an argument about having a purpose in life.

I think I accused you of having no ambition."

Maggie dropped her gaze, a little embarrassed by the memory. "And you told me that maybe one day I'd want something more than I wanted to be famous. That someday something else might seem more important. And to be honest, I thought you were crazy. I couldn't imagine wanting anything more than I wanted to succeed." She shook her head and fell silent for a moment.

"And now?" Lena prompted.

Maggie looked up at Lena, then glanced out at the yard, watching the children. "And now I understand," she said finally. "I love my job. And I dream about winning the Regent. But it isn't worth it if I don't have a home and family to come back to. My life can't be just about what I do, as much as I love it. I need something more. I want something more."

Lena smiled, her eyes shining with those words. "I'm so glad," she said.

Maggie nodded, staring out across the bluff to the water beyond, glinting like quicksilver in the afternoon light. "When my mom was dying, I asked her if she was sad about going so soon, if she felt like she'd accomplished all she wanted to do. And I remember what she told me." Maggie paused, her mouth turning up at the corners as she recalled her mother's words.

Ana had been bald as an egg, sitting cross-legged on a hospital bed when Maggie asked her the question. She hadn't hesitated for a second in her response. "She said we just get this one brief life. We don't know how long it will last. And the most important thing we can do is to use what we have in our hands to care for the people we've been given to love. She said she had done two good things in her life. She'd loved me the best she possibly could, and she'd tried to make the world a better place because she'd been in it. She said in the end, that's all that matters." Maggie closed her eyes against a sudden prickle of tears.

Lena reached over and took Maggie's hand, her fingers cool and smooth. "She was right," she said simply. They sat together in silence. Maggie was wrapped in memories, thinking of the life she'd lived, of Marco and the long years she had shared with Lena in friendship.

After a few moments of silence, Lena broached another topic.

"I'd like to have the memorial service before you leave."

"If you feel ready," Maggie said. The silver urn had been carefully stored on a top shelf in the kitchen, set beside the good lace tablecloth and a tarnished silver tea service.

"I don't know if anyone is ever ready for a good-bye like this," Lena answered, "but I want us to be together when we say it."

Chapter Twenty-Eight

On a bright and cloudless morning, they gathered to bid farewell to Marco Firelli. Lena wore her pale-blue suit and high heels and carried the urn filled with Marco's ashes. Ellen, clad in a white-and-navy-blue floral-print skirt and blazer, had dressed and combed the children into order. The boys, hair parted on the side and slicked down with water, were subdued in their dark suits and shiny shoes. Gabby had picked a handful of wildflowers, which she clutched tightly in her fist.

Maggie, at a loss for appropriate clothes, had donned the simple black travel dress she carried with her everywhere. It was perfect for the unexpected art gallery opening or evening out, and also, apparently now, for funerals. Griffin roared up to the house on his motorcycle, a black cassock tucked up around his waist, wearing a white collar, looking solemn. He dismounted, rearranged his clothes, then ruffled Gabby's curls and patted each boy manfully on the back.

"Are you ready?" Griffin asked, offering Lena his arm. She nodded, tight-lipped, taking his arm with one hand, her other holding the urn tucked firmly against her chest. They headed around the back of the house to the nearby bluff Lena had chosen for the memorial service. Maggie walked beside the children, holding Gabby's hand. In her other hand Gabby clutched her bouquet, picked "for Daddy's going-away party." That was how Lena had explained it to them, as a celebration of their daddy and a chance to say good-bye to him.

Just at the edge of the Firellis' yard, the whole party came to a halt. Maggie glanced up, a jolt of shock running through her from head to toe when she saw the man ahead of them in the path.

Daniel Wolfe stood in front of Lena. Dressed in a simple black suit, he was clean-shaven and his hair had been cut. He looked like the photos Maggie had seen of him from his New York days, a little older perhaps, still with a hint of sadness around his eyes, but strikingly handsome. He was carrying a bouquet of white flowers—a mix of roses and daisies. His gaze strayed for one second to Maggie, his eyes locking with hers, but then he turned to Lena, proffering the bouquet. Maggie thought her heart might fly out of her throat. She couldn't breathe.

"Mrs. Firelli, I'm Daniel Wolfe. I'm responsible for the accident that claimed your husband's life." He spoke directly to Lena, his attention unwavering, though Maggie could see his hands trembling. How bold he was to do this, but how difficult it must be. It seemed almost foolish for him to have come. Had he known they would be saying good-bye to Marco today?

"I know who you are," Lena said evenly. The

color had drained from her cheeks. She looked like an alabaster statue, graceful and remote. Griffin moved a little closer to Lena, a protective gesture.

Daniel nodded once, then pressed on. "Father Griffin told me you were having a memorial for your husband today. I don't want to intrude, but I came to say how sorry I am—"

Lena held up her hand. She was wearing short white gloves, just like the day Maggie had met her so many years ago at Rhys.

"Apologies may be necessary, Mr. Wolfe. And if you feel you owe me one, I will hear it. But please know I hold no blame toward you in my heart. It was an accident, a tragic accident. I know that. I hope you know that." She spoke calmly, with not even a tremor in her voice. "And while we certainly regret the outcome, we can't change what happened. There is no blame in this, except perhaps that we cannot see the future and we cannot turn back time." She smiled a little sadly. Maggie stared at her, in awe of Lena's grace and absolution.

Lena continued speaking. "You have a good heart, Mr. Wolfe, and I am grateful for your generosity. We are going to say our good-byes to my husband now. Would you join us?" She reached out and took the flowers from his hand. "I think Marco would have liked that."

Daniel nodded wordlessly, then fell in step

beside Ellen, who turned and gave him a look of newfound respect.

Together they finished the short ascent to the bluff. They walked slowly, their shoes kicking up little puffs of dust on the path. Maggie kept her eyes glued to the lean, sober figure in front of her, dark head bent slightly, walking purposefully behind Lena. Something had changed. She could see it in the set of his shoulders. He looked like a man set free. But why? Had he seen Eli, begun writing poetry again, been reconciled to his wife? This was the thought that had been eating at her since his disappearance. What if he went back to his old life in New York and she never saw him again? Or if the next time she saw him it was in the pages of a newspaper, accepting an award, handsome in his tuxedo, his arm around his once-again wife?

With brutal honesty Maggie acknowledged she was not ready to say good-bye to Daniel Wolfe. Quite the opposite, in fact. It surprised her how glad she was to see him, how her heart rose at the sight of his face.

They stopped in a grassy open place on the high bluff overlooking the water. A light breeze lifted the hem of Griffin's cassock and tousled the boys' slicked-down hair, bringing with it the briny sweet smell of the sea. The sun was ripe and warm, the sky a vivid blue where it touched the darker horizon of the water. Maggie took a deep breath, inhaling the scent of rotting kelp and dusty black rocks, the spice of dry evergreen needles warmed in the sun. It smelled like home. She swallowed hard once, then again, trying to dislodge the tight knot in her throat, composed of equal parts grief and hope. They formed a semicircle facing the water. Maggie held Gabby's little hand, a trifle moist in the heat. Daniel moved to stand on Maggie's other side, and she glanced sideways at him. He was looking at her intently. It made her nervous.

"Maggie." He said her name softly, just the one word.

Her heart was thrumming in her ears. She dropped her own gaze, concentrating instead on Griffin as he faced them and spread his arms, waiting for a moment to begin. Lena stood to one side, resolute, still holding the bouquet from Daniel, the silver urn at her feet.

"I saw my son," Daniel whispered, leaning in toward Maggie. She could smell him, cedar shavings and a hint of roasted coffee beans. She glanced at him, noting the small smile playing about his mouth, an expression she was unused to seeing him wear.

"And?" she asked.

"I'll get to see him more. Kate agreed to that."

"Your wife," Maggie murmured, feeling instantly nervous.

Daniel shrugged ruefully. "Ex-wife. She's engaged to her chiropractor now. They seem very happy. I think he'll be a good stepfather for Eli."

Maggie exhaled in relief, not realizing until that second that she'd been holding her breath. "And what about you?" she asked boldly, keeping her voice low.

"Happy to be here," he said. She glanced up at him, and he held her eyes for a few seconds. She broke the gaze, elated and a little embarrassed.

"I got the envelope," she said at last, keeping her voice low. She saw Ellen glance over at them with a curious expression. Lena was dabbing at her eyes with a handkerchief, and Griffin paused for a moment to give Lena time to regain her composure.

Daniel raised an eyebrow. "And?"

"Lena can keep the house, thanks to you." Maggie gave him a brief, searching look. "Where did you get that kind of money?"

He shrugged. "Part of the divorce settlement. Kate got the brownstone, and attorneys make more than poets, even famous ones." He grinned ruefully, and she smiled in return. Griffin cleared his throat, and Maggie quickly turned her attention to the priest as he began the memorial service.

"We're gathered here today to celebrate the life of Marco Firelli, a man who was many things to many people. To Lena, he was a husband of more than nine years. For Jonah, Luca, and Gabby, he was a loving father. For Maggie and Ellen, family. For me, Marco was a man I didn't get to know as well as I would have liked. I think we might have been friends. For Daniel"—he inclined his head in Daniel's direction and Daniel stiffened—"Marco was a man who gave a great gift, a sacrifice to save another's life. And for many others, Marco remains the artist behind works of great beauty that celebrate the human spirit. Marco Firelli was a complex and many-faceted man, a man with an amazing gift for architecture and with a passion for life, a man who will be greatly missed, most of all by those gathered here."

Griffin made a gesture of invitation to Lena, who handed the bouquet to Ellen and picked up the urn. She stood a few feet from the edge of the cliff and took off the lid. For a moment she clutched it to her chest, the urn rising and falling with her breathing. Tears made silver tracks down her face. Maggie brought her hand to her own cheek, finding it wet. It felt surreal to be here, with the sun sparkling on the sea, all of them gathered around the urn containing the earthly remains of the man she had loved and yearned for all these years. Beside Luca and Jonah, standing stoic in their identical suits, Ellen was crying into a handkerchief. Griffin spread his arms in benediction.

"So, Marco Firelli," he intoned, "today we commit your spirit to our gracious Lord. We say good-bye to your earthly form and trust that we will be reunited with you in the life to come. We call upon the grace and mercy of God, and ask that he take you into his arms and carry you into eternity with him, amen."

Lena glanced at Griffin. He nodded. She set the urn on the ground and hesitated for a moment, then scooped up a handful of ashes. Fine dust sifted through her fingers, swirling away on the breeze. She turned to the sea, tossing her handful of ashes to the wind. They blew out over the cliff, dissipating on the surface of the water. Next it was Jonah's turn, then Luca's and Gabby's. The boys were solemn and stoic, though Luca's lip trembled as he released his handful of ashes. Gabby was crying as Ellen helped her scoop up the ashes in her little hand. Then it was Maggie's turn.

Griffin motioned to her. Maggie felt a hand on her back. Daniel, urging her forward. She stopped at the urn and bent down, letting the ashes sift through her fingers. How strange that this would be the last time she would touch Marco. With a brief flash of his face, the rasp of his beard, the taste of him—rich red wine and olives—she felt her cheeks flush. How long ago that was. So many years in between that memory and now, years when she had denied herself the making of new memories, holding on to a desire that had been doomed from the start.

She glanced back at Daniel. He was watching her, his dark eyes warm and intent. She was drawn to him in a way she couldn't describe, drawn to the soul she caught glimpses of in his poems, drawn by the fact that he was open to her in a way Marco had never been. He was flesh and blood standing before her, and with him the possibility of things to come. Maggie straightened, her handful of ashes already slipping through her fingers.

"Good-bye, Marco," she murmured softly. The wind carried away the words as she said them. She flung the ashes out into the wide blue where sky and water met. "I will always love you, but today I'm letting go."

As she made her way back to her place in the circle, she was dimly aware of the others. Ellen sniffling. Griffin beside Lena with his arm around her, comforting her, his auburn head bent over her fair one. Luca scuffing the toe of his shoe in the dirt. All she could feel was an incredible lightness, a sense of limitless possibility. Her heart was rising like a helium balloon in her chest, filled with elation at the budding realization that what had seemed like the end might in fact be just the beginning.

On impulse, Maggie reached out and grabbed Daniel's hand. He glanced at her, surprised, but did not pull away. She faced forward, looking out at the horizon. After a moment he laced his fingers through hers, his own warm and strong, hers a little gritty from the ashes. She closed her eyes.

"Look," Gabby shrieked, pointing out toward the water. A single porpoise was arcing through the waves. It came gradually closer as they watched, a dark and solitary shape.

"Hey, I think it's the one from the beach," Luca shouted.

The three children ran to the edge of the rocks, Ellen in close pursuit, catching at their collars to stop them a safe distance away from the cliff.

"Is it him?" Gabby asked as they waited side by side for the porpoise to crest again. It did, nearer the shore. Even from where Maggie was standing she could see the vivid white wheal of the scar above his flipper. He came as close as he could to the shoreline and then veered away from the jagged line of half-submerged rocks.

"Yeah," Jonah said, his expression amazed. "It's him. It worked."

Maggie shivered as she watched the porpoise. She stared at the animal, at the long white scar on his left side, struck by a vivid memory—Marco unbuttoning the top two buttons of his dress shirt in the cafeteria at Rhys, showing her the long white knife scar that roped across his left collarbone. It had to be coincidence, and yet . . .

"It worked," Luca repeated in awe. Gabby shrieked with glee, clutching her hands together in excitement, watching every move the animal made. Ellen stood behind them, still clutching tightly to the two younger ones in case one of them made a mad dash forward over the cliff edge. Lena and Griffin stared out at the water, their expressions puzzled.

"Yeah." Jonah nodded, not taking his eyes from the back of the porpoise as it headed to open water. "It's the sign. Dad's telling us he's okay."

Maggie squinted against the glare on the open water. The porpoise was now just a dark blur against the distant swells, swimming out into the Strait, away from them. Gazing out at the sea, she thought once more of the quote Griffin had spoken that day in Lena's hospital room when all the world had seemed so dark, the words of the mystic Julian of Norwich, "All shall be well, and all shall be well and all manner of thing shall be well."

Griffin had been right after all, she reflected, tilting her face up to the warmth of the sun. She squeezed Daniel's fingers, reveling in the fact that he had returned, that he stood beside her, flesh and blood. She was open to whatever came next. "I'm ready," she whispered, her heart swelling with an unexpected thrill of hope.

Somewhere in the open space of sky behind them, a lark began to warble. Another joined it, dipping and swooping in the morning light, their voices ascending through the air in a sweet and trilling song of benediction and farewell.

Discussion Questions

1. How does Maggie's definition of home change over the course of the story? How would you define *home?*

2. How does the recurring quote by Julian of Norwich, "All shall be well, and all shall be well, and all manner of thing shall be well," play out in the novel? Do you agree with this quote? Why or why not?

3. What role do San Juan Island and the natural world play in the story?

4. How do the supernatural/transcendent aspects of the story interact with the natural world? How do the beckoning ceremony, the larks, and the porpoise contribute to transformation or breakthrough for the characters?

5. What are the central motivations of the main characters? Compare and contrast the motivations of Maggie, Lena, Daniel, and Marco. How do they change over the course of the story?

6. Are Maggie's decisions selfish or selfless throughout the story? How do her decisions impact her life and the lives of those around her?

7. How are the characters in the story bound by their pasts and unable to move forward? What helps them finally break free?

8. What character do you most identify with and why?

9. Maggie is said to have a gift for revealing "hidden and forgotten things." How do you see this gift playing out in the story? How does it play out in her own life?

10. What are the strong themes you see woven throughout the story?

11. What are the central underlying messages of the novel? Do you agree with them? Why or why not?

Acknowledgments

Books are very much like babies. You may birth a baby yourself, but it takes a village to raise it well! There are a number of wonderful people who acted as the village for this novel. I want to thank all of them. A great big thank-you to . . .

My very capable, reassuring, and enthusiastic editor Karli Jackson, who helped guide me through this publication process with such clarity, warmth, and positivity. Karli, I'm so glad it's you! Also Kimberly Carlton and the rest of the excellent Thomas Nelson team, who consistently exhibited such professionalism, dedication, and above all kindness as I navigated the path of publishing my first novel.

My super agent Chip MacGregor, whose steady demeanor, wise counsel, and unflappable belief in this story instilled me with confidence and hope. He politely let me ambush him at a writing conference many years ago and then gave me a chance as a new author. Chip, thanks so much for taking me on. Our coffee shop meetings and Skype calls—whether from a seaside manor in Ireland or the darkened kitchen of a café in Paris in the middle of the night—are always educational and entertaining. I'm so glad you're in my corner.

My wonderfully honest and wise test readers—Sarah Smith, Adelle Tinon, Elisa Gonzalez, Adrianne Oglesby, and Carmelita Clarke. Their constructive criticism and clever insights made this story stronger.

Davide Neri, for Marco's Italian translations and for all the delicious treats he brings us from Bologna. Chad and Amy Strobach, for their photography smarts and engagement with the arts and humanitarian causes worldwide. Any technical errors in the novel are entirely mine. Pam Rempt, for sharing her love of San Juan Island and her extensive island knowledge with me. Jonathan and Su Jin Wilkinson, for providing transport and their internet at four in the morning in Busan, South Korea, so I could connect with the Thomas Nelson team for a crucial meeting. Now that's hospitality!

Last and most importantly, my wonderful family. My husband, Yohanan, who is my strongest supporter, an insightful editor, and a thoroughly good man. Yohanan, I love you and am so thankful for you. Thanks for your keen insights, for your patient interest in my stories, and for giving me the space to do what I love. Thanks also for giving me the gift of San Juan Island and the Pacific Northwest. You are my favorite. And for Ash and Bea. You make the world a better place.

Books are produced in the United States using U.S.-based materials

Books are printed using a revolutionary new process called THINKtech™ that lowers energy usage by 70% and increases overall quality

Books are durable and flexible because of smythe-sewing

Paper is sourced using environmentally responsible foresting methods and the paper is acid-free

Center Point Large Print
600 Brooks Road / PO Box 1
Thorndike, ME 04986-0001 USA

(207) 568-3717

US & Canada:
1 800 929-9108
www.centerpointlargeprint.com